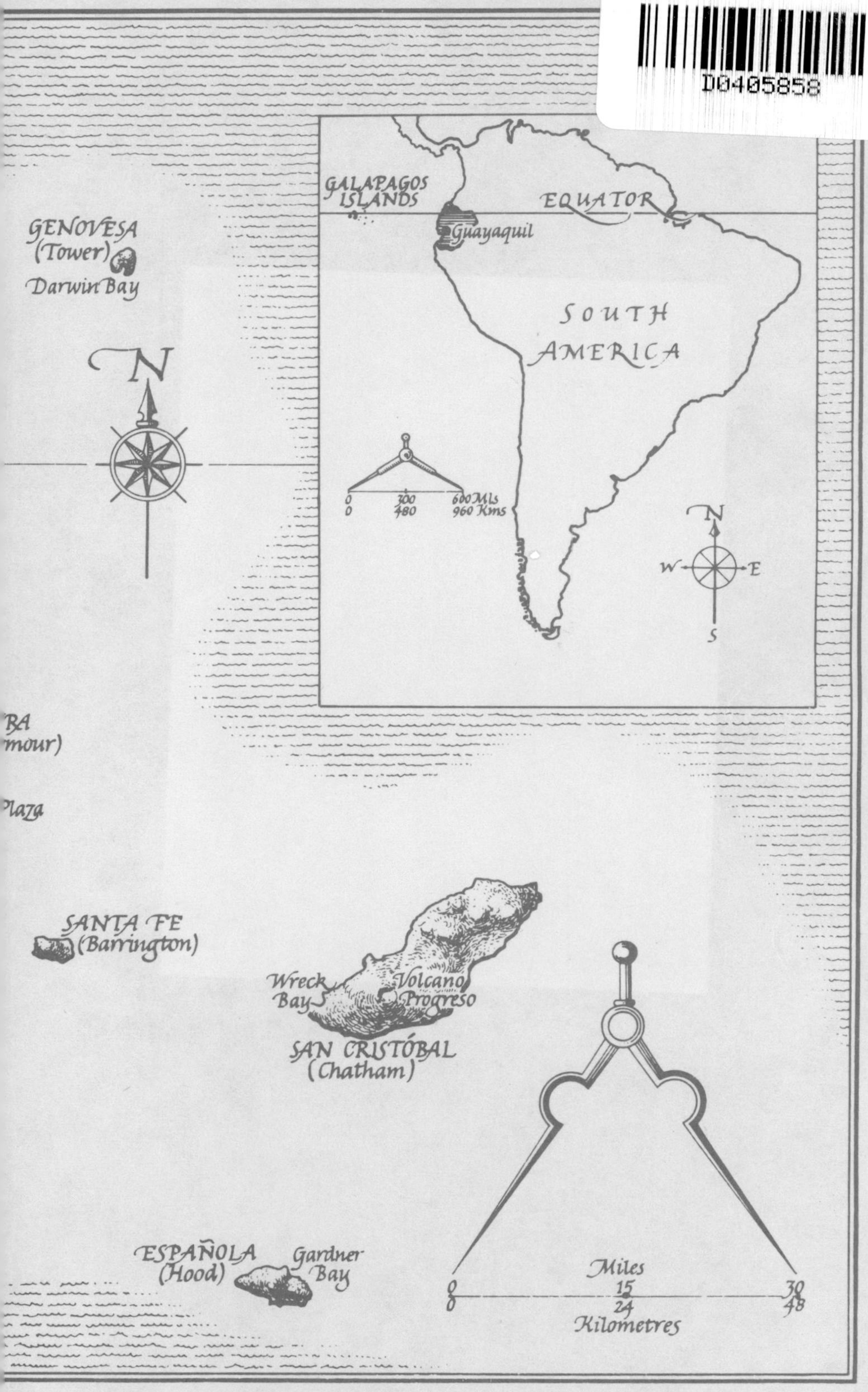

GENOVESA
(Tower)
Darwin Bay

N

BA
mour)

Plaza

SANTA FE
(Barrington)

GALAPAGOS
ISLANDS

EQUATOR

Guayaquil

SOUTH
AMERICA

0   300   600 Mls
0   480   960 Kms

N
W   E
S

Wreck
Bay

Volcano
Progreso

SAN CRISTÓBAL
(Chatham)

ESPAÑOLA
(Hood)

Gardner
Bay

Miles
0   15   30
0   24   48
Kilometres

D0405858

OMNIVM LVX CIVIVM

BOSTON
PUBLIC
LIBRARY

My Father's
Island

My Father's Island

A GALAPAGOS QUEST

JOHANNA ANGERMEYER

VIKING

VIKING
Published by the Penguin Group
27 Wrights Lane, London w8 5TZ, England
Viking Penguin, a division of Penguin Books USA Inc.
40 West 23rd Street, New York, New York 10010, USA
Penguin Books Australia Ltd, Ringwood, Victoria, Australia
Penguin Books Canada Ltd, 2801 John Street, Markham, Ontario, Canada L3R 1B4
Penguin Books (NZ) Ltd, 182–190 Wairau Road, Auckland 10, New Zealand
Penguin Books Ltd, Registered Offices: Harmondsworth, Middlesex, England

First published 1989

1   3   5   7   9   10   8   6   4   2

Copyright © Johanna Angermeyer, 1989

Grateful acknowledgement is made for permission
to reproduce the following copyright material:

Lines from 'Moonlight in Vermont' (Blackburn/Suesdorf)
© 1944 and 1945 Capital Songs Inc. Copyright renewal
© 1972 by Michael H. Goldsen Inc. Lyrics reproduced
by permission of Chappell Music Ltd and Criterion Music Corporation.

Lines from 'You Must Have Been a Beautiful Baby'
(Warren/Mercer) © 1938 Remic Music Corp., USA.
Reproduced by permission of B. Feldman and Co. Ltd, London WC2H 0EA.

Every effort has been made to trace existing copyright holders.
The publishers would be pleased to hear from anyone they have
been unable to acknowledge

ISBN 0-670-82732-0

Library of Congress Catalog Card Number 89-40320
(CIP data available)
A CIP catalogue record for this book is available from the British Library

All rights reserved.
Without limiting the rights under copyright
reserved above, no part of this publication may be
reproduced, stored in or introduced into a retrieval system,
or transmitted, in any form or by any means (electronic, mechanical,
photocopying, recording or otherwise), without the prior
written permission of both the copyright owner and
the above publisher of this book

Printed and bound in the United States of America

*To my mother, Tony and Johnny,
and the memory of Mary*

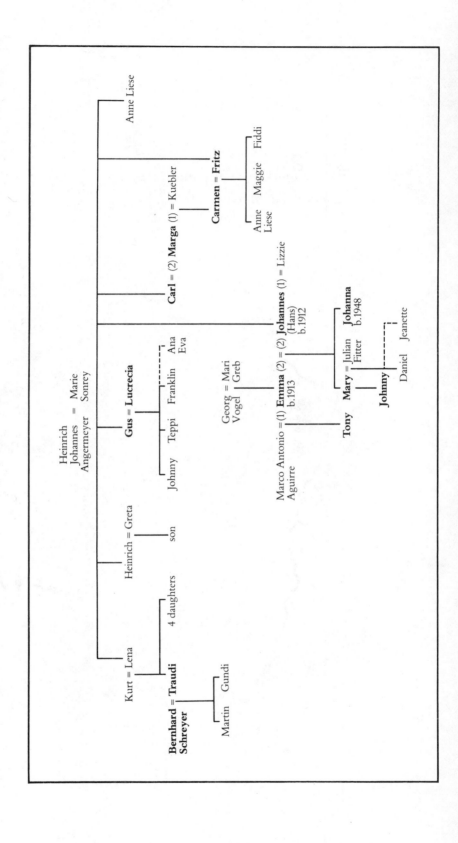

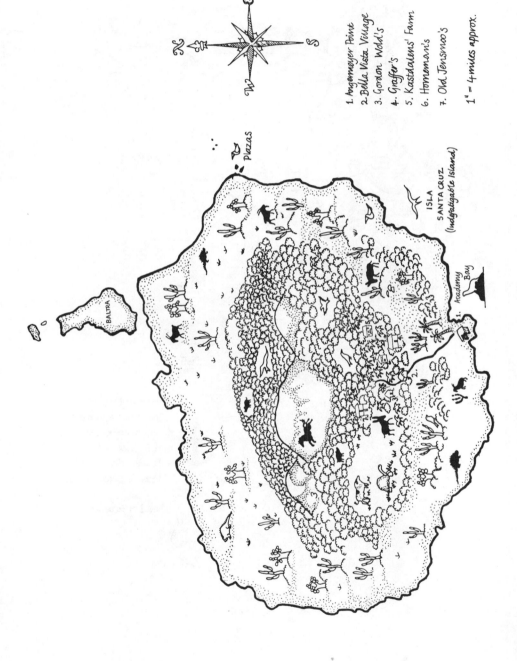

Plazas

BALTRA

ISLA
SANTA CRUZ
(Indefatigable Island)

Academy
Bay

1. Angermeyer Point
2. Bella Vista Village
3. Gordon Wohl's
4. Graffer's
5. Kastdalens' Farm
6. Horneman's
7. Old Jensmoo's

1" = 4 miles approx.

N
W
E
S

THE OLD TRAIL

6.

Pelican
Bay

5.

4.

The
Village

NYMPH
LAGOON

The barranco
3.

ACADEMY BAY

1.

2.

Salt
Lagoon

DIVINES' BAY

DEVIL'S KITCHEN
↓

1. Angermeyer Point
2. The house on the beach
3. Our house on the barranco
4. Herr Kuebler's house
5. Pelican Bay House
6. Haeni's Brackish Well

5" = 1 Mile approx.

Contents

Illustrations

Parties and music
Fritz with Gordon Wold and Graffer
Alf Kastdalen
Maya Kastdalen with Lala
Below the barranco
Carl and his iguanas
Carmen's first kitchen
Fritz, Carmen and Anne Liese
Lucrecia with Johnny, Teppi and Franklin
Tante Marga with Anton the sea-lion
Carl with Ani-Ani the iguana
Mary, Tony and me in Nebraska
My class picture, c. 1958
Mary and me in the highlands
Johnny
Tony with his son
Mary, Julian Fitter and their son
Carmen and Fritz with their daughter
The 'muelle'
Carl on his boat
Fritz and Carmen

Colour Photographs

All the colour photographs except two were taken by my husband, David Fox. The first colour photo, sunrise over Santa Cruz, was taken by my nephew, Daniel Angermeyer Fitter. The photo of the mangrove in the second colour section was taken by Barbara Reed. I am very grateful to all three for allowing me to choose from the huge selections, all of which I would have loved to include.

Acknowledgements

This story could not have been put down without the help of Carl and Marga Angermeyer, Carmen and Fritz, Gus and Lucrecia, Traudi and Bernhard Schreyer, Julian Fitter, Mary and all their children. I thank them and the Divines, the DeRoys, the Kastdalens, Mrs Horneman and so many other Galapagueños for their generosity to my family, their unique sense of adventure and the patient hours some of them spent talking into my tape recorder. The loan of priceless photographs was most unexpected and greatly appreciated. I am grateful for the kind assistance of the American Historical Society of Germans From Russia, the people of St Mawes and Mrs Joyce Sellens.

I thank my mother for remembering, and Dr John Treherne for insisting I write. The next one is for David.

My Father's Island

1

Show 'n' Tell

'... One nashun unner God, invisible ... with freedum an' justice fer all.' Miss Bean turned, thin hand lingering on the 'I Like Ike' badge pinned over her heart, and scrutinized me as I quietly shut the classroom door. Her spectacles with the silver butterflies on the rims slowly slid down her ski-jump nose and rested at the tip. Twenty-six ten-year-olds watched me carefully deposit my brown paper bag in the row of shiny lunchboxes on the shelf over the coat rack. I moved slowly, as I'd seen Gary Cooper do in *High Noon*, taking his sweet time moseying down main street, deliberately postponing the inevitable showdown. He would have hitched up his britches and chewed inscrutably on a thin piece of straw, fingers flexed, ready to draw cold steel. But Cooper bit the dust as mingling smells of Listerine, shoe polish and frothy powder paints in assorted jam jars by the art sink pinched my nostrils. Red, blue, yellow and black, all we needed to produce dripping-wet pictures for our mothers to stick up on the fridges at home with strawberry and banana magnets. I paused by the easels, aware of all their eyes on my back.

Might as well get it over with, I thought grimly, stopping at the usual spot by the chart of United States' presidents. Squaring my bony shoulders, I recalled last Saturday's Double Western Matinée Special. Indian braves in war-paint had tied the hero to a stake and, in a frenzy of savage excitement, stacked kindling under his feet. As the flames crackled and his boots began to sizzle, the hero just stood there cool and confident in some last-minute plan he'd devised to save himself and the bird-brained blonde screaming hysterically from within Cochise's wigwam.

I

Cool and confident, I eyed Miss Bean. With her hair parted in the middle like that and slicked down over her ears, she looked more like Popeye's Olive Oyl than a fierce Apache. Though I didn't find her in the least bit comical, I did not find her frightening either; just inhibiting. How would she look, I wondered, in squaw-chewed moccasins and a porcupine-quill jerkin?

Chin tilted back defiantly, I waited for the flames to lick my hand-tooled cowboy boots. Miss Bean readjusted her glasses, gave the class their cue to light the pyre and they all joined in chorus:

> 'Who is late to school again?
> School again, schoooool again?
> Who is late to school again?
> Jo ANNE is ... shame ... shame!'

That over, I quickly found my place beside Dennis Lizonbee, the chiropractor's son with the Colgate smile.

'It's Jo HANNA ... with an "h"!' I muttered as loudly as I dared. Every morning they got it wrong and every morning there were perfectly good reasons for being late, although stringy Miss Bean never wanted to hear them.

Why, that very morning was a good example. I'd laid out my school clothes the night before with every intention of getting a good start, and I awoke especially early to feed all my animals. I wolfed down breakfast and had opened the gate to go to school, when there in the back yard I spotted my duck's white body floating heavily in his pool like a drowned airplane, beak submerged among the lily pads. I shouted and my older sister Mary dumped the laundry basket and came running. For twelve frantic minutes she vigorously rubbed Pico's soggy chest with our best fluffy towel, pausing now and then to breathe gently down his gullet, her soft blonde hair hiding the compassion in her big blue eyes which I found touching, knowing how she felt about my pets.

I moved Pico's limp wings up and down, gulping back sobs of remorse at having installed the duck diving-board on which he'd obviously banged his head. My other ducks gathered round in silence. Finally, after the fourth kiss of life, Pico's pale feet had waved weakly; water had streamed out of his orange nostrils and, rustling his feathers with bird-like embarrassment, he'd righted himself and waddled off, pals circling and quacking solicitously.

I'd wanted to embrace Mary. She had not even complained about the best fluffy towel. But I didn't embrace her. We didn't do much of that sort of thing in our family.

Once I'd assured myself that my duck had not suffered brain damage, I'd disobeyed the house rules and served the whole flock a thanksgiving feast of Wheeties while Mary was busy shaking off leaves from the wet wash.

Then, mounting my fastest dream stallion, the grey with black legs, I galloped off through the California morning, jumping cracks in the sidewalk but resisting the usual temptation at the corner drugstore to peel the dead bark from Todd, my favourite eucalyptus tree. I was probably already late for 'One nashun unner God' so I ran especially fast, because this morning, for the first time in my life, I would raise my hand for Show 'n' Tell.

The tall windows of the ivy-covered school stared back like empty eye-sockets; the flag already flying, with the brown bear of the state flag beneath it. I squeezed my heels into the steaming flanks of my steed as we approached the big doors, but he flatly refused to go faster than a stilted trot. Removing his bridle and slapping his rump like John Wayne always did, I turned my horse loose to graze on the school's lawn bordered with date palms and pepper trees, where he would be waiting when I was released for recess. The Duke always wore dusty chaps and a sweat-stained leather waistcoat, high-heeled boots and spurs that jangled when he walked. I dusted off my own blue gingham dress and yanked up my white socks, thinking how different life would be if only I could wear faded blue jeans to school, with a red neckerchief...

The big doors were ominously quiet as I pushed them open. I liked the school doors; they'd once been trees and seemed the most natural thing in the entire building. The janitor rubbed down the principal's oak door every afternoon. He said it was

3

to remove all the sweaty handprints of naughty children sent through it. I paused there and caught my reflection in its shine. I did not think I looked particularly naughty. Tiptoeing down the long hall of shadows, I removed my holster before opening the door to Miss Bean's classroom. Every morning I imagined they were saloon doors, and when I swung them open my teacher, the bartender, would be drying shot glasses and saying, 'Whadllyahave, pardner?' Instead she always glowered with disapproval and acute dislike.

The fact that Miss Bean hated me was no surprise. It showed clearly on her face every morning when she gave the class its note to sing the 'Who's Late to School' song. But after last night I didn't care any more. After last night, nothing could hurt me or make me feel inferior ever again.

As usual, once they'd sung the 'Late to School' song and the giggling subsided, the class forgot about me. While Miss Bean droned on about plans for the coming April Jelly-Bean Hunt, I silently rehearsed what I was going to say for my debut. I had never submitted anything to Show 'n' Tell before, because things that happened in my house just weren't discussed at sharing time.

I'd tried hard to be the average, well-adjusted, bike-riding American kid, but I'd known this was impossible the day Mrs Pearce, the lady next door who wore six curlers under a net in her blue-tinted hair, sat me down to strawberry Kool-Aid and brownies made from a package mix. As we sat in her spotless formica kitchen, she lit one Camel after another between cups of strong black coffee. The floor was partially covered in newspapers because she couldn't house-train her three Pekineses. Flicking ash into a sickly potted fern in the window, Mrs Pearce rested her fat elbows on either side of the coffee mug and brought her face close to mine. Her right eye had a permanent squint from years of avoiding the curling smoke.

'Well now, tell me – where is it y'all come from then?'

'Who, me?' I asked, brushing off the crumbs.

'Yeah, well, you ... yer folks, y'know.'

I swallowed the last bit of cake and eyed the battalion of ant poisons, fly sprays and roach pellets by the cake-mixer, their ominous smells mingling with bleach, Pine Clean, Air-o-Fresh and Peke pee. I was in a dilemma. I knew exactly what Mrs Pearce wanted to know. The Bible said I shouldn't lie, but how could I possibly tell her the truth? Especially as it wasn't any of her business.

'Well, I was born in Nebraska, 'cause that's where my Grandma lived and my mother was born in Russia but she isn't a Communist or anything and my sister was born in South America and so was my half-brother only Mom married his father first who was an Ecuadorian pilot but my father was German but he wasn't a Nazi or anything and that's why he left Germany because he didn't like wars and neither did his brothers, see? So that's why they sailed off to the Galapagos Islands to live and my Mom lived there too in a bamboo hut under palm trees on a beach and when they weren't climbing volcanoes and having adventures they were painting pictures in Ecuador because they were artists and they liked to play music too. Only my mother came back and we moved with Grandma to California because it's warmer than Nebraska and we lived in the desert once but it snowed and I had a puppy there with spots but it died.'

I spoke quickly, more words than I had ever rattled off to anyone outside of our family. Mrs Pearce stubbed out her cigarette and gave me a long hard look. I had told her the truth, but not the truth she'd been hoping for. What she really wanted to know was what had we done with our stepfather, who had not been seen in the neighbourhood for the past five months, and she wanted a second instalment on the drowned-sailor story I'd told her to explain about my sister. I hadn't actually said that he was drowned ... I'd only said we thought he might have. Only the sailor was made up.

I caught sight of myself in the sparkling chrome percolator and hurriedly wiped the pink moustache from my upper lip with the back of my hand; napkins had not been provided. The un-refilled glass before me hinted it was time to go home. Exiting past the glass eye of the tumble-dryer, I pushed open the taut screen door, but stopped mid-squeak to listen. Mrs Pearce was speaking to Mr Pearce, who spent the whole day in an Ezeeday Rocker, reading *Field and Stream*: '... sneaky little kid ... trying to hide something, I can tell.' I hated her then; because I had given in for the price of brownies. I had talked about things too precious to mention; Mama's best stories; and because Mrs Pearce had said I was trying to hide something. And because she was right.

Our ex-stepfather had started taking Mama out when I was five. She was lonely and I had chicken-pox. One night he took Mama and me to the Peter Pan Drive-In, where green ladies served giant hamburgers, fries and malts as we sat in his Ford. I wasn't allowed out in daylight because of my spots so, since I got to go out in my pyjamas and because I wasn't usually allowed that kind of food, I thought the man charming. Well, one does.

Then Mama married Mr E. and I changed my mind. So did Mama. I don't know what my older brother and sister thought of him in the beginning, but I once overheard our Russian grandmother ask Mama how she could 'throw herself away' like that ... especially Mama, who had a university education. Grandma had sounded empty when she'd said it.

Mr E. had a typewriter-repair business that went bankrupt from time to time and kept us on the move from one end of the state to the other, towing a rented U-Haul trailer, dodging his business debts. Memorizing new telephone numbers, strange routes to school and always being the new kid in class seemed as normal to me as tinned beans. But with no roots holding on to any particular soil, we were the last piece of the American jigsaw-puzzle which never fitted in.

Mr E. had ambition; big plans. But he spent most evenings drinking beer which the liquor store wrapped in brown paper bags (the wrinkled ones I took my lunch to school in the next day). Watching *Victory at Sea* reruns, he'd tell the same stories about the navy and the war over and over. The most exciting thing about Mr E. was that he was one-eighth Cherokee Indian and looked like a cowboy. He knew I didn't like him because he'd cook a 'mess' of black-eyed peas and make me sit at the table until I'd eaten every last one. I hated Okie food. You would have thought he'd have hated it too after being so eager to flee Oklahoma with his family during the '30s dustbowl depression.

He called us snobs because we liked Mozart and read library books. He had two records: 45s of 'Cool Water' and 'How to Teach Your Parakeet to Talk'. Only we didn't have a parakeet. He didn't want pets. Often he'd try and make me like him by promising me a pony when his 'ship came in'. I used to say I wanted a real horse, not a pony. It was a cruel thing to say. I wasn't a cruel child by nature and didn't feel better for saying it.

Now he was gone and things were better. I didn't have to hide my books with the small print; I was allowed pets. We gave thanks before meals and I took violin lessons. The teacher said I had talent – which I found amazing, coming from a perfect stranger. Music lessons were on Wednesdays, so that became my favourite day. Still we weren't normal and that's all I wanted then; to be ordinary and inconspicuous.

It would have helped if Mama hadn't needed to work so hard, if she could have stayed home all day baking cookies and watching television; if I needn't have packed my own school lunches in wrinkled paper bags; if we'd had a dog from the animal shelter and a real father who mowed the lawn and fixed bicycles on Saturdays.

Often I'd sit out on the sagging back steps of our clapboard house, just willing something to grow in the packed dry earth of our yard. Distant cheers from vacant-lot baseball games, shrieking children dashing through sprinklers, husband and wife arguing over the dent in the Pontiac, metallic wet sound of cars being hosed down all fused together in a chant: 'You don't belong, you don't belong.'

To confirm this, behind me through the patched screen door Mama would belt out Russian dance tunes on her old accordion. Sauerkraut steamed. Dark rye bread with caraway seeds rose out of tins near the oven. Hammering sounds confirmed that my sister Mary, sixteen years old, was hanging another Van Gogh print up on the wall. Instead of one of those nice landscapes of fighting stallions in the moonlight or the snow-covered Grand Tetons that you could buy in department stores, we had to look up at Van Gogh's bandaged head where he'd cut off his ear and sent it to some woman. Mary was arty and liked things to look nice. But when she began wearing leotards around the house and dancing in the kitchen with finger cymbals, I was afraid she was turning into a beatnik. But Mama said it was all right and with all my nine-year-old's wisdom, I understood.

About a year before, I'd gone into Mama's bedroom to get my violin out of the closet to practise. I noticed a new candy-striped dress hanging there. I pulled it out and began to laugh. The newest rage was the sack dress, a shapeless thing men across America were complaining about. It looked like a maternity dress, they said, and there were demonstrations in the parks and parades down Main Street in good-natured protest.

I ran into the kitchen waving the dress around and shouting, 'Hey, who's expecting? Ha, Ha!'

Mary was slicing tomatoes for dinner and arranging them on a willow-pattern plate. Mama was chopping big yellow onions to fry. Mama did not look up. She just said, 'Your sister is.' Then she slid the yellow onions into the frying pan. Mary went on arranging the tomatoes just so. They looked perfect on the blue plate. Like I said, she liked things to look nice.

I hung the dress back in the closet and got out my violin. I didn't practise for long. The smell of onions wafting through the house didn't make me hungry.

Mary named him Johnny. The hospital wouldn't let me in to see the baby or my sister because children under sixteen weren't allowed, although my sister was only fifteen then. Mary sent me hand-painted cards of girls in braids with freckles across their noses like me. I sent back pictures of cats. I couldn't draw girls.

Johnny looked like the blond, blue-eyed baby on the Gerber infant-food jars – the tapioca and apricot kind, I think it was. He was the best thing that ever happened to me up until then, but Mama said I mustn't talk about him at school; or at the library where she worked. She'd lose her job. But no one told me what I should tell Mrs Pearce, so that's why I made up the story about the young sailor lost at sea. Grandma always said my making up stories was too close to lying for comfort. But it kept Mrs Pearce from bothering Mary with questions.

Anyway, soon after the baby came home the judge gave us a divorce from our stepfather. Mama said it was on biblical grounds, but that was something else you didn't talk about at sharing time. I'm not sure how I knew that Mr E. was the father, but I was right.

Then there was my half-brother, Tony. At twenty, he went to college and was, according to Mary, an intellectual. He kept a tarantula in a box with a wire-mesh lid beside his bed. Every evening he let it out to tiptoe around his room, exploring shoes, tennis rackets, the cuff of his blue jeans, or, to my horror, stroll up my brother's bare arm.

Because his teacher said he had to, Tony chloroformed beetles and moths, speared them with sewing pins, attached tiny Latin labels and stuck them in neat rows on a cork board like sun-bathers at the beach on Labor Day weekend. Unborn things floated motionlessly in dill-pickle jars and a poster of the repro-ductive cycle of the common cockroach adorned his bedroom wall.

Our Russian Grandma died on a Wednesday and the day lost its charm. We passed by Grandma Mari's coffin where she slept in a lovely pink négligé like movie stars wore. Like me, she'd always liked movies. Her hair was done and she wore rouge on her high cheekbones. She looked happier than when Mama had married Mr E.; in fact, she looked so alive that I wanted to crawl into that coffin with her and explain why I'd made up the story about the sailor. I remember thinking, 'Don't go yet ... there are things I want to ask about the old days.' During the funeral, Mary whispered to me that I could cry if I wanted. But I couldn't. We didn't do much of that in our family.

Grandma left some especially fine things: a rosewood carving of a Chinese lady, hand-carved Russian spoons made by her father, a Jivaro Indian headdress and a box of recipe cards. All these were in a small pine chest my young grandfather had made over in Russia shortly before they'd emigrated. Mama had slept in the chest as a baby. Grandma Mari also left us the television which changed my life.

Every Thursday night, Mama, who usually frowned when

we watched television, saying that *I Love Lucy* and *Queen for a Day* would warp our minds, actually insisted we eat supper in front of *Travel to Adventure*. She said it was good for us. The programme took armchair explorers all over the world; the black-and-white films usually made my sister seasick.

That Thursday we balanced bowls of chicken soup on our knees and watched as a jagged coastline topped with twisted bare trees and thick cactus forests appeared on the screen. Gulls swooped over buttresses of lava rock. Rows of sea-lions dozed on a beach. A mass of black reptiles slithering into the sea struck a chord in Mama and she rose, spilling hot soup down the skirt of her dress. Her face was flushed, she looked as though she'd just won a fabulous prize. 'It's Galapagos!' she cried incredulously, leaping forward to turn up the volume.

'There's Uncle Gus!' Mama was shouting. '... And your cousins!' A bare-chested man sat in a dinghy. He rowed along a low cliff until he reached a partly built house and climbed out. When he stood up you could see a sheathed knife on a belt round his waist. Three children waiting there waved at the camera and followed our uncle, jumping nimbly from rock to rock. There were more rocks than I'd ever seen in my life; tumbled in heaps by the sea. The children waved to the camera and then a deeply tanned boy my age ran off and brought back a well-built man, taller than Uncle Gus and wearing a Robin Hood hat. He was the handsomest man I had ever seen, even better than Cary Grant when he swept off his hat with a flourish and invited the camera into the rock house which he was building. 'Meet the Duke of Galapagos,' said the narrator.

'That is your Uncle Carl and there is Aunt Marga, his wife, and her daughter Carmen, who is married to your Uncle Fritz,' Mama announced. Aunt Carmen was young, pretty and holding a little boy in her arms. Marga was fair, with a Dutch-boy haircut. She stood in the house Carl was building for her and pointed proudly, explaining inaudibly to us where this and that would go.

'... These children were born in paradise ...' continued the narration. '... They have never seen an automobile or shopped in supermarkets. Their toys are the wild animals who live beside them and school is the sea, the stars and the stories, told to them by Carl Angermeyer, of the world he and his two brothers left behind in Germany.'

'Hey!' I shouted. 'He means four brothers! Why don't they mention our father?'

Everyone shouted for me to be quiet. 'Well, he was there too, wasn't he?' I insisted. 'Once?' I whispered.

There in Galapagos, six thousand miles away, my Uncle Carl picked up a huge iguana and stroked its belly. The reptile grinned foolishly and closed its small eyes. Carl looked straight at the camera and smiled with all his white teeth, and I fell in love as only a ten-year-old can.

The film was scratched and badly edited. A picture of a tired but attractive young woman with dark eyes jumped to the screen. Her tiny waist and slim legs were accentuated by a very wide skirt. Aunt Lucrecia, Gus's wife, stood in front of a weatherbeaten door and played a concertina, tapping her foot and smiling. I wished we could hear the music. Mama said she bet she was playing the *Beer-Barrel Polka*, 'Lu's favourite,' she explained.

In the shade of a stand of mangrove trees by the sea, a tall, slender man bent over a rustic workbench. His shoulders were broad and his quiet manner reminded me of a story in school about Abe Lincoln as a young Kentucky woodsman. Uncle Fritz pointed to a graceful sloop bobbing in a shaded lagoon, which he had just built from island timber. He held out a massive hand with tapered fingers. On his palm were two-inch nails cleverly crafted from copper wire.

'. . . And for those with a sense of adventure and the courage to confront the odds of living in hell . . . or is it paradise? To the Angermeyers, anyway, it has been home since they left war-torn Germany in the 1930s. Three brothers who weren't afraid to do the impossible.'

Mama caught my eye before I could utter another protest. 'They don't have time to tell about the fourth brother,' she whispered.

Was it such a long story, I wondered?

Then our Galapagos family, whom I'd always known existed but had never expected to see, stood together on the beach. Carl lit his pipe and sat down on a large rock. Gus squinted into the sun and looked philosophical. Fritz smiled and folded his long arms over his bare chest. The women waved goodbye and turned to go. I wondered what they were going to make for supper that evening. The tanned boy bent over and picked up a baby sea-lion. It was covered in fine sand and sneezed sleepily into my cousin's gentle face.

Suddenly the camera focused on a high cliff with nesting birds and then back to the sea with dolphins jumping in the foam of a boat's prow. At my side Mary groaned softly as the waves rose and dipped.

'This stalwart Swiss Family Robinson has struggled for twenty years in this harsh and difficult land. Hunting for survival, they made their own shoes, delivered their own babies, built houses from lava blown from the bowels of the earth, and they survived. Yes ... a forbidding land for men and women with strong souls and a thirst for ... TRUE ADVENTURE!'

The last frames showed a lush jungle on the side of a volcano. Wild horses with flying tails galloped madly, startled, into the tangled forest of what looked like orange trees. A black-and-white sunset taken from the deck of a moving yacht bobbed up and down, up and down, as Galapagos merged with the horizon and disappeared from view.

Outside through the screen door, traffic on Arlington Street whooshed past. Supper dishes were washed and dried in silence; teeth brushed; baby tucked into his cot, cat let out and home-work forgotten. Each of us was lost on a private island of thought and dreams. I padded in my pyjamas to Mama's room to say goodnight and somehow make the evening linger. She did not hear me. I opened the door a crack and saw her sitting on the double bed brushing her dark hair. Suddenly she put the brush down and bent over a shoebox.

It was dusty, the string yellowed. Gently Mama untied the string and tipped the box on its side. Out over the patchwork quilt spilled the proof of past joys and sorrows. And to me, watching from the shadows, visions of a childhood faraway and impossibly out of reach.

Mary and I nestled like amiable spoons in the bed we shared. I lay for some time listening to the baby's regular, comforting breathing. Mama's light seeped from under her door and into our room until late. I found out much later that she was writing a long overdue letter.

'Mary,' I whispered, 'what happened to Hans?' I usually called him Hans. Father sounded so personal for someone you'd never known.

'He died.'

'Why do people die?' There was a long silence. Johnny turned in his sleep and began to suck on his tiny fist. 'I asked Ronnie Fink's father once ... she's a girl in my class ... her father's a preacher and he said it is God's will. He said that Hans was such a good man that God wanted him up in heaven with him.'

'What a stupid thing to tell a little kid,' said Mary.

'Yeah, that's what I thought.' I waited. Nothing. 'I mean, God must know we need him more down here?' I persisted.

'Yeah. What a dumb thing to tell a kid.'

'Yeah. Mary? You still awake?' My sister rolled over; a sure sign that I was meant to shut up.

'Yes, for one more second, so this is absolutely, positively, the last thing you are going to utter ... OK?'

'OK.' I cleared my throat. 'When Mama tells us about the old days, why doesn't she ever talk about how Hans died?' There. I'd said it at last.

A long pause.

'It's too sad. Some day you can read the letters,' she said, yawning. 'When you're older.'

I knew what she was really saying. The whole family claimed I was 'too sensitive'. The dictionary defined this as 'acutely affected by external impressions or susceptible to influence of light'. It was similar to what they'd said when I'd had chicken-pox and had to be kept in the dark. They reminded me that if I watched sad movies I didn't sleep at night. They also said I had a 'nervous stomach'. It was true, I threw up a lot; but that was only when I read in the newspaper about the old lady whose twenty-seven cats had to be put to sleep because she went into hospital. The others were always trying to protect me from things. But I had definite ideas about who was really sensitive in our house.

'The letters', I knew, were kept in that dusty shoebox that I'd seen Mama take out from under the bed. Father's mandolin was kept under there also. Along with the letters were old photographs and newspaper clippings dating back long before I was born. There were also drawings of full-rigged ships in distress in stormy seas, hand-painted cartoons of penguins and iguanas cavorting on the rocks of Galapagos, bits of hurriedly written music on yellowed paper, and house plans, lots of house plans. I'd only seen these once and had always wondered about their meaning. But the letters, written in German and English, were tied up with faded ribbon and the knot was tight.

Long after Mary's breath slowed and deepened, I lay awake. Questions flooded my brain and would not let me sleep. Why had we left Galapagos? And how – how were we going to get back?

'Well, Joanne, didn't you have your hand raised for Show 'n' Tell?'

I went bravely forward to address the fourth grade.

'Last night ...' I began –

'Speak up, Jo ANNE, the back of the class can't hear you.'

'LAST NIGHT ... I saw my uncles on the television and they live on the Galapagos Islands and have lizards that swim in the sea and seals for pets and they hunt goats and fish and play the accordion whenever they like and my Mom says they wash the dishes and their shorts in the sea and never wear shoes and there are wild stallions running in the mountains and some day ...'

'WHERE did you say this was, Jo ANNE?' Miss Bean squeezed her eyes at me over her butterfly glasses. 'Can you show us on the map?' She looked encouraging and pulled down the map of the United States and Canada.

'It's not on that one, ma'am.'

Miss Bean gave me her look reserved for children who spilled milk and pulled down the map of the world, which was rolled up over the blackboard like a window shade. Pursing her lips, she said, 'Now show us where these islands are, whatever they are called.'

'The Galapagos Islands are...'

'The gallapin' islands!' mimicked Curtis Smogett from the rear of the class. He and the other boys who picked their noses sat at the back. Their cries started up like gulls after a tasty morsel.

'The gallapin' islands!' They shouted louder, accompanied by gales of laughter. Erasers were launched and spit balls fell like confetti into the tadpole tank. Brian Woodhouse (whom the girls called 'Woodlouse') jumped on Curtis's back and he began to gallop around the desks. Miss Bean thrashed her desk with the big yardstick, and in the afterquake several large Encyclopaedia Americanas toppled over. In the silence that followed, she handed me her yardstick and I felt a sudden supreme power surge through my arm.

'Now then,' she continued with renewed composure, 'please show us where the Galampagins are.'

I glowered at Woodlouse, daring him to start up again, but the nose-pickers slouched down like subdued circus lions. I strolled over to the world map and searched the equator off the coast of Ecuador as I had searched so many times before during geography class. They were not there. They never were.

'Er ... mmmmmm ... they aren't on this map either. It's too big. They should be right here.' I said pointing with the yardstick which suddenly felt very limp. There was a dead silence. 'They are very small islands,' I said in a very small voice.

'Thank you, JoANNE, that was very interesting. Now Marjie, did you have your hand raised?' Marjie came forward with a Shirley Temple smile, her Brownie uniform crisp, merit badges adorning her flat chest. How I envied her her shiny new Minnie Mouse lunchbox. Her mother, who wore an apron all day at home, packed Marjie's lunches. Marjie's bologna sandwiches were lovingly entombed in Tupperware alongside two regulation carrot sticks and twin pack of Hostess cupcakes, one of which she always gave to Dennis Lizonbee – the handsomest boy in class. Of course he ate it. He wasn't allowed junk food at home.

'Last night,' she began, 'my baby Tommy...' I groaned inwardly. Not baby Tommy again! Every single Friday Marjie told us about her kid brother.

Dennis Lizonbee turned and offered me a dried apricot from his pocket. 'I saw that programme last night,' he whispered. 'It was neat! Are they really your uncles?'

'DENNIS? Would you care to share whatever it is you two find so interesting with the rest of the class?' queried Miss Bean.

'No, Miss Bean.'

Marjie beamed at Dennis and pressed on. Someday she would marry a promising executive, drive a sky-blue station-wagon, have three kids, attend PTA meetings and play bridge every Tuesday afternoon with 'the girls'.

Dennis smiled at me out of the corner of his eye and slipped me his last apricot.

2

The Robinsons of Galapagos

Weeks later Mama went to Dennis Lizonbee's father to have her neck cracked and came home with a copy of *Argosy* magazine which she'd found in the waiting room. The receptionist had insisted she take it. Amazingly, on the cover was a picture of Gus and Carl sitting on giant tortoises.

'THE ROBINSONS OF GALAPAGOS' said the cover. After Show 'n' Tell I'd begun to wonder if my uncles really existed at all but here they were again, looking as daring and dashing as Douglas Fairbanks and Robin Hood. Unfortunately, the article was written by someone trying to sound like Uncle Carl and not sounding, according to Mama, like him at all.

'Your uncles mix up their languages and invent words when they can't think of the right one.' She read the article aloud to us all as we looked over her shoulder.

'Santa Cruz, one of the islands in the Galapagos chain, is a lava-encrusted remnant of a prehistoric era, a speck of hostile land humping unexpectedly out of the Pacific wastes. This is my home. Now and then, hopeful escapists make half-hearted, futile attempts to settle here. Growing bitter and disillusioned, they soon leave, calling the place a hell-hole. My brothers and I have fought life-and-death battles with Santa Cruz for more than a quarter of a century. We think we've won most of them.

'If you were to join us and the handful of permanent settlers here, you would have to give up radio and TV. We have no telephones, no newspapers. We do without cars, stores, policemen and all the other amenities of civilisation, including doctors. What do we have in place of modern life? Well, we have three things you'll never find in your comfortable, civilized cities: a daily dose of adventure, complete freedom and the rare kind of zest that comes only with survival on the most elemental level. While you relax in front of your television sets, we catch sharks with our bare hands, wrestle wild pigs and play with monster-like beasts left over from the Stone Age.'

'Why do they catch sharks with their bare hands?' I asked. 'Why don't they use a rock or something?'

'They have to write that way in men's magazines,' Mary said. '. . . All guts and blood . . . the kind of stuff Mr Pearce reads.' I looked long at my sister. How did she know what he read? Had she been next door? Had they been asking her about the sailor? Mama read on.

'The Captain of the old schooner which left us ashore thought we were crazy. Four youngsters pretending to be Robinson Crusoe. "Do you have any idea what you've let yourselves in for?" he asked us. We did not answer but it struck us, as we surveyed the tortured coastal wilderness of rock, cacti and prehistoric lizards, that we had removed ourselves out of our own time and age. We were going back to the very beginning of existence.'

A year later they'd built a house in the lush highlands, caught and domesticated pigs, some goats, hunting dogs. Their fruit trees and vegetable patch were producing luxuriantly. Then, overnight, the four brothers realized just how isolated they really were.

Fritz and Gus, the youngest and the eldest, had gone wild-boar hunting. After some time they cornered a hairy monster. It charged without warning. They did not stand a chance. First the boar caught young Fritz in the legs with its massive tusks. Then it went on to throw Gus high in the air. Gus landed stunned, semi-conscious. Through his blinding pain, Fritz realized the boar would charge again and there was Gus, just sitting there, giddy and defenceless. The beast lowered its huge head, pawed the earth and snorted. Fritz rose with difficulty, using his rifle as a crutch. The very moment the boar charged, Fritz leaned against a tree to steady his trembling hand and fired twice. Both bullets struck the beast's heart. He thudded to the ground, twitched and died. Then Fritz fainted.

Gus carried him back to camp. The brothers examined Fritz's leg; the muscle was hanging out, a chunk missing. There was no doctor within six hundred miles and the wound required expert stitching. Hans had had some medical training but nothing like this. They had no iodine, certainly nothing against tetanus, not even any alcohol left. Out of desperation, they bathed the gruesome wound with lemon juice and bound it up in the cleanest cloths they could find.

Fritz soon became feverish. He begged all night for water. The leg festered and swelled. The brothers gathered outside of hearing distance. The wound would have to be lanced. Who would do it? They would never forgive themselves if their brother, a mere twenty years old, died. Had their coming to the islands been a senseless, irresponsible mistake?

While they planned the operation, Fritz rose quietly, limped to the campfire, heated his knife till it was red hot and lanced his own leg. His fever broke; the swelling went down. Within a week he was out of danger.

Hans voiced what they had all been thinking. 'We must build a boat to be able to get help if there is another accident.'

'It says "Hans", d'you hear? Our father was there, you see?' I said, trying not to let the choke in my voice come through.

'Of course he was there,' said Mama, looking down at me strangely, 'Where else did you expect him to be but with his brothers?'

Their three faces looked at me, a trinity of amusement and slight bewilderment. They couldn't possibly know how little I understood, how confused my sense of our past was. Embarrassed, I punched my brother in the arm, as though I'd merely been joking. Mama told us to stop horsing around and continued reading.

The other two dozen or so settlers living on the island scoffed at the Angermeyers' plan to build a boat. Even if they found the right timber, how would they get it out of the bush and down to the beach without a road, let alone wheels of some kind? It was impossible; they had no rivets, nails, screws.

But in time, with mind-boggling obstacles to overcome, the

brothers had built a small sailing boat. They'd been raised around boats, playing on rivers; a boat meant freedom. Now the island really felt like paradise.

The article ended with Uncle Carl's words:

> 'Why don't you come and see us? We'd welcome your visit. I've still plenty to tell you about our adventures. Plenty of peace and quiet on Santa Cruz. We can talk at leisure about everything.... Come to stay. But don't plan on staying unless you're ready to accept life on a lonely, abandoned, sun-baked bit of lava land. It isn't easy. You'll need every bit of your courage, your intelligence and your will.'

I sat back stunned. It was as though I'd been sitting at my uncle's side and he'd whispered those words right into my ear, for me alone.

But how in the world could we, a fatherless family with no skills, little muscle and even less money, ever hope of joining the Angermeyers on their lonely paradise out in the middle of the sea?

The next morning during arithmetic class I figured out that with my meagre weekly allowance it would take approximately twenty-nine years, four months and sixteen days to save the fare to Ecuador. Then I'd probably have to find a job cutting sugarcane in some forsaken jungle to raise the boat passage out to Galapagos.

'...JoANNE...JoANNE!' Miss Bean stared at me from the blackboard where she'd drawn what looked like limp balloons. '...Now if Barbara took two and Henry took three, how many chocolate eggs are left in Sarah's Easter Basket?'

I blinked away the blazing tropical sun from my daydream and Miss Bean turned her back in disgust.

Spring turned into a sizzling June of lemonade stands, Roy Rogers reruns and frying-pan sidewalks. Summer vacation was the closest I could get to paradise and I forbade myself so much as to think about Miss Bean or ever returning to school.

I began riding imaginary horses to meet Mama's bus down on the busy intersection of Magnolia Avenue and Arlington

Street. On that corner was a shrine dedicated to 'The Original Navel Orange Tree of California'. If I pushed my skinny shoulders through the wrought-iron railings surrounding the old squat tree, I could just manage to reach some of its branches and plunge my nose into its perfumed blossoms, which were about to form tiny oranges. I'd close my ears to the traffic and dream of riding through wild orchards on a Galapagos stallion and, when I felt thirsty, simply biting into big sweet oranges and letting the juice run down my chin. Then Mama's bus would pull up, belching black fumes, and we'd walk home together.

As Mama eased off her Dr Scholls, I'd watch her eyebrows. Russian eyebrows, I called them. If she'd had a hard day, they'd knit together over her dark eyes like ferocious protective caterpillars, and I'd leave her alone. But if they looked tame, I'd chatter about this and that and she'd patiently divide her attention between me and the newspaper. If I waited long enough, she'd bring the top of the paper up to the bridge of her nose then slowly begin to raise one eyebrow and then the other, faster and faster. They'd gain momentum like a turbo engine, while her eyes took on a deliciously wicked glint. Then, once she'd reduced me to a giggling jelly at her feet, she'd calmly resume reading.

Mama was never demonstrative; no hand-wringing when we were late home from the Saturday matinée downtown. No mushy talk when we got good grades or nagging when we didn't. She was understanding, intelligent and had a zany, quickly ignited sense of humour which sometimes frightened me it came on so suddenly. But the raw-edged emotions, the sadness, anger, longing ... all those were let out only when she opened her accordion case. I had many questions about our past, but I never asked. Tonight, I would tell myself, if her eyebrows are tame, I will ask about the old days. But then she'd disappear upstairs while we washed dishes and soon I'd hear the pop-popping of her accordion case being snapped open. While I dried the knives and forks, dreamy waltzes, tangos or oompah polkas would fill the house. We took the responsibility of being her children very seriously, adjusting to the moods of Pandora's Box. But if Mama played a Russian kamaranskia, slowly at first, then getting into her stride, faster and faster, her bellows billowing back and forth, I'd simply give up any notion of conversation and go and watch the *Ed Sullivan Show*.

Perhaps the real reason I simply did not ask Mama straight out about the old days with Hans in Ecuador and why we'd ended up back in America was because I was convinced my own version must be better. Living in the shadow of Hollywood and Disneyland, I daydreamed in Cinemascope, inventing stories with impossibly complicated plots, designing stage sets and choosing splendid casts of characters. I regularly fed my imagination and kept it close by even as I slept, like a glass of water on the bedside table. I knew what had happened to Hans, but preferred my version that he'd really been lost in the Amazonian jungle while searching for Atahualpa's treasure. This meant that he wasn't dead at all but suffering from amnesia and living with headhunters who befriended him because he looked like a blond god. One day I'd hire a canoe, find Hans, tell him who he was, trim his beard so Mama would recognize him and take him home.

Grandma's television blew up that summer when I was ten; right in the middle of *The African Queen*, when they were picking off leeches. I ran and phoned Mama at the library.

'You sure it won't work any more?' she asked in what I detected to be hopeful tones.

I explained I'd already kicked it, bent its antenna and checked the fuse-box in the kitchen, but it was done for. To my utter dismay she cheerfully said we'd 'get along without it'.

I was speechless. Then I recovered enough to list all the programmes we'd be missing that very evening. She told me to stop screeching and, typical of a librarian, read a book instead. Then she said she was bringing home a surprise. 'Wait till you see it . . . you'll be so excited.'

I returned to the vacant face of the TV and gave it one last kick. Some surprise, I grumbled. She'd probably bought a carton of Baskin Robbins new flavour number 30. It would melt in her handbag and people on the bus would stare as she dripped down the aisle. I decided I wouldn't meet her bus that evening.

When I met her bus, Mama's handbag did not drip as she stepped down on to the sidewalk. She wouldn't say a word about the surprise, she just smirked all the way home.

I eased off her shoes for her so she wouldn't waste time. Then she called Tony down from his homework, and Mary, who was bathing the baby, and drew from her handbag a small, yellowed envelope speckled with mysterious brown spots and bearing Ecuadorian stamps.

'It came this morning. It's from Uncle Gus. I wrote to him the night after we saw that travel programme and I sent school photographs of you all.' She seemed unable to control her excitement as we crowded around her armchair. My stomach felt queasy and my teeth throbbed as I clenched my jaws. None of them, not even Mama, knew how important that letter was to me. It would confirm once and for all that the wonderful Angermeyers of the Enchanted Islands were a part of us, that someone called Hans had really existed and that my dreams would all come true. Mother read:

Academy Bay, Galapagos
1958

Dear Emma,

Thanks for your letter. Tomorrow they say there shall be a boat so this is my writing night.

It was sure nice to hear from you. I'm glad that you have a good job which, I believe, you must like. I think California is a good place to live in and your children, Emma, they look swell, pretty and big they have grown. Yah, there we see again how fast the time is flying by ... even down here where things go so slow. We are always busy, plenty time, no time at all.

We still have our parties, music – music. Everybody plays something, accordion is *la moda*. Carl plays the guitar, Marga the violin, Fritz is beating any kind of drum – even an old frying pan – or the spoons.

That's life and they say life begins at forty and there is quite something in that, quite something.

I've been telling a little from here. Let me know if there is anything I can do for you. Everybody sends regards and I am wishing you and your children all the best of luck.

Till next time,
Gus

PS The tuna boats you ask about ... the last one came three or four years ago – very seldom we see them from a great distance on the horizon.

So. That was that. Tangible evidence which proved one thing all too clearly: the fabulous Angermeyers were thousands of miles away, living in paradise surrounded by dragons and volcanoes while we sat deep in thought, a sea of commuter traffic roaring by outside the screen door, a broken television in the corner and the six o'clock news blaring over the kitchen radio.

Poor, well-meaning Uncle Gus, how intensely I hated him with unreasoning passion. California was *not* a good place to live. Mama's job consisted of wading through dusty books written about other people's adventures and we, four people and a baby, ached inside for something unknown and out of reach.

'He never expects to see us, does he?' I said, breaking the silence. '"Wishing you and the children all the best of luck" and goodbye! Well, I'm going to Galapagos even if the rest of you don't want to and when I get there I would just like to see the expression on Uncle Gus's face!' I ran out, slamming the screen door for punctuation.

The air around the Original Navel Orange Tree smelled tangy and sweet. In the evening shadows I gripped the iron bars and climbed over the fence, catching my shirt on the top spike and bruising my knees painfully.

'You spoiled ninny!' I shouted. 'Just look at you standing there like a boring great oaf! Boring ... *Boring!*' Dashing about madly, arms swinging, I kicked the tree trunk and grabbed viciously at its carefully tended branches laden with dangling baby oranges.

'He never ... expects ... to ... see us!' Confused and helpless, I shook the padlocked gate and glared back at the car lights flitting by in regimented rows. I sank down by the plaque at the old tree's foot and wept. After what seemed a long time, exhausted and worried that a neighbour walking the dog might recognize me, I climbed out, wandered home, tiptoed upstairs and, still clothed, slipped in between the cool sheets.

Mama came in and sat on the edge of the bed, ignoring my pretence of instant sleep.

'You really want to go, don't you? More than anything?'

I snored softly.

'Well, listen, we all want to go and maybe, just maybe, we can.'

I bolted up in bed. 'But how? We don't have any money!' I hissed, keeping one eye on little Johnny, who began to stir. 'You know we can't.' My eyes began to fill and I dipped my head so she wouldn't see. Then she held me close. It felt exquisite but unusual. The moon's face peered at us through the window and I was reminded of something long ago ... something excruciatingly important ... Mama's button pressed into my cheek painfully but I did not move; and I could not remember what it was her holding me close reminded me of.

'You know that hacienda I've told you about in our stories?' Her heart beat faster under the button.

'The one in Ecuador that belonged to Tony's grandfather ... near the volcano?' I asked doubtfully. She hadn't told me much about it.

'Yes. Well, you see, some day, when Tony is twenty-one, he will inherit his third of that property and he will be a wealthy man. He will have to go down and take care of what is his, and it's such a big place, he will need our help, maybe.'

I allowed this astounding piece of news to sink in, but she mistook my silence for disappointment.

'It isn't so far then to Galapagos.'

I sat up even straighter, but she laid me back on the pillows. Perhaps I would get to the islands before I grew old after all. My brother was already twenty.

'Are there horses on the hacienda?' I asked.

'Oh, there must be dozens and dozens – and llamas and donkeys and cowboys, cattle, servants and Indians and ...'

'But how many horses?' I interrupted her, a bit uncomfortable at her sudden vehemence.

Mama seemed far away for a long time. Then, remembering me, she answered, 'There were – about ninety. I can't remember exactly.' She pushed the hair back from my forehead and, forgetting I still had my clothes on, began to tuck in the covers like they do in movies about distressed kids whose dogs get run over. I enjoyed it intensely but after some quick mental division I had to jump out of bed.

Forgetting the baby in the room, I pounded Mama on the back and then hugged her clumsily. 'Then good ol' Tony owns about thirty horses. Wowee! Boy oh boy!' I knew for a fact that my brother did not particularly like creatures with only four legs, so I dashed off to his room where he was studying for extra summer credit and asked what he would do with his herd.

'Oh, grind them into dog food I suppose,' he said glancing up from his trigonometry.

'Will you give them to me?' I asked seriously. 'Do you think we really will go there to your hacienda; to Galapagos?'

'Sure,' he said, far too easily to be convincing. 'Anyway, why do you think I've been slaving over those books on agronomy and soil erosion for all these years? Look, when we get there, I'll give you all my horses, OK? Now get lost or I'll get out my spider.' He frowned, burrowed back down in his calculations and I left immediately.

From then on I smiled a lot at my brother. He said it was ingratiating and entirely insincere. I still smiled. I even admired his tarantula one night and he tested me by offering to let me feed it mealy bugs. I settled for stroking its hairy, pipe-cleaner leg. I would have done anything for a horse.

Neighbourhood kids heard about our television and thought Mama a monster not to get us a new one. But I had to admit we were finding plenty to do without it. Mama seemed less tired at night, and began telling us stories out on the porch. Mary hung more Van Goghs and spent her allowance on sketch-pads and paints. Tony joined a record club and a new sound filled our little house every month: Brahms, Bartók, Brubeck and, once, an LP of authentic earthquake sounds from around the world. He said his collection would be an investment against boredom in Galapagos. I wondered what kind of lunatic would sit in paradise under a coconut tree listening to the groaning of the earth's crust. Mama promised she wouldn't let him take the record that far. She also reminded me that Galapagos wasn't paradise and that there weren't many coconut trees on the islands. But I must not have listened.

That summer I started collecting animals. They just seemed to arrive at the door; injured birds, abandoned goldfish, people's unwanted ducklings won at the county fair by throwing dimes into glass plates, rabbits with teeth problems, homeless hamsters.

Little Johnny, now a year and a half old, had what I considered to be a poetic look about him, a compelling depth in his blue eyes, a humorous turn to his mouth of one much older. He invented names for us all; I was Tanni. Mary was Loli. Tony was Bone. I found it disturbing that he called my Mama, his Mama. But when I tried to get him to call her Grandma he became confused. Besides, Mama at forty-five didn't look like a grandmother; Mary, sixteen and growing prettier every day, didn't look like anyone's mother and I didn't feel like an aunt.

That summer Johnny and I spent most days playing outside or cleaning my cages in the backyard. Of course he was really no help at all, but so funny I'd laugh until my sides ached. Maybe I laughed too loud, because I'd hear Mrs Pearce's screen door squeak and soon her head would be staring at us over the back fence, eye squinted as ever against the curling smoke. One evening, while Mama watched me shovel out the rabbit droppings, she commented that if we moved to Ecuador I'd have to face leaving my menagerie behind. She suggested I start thinking now of new homes for them all. I felt a lump in my throat, not only for my animals, but because it sounded like we really might go. My heart so swelled at the prospect, I found it hard to speak. As usual, I made a joke out of it, saying that I'd re-house my creatures if Tony gave up his earthquake record and if Mary left behind Van Gogh's bandaged head. Mama laughed dutifully but as I watched her go back inside I suddenly realized that she'd been planning our return to Ecuador for some time; her reluctance to adopt 'American' customs, the travel books brought home from the library, the firm refusal to replace our broken television. Slowly but surely she had weaned us from the American Dream. She had never really wanted to fit into the American jigsaw-puzzle at all.

The subject of moving cropped up at the supper table more and more. We now had a common goal, a no-longer impossible dream. We sat out on the porch almost every night that hot summer when I was ten. Moths fluttered around the light so much that we had to turn it off. Once the commuter traffic died down and all was still, Johnny would fall asleep on Tony's knees. Mary would invite the cat on to her lap. I'd make a pitcher of lemonade and put two ice cubes and a mint leaf in every glass, because Mary was particular that way. Once we'd all settled down, crickets would start to fiddle in the weeds of our flower bed. Then Mama would say: 'My parents and I used to sit out on our porch like this in Lincoln, Nebraska. We'd take turns churning homemade ice-cream, and neighbours would stroll by, saying, 'Guten Abend, Herr Vogel,' and we'd tell them to sit down and have some ice-cream. My Mama was famous for her ice-cream. Then someone would start to tell about the old days.'

My heart leaped every time Mama said that. And one night I handed her a glass of lemonade and said, 'Mama, you tell us about the old days.' And she laughed and said, 'Oh, I already told you over and over.' But I would insist and Mama would start; slowly at first, but then, like a kamaranskia dance, there would be no stopping her. Now, I couldn't be sure, but it seemed to me, that summer when I was ten, that even the crickets stopped their sawing and listened to my mother's story.

3

My Mother's Story: Capitán Marco

I suppose you could say it all began back in Russia in that spring of 1912 when Jacob Baltzar rode into town. Now Jacob was an honest horse trader, and, even more unusual, he spoke fluent Russian. This was quite uncommon, you know, because Russian Germans rarely left their isolated villages. But Jacob did business in Saratov and liked being able to eavesdrop in the taverns, so he could bring home with him the capital's latest gossip.

My Mammushka always suspected Onkel Jacob embroidered his facts during the long ride south across the steppes home to Wiessenmüller, because by the time he rode into town he always had colourful stories to tell; stories that were retold over and over during the long winter nights. She used to say the winds howled outside like starving wolves and the blizzards in the Volga region were so bad the villagers had to dig tunnels through the snow to check on neighbours in the next house.

It was Jacob's business to buy thin, skittish colts up north and bring them home to graze on rich summer grass and then sell them in Saratov for a profit. The children of Wiessenmüller always ran out to greet Jacob when he arrived and he would laugh and make his ponies prance and snort for them. But one particular day, Mammushka said, he rode in looking very subdued, and his ponies shuffled tiredly. The town gossips immediately blamed Jacob's wife, of course, saying he was making too many trips to Saratov because he had to pay for her new parlour.

Now Frau Vogel, the cabinet-maker's wife, had a parlour *and* a silver samovar, so naturally she insisted Jacob come to her to tell his tales. Her spotless kitchen would fill up with people all watching Jacob eat Frau Vogel's famous piroshki and drink tea laced with watermelon syrup. Your grandmother used to make her recipe, do you remember?

Anyway, when Jacob finished, he would always wipe his black moustache, carefully fold his napkin and then, copying the typical drawn-out Russian way, begin.

'Last night ... out on the steppes ... as I rode from the great city of Saratov ... home to Wiessenmüller, home of my father and his father before him ... I, Jacob, sure as I sit here, saw ... the *Devil*!'

Mammushka used to laugh, telling how Frau Vogel got up and quickly shut the window as if the Devil himself might be lurking outside at that very moment! Jacob said he had staked out his ponies the night before, as he always did, and made a small fire and went to sleep on his saddle with his gun nearby in case of wolves. His ponies were huddled together, everything seemed all right and he fell asleep.

Suddenly, he awoke to a terrible sound of the earth rumbling beneath his ear.

'Who is there?' he called out. There was no moon, but the ponies were shining in an eerie glow. 'Who is there?' he repeated. Then he heard thunder like a thousand hooves. His horses began to scream, bolted their stakes and stampeded off. Jacob leapt to his feet to catch them, but fear made him turn. And there he saw – the huge eye of the Devil shining down on him! Clouds of smoke billowed from the devil's mouth and it screamed hideously. Poor Jacob began to run, his heart banging. But the demon kept chasing him. He ran faster and faster, but at last his poor legs buckled. He fell to the earth. His time had come. The beast spat fire and smoke over him and screamed so loud his ears crackled. Covering his head like this, he shouted '*Da! Fress mich!* Eat me!'

Of course when he was not killed he looked up and saw the monster fly right past him, glowing sparks flying from its long iron tail, smoke pouring from its black head. You understand? It was a train! He'd made his camp beside iron train-tracks.

Apparently the Tsar's railroad was crisscrossing the steppes from Saratov down to the Caspian Sea; from the Don River to the Ukraine, and this worried Jacob, for it meant the Russians were moving closer to their settlements.

Worst of all, Mammushka always told me, was the rumour that another war was brewing and that all the promises made by Katerina the Great would be broken and Russian Germans would be conscripted into the army. Of course the young men, who did not remember the Crimean War, scorned this. But their fathers and grandfathers recalled too well their bitter years in the Tsar's army: the floggings, the persecutions because they were neither German nor Russian, the starvation, their frozen feet wrapped in rags with hide from dead horses. In desperation some men had even inflicted injuries upon themselves so they would be rejected by the army. My Mama said every village had its blind, deaf or lame men to add to those mutilated in battle.

When Jacob rose to go, he said to those assembled, 'Whose cannons will our young men feed this time?' There was no time to waste. In the larger settlements he had heard about secret meetings, agents encouraging families to get out and go to America. All you needed was a sponsor to guarantee work. The real problem was getting the papers to get you past the Russian border.

Before Jacob left, he warned everyone to watch their tongues. Spies were everywhere and now, with this train, reports would get back to the officials very quickly. People were being sent to Siberia merely for criticizing the authorities.

Now, my mother, your grandmother Mari, was a young girl of about sixteen when all this happened. She had heard about America from her teacher who used to fill her pupils' heads with stories of, oh, all sorts of wonderful faraway places. This Mademoiselle Irina Avdyeevna was very outspoken too, encouraging my mother to get a high-school diploma and even go on to university, which was unheard of for a woman in 1912! My mother remembered all the times her teacher had spoken out against injustices and the government. She would have to be warned. Mammushka said she felt afraid that afternoon; the reliable world she knew was falling apart and, worse, when she got home, she found the *Freir*, or matchmaker as we would say, in discussion with her parents.

It was suggested that my mother should marry the cabinet-maker's son, Georg Vogel. But Mama was headstrong and wanted an education. Her mother, Frau Greb agreed. But Herr Greb, the village Burgermeister, though he respected education had six daughters to marry off and Mari was the eldest. Georg was a hard worker and came from a good Lutheran family. With his skills and her brains, they would do well in life. Mammushka could take her exams and get her diploma, but university was out of the question. The wedding would be in early June, and that was that.

Of course, my mother's teacher was unhappy at the news. But she told her that dreams come true, not just in books but sometimes in real life. 'Mari Katrina,' she said, 'you are stubborn and you have a good mind. You could make things happen.' And of course my mother never forgot those words.

One day in late spring Mammushka sat in the schoolhouse. She had passed her examinations and her diploma hung in a place of honour in her parents' parlour. She was very proud as Mademoiselle Irina passed among her pupils praising their accomplishments. Suddenly the door burst open and about five or six soldiers grabbed Irina Avdyeevna and carried her kicking and screaming out to a black coach and drove her away. The older boys chased after but she yelled from the coach for them to keep back. They never saw her again.

My parents were married in June and moved in with the Vogels. My mother was philosophical about it all; she respected her in-laws and they treated her well. Frau Vogel kept a clean, pleasant home and had more status now that her son had married the Burgermeister's daughter. With such an industrious new daughter-in-law to help with the chores, she had more time on her hands to gossip with her friends in the town square. Every day her cronies would ask Frau Vogel the same question and every day she shook her head and said no, she wasn't to be a *babushka* yet.

Georg had made a small pine chest, at his mother's insistence, for storing baby clothes. My mother knitted a few little caps and embroidered a small blanket, but she was far more interested in the old schoolbooks kept in that little chest. When everyone had gone from the house she would open the lid, sit on the bed and read poetry and leaf through the pages of the book which interested her most of all: geography. She told me that she would play a little game; closing her eyes, pointing blindly to some place and then opening them to see what part of the world she had chosen. Often she let her mind stray to the summer days when Mademoiselle Irina had taken her pupils out on to the steppes for picnics among the wild poppies. The sun would warm their backs and their teacher played her little accordion and told of faraway places she herself had never been to.

Now Georg, my father, was kind and dependable, but Mama found him unimaginative. Little did she realize that he had taken to heart what Jacob Baltzar had said. That winter, he wrote to his father's distant cousin in America. Five months later Father got a reply which made him lean against his work bench in amazement. '*Natürlich*,' wrote dear, wonderful Uncle Henry, 'of course we will sponsor you and your wife Mari to come to America!'

Father decided not to tell Mother right away. The winter had been severe. She had been ill. He would tell her in a few weeks, he thought, after the baby was born. Well, two days later he received terrible news. An official-looking paper came. In three weeks he had to report for duty in the Russian Army! Of course, he had to tell my mother then! What were they going to do? How could they get out without documents? That's when Jacob stepped in. He had bought papers and tickets for himself and his wife to leave Russia. But, while making his last journey into Saratov with a string of yearlings, he was kicked so badly in the ribs, the doctor forbade him to go. Jacob insisted my parents go instead, that he and his wife would come later.

Naturally, the Grebs and the Vogels were very upset; none of them had ever been away from the beautiful district where the land was rich and food plentiful for those who worked hard. And of course no one knew for sure that America would be any better than Russia, and now their long-awaited grandchild would be born thousands of miles away. But they had no choice, you see. Frau Vogel gave Mama a large loaf of rye bread, sausages and watermelon pickle for the long journey to the border and Grandmother Greb gave her daughter her Bible, some wooden spoons Herr Greb had carved and Mama's beloved high-school diploma in a frame. They helped my parents pack a few belongings in that little pine chest and tucked rugs around them in the sled. They left Wiessenmüller very early one cold morning, removing the bells from the horse's harness, for no one must be aware that they had gone in case the soldiers came looking for Father. Poor Mammushka was in shock. She kept looking back and saying she could not leave behind the beautiful cradle Father had made for the baby.

When they got to the border they had to wait many hours for their papers to be inspected. Many people were turned back and my father was terribly worried that the authorities would see that he, being a red-head, did not match the description on Jacob Baltzar's documents. Terrifying stories were going around about cruel punishment for anyone deserting the army. It isn't surprising, I guess, that I was born unexpectedly, in the Red Cross refugee station. I was named after my mother's youngest sister. You know that pine chest your Grandma Mari left us? It has a domed lid. Mammushka turned it upside down and that was my cradle.

Just as Grandfather Greb predicted, my parents did well together. Nebraska was a good place to live and by the 1930s Father had his own construction business. But I guess he could never quite understand why my mother was so restless. After all, she had a nice house with a basement and a parlour and a player-piano. But that wasn't enough for Mama. She found a job as pastry chef in Lincoln's finest hotel. As she wished, I learned to play the accordion and went to university. My father couldn't see the sense in studying art and Spanish. Such a silly waste of time, he used to say. If only he had known!

Now in our family we have always followed the German–Russian custom of cleaning the house top to bottom on Saturdays. We waxed the floors, dusted, shampooed hair, polished our shoes, ironed, canned pig knuckles, brewed homemade beer and hosed down the sidewalk. Then, in the evening, Mama and I would get all dressed up and go downtown to the talking pictures. Mama loved the movies. For days after she would hum Fred Astaire songs around the house. When the picture finished, we would walk home, strolling by the department-store windows, looking at the latest fashions. Mama was awfully clever about copying dresses for me.

One night we were admiring the mannequins in Gold's Department Store. Mama was chattering away in German, saying that I'd look good in this and that. Suddenly she nudged me. There were three dark figures staring at the men's fashions in the next window. I heard one of them speak. I whispered to Mama, 'They're speaking Spanish!'

'Go on, say something to them! Here is your chance to practise.'

But I couldn't just walk up to strangers and begin talking to them. So Mama says, 'Well, if you won't, I will!' and she marches over and says *'Buenoos nocheeese.'* Well, I just about fainted with embarrassment. But the young men's faces lit up. In broken English they told her that they had just arrived from Ecuador, South America, and were studying flying at the Charles Lindbergh School of Aviation.

'Did you ever hear of such a thing?' Mama turned to me. 'Coming all that way from South America just to fly an aeroplane!' And then she asked them to explain the principles of aerodynamics to her. The tallest one of the group looked too much like Tyrone Power for his own good, I thought, and he was a shameless extrovert. When he ran out of words to answer Mama, he stretched out his arms and began soaring up and down the sidewalk making aeroplane noises. His friends thought it was hilarious. So did Mama. She clutched the arm of his overcoat and invited him and his friends home for coffee in our basement! I was shocked. Strangers were always shown into the parlour, you see. And then Mama invited them to a big wedding the following weekend!

'Mama!' I said later, when we were washing the dishes. 'How

could you invite them to a Russian–German wedding? What will everyone say?'

'They will say what handsome young men come from that Ecuador place. They will say how they would like to see their daughters marry somebody more interesting than a flat-footed farmer who dances like he was stepping over cowpats. Anyway, don't you worry about those three,' she said. 'They are not after Russian–German *hausfraus*. All they want is to eat good Volga–Deutsch food and not feel so homesick. You don't understand what it is like to be a stranger in a foreign land. I do.'

Our weddings lasted three days, you know. I played my accordion with the band and those Ecuadorians, Alfonso, Luis and Marco, ate and drank and seemed to have a good time. When we musicians tired, a record would be put on the Victrola so the dancing never stopped. Now, I didn't see her do it, but thinking about it now, I bet it was Mama who brought a tango to that wedding. Next thing I knew, the tall one was asking me to dance. No one else danced. Marco said later that I was the only girl on the prairie who knew how to tango. You see, Mama and I had seen it done in the movies and had practised it down in our basement.

In the weeks that followed, Marco came by the house a lot. We learned that he came from what sounded like a rather aristocratic family in Quito, the capital city of Ecuador, high in the Andes. I got the impression that his mother was a bit eccentric; going off to Mass early every morning dressed in black, with rice-powder on her cheeks. She hadn't wanted Marco to leave the country or become a pilot. His elder brother had died and Marco was in line to manage their estates. Doña Aguirre, as she was called, even went to the archbishop, but he could not change Marco's mind.

He answered an ad. in the paper for the Lindbergh Flying School, which offered courses in Spanish. But, he said, when he got off the train in Lincoln, his heart sank; all those endless miles of prairie, not a hill in sight, and he had come to Nebraska to learn how to fly in the Andes.

Now Mama had saved up some money and bought a small car. So every week she took the three boys and me skating, to the museums, on picnics or to the movies. Their English improved a lot and they did well in their courses. Soon they were flying over Lincoln. Marco invited me up once and we flew over the magnificent State Capitol Building and even over our own house. I could see Mama waving down there. My father wasn't convinced that flying was a good idea.

When we landed Marco said he would need much more powerful planes to fly in his country because the Andes were 20,000 feet high in places – so high their heads were lost in cloud and covered in snow. Some day, he said, flying 16,000 feet high would be normal. He said that one day he would be the greatest pilot in Ecuador. Then he laughed and added there was only one other pilot in his country. Well, I couldn't say much to that; the wind was so strong up in that plane, you know the old type like in the movies, the spit had been blown right out of my mouth and I could not find my voice.

In June, after graduation, I went down to Oklahoma to visit the Baltzars. I had a wonderful time and came home full of tales of cyclones ripping the doors off barns and Jacob's dashing sons roping wild mustangs and being chased by runaway steers. I noticed Marco was very moody one day when he sat in our basement. The more I chatted, the more quiet he became. I didn't know what was wrong with him and when he didn't come by for a whole week, I thought it very unusual.

The next weekend Mama packed a big picnic with fried chicken, lemonade and chocolate cake. We got into her Olds-mobile and set off to pick up the boys. Mama made me sit in the back, which was all right with me. But when the boys got in, she made Alfonso and Luis sit up in front with her and pushed Marco in the back with me, which was very silly, as we could all see that they didn't have enough room in the front and that Mama could barely reach the gear-stick. Well, my Mama behaved very strangely, driving at a crazy speed, screeching round corners. I thought she had gone mad. I noticed Alfonso crossed himself a few times as we nearly ran someone down. Mama had her rearview mirror at such an angle you just knew she couldn't see the traffic behind. Marco and I were sliding every-which-way over the slippery seats in the back. Suddenly to my surprise Marco grabbed me and kissed me! And just as suddenly, Mama slowed down the car, smiled and readjusted her rearview mirror.

> 16 August 1936 – Lincoln has a number of brides this Sunday, blithe young creatures defying gravity as they float about in rosy clouds of romance.
>
> But to none, as she goes up the Lohengrin Lane, will come quite the romance of Miss Emma Vogel. For her bridegroom is First-Lieutenant Marco Antonio Aguirre, twenty-six years old, of his country's aviation department.
>
> The slender, dark-eyed young man will be serving as assistant instructor in the army flying-school established about a year ago in Guayaquil, coastal city of about 120,000 in Ecuador.
>
> . . . Very eager to return to his native land, he takes with him a very slim young wife, Emma Vogel until today. Her life has not waited for South America for all its glamour. She was born in Russia. Ecuador takes her to the south, to the blue Pacific waters, very far from those Baltic shores of her infancy.
>
> *Lincoln Sunday Journal and Star*

For a girl coming from the prairies, it was unbelievable to find myself high in the Andes surrounded by majestic green mountains with their heads lost in cloud! We arrived by a train pulled by an old-fashioned, wild-west engine. It was cold and gloomy that afternoon and my head was swimming with the altitude. All I wanted in the world was to lie down on a soft bed and go to sleep.

No one met us. We had to hire a very tired-looking Cadillac to take us to the hacienda. Marco's face was so happy when we drove up the drive, but when we stopped at the door he looked like a stranger. Black crêpe was still draped there to mourn his brother, who had been dead for years! He got out and yanked it down, saying, 'I told them to take it all down before we arrived. I told them!'

There were no servants in sight to help with the bags, no welcome wave from the window, but I did notice a thin, pale hand close a curtain. A servant showed us into a drawing room where my new in-laws were waiting. You can imagine my dismay when I saw the room was full of relatives. They were silent as I was shown to a red velvet Louis XIV chair. Of course my Spanish was not up to the polite conversation which followed, and Marco was carefully placed far away from me at the opposite end of the room. I was pretty sure I saw Doña Aguirre smile at my predicament, and it didn't take me long to realize that I was a great disappointment. I found out later that they all felt that if Marco had to bring a *gringa* home, at least he could have chosen a big blonde one.

Unfortunately, Marco's work, setting up an aviation school down on the coast, took him away most of the time. I was left in that cold house alone. I said I didn't mind roughing it, you know, I would have preferred going down to Guayaquil with him. But he said there wasn't any time to build accommodation for married couples because all their effort was going into finishing student barracks and draining the runway, which flooded constantly.

Well, I tried to entertain myself, but I missed having books and, although I had my accordion, I didn't feel like playing it with my sourpuss mother-in-law stalking the corridors. So one day I slipped on my coat and went into town to the market. It was very exciting, seeing all the exotic fruit being sold on the cobbled streets by Indians. I was elated and came home with a basket full of chirimoyas, guayava and three kinds of banana. But my sister-in-law met me at the door. I could see by her astonished expression that I had done something very wrong.

'Oh, but you must never go out alone to the market!' she said. 'No, you must hire an Indian to carry your parcels home!' As Señora Emma de Aguirre, she said, I must always appear to be feminine and '*delicada*'. Otherwise, what would the '*gente decente*' think?

But I soon realized that Latin women had it all worked out; even in the church, wasn't a so-called helpless woman hailed to be the very mother of God?

With time, I learned all the rules. I shouldn't talk to Indians unless it was to give them orders, which I couldn't do anyway, since my mother-in-law ran the household. But I'll tell you, as lowly as the Indians were meant to be, I began to suspect that the prettier girls were more than servants in families with young squires.

It was a pretty big culture shock for me and I rebelled against most of it. One day, chaperoned or not, I took myself into Quito to explore the old streets. It really was a most fascinating city; like a jewel cupped in between the folds of the Andes. I always wished Mammushka could see it and sent her long letters and sketches of the things I discovered.

Marco flew home when he could. He wasn't happy at seeing me stuck in his parents' house, but he would say, 'Emmasha, things are really beginning to happen now. A famous German pilot, a war hero, is coming here to discuss my ideas for an airline. All we need are alternative air routes mapped out over the Andes. Just think what it will mean for Ecuador! Instead of the two days needed to come up here by train, we will do it in an hour!' He would get very excited and promise to take me up as soon as he had a safe route mapped out. He said no one could imagine what it was like to fly over the Andes like a condor, with God's own view of the world.

I used to worry a little about that German war hero. His name was Major Hammer. Father had been sending me clippings from home and there was a lot about the state of affairs in Germany and Hitler. I didn't like the sound of the Youth Movement and I wondered what this Major Hammer's real interest was in little Ecuador. Of course, I could not share these thoughts with anyone, least of all Marco, who almost worshipped the man.

Marco arrived unexpectedly one day and, handing me my coat, he hurried me out to a waiting car. We drove into the oldest part of the city, to a cobbled street I'd always admired and had sometimes sketched. Marco dragged me up the street and, huffing and puffing, we stopped before a large, medieval-looking door. Then he took a big iron key from his pocket and let us in.

'Our house!' he said grandly. I didn't know what to say! A fountain gurgled in a paved patio. There were doves on the roof-tiles. There were five rooms below and an exterior staircase leading to five more above. There was a wonderful view of the street in the front and another of the volcano Pichincha, which towers over the city. It was really too grand for us and I couldn't understand where he'd found the money.

'I borrowed it from my father,' he said. His mother didn't know about it. Well, although I was tickled at the idea of putting one over on my mother-in-law, I didn't like being in debt. Still, for me, it meant freedom and I tell you I enjoyed the months that followed. We hired a few servants – a doorman named Don Benito, who only had one leg but somehow would double as a handyman, an Indian cook and a young girl, Pastora, to clean and wash clothes. I sewed bright curtains by hand, bought big pots of geraniums at the weekly market just outside the door and soon the house on Rocafuerte Street was home. Now I could speak to Indians when I liked and I even made friends with a blind beggar on the corner who played a wheezy accordion. Of course, I played my accordion when the mood took me and I carried my own parcels about town. My treat for the week was taking tea down in the fancy Hotel Metropolitano; it was the fashionable thing to do, you know, there was a three-piece orchestra that played all the latest hits from Europe. It was so respectable there that I could even go alone when Marco was away and it was on one of these visits that the accordion player, who I discovered was a Russian named Boris, came and sat at my table. When he found out I'd been born in Riga and that I played the accordion he begged me to join his little group. He said I should come that evening to practise with him and his boys. However Marco came home that night with the rumour that there would be a revolution the next day. The streets were not a good place for me to be.

But I did play tangos and polkas on the radio quite regularly. I knew Marco could hear our programme way down in his jungle hut and, I guess, it made him seem closer. Sometimes, when I thought he was still down on the coast, he would appear through the door, goggles still around his neck just to impress me, I think. He was always full of his latest adventures. The German had said this or that, they'd climbed up to this or that altitude; they had looked straight into Cotopaxi volcano, or seen bears climbing its snowy sides or condors flying above its crags. Sometimes they dipped over the jungle and spotted headhunters paddling canoes up the brown waters of the Amazon. In the beginning I thought he was exaggerating, but with time I learned that he didn't even report to me his more daring exploits for fear I would worry.

One morning when Don Benito brought me the *Comercio* newspaper at breakfast, I opened it to see headlines about an 'Emergency Landing in Sigchos'. Well, of course I was really worried, but it was another pilot, named Olivas. There had been a terrific storm in the jungle, completely blocking this pilot's route through the mountains to Quito. When they lost radio contact with him, Marco volunteered to search. The paper said he took off in torrential rain that afternoon. But to everyone's amazement, Marco found Olivas's plane down in a jungle clearing far away, in the remote village of Sigchos. He was very pleased with himself when he came home that night. He had been promoted to captain and, with the better salary, we could pay off our debt. But Marco was even more pleased when he found the baby shirt I was embroidering.

Naturally, Doña Aguirre took more interest in me when she found there was to be an heir. She told Marco to give me the family diamond, a huge rock which was too big for my hand.

Marco's flying school was doing really well. Major Hammer brought his famous 'Blue Bird' plane to Ecuador. That was how serious he was about Marco's plans to form 'La Sociedad Ecuatoriana de Transportes Aereos'. They had financial backing. As I said, I didn't care much for this German, but if it meant Marco was able to spend less time on the coast, I was happy. The rainy season came in December. The poor pilots lived in a quagmire! The insects were awful and the heat so bad, Marco said, they dripped perspiration all day and night. The jungle grew incessantly. It was a constant enemy, you know, trying to swallow up the runway. So I wasn't surprised when Marco couldn't get up to Quito when Tony was born in late February. They sent his daddy a radio message, but a third of the airstrip had been washed away and he was grounded.

We had good weather in Quito. They said it was the city of eternal spring, but we did get a lot of fog rolling down Pichincha. It crept by the Hospital Militar where I was. I enjoyed watching it swirl by from my bed and hearing the street vendors shout below in the street. But one morning, when Tony was about three or four days old, I lay in bed after breakfast and wondered why the streets were so quiet. All I could hear was a sound like chains being drawn over the cobbles – or heavy boots. It went on and on. I was very curious but I didn't like to get up because I was a bit giddy. Still, the noise got louder and louder. Then I heard low moaning. I thought I was hallucinating, but the moaning turned into a trumpet. Then I began to giggle because I realized the military band must be practising. Marco used to warn me that he wouldn't take me to any more military functions because the minute the band started to wheeze and honk on their beaten-up old instruments, I couldn't keep a straight face through the national anthem. But this was really the worst din I'd ever heard. I got up from bed. I managed to get to the window and look out. Then I saw the reason for the morbid horns. A funeral procession was passing below. The horse-drawn hearse was draped in black – it had gladioli on the top. I could see it was someone very, very important; the dictator was there and the archbishop. And then I saw my mother-in-law.

The doctor told me later that they hadn't told me about the accident because they thought it would be too much of a shock.

1 March 1938

YOUNG ECUADORIAN WHO STUDIED FLYING HERE AND
MARRIED LINCOLN GIRL DIES IN AIR CRASH ON WAY TO
SEE HIS BABY

Death rode the plane that was taking Captain Marco Antonio Aguirre to see his new son, and he died in the high Andes before he saw the little mite.

His young widow will find consolation in the fact that Captain Aguirre was greatly loved by many and the funeral was an exceedingly large one in which the dictator, together with members of his cabinet, were present.

Learning of the birth of his son, he left by plane with Major Hammer, a well-known and expert flyer who for many years has travelled in South America and who had an exceptional war record in Germany.

They must have encountered heavy fog and sleety rain in trying to cross the cordillera and before Major Hammer was able to see the danger, their plane struck one of the crags of the Andean range.

Lincoln Sunday Journal and Star

4

My Mother's Story: Hans

Do you know, it was 1939 and still we did not have tomatoes in Ecuador? I had heard that an Italian had imported some seed and that we would be seeing them in the marketplace eventually, but every week I looked up and down the stalls, and no tomatoes.

I loved standing on my balcony and watching Rocafuerte Street on market-day. Early in the morning Indians arrived from the countryside and set out their blankets and baskets full of yellow corn, potatoes, onions, green bunches of fresh herbs and tropical fruit. Mind you, by noon some of the fruit got trodden on and began to give out a sickly-sweet smell, but the afternoon rain came and gave the street a good wash. Every afternoon the rain came; Don Benito said you could set your watch by it, but then, he was never on time.

That morning in September, I got ready to go out to buy Tony some new shoes because he'd given his away to the boy who sold lottery tickets outside our window. I grabbed my basket in case I found any tomatoes, and was just about to leave when Don Benito handed me the morning *Comercio*. The headlines shouted that Great Britain was at war with Germany. It was a blow. I should have expected it, but we had lived a simple, secluded life up till then in Ecuador. Our revolutions were quite harmless. Your grandfather sent me clippings from the *Lincoln Sunday Journal and Star* often, so I should have seen it coming. All the Volga Deutschen left in Russia who had survived the First World War would be in trouble again; rounded up and sent to camps or worse. Germans in America also had problems. Mammushka wrote that she had been talking to a neighbour lady in German one day on the street, like she

45

always had, and a policeman came up to her and said, 'We don't allow that kind of talk in our country, lady!'

Well, I remember thinking it was too beautiful a morning to think about terrible news. I decided that that afternoon I would take little Tony up to the waterfall on the side of Pichincha for a treat. We loved hiking up there for picnics and when Tony fell asleep I would often sketch the lovely view of Quito.

I remember I could barely get out of my own door that morning. Big pink onions were stacked against the wall of the house, a woman had a large enamel basin full of roast pork, everyone was haggling and roosters were crowing. But over all the noise I heard a deep foreign voice shouting. It came from the cheap *pension* across the street, the *pension* that had just installed a telephone. Of course this hadn't been connected properly and it rarely worked and, besides, the Indians kept lifting the receiver to hear the dial tone. Then I was sure I heard a bit of German.

There were so many Germans coming to South America! In one of her letters Mammushka had said at least America was safe from that German 'nincompoop', as she used to call Hitler. Mama came down to Quito, you know, soon after the accident. She was so excited, I remember, and kept saying, 'It is just as I was reading in my books!' Dear Mama, you know, she made so many friends in Quito, and when she found out they had no ice-cream, she went into business with an Austrian who had a struggling coffee house. He told her she would never find enough ice in Ecuador to make ice-cream. But Mama hired an Indian to run up Pichincha's sides and bring ice down on his back – wrapped in leaves. And the Austrian's business became a big success. Anyway, you want to know about that German making the telephone call.

He kept shouting, '*Barco! Barco! Cuando? Bitte? Bitte?*' He was very tanned, like someone who spent a lot of time out of doors, and his hair was very blond. I think that if he had been dressed smartly – like I thought a Nazi would have dressed – I would have walked on down the street looking for tomatoes. And if he had been too shabby I also would have walked by. But his jacket was washed and carefully pressed, though you could see it was patched at the elbow. Well, I wasn't the only one who noticed him; a crowd of Indians had gathered round him, which seemed to irritate him even more. '*Allo? Allo?*' he kept shouting into the telephone. Finally I spoke up in German and asked if I could help. I explained I spoke Spanish. He gave me the receiver.

'Please,' he said very formally, 'I am speaking to the Guayaquil Port Authorities. I need to know when the boat is leaving for Galapagos.'

I thought I had misunderstood him. 'To where?' I asked.

'The Galapagos Islands.'

Well, I shouted into the mouthpiece and a faint voice said the ship would not be leaving for weeks or even months, because it had engine trouble. That poor German looked so depressed by this. I said I had to walk down the street anyway so we went together towards his hotel, talking about the bad news of the war. I could barely keep up with him, his stride was so long, like a sailor's I thought. He seemed distracted by the bare-bottomed babies playing under the fruit stands and the thin dogs staring at the basins of roast pork. When we paused at the corner and I gave the blind accordion-player a few coins, I noticed the German frowned at the chipped enamel cup between the beggar's cracked feet. I remember saying, 'I always give him something – he cheers the street up a little, don't you think?'

Well, the German said very little, but his nose seemed to find the smells objectionable and I began to feel a little apologetic and said in the afternoon the street would be washed by the rain and smell as sweet as carnations by morning. I thought to myself, why should I feel defensive?

When we walked past his hotel I was just about to say goodbye to my silent companion, with some relief I might add, when an Indian trotted past us thrashing a donkey. It was an old donkey and it slipped on the cobbles and fell under its load of charcoal sacks. The Indian began beating the animal, who closed its eyes. You couldn't help noticing that its flesh was scarred where ropes had bitten into its hindquarters. Well, it was as though something snapped inside the German. He caught the Indian's arm and wrenched the stick away. I thought for a minute, that he was going to beat the Indian. The Indian clearly thought so too, because he whipped off his hat and put on a pathetic expression. But the German ripped the sacks from the donkey, shoved them into the Indian's arms, pulled the poor beast to its feet and cut the ropes from under its tail, all the while shouting in Low German. Of course the Indian was very impressed, but he did not understand a word, so I told him: 'This *gringo* says that if you ever mistreat a donkey again, he will find you and likewise beat you!' That Indian nodded quickly, mumbled something and shuffled off with the donkey.

When the German had calmed down he apologized for having embarrassed me. But you know, I told him I'd been wanting to do something like that for years! Suddenly I realized he was suffering from acute culture shock. I remembered Mammushka's words, 'You don't know what it's like to be a stranger alone in a new country.' But of course, I had been living in Quito for three years. I knew all right; and so I invited the German back up the street to my house for coffee.

As I knocked at the big door, Johannes, that's what he said his name was, asked me, 'What was it that Indian back there with that pathetic donkey said to me when he left? I did not understand.'

'He said you have the hair of Jesus Christ.' I tried so hard not to smile. First Johannes looked very angry. Then he burst out laughing. Finally, he said, 'I haven't stopped that Indian from beating his donkey, have I? Tell me the truth.'

I said, very seriously, 'I think he will not beat that donkey as long as he remembers that look on your face. You were most impressive!'

The German seemed quite satisfied. He pounded on the door for me.

'He will beat his wife instead,' I added.

Do you know, when Don Benito opened the front door he found me laughing with a stranger. He looked very shocked. I guess I had not laughed in a long time.

I couldn't believe he lived on the Galapagos. No one lived on those islands but reptiles. But he assured me that he was a colonist. He and his four brothers had escaped from Germany, not wanting to have anything to do with Hitler. But the eldest brother had turned back because of poor health.

'Now it is just my three brothers and myself,' he said in English. Actually, Hans – I called him Hans then – spoke better English than I spoke German.

'*Ja*,' he told me, 'my brothers and I used to go everywhere together, *nein*? We were noisy I guess, because pretty soon the Nazis began to watch us, noticing that we did not wear the armbands of the Youth Movement.'

They didn't agree with all that and their mother said the Devil himself was stirring up trouble on the earth. There would be another war. Hans said she was a very determined lady and wanted her boys to get out of Germany before it was too late. You see, when their father had been sent to fight in the First World War, their mother was so sick with worry she began to read the Bible for comfort. It became quite clear to her that no man had the right to kill another. So she wrote to her husband in the trenches, quoted many chapters and verses and told him he had better stop killing people. Hans used to laugh and say, '*Ja*, my father agreed with her, but he noticed an officer behind his back ready to shoot him if he got up and said, "Well, my wife says I have to stop shooting people so I am going home now." Anyway, Father began shooting over the Frenchies' heads.'

As little boys they'd always played Robinson Crusoe; it was their favourite book. And when as young men, they met an old sea captain in a tavern, who told them that the Galapagos was like paradise, with fruit on the trees and plenty of fish, they wanted to go there. The idea was to make a home for their parents to join them later. Well, their parents sold the family home and bought a beautiful boat which they named the *Marie*, after their mother.

They hid provisions on board keeping visible only tackle and enough food for a few days, as though they merely planned to go on a fishing trip. The harbour police were curious, stopping by their mooring, climbing on board now and then to observe the repairing of the *Marie*. The last day they had a little get together, just the five boys, the wife of the eldest brother, their two sisters and their parents. I have often thought how their mother must have suffered, saying goodbye to all her five sons in that way. Hans said that she insisted on washing their clothes while the others sang and played music. He said he saw tears stream down her nose. But she insisted it was merely steam. You can see her washing the clothes in a photograph we have. That night, before it was time to go, your grandmother Marie borrowed a cap. Into it she put five little photographs of herself and passed the cap to each of her sons. When each son had taken a picture, she told them to read the proverb written on the back. When they had done this, she said each one had chosen exactly the one she had intended him to. We have Hans's somewhere. It is a rhyme in German, something like: 'Unless a man builds with God, he labours in vain.'

Hans came up to see Tony and me more and more. He began doing chores for me – repair work on the house. He said I should get out more and he was right, but I was afraid to leave Tony. Doña Aguirre was always difficult after she 'borrowed' him. Didn't I ever tell you that story? I'm sure I did.

Well, when he was a baby, I never had Tony baptized. I thought everybody should choose when they grew up, like Christ did. But my mother-in-law didn't agree, so one day while I was washing my hair, she sneaked into the house while Don Benito was out, grabbed little Tony and rushed him down to the nearest church. Pastora saw her do it but was afraid of the old woman. When I found out I ran after her, but it was too late. His being baptized didn't bother me so much, I knew he'd still make up his own mind, it was the way it was done and I was afraid she'd try to take him for good some day.

I tried to pay Hans for his work, but he was proud and wouldn't hear of it, so I sneaked money into the pocket of his jacket when it hung on the peg. I couldn't give him too much or he would have caught on so, when I found out he was an artist, I bought him some pencils and sketch-pads. His work was very good, a lot of ships against Galapagos backgrounds.

I asked him if one of the ships was the *Marie* but he said no, she'd never made it to the islands. They'd been caught in a storm off the coast of England. His younger brother Fritz had chopped down the mast to save the ship, and they'd been stuck in some little Cornish village for a year while they made repairs. They told the British authorities that they were sailing around the world, not a word about Galapagos or sneaking out from under the noses of the Nazis because they were afraid harm might come to the family left behind, you see.

INTERESTING KETCH IN ST MAWES

Considerable interest has been aroused in St Mawes by the arrival of the German ketch *Marie* of Harburg, near Hamburg. This vessel is owned by five brothers who comprise the crew, together with the wife of the eldest. They are planning to sail around the world but have no fixed schedule or time limit. Their captain is Herr Heinrich Angermeyer, the eldest of five brothers, who is a talented artist and who has executed many drawings of the places they have already visited.

Like so many of their compatriots, the whole crew are beautiful singers and on their visits ashore have delighted many in the village by their charming renderings of various German folk-songs. Their ship, *Marie*, is a ketch of about 90 tons, built over forty years ago in Denmark for the King as a present for a lady of the court and is an exact copy of an old Dutch galleas, and her charming old-world look, with her figurehead and quaint stern, has drawn the attention of many yachtsmen in the neighbourhood.

Cornish Echo

We phoned the port of Guayaquil more than once but his ship, the *Don Lucho*, wasn't going anywhere so he relaxed and began to enjoy Quito. On clear days the three of us walked up to the waterfall with a picnic, and sketched and talked. He told me he had been married before, to a ballerina he'd met in Denmark. That was why he was on the mainland, so they could divorce. She had been desperate to leave Europe, but she wasn't the rough-and-tumble type. She didn't like Galapagos. I could tell by the way he said it that in fact she had hated the islands. He used to say, 'Living on an island is like any affair of the heart – you must be dedicated.'

One day Hans finished building some cupboards for me. I wanted to celebrate so I suggested we go to the Hotel Metropolitano for tea, explaining they had live music there. 'Music?' he said. 'Music? But I love music!' He insisted on paying, so I was relieved that I had put quite a few coins in his pocket the night before. Well, toasted chicken sandwiches and tea became a ritual after that. Hans and I loved watching the solid bourgeois families and pampered dowagers who gathered there every afternoon at four o'clock to eat gooey cakes and listen to Boris, the Russian accordionist.

Boris came up to our table one day and said, 'For weeks you come here with this gentleman and only now I remember who you are! You are the Russian lady who wouldn't play with us. Why you did not come that evening, what was it, two years ago, when I invited you to join our little band? We waited and waited. My boys and I, we wept. Always we were hoping you would return and play with us!'

Boris embarrassed me a little. He had bright red hair and spoke very loudly. All the *gente decente* began to look around at us. I told him quite matter-of-factly that my husband had said it wasn't prudent for a woman to go out at night, especially since it was 1938 and there was a curfew – there were rumours of a revolution.

'Revolution? Revolution? But Madame, when did a revolution ever stop a Russian from playing music, eh? Tell me that!'

Still, I said, my husband said a respectable married woman could not go out at night alone.

'Aha!' he cried. 'But here with us you would not have been alone! Now I, Boris, am alone! The rest of my band have gone, probably to look for Atahualpa's treasure. So you see how you broke their hearts for playing? They wept for you and your accordion when you did not come.'

Then Hans turned to me. 'You play the accordion? *Mensch*,' he said, 'why didn't you tell me? Come, you must show me at once. I also play! I play anything: accordion, mandolin, cello, guitar – even the spoons! *Mensch*, I cannot believe you never told me!' Hans paid the waiter. Boris winked at Hans and launched into a Russian waltz. Hans grabbed me then and danced me out of the door. You should have seen the respectable dowagers stare at us. Boris just grinned and grinned as he played. When I could catch my breath I said, 'You just wait till my mother-in-law hears of this!'

Hans was in such a crazy mood. He just laughed and said, 'Send the witch to me – you send her to me!'

I hadn't played my accordion for so long, I was afraid I'd forgotten how. But Hans fetched his mandolin from his hotel and we played and played. The patio rang with music and Don Benito even tried dancing on one leg.

It didn't take Doña Aguirre long to hear about the waltz in the Metropolitano. She showed up one morning as I was eating breakfast, and demanded to know who he was and what he did for a living. I told her. 'Galapagos?' she shrieked. 'He is a colonist in Los Galapagos? Only *criminales* live in that place – desperadoes – men banished by God and decent society. You knew this and yet you allow this person into your home, exposing my grandson to him?'

Of course, she claimed that the German was after Tony's inheritance, although she had made sure this had been so tangled in red tape when Marco died that I doubted whether Tony would get any of it anyway. Then she went too far. In such a sweet voice she said I was young still, I had life ahead of me. If I wanted to go off with my German, that was understandable. She would give me money – she suggested an amount. I could go home to my country. She would raise little Tony, or Marquito as she called him, as his father would have wished, in Ecuador, where he would carry on the family's name with honour. She offered to double her first offer.

When Hans came, he said I shouldn't waste my fury on such a woman. What we needed was a lawyer. After a month of wrangling, we settled that Tony would receive his inheritance when he came of age, and I would get an allowance from the estate.

In 1940 – I think it was July – the *Comercio* reported that the Battle of Britain was on. They said large areas of London were heaps of rubble. Children were being evacuated. But Hitler's losses were also heavy and he was preparing to attack Russia. Hans said he would never be able to fight a war on two fronts.

He said the end would be quick and bloody. He was very worried about his parents. He hoped his brothers out in the islands would have news of them. A few days later, Hans showed up rather breathless. His ship was leaving. He had to catch the morning train. I said that was wonderful, he would soon be home in the sunshine, out of the drizzle of Quito.

No he said, it being July, the garua would have started. He explained that this was a fine mist that blew over the islands from the sea, turning the nights fresh and helping the crops in the hills to grow. He had a lot of work waiting for him back on his little plot of land. Things grew so quickly in the rich volcanic soil, he said. Once his brother Carl had forgotten his shovel out in a field. The rainy season began. When Carl finally returned to that field, he found a crop of shovel trees growing.

Then, seriously, he said that he had planted some bananas, papaya, coffee and cabbages. The wild pigs or rats would have eaten his cabbages by now. Then he said a curious thing. 'Does the idea of rats bother you?'

'Rats? Have you walked around Quito late at night?' I asked. But he wasn't listening. 'I have much work to get back to.' He said nothing for a long while. 'Then there is my horse,' he said at last.

'Oh?' I said.

'You will think me crazy,' he blurted out, 'but I have the most magnificent horse. I didn't really need one, you understand, but when I saw him shining on the hill, like a golden statue, the colour of the sun, I knew I must have him. I remember as a boy, second to wanting a boat, I always wanted a stallion. I lost my head; I traded a perfectly good steel knife for him! Only then did I discover no one had ever managed to ride him.'

I had to smile when he told me. He looked so boyish all of a sudden. I said, 'But you bought him anyway?'

'*Natürlich*,' he said. 'I only managed to climb on his back once. Then we went like the wind, I tell you, like the wind! It is childish, *nein*? In Galapagos a strange thing happens to me. I feel like – like I could never grow old. We men, we live in fear of looking foolish. We all pretend to be grown up, and so we deny the child in each of us, refusing to let it come out and play.'

He left his mandolin with me. He said the damp in Galapagos was bad for it.

I thought of returning to Nebraska after he'd gone. Tony didn't know much English. I could teach school. But somehow, I just couldn't imagine myself in Lincoln. In Ecuador I was a foreigner, but back in the States I would be a stranger. So I stayed on and taught school in Quito. About six months passed. One cold afternoon I came home from work to find Don Benito in the entrance, all excited. He pointed upstairs and danced a little jig. I thought he'd been drinking. Well, I found Hans upstairs with Tony on his knee. He'd come back for his mandolin, he said. Pastora served tea. I asked him about his property and his family. He hadn't heard from his parents, he said. His land had been overgrown when he returned but he'd been working hard the past months. I asked him about his horse.

'It nearly kills me every time I ride it,' he laughed.

He and his brother had tamed a wild sow. One day they would have piglets. But he and his brothers weren't farmers. They needed a boat. They had found good, hard wood for building one, but it would have to be hauled out of the bush. One day they would have their boat and fish for bacalao. They could sell it to the mainland at Easter time when the entire country ate fish soup. He asked me if I'd ever eaten fanesca, this fish soup. I said I thought it was awful stuff, thick, like porridge. He said he didn't like it either. I knew he hadn't come eight hundred miles to discuss soup. And then he asked me to marry him!

We took a bus to Machachi outside of Quito, away from prying eyes. Haven't I told you this story? You sure? Well, the Justice of the Peace was out with a bunch of Indians harvesting potatoes when we arrived. He shouted irritably that he was too busy to marry anyone. But Hans found two Indians in a cantina anyway and paid them five sucres to be witnesses. Still the judge refused.

'Then, when your potatoes are dug?'

'Only if I finish before six o'clock. I don't marry people after six.'

We waited and waited in his stuffy office. At ten to six, Hans stood on a rickety chair and moved the hands of the clock back to twenty to six. The judge came in, wiped off his hands, looked at the clock, grunted and went outside again. Fifteen minutes later he was back. The clock now said ten minutes to six. I think the judge was suspicious but he dragged out a thick ledger anyway and put on his spectacles. Hans shook the two Indians awake. They assured him that they could sign their names. Hans said he didn't want any Xs on his marriage certificate. They said no, no, the nuns in the convent had taught them. The justice pointed his dirty finger at a dotted line. The Indians wrote their names on the document. The judge snapped the book shut and mumbled something about happiness. Hans had a better way of summing it all up. He put on my ring and said simply, '*Du auch du*,' 'You and me.'

The only taxi we could find for hire had one working head-light, which pointed downward. An hour later, when we sped down the mountain road into Quito, we discovered it had no brakes either! We could only hope that we would meet nothing coming from the opposite direction. In spite of this, I felt happy. We had something the *gente decente* would never understand and could never take away. Suddenly Hans began to laugh! He laughed so hard the old car shook. The driver took his eyes from the road and turned in his seat, laughing with Hans, though he had no idea what the joke was. Finally Hans wiped the tears from his eyes and showed me our licence. 'Oh, *mein liebchen*, whatever will the *gente decente* say now? That old *dummkopf* has married you to one of those drunken Indians I pulled off the street as a witness!'

Mama stopped there. She said so much storytelling had worn her out and besides she couldn't remember much more.

5

Kettles, Castanets and Old Rats

My brother turned twenty-one with little fanfare and even less money in the bank. He took odd jobs bagging groceries, herding trolleys around supermarket car parks, and then he signed on for a summer job with the Forestry Service. He thought it would be good experience for when he took over his third of the Aguirre estate but in fact what Tony did all day was scrape dead rattlesnakes from the state highways. Inexperienced out-of-state drivers would run over snakes, embedding the heads, poison sacs intact, in their tyres. When they stopped to change what they thought was a normal flat, they would often get bitten by dislodged fangs. So Tony and another college recruit roamed the roads that summer with shovels and gunny-sacks.

Although it wasn't what I had in mind for him, my brother appeared to thrive on the outdoor life. He came home tanned as a Mexican, bulging new muscles on his slight frame and assuming what I considered to be airs of the landed gentry.

My sister nagged me constantly. She said Mama didn't have time to do it. It got worse when the school nurse claimed I had funny feet and recommended 'substantial oxfords with arch supports'. Mama agreed with me that my feet looked perfectly strong, but Mary insisted I must wear oxfords in order to have beautiful legs and wear high heels someday. I said where I was going, I didn't need high heels, but she got her way. The shoes were stiff and made me limp like I'd had polio as a child. I kept turning my ankles, so Mary decided I had weak ankles as well. When I turned eleven she began staring at me when she thought I wasn't looking and mentioned 'developing' more than once behind closed doors. Mama finally brought home a book called

The Growing-Up Years. I propped it up on my pillow every morning and compared myself to the chart. We would have to hurry if I was going to reach Galapagos before I grew up.

My chances seemed no better than Peter Pan's. Mary announced it was time I stopped playing Robin Hood in the vacant lots and riding invisible horses to school. She hid the long-bow Mama had made for me and dragged me down to Penney's pre-teen department and fitted me for a training bra in front of thousands of spectators. She made me promise never to go shirtless again. Mama wasn't there to defend me so I gave in to avoid a further scene. Going home on the bus, I thought of my Galapagos cousins. They were most likely at that moment shirtless, climbing coconut trees and swimming nude with sea-lions. The girls had probably never heard of training bras.

If we ever got enough money to join them I knew exactly how it would be. The island would appear through the sunrise. The five of us would be standing on the bridge of a white steamer sailing nearer and nearer Academy Bay. Sea-birds would fly out to greet us. My brother, with three days' growth on his chin, would look rough and ready. Mother would look pensive, holding Johnny's hand. I would stand on the bow of a ship with a Jim Bowie knife strapped to my waist. My cousins, asleep in palm-frond hammocks, would awaken to the thumping of the ship's engines. Hurriedly, they would wash their faces in huge mother-of-pearl shells, wrap loin cloths around their hips and run to the cliff to greet us. When they saw us waving, they would clench knives in their teeth (in case of sharks), dive gracefully into the sea and swim out. Climbing up the rope ladder, dripping wet, we would shake hands. My cousins would place a shark-tooth necklace about my neck. Then, with a defiant glance at my sister, sweltering in her Tummy-Trim girdle, underwired brassiere and high heels, I would strip down to my best red underpants and dive into the sea.

The bus stopped at our corner. Grabbing my bra box, I lurched down the aisle after Mary just before the doors whooshed shut, remembering I did not yet know how to swim.

It was all right for Mary to be feminine; she was so blonde, so blue-eyed, so gorgeous. You could tell every Saturday when we walked home from the Fox Theatre matinée. Boys in hot-rods, the Everley Brothers blasting over their radios, kerb-crawled alongside us commenting on my sister's finer points. Mary always threatened to do one of her fake Russian accents on them but never did. So, fed up one evening, I turned on them. Fingers prying apart my mouth, I dragged one foot hunchback-style and glared at them cross-eyed. Mary turned violent shades, jerked my arm and marched me home, scolding all the way. 'You will grow up whether you like it or not!' It sounded like a threat to me. Coming from her, a mother at fifteen, maybe it was. I shouted back that I was glad I had swamp-water eyes, freckles and frizzy braids. 'I wish I had braces on my teeth,' I screamed, running home ahead of her, turning my ankles repeatedly.

By the time school ended and the summer came around, my brother had enough money saved to go and seek his fortune. Letters were sent to Ecuador. Old Doña Aguirre and her husband had long since died; their only daughter had married an ambitious lawyer who was now a judge. He replied to Mama's letters with long-winded, flowery phrases. Mama said he didn't say an awful lot, but appeared to welcome his long-lost nephew's emergence.

Mama polished Tony's Spanish every day. Nothing but Spanish was spoken now at supper. If you couldn't say it, you looked it up in the dictionary while your food got cold. I sounded foolish when I spoke. I sulked and fidgeted. Proud people do not learn languages easily.

Tony bought a suitcase from the Salvation Army bargain basement. It looked enormous but he packed and repacked, moaning that he could never fit everything in. He sat for long periods cross-legged before his bookcase, looking lost.

In August 1960, after many hugs and parting words of wisdom, he boarded the steps of a Panagra plane and set off. His room seemed small without him: bare without his little jars and smelly gym-shoes. I went through his trash can and rescued the cockroach poster, but it was faded so I threw it away.

September pushed the summer away rather rudely. I was now a teenager. I felt quite ill, for everyone knew what happened at junior high school. You had to undress after gym class and take showers with hundreds of naked girls.

My sister, on the other hand, was ecstatic. Mama found a motherly babysitter with big bosoms for Johnny. Mary was going back to school. They had a 'confidential' file on her. Worried about what she was going to tell the kids when they asked her where she'd been for the past two years, I offered her my drowned-sailor story, but she said she'd be all right.

The first day of school Mary, dressed in her wide-hooped skirt and bobby-socks, fell in step with the other girls as though she'd never been gone.

Tony's first letter arrived. Written on airline stationery, it began with the dreary details all maiden flights inspire; take-offs, landings and who you sat beside. But when he reached Quito the writing became cramped and excited. Did Mother know that if Otavaleño Indian men cut off their braids they'd be banned from the tribe? He'd seen one squat Indian carry a chest of drawers on his back down a slippery cobbled street with merely a rope tied about his head. Roasted beetles were sold on the corners. They were a bit tasteless but the vendor would salt them if you asked. His father's compadres greeted him like one returned from the grave. 'They say how much I resemble El Capitán, but complain that I'm too serious. I am constantly invited to make speeches. Little do they realize I can barely understand what they say.' As for his horses, he wrote to me, the ones mentioned in the will had all died of old age. He vowed he would personally see that I got a wild one in Galapagos ... but not too wild. His uncle had horses; huge stallions with rolling eyes who pawed the ground. He would have to ride one soon to tour the estate with his uncle.

Meanwhile, on the edges of California's leafy suburbs, we girls paraded through tepid showers like plucked chickens on a conveyor belt while our sports teacher, an ex WAC, perched on a stool with a stopwatch. After the initial week when every beet-red girl tried to cover her vital parts with a towel the size of an oven-glove, we ceased to care what the next fat or thin body looked like and school became routine.

Tony's second letter arrived. He had been taking a closer look at his new life. Why did the Church have such a grip on these people? Had Mother seen the painting of hell in the Iglesia Compañia? He felt clumsy and humourless next to his suave uncle. It wasn't honourable, being this wealthy by birthright.

Mother said it was merely culture shock. She wrote telling him to be patient with himself. It was a good sign, she told us, that he was now signing his letters 'Marco Antonio'.

A year later, on a Saturday in September, Mary and I did the usual Russian–German attack on the house, as Grandmother Mari had taught us. After the cleaning and polishing, we washed our hair, folded the wash and scrubbed the sidewalk outside. The phone rang. Tony's voice crackled over mountains and seas.

He had found Mama a teaching job in the American School where she'd taught eighteen years before. They would pay her fare if she could come in two weeks' time.

Two weeks; the dream stared us in the face.

'We'll never do it,' I ventured, wringing out the mop.

'We will,' answered Mary quietly, screwing on the cap of the furniture polish. She phoned the library. Even from where I sat, I could hear joy in Mama's voice.

That night we worked it out. We could barely scrape together the money for my fare and Johnny's. Mama could leave one month's rent paid, but Mary would have to take a part-time job with the telephone company. She could sell the old Studebaker and our furniture, if anyone would have them. The Russian chest, Father's mandolin, books and valuables could be shipped down when Mary could join us. It sounded so simple. For someone of eighteen, my sister looked awfully determined.

Emotion banged into reason as I lay in bed, my eyes wandering over the familiar room, generously excusing the faded wallpaper, suddenly loving the ugly chest whose drawers never fitted. I rose and looked out the window to the back yard. Mary had always been embarrassed by my zoo. If her friends visited, she always said that that corner of our yard was occupied by a hopelessly eccentric old neighbour-lady. I thought it looked nice, the way the rabbit hutches were lined up like a trailer park behind the duck pond. The animals would all have to go . . .

I went to brush my teeth. The bathroom mirror showed a pale, unadventurous-looking stranger. Suddenly I understood the expression in my brother's eyes before he had left home; the apprehension, sickening excitement and dwindling determination. It was the way Mari Vogel had felt when the sleigh set off from Wiessenmüller. It was what Marie Angermeyer had felt on board the boat when she'd grasped Grandfather's arm and told her boys, 'Never be homesick and never come back.'

Ronnie Fink, my best friend in the showers, had been to Tiajuana, Mexico, when she was twelve. On my last day in school she embraced me and warned me about Latin lovers.

After many hours of flight we landed in Panama and spent the night in an unfinished hotel beside a dark jungle pulsating with nocturnal noise. Flying insects flew at the light outside our door and the next morning we saw the underbellies of hundreds of magnificent moths and four-inch-long beetles which had attached themselves to our screens.

We set off for Ecuador, but our plane lost an engine over Cali, Colombia, so we spent another night there. By this time seven Ecuadorian air cadets had learned that Mother was the widow of their illustrious hero, often quoted in their textbooks. As we boarded the plane the next morning, they became our guard of honour, sitting Johnny on their knees and chatting incessantly to Mother. I felt it useless to pass on Ronnie Fink's warning.

Jungle passed below us like steaming broccoli. When we reached Ecuador one of our entourage told Mother that he had told the pilot that she was on board. We would fly the route into Quito which Capitán Aguirre had mapped out. It would be like flying through an avenue of volcanoes. As a special treat we would circle Cotopaxi, the world's highest active volcano. I glanced at Mother, but she just smiled pleasantly.

We began to rise and fall. The passengers, mostly businessmen and plump women, got very excited and ran from this side of the plane to that for the best views. Johnny screamed with glee every time we hit an air-pocket. Then our wing dipped and I began to feel sick and clammy. Ghostly clouds grasped at us with witches' fingers, beckoning us closer and closer until we were looking straight into Cotopaxi's bottomless cauldron. Our engines seemed to shake the mountain, for powdery snow on the volcano's edge crumbled, was instantly lifted into a whirl-wind and disappeared, swallowed by the depths; as we would be if we fell. The earth's jaws would crush us like a beast mauling a little bird. My head pounded with fear.

'You see how skilful are Ecuadorian pilots these days?' said the cadet proudly. 'See how he nearly brushes Cotopaxi with our wing-tips? Clearly, if we venture too near all the snow falls down in – how you say – an avalanche. Also if we fly too near, the plane gets –' he made a gesture with his hands and a sound like a toilet flushing. 'It is *magnífico*, no?'

I begged Mama to order the pilot to stop showing off. She said you could not say things like that to Ecuadorians; they were very sensitive.

At last Quito lay below us at 9,000 feet. An Indian wearing an earth-coloured poncho and black hat squinted up, quickly herded his sheep and llamas from the runway, covered his ears and turned his back as we landed, obliterating him in the fumes and dust of the twentieth century.

Tony looked no different now that he was rich. He stuffed us into a battered taxi Mother said she remembered seeing fifteen years before. He had rented a small house with a beautifully tended garden on a steep hill opposite Pichincha. A square-shaped Indian named Ophelia, with glossy braids and a keyboard smile, opened the gate and insisted upon carrying all four suit-cases at once. She would have taken my violin case if I hadn't clutched it tight.

While Ophelia prepared lunch, the four of us sat out among the snapdragons and butterflies. Pichincha scrutinized us like a craggy-faced judge wearing a white-powdered wig of snow and a thick cloak of eucalyptus forest up to his chin. Quito, the oldest city in the New World, stretched out between his raised knees, with her winding streets, red-tiled roofs and white houses full of *gente decente*.

A miracle had happened. We were sitting beneath the same sun Atahualpa had worshipped. Beyond the Andes lay the jungle, then miles and miles of bananas, the port of Guayaquil, six hundred miles of sea and – Galapagos.

Tony announced sleepily that we were invited out to the Aguirre hacienda to lunch the next Saturday. There would be a horse saddled and awaiting my arrival, he added calmly.

I had jodhpurs which Mama had bought from the Salvation Army on impulse, and fine English-leather boots. Only their owner must have had one foot larger than the other because I had to scrunch my toes excruciatingly to wear the right one. For weeks I had limped up and down Arlington Street trying to break them in, until the cramp got so bad I had to walk home barefoot.

When Mama found a red jacket as well, I dressed in the whole outfit and limped around the block. Mr Pearce next door, adjusting his lawn sprinklers, would shout, 'Hey, I jest seen yer horse – he went thataway! Ha ha!'

Ophelia announced lunch. I was not brave about food like Mama and Tony. The soup was bright green with slivers of potato floating in it like small canoes on the Amazon. The salad was safe, Tony announced. He had drowned all the amoebas by soaking the lettuce in permanganate. Afterwards he had washed his feet in the water, which was very good against athlete's foot. The little bits of meat was cuy.

'What's cuy?' I asked suspiciously.

'The national dish,' he answered, pouring himself a glass of wine. Ophelia appeared with potato cakes with cheese melted in the centres. Tony called them 'yapping gauchos'. I imagined Argentinians camped out on the pampas sipping maté from gourds and howling at the moon while their potato cakes fried. Then Ophelia poured peanut sauce over my lunch. It had no more taste than if you'd soaked an empty Skippy peanut-butter jar overnight and drank the juice. Dismally I looked forward to dessert, but this was a wedge of orange papaya with a slice of lime. Ophelia smiled as she watched me eat it so I smiled back, but it tasted like shoe polish smelled.

Tony said eating papaya seeds on an empty stomach was a cure for intestinal worms. He had a habit of discussing biological functions at the table; also tales of plague, scorpion-like creatures that live on the human eyeball and such-like. Mama always said to ignore him, but he took my silence for scepticism.

'Ophelia knows! She has countless old cures – you know, Inca secrets passed down through the centuries.' He called for her to tell us about her bloodshot-eyes cure. I knew this would interest my brother for he, like other intellectuals, always read late at night.

'Oh, *sí*,' offered Ophelia enthusiastically, 'one drop of mother's milk in each eye – it must be straight from the breast!' As my brother translated this I turned very red.

Ophelia served coffee. With great seriousness she said she had spotted several bats flying about the garden at night. So, while she had it in mind, could she please have a few sucres to buy rat-poison tomorrow at the plaza?

Mama looked perplexed and a little tired. 'I think the altitude is affecting me,' she said fishing about in her handbag and absent-mindedly handing the bewildered Ophelia two American dimes and a nickel.

'Bats,' Mama said slowly, 'don't do any harm really – I believe they eat insects –'

'Oh no, no,' said the girl staring at the unfamiliar coins and politely slipping them into her apron pocket. 'I don't poison the bats, oh no, I only poison the rats!' She poured Mama another coffee and explained very slowly, as one does to someone with sub-standard intelligence. 'Only the rats – the old rats which turn into bats. You see, that is how I know we have rats! Because we have all those bats flying around every night in the trees of the garden!'

Mama went off to rest with Johnny. Later that afternoon she would take Tony and me to Rocafuerte Street.

As we walked past the neighbour's house towards the bus stop, a dog resembling a timber wolf leaped out, snarling through the wrought-iron gates. The rich kept watchdogs which, Tony explained, were always named Tarzan. Households of any standing had at least three maids, and a gardener, and their houses were surrounded by high walls encrusted on top with bits of broken beer bottles embedded into the plaster like sloppy cake decorations.

The neighbours' eyes followed us from behind parted damask drapes. Were we rich though we only had one maid, I wondered?

Few people could afford automobiles. You could go anywhere by bus. Even the wealthy caught the Colectivo to work. The middle class took El Especial for half the price, but the poor waited for El Bus for two centavos. El Bus was easy to recognize with its small windows, people hanging out of the doors, statues of saints surrounding the driver and electric Christmas candles wired over the dashboard to inspire faith.

How comforting. One simply got on the right bus and announced one's position in society. We waited for El Colectivo but, to my dismay, El Bus came lopsidedly up the hill, bulging arms and legs like a basket of spider plants.

'You jump on through the back door!' Tony shouted as the bus slowed. We hopped up, assisted by a scrawny conductor half my size who held on to my elbows longer than I thought necessary.

Losing sight of Mother, I crawled into a seat between two fat Indian women dressed in full skirts and shawls with two hats each on their heads. Mother had explained that their good hat was worn on top in fine weather, and was switched to the old one when it rained. The woman on my right held a baby in swaddling bands, its limbs immobilized like a miniature mummy. The woman on my left held a greasy newspaper from which she gobbled fried pork and tough-looking corn on the cob. She pried each kernel loose with a long, dirty thumbnail. Between bites she belched contentedly and wiped her hands on her skirt. I looked away, realizing I'd been staring.

But staring did not appear to bother Ecuadorians. I looked about me at the crush of brown people jockeying for positions in the aisle where they attempted to cling to the overhead bar. They were all staring; at me.

The baby broke wind. I tried to look out of the window but could see heads no matter which way I turned. The baby wailed. Its mother whipped out a big brown breast and stuffed an even browner nipple into its mouth. Mortified, I glued my eyes to the back of the Indian ahead, but there was something wrong with his neck, for the shaggy head wobbled back and forth until I feared it would fall off. Then he groaned, rose unsteadily and addressed his fellow passengers, waving a bottle.

'*Viva el presidente!*' he hiccoughed. '*Viva los pobres pecadores de este mundo tan bello, tan precioso...*' Then he spotted me and brought his watery eyes closer. I looked around for Tony. With a crooked grin which the Indian either meant to be charming or threatening, he drew closer and closer whispering in pickled tones, '*Gringa bonita – gringa preciosa!*'

The corn-cob lady insulted him in what I assumed was Quechua and pushed him back into his seat. A moment ago so joyous, he now began to weep, between sobs sipping from his bottle. Then he grabbed a chicken from the woman next to him and cradled it in his arms like a dying friend.

Just as the smell got to my stomach, Tony appeared to say we were getting off. I crawled over the baby and skirts, squeezed through the throng of the narrow aisle, unable to see my body from the waist down. A rooster crowed nearby and I stepped into what felt like a basket of fresh bread. Someone shouted '*Caramba!*' as I tried to wrench my leg from several warm bodies behind me. A man with two teeth whispered those words again, '*gringa bonita!*'

Tony caught me as I fell off the bus. There was a flea on my neck he said as I buttoned my blouse and straightened my skirt. He grabbed for it but missed. 'Rats! It got away. The next time you get a *pulga*, pinch off the head, otherwise they go on sucking. With lice it's trickier. I think the Indians usually bite them in two.'

Passing many shops owned by immigrant Europeans and Jews, we reached the Plaza de Independencia. Flowers were arranged in splendid triangular beds at the foot of a huge central monument. Every park bench was occupied by gentlemen in pin-striped suits discussing politics and spitting in the gladioli. Shrouded widows shuffled off to Mass. Younger men bent breathlessly over marble games, the dirt before them littered with gambled money. Ragged shoe-shine boys ran circles around each other searching for dusty shoes. Half of the city's inhabitants flocked to El Teatro Bolívar to see the latest American film. In competition the cathedral bells rang out, clanging like tin washtubs beaten with soup ladles. Quito, it was said, was a city of one hundred churches and, as if to confirm this, it seemed a hundred terrible bells rang out like old alarm clocks: clang, bunk, ping and pong. The cathedral's doors were thrown open. Dogs scratched in the entrance. Inside a hum of bees rose as Mass got underway. The walls were resplendent in melted Inca treasure, as though the roofs had been lifted and hot gold poured over altars, pillars and posts.

Mama wandered on, turning left and right along the cobbled streets. Tony insisted I walk on the inside of the pavement, explaining it was customary as things were often thrown out of the upper windows. He did not say what. We passed a cantina. Tony steered me away from a wall where five men stood in a row studying a torn, out-of-date bullfight poster, their legs spread. I asked what they were doing.

'Peeing,' he said.

The street was deserted except for a wizened old beggar playing an accordion so tiny, so infirm, its bellows wheezed, giving off faint whispers of music. Mama stopped to talk with him, touching him on his emaciated shoulder. She gave me coins to drop into the chipped enamel cup held between his feet. The feet were bare, the heels so cracked that they resembled those of a badly repaired statue. My face flamed when I realized how I'd been staring, but then I saw the man's shrunken eyes.

Mama pointed to a rusty sign overhead. Calle Rocafuerte. Each of us climbed the hill alone. The cobbles underfoot were burnished brown, grey and blue; the very stones Father had stepped on, rushing up to visit Mama. I paused to catch my breath, my throat tight. The silver waterfall glistened like tinsel on Pichincha's side, just as Mama had described. A white cat sat sleepily in an archway, opening its green eyes as I passed. I could hear a guitar being strummed somewhere in the shadows of an inner courtyard. Each balcony had flower-pots overflowing with geraniums, and the air smelled of carnations.

An overhead sign creaked: Hotel Europa. Where Emma had met Hans. The telephone was still there in the doorway, its wires frayed and twisted. I turned slowly, knowing the house would be directly across the street.

Mama stood before a weathered carriage door set in a high wall. A narrow door within this large one opened and a grey old man with a crutch, his right trouser-leg pinned up, hopped through the opening. He looked like another beggar as he reached out his hand to Mama, as though pleading. Mama embraced him and then they shouted questions, neither waiting for the answers. Don Benito's clothes had once been fine, but now were carefully patched. He took a clean folded handkerchief from his breast pocket and dabbed his eyes, glancing up repeatedly and taking Mama's hand as though to make sure she was real and not some apparition from the past. Mama told us to hurry, Don Benito would show us the old house as the owners were away in the country.

A cool passageway led into a sunny courtyard. In the centre a fountain gulped tiredly, its basin cracked and mended, green slime collecting where it leaked. Doves cooed up on the roof-tiles and underfoot the floor of the patio was inlaid with oxen vertebrae set in intricate patterns of circles surrounded by round river pebbles. A potted tangerine stood against a fine staircase leading to rooms above, each opening on to a continuous balcony overlooking the patio. The roof sagged. The walls were covered in a hundred coats of whitewash. The whole effect was beautiful. For once in my life, something was just as I had imagined it would be. It was a fitting place for one's parents to fall in love.

Don Benito, still overcome, waved his arms extravagantly, reliving the moment he had opened the door 'merely to take my Sunday stroll and there had stood Señora Emma – like twenty years had never been!' Then he glanced over Mama's shoulder and paled as he saw my brother.

'Santa Maria, he is the ghost –' The old man crossed himself. 'I do not believe what I see. Little Marquito grown into such a man so like his Papá!' He took Tony's hand reverently. My brother looked embarrassed. 'Everyone said he would become *el presidente* if only – but – always joking he was, making us laugh, you know? So tall. Young. It was not really so long ago, was it – not really?' He caught his breath like he was about to say something, then decided against it. 'And you, Don Marco, you remember this house where you painted the doves and we had to wash the poor things in the fountain? You remember how you gave away your little *zapatos* to the poor boy who stared at you through the window?'

My brother hated baby stories. He pushed me forward, saying, 'The youngest daughter of Señor Hans.'

Don Benito's hands were rough like a gardener's; his eyes full of memories.

'Ah, the daughter.' I felt ashamed, but I was glad my sister wasn't there. The kind old man would have held her hand instead of mine, looked at her hair and blue eyes and not noticed me. 'He was a gentleman. So cultured, very European; not like us in this country. We know nothing from the outside, nothing! Your Papá had seen the world – he had seen everything, I think! People would look at him coming up the hill, he was so golden. I would hurry to let him in. On cold nights he and I had our little drink of rum; just a little one to keep the rot from my stump. When we were warm, I would announce him to your *madre*. Marquito would run and grab his legs, begging for a picture. He could paint, did you know? Oh yes, a *gran artista*. And stories too of those islands, I forget what they were called, but stories so incredible one would not believe them if one did not know him to be honourable. Sure, he could not speak Spanish so well, but when he ran out of words your *madre* would translate as she does for you now. Oh, but they were happy days were they not?' He turned to Mama. 'Such music and singing – you remember the mandolin?'

'I still have it,' said Mama, smiling.

'Don't tell me – you still have – and you, señorita, do you play your Papá's mandolin?'

I nodded. I did not play it, but I silently vowed I would learn.

As Mama walked up the staircase Don Benito told my brother, 'This has been a happy house but later – much tragedy your mother has seen. She is so brave. Here we say – the heart must weep before the guitar can truly sing. Did you know your grandmother? What a lady! When she came here to cheer your mother, she made bread with cinnamon and raisins. Then she made ice-cream.' He pointed to Pichincha. '*Sí, sí*, with the snow! I used to sit on the top step there, polishing the silver and watching for the little Indian bringing the ice down, wrapped in leaves on his back. He ran so fast it barely melted, and your grandmother would be waiting for him, her apron on and a big spoon ready. It was the first ice-cream in Ecuador, maybe in all of South America, what do I know? She died, no? Yes, well, the good die, the same as the wicked. At least the good are rewarded by God.'

Talk of God made me uncomfortable. I ran to the top step, half-expecting to see a bandy-legged Indian trotting downhill. Instead storm clouds gathered. Don Benito took out a tarnished pocket-watch and smiled knowingly. Several teeth were missing. 'It will rain in seventeen minutes. Every day the same, three o'clock.'

I thought this fanciful, but smiled and joined him down in the patio, trying to express my gratitude in Spanish. He pretended to understand me and shook my hand warmly. We promised to return soon and rushed down the hill as low clouds reached the rooftops.

The guitarist at the bottom of the hill had stopped playing. The white cat had gone, in search of a warm place to curl up, no doubt. Mama and Tony vanished round the corner but I turned and looked back at Calle Rocafuerte. If I lived in Emmasha's house, I thought, I would throw open my shutters early each morning. Doves the colour of a rainbow would rise like fountain spray. The air would smell fresh as snow. A frizzy-haired Carmen on the next balcony would burst into arias. Seeing me, she would call out '*Buenos dias!*' and, waving a wilted rose, bend far over the railing looking for some special gentleman, her bosoms rising above the lace of her bodice.

It was a street of dreams come true, a child's dream, a lover's dream, the dream of whoever it was I would become in this land.

A distant church clanged. Three o'clock. 'Clunk, ping, bim, bim, bim.'

In spite of his crutch, Don Benito bowed elegantly to me from the crest of the hill. Low wisps of fog rolled down the lamp-posts, over the kerb and up his good leg, turning him to cool shadow. I felt the first raindrops on my face and turned to go. But before I did, the figure on the hill grew taller, with two straight legs and a curly mop of blond hair. I answered his wave. The figure laughed, turned and with the long strides of a sailor, strode back through the little door. I was sure I saw a mandolin in his hand.

6

The Inca Princess

The next Saturday I limped into breakfast wearing my jodhpurs and boots. Tony, buttering his roll, said calmly, 'You know, of course, that women in this country don't wear trousers in public. Naturally I don't care what you wear, but you're always going on about how people stare at you. You wear that get-up ...'

My cramped toes made me irritable. My boots were excruciating. 'Staring?' I snapped. 'Staring? I wore a perfectly normal dress last Sunday on that wretched El Bus and you saw them stare. That fat man with the cigar sitting next to me not only stared, he whispered "*Mi corazón*" something or other all the way home. I don't even know what it means.'

Mother buried her nose in the *Comercio*.

'Well?' I could stand the pain no longer. I sank into a chair and pried off the boots.

My brother hemmed and hawed, deliberately spreading guava jam on his roll and asking Ophelia for more hot milk.

'Well?' I demanded. 'What does it mean?'

Mother told me to lower my voice.

'It means – er – uh – my heart,' Tony mumbled through crumbs. '*Mi corazón* means my heart.'

'That's the stupidest thing I've ever heard. What's the matter with their hearts? Why don't they see a doctor or something! And "*greengeeta preciosa*"? What does that mean?' Ophelia returned with the milk and stayed to listen with great interest.

'Well, if you must know, it means precious little foreigner.'

'*Precious? Precious?* And "*greengeeta linda*"?' I asked, my face reddening with enlightenment.

73

'Er – uhm – pretty – little foreigner,' he mumbled defensively into his boiled egg.

'You mean to say they're *flirting* with me? I'm only thirteen, for crying out loud!'

Stomping in stockinged feet back to my room, I threw open the wardrobe doors. 'I'm only a kid!' I shouted to the limp forms hanging there. I hated dresses, and I was going to spend the rest of my life in one. Slowly I undressed, studying myself in the mirror. I was looking older; haggard in fact. Slipping a gingham dress over my head, I put my beloved jodhpurs and boots into a paper bag to take along.

Entering the dining room I overheard Mother saying to Tony: '. . . wear what she likes . . . don't want the *gente decente* to get to her.'

Tony's Uncle Hernán did not have a stallion with fiery Spanish blood in its veins saddled and waiting for me. As our taxi pulled up outside the hacienda he bowed gallantly over my hand and apologized. Every one of his horses and *vaqueros* had been called out to round up cattle that had escaped through a broken fence on Pichincha's south side.

He led us into a shabby but elegant drawing room smelling of polished floors and mothballs. It was undoubtedly the very room Capitán Marco had entered with his young bride to be scrutinized by the august Aguirre relations assembled there. I pushed my paper bag under the red velvet Louis XIV chair, hoping no one would notice it.

I had worried about what we would say regarding Johnny. But he was introduced simply as 'Juanito'. Everyone assumed he was Mama's, and we did not enlighten anyone.

Aunt Anita, a small, aristocratic-looking woman, passed a porcelain dish of sweets with sickly centres, wrapped in coloured foil. Everyone sipped sherry, and struggled to find something to say. My brother's five cousins stared at me and I began to fidget. Wondering if they still had the locked room with Capitán Marco's medals and uniforms mouldering away, I asked stiltingly for the '*servicios*' and was led away by a servant down a long corridor to a stark little room.

A pitcher and basin stood on a plain dresser. There was an ugly pull-chain toilet in one corner beneath a high window. No curtains. No yellow sponge duck in the bathtub; there was no bathtub. How did they bathe? I could not imagine Uncle Hernán outside on sunny mornings, like Ophelia in her underwear, scooping ice-cold water out of the laundry tub and sloshing it over her sudsy body. Perhaps the wealthy did not bathe at all. Perhaps this was why all the best shops stocked so many bottles of French 4711? When I'd finished, I wandered back along a different corridor. I could easily pretend I'd lost my way. A few bedroom doors were open. Plain crucifixes hung on monastic white walls. No teddy bears, posters or half-read novels on bedside tables. I felt chilled and buttoned my sweater, but it was more than draught which hit the nape of my neck; it was as though Doña Aguirre were following me, prohibiting my prying into past secrets and tragedies. I determined to find the locked room, but first came upon a dark, smoky doorway.

Adjusting my eyes to the medieval gloom, I picked out the shadow of a woman stooping over pots and pans which sizzled and steamed on a charcoal fire. Bunches of fresh herbs hung from low rafters. About the woman's skirts numerous furry creatures scampered over the dirt floor of my brother's aunt's kitchen which, presumably, the grand lady herself never entered.

Following the sound of polite conversation back to the drawing room, I arrived just in time to see my brother hold out a practised arm to his aunt. The eldest of his cousins did the same for Mother. To my surprise, Uncle Hernán clamped my hand in the crook of his arm and we entered the dining room not unlike Rhett Butler and Scarlett O'Hara. Lesser cousins followed in our wake.

The long table was shrouded in linen. In panic I counted more silver than I knew what to do with, glittering beneath a small chandelier. Mother was seated in the place of honour. She was not the same woman who had plodded home from the bus stop and eased off her Dr Scholl shoes every evening. Johnny had his hair slicked down and wore blue bow-tie and jacket, but he kept giving us away by removing the pressed handkerchief in his pocket, unfolding it and staring at it as though he'd never seen one before.

Consommé was served. Then the servant brought out a salad of anchovies and olives. I hated olives. I swallowed them whole, washing them down with wine because I didn't know what to do with the pips.

Silver salvers appeared. When one got to me and the maid lifted the dome, I choked back a scream. There lay a small roasted corpse on a bed of shredded lettuce, its legs outstretched as though still running for its life. The teeth grinned. The eyes were baked black in the thin skull. The *muchacha* smiled, waiting for me to pry off a piece. I could not. I simply could not. She handed me a fork. Reluctantly, I broke off a back leg and hid the limb under a mound of rice and vegetables on my plate and quickly drank more wine.

The maid passed to Uncle Hernán's side with another salver. '*Excelente!*' he exclaimed as he served himself the whole animal, head and all. I was aghast. I had been meant to eat the whole corpse. One rat per person. I gulped some wine. And some more.

Everyone nibbled daintily at their hideous main course.

'Cuy!' said Uncle Hernán in English. 'Especially for you!'

I caught my brother's eye and mouthed the word '*Rat?*' when no one was looking.

'*Guinea pig*,' he mouthed back. 'The national dish.'

I thought of all the tousle-headed creatures in the pet shop back home. Then I thought of the small rustling animals in the hacienda's dark kitchen. They lived on the floor in there. When the cook felt hungry, she conked one on the head. I felt dizzy and drank more wine. Following accepted etiquette, we left bits of everything on our plates; otherwise your host would think he had not given you sufficient food. In my case, I left more than the others.

After dessert and coffee we retired to the drawing room. The men and boys undid their jacket buttons. The sun streamed through the windows over the parquet floor. I felt very sleepy and had to jerk my head up. Outside somewhere were the herds of horses and llamas and cowboys and Indians Mama had told me about that night while sitting on the edge of my bed. It wasn't her fault. Things changed. She always said I imagined too hard.

During the following weeks we were invited to the more splendid houses of Quito. Old ladies planted kisses on my cheeks, complimented Mother on producing a daughter with such an abundance of hair, seated us on carnivorous stuffed chairs and served us tea and pastries from the Viennese bakery. My apprenticeship in the art of small talk was furthered as we discussed the garden, stroked the cat, admired the family portraits on the walls and pretended not to notice when the Pekinese sneezed on the strawberry tartlets. At weekends we were taken to fiestas held on haciendas in the warm valley outside the city. Steers were roasted on spits, orchestras played tangos. The men drank imported whisky and pontificated about the current dictator. Tony and I usually wandered off, I afraid someone would ask me to dance, my brother worried he'd be asked to make a speech.

Mary wrote, saying she'd sold everything she could and complaining about my hamsters which had gone wild and nested in Mama's sheet music. A crate of household goods was coming by ship. We would have the first washing machine in Quito, Ophelia boasted to all the neighbouring maids. Mary would join us as soon as school finished in June.

Johnny, being blond and blue-eyed, was a big success in kindergarten. My beginnings were less auspicious. The school uniform was too big, my socks kept falling down and everything we did required either Spanish or breathing. I could do neither. Even hurrying to class left my lungs tearing at the seams in the thin air. In literature class we memorized ancient Arabian poetry. Well, I assumed Sheik Ass Pehareh was Arabian, or maybe a Persian poet, until two months later I saw the name written: Shakespeare.

I wasn't surprised when I was sent to the school's principal, a formidable American woman who walked like a chicken in hobnailed boots. She tried to comfort me, saying, never fear, I would learn Spanish through osmosis. I looked this up in my brother's old biology textbook. 'The tendency of a solvent, when separated from a solution by a suitable membrane (often animal or vegetable), to pass through the membrane so as to dilute the solution.' While waiting for this to happen I collected the worst grades in the school's illustrious history.

I did pass cooking class, however. Doña Magdalena wore a frilly apron she'd bought in Miami and darted about her tidy little kitchen measuring and mixing while we señoritas sat at the big table filing our nails or reading Donald Duck comic books from Buenos Aires. Once the dish of the day was in the oven, our *profesora* would wipe her floury hands and dictate the recipe. We wrote this out in three colours of ink, which looked rather splendid. Then we ate.

For our mid-term exam we purchased cake-decorating sets and were each given a square of paper. There was a deathly hush in the room as we all studiously squirted out tiny baby shoes – rows and rows of pale pink and blue baby shoes.

I asked one girl what they were for. Apparently when we all married and had babies we would be required to decorate many cakes for our other friends who were having babies. I asked if we shouldn't be learning to cook – a little, I ended apologetically, for she looked at me aghast. When we married, she reminded me, we would have servants to do all that. Our husbands would make the money to pay the servants. The servants would make the food and we would make the babies.

As summer holidays approached, most of my classmates said their rich Papacitos were taking them shopping in Miami, New York or Paris. I said nothing about Galapagos, for our geography professor had pronounced the islands fit only for reptiles and hardened criminals.

I became confused as to whether my family was rich or not, so I decided to have a good look at the poor who lived in an eroded cliffside behind our house, reached by a worn path along a ravine where landslides were common. Every rainy season the fire brigade was called out to dig someone out from the mud. Babies with runny noses waddled in the dirt of Guapulo. Old women with cracked feet trudged up and down the cliff with eucalyptus branches strapped to their backs for firewood. Mangy dogs fought over potato peels. Young tailors sat in the sun, bent myopically over their stitching, growing old early. I had seen old movies about families with no money who 'did not know they were poor', but these people knew. However, like most Ecuadorians, they were proud, hospitable and generous to a fault. That is what baffled me. They knew I lived at the top of the ravine, meaning I was rich, and still they gave me bananas, bread rolls, cuttings for our garden and, once, a thin young rooster which we were meant to eat until I named him. And I never knew what to give them in return.

So there were the rich and the poor and almost no one in between except maybe Alberto, an Italian from Chicago who ran a small grocery store in our local plaza. Alberto had a doughnut machine in his parlour and tried valiantly to invent a batter that would rise in the altitude. One day, he promised, he would make doughnuts for all of Ecuador and give up the grocery business, which he and his children hated. But baking at 9,000 feet was complicated. No one left Alberto's house without a bag of greasy rejects.

Once a month the Catholic priest of our plaza showed Mexican cowboy films on the wall of the unfinished church there. The ravine people came in throngs to perch in trees, on park benches or watch from friends' balconies. Women sold whole roasted pigs and hominy grits doused with hot aji sauce. Others ladled canilazos, a hot, laced cinnamon punch, from dirty enamel buckets. Fearing amoebas or hepatitis, I always dropped by Alberto's for rejects and ended up with simple indigestion instead.

The films were dreadful. The soundtracks rarely worked, the projectionist, having drunk too many canilazos, couldn't aim the picture, so *vaqueros* galloped down the spire and on top of onlookers' heads. The audience did not care. Snuggled deep into their ponchos against the chill, they cheered the man in white, booed the one in black and were happy if the hero married the señorita in church before we all went home. Ophelia said it was all very '*romantico*'.

She and her sister Maria chaperoned me. The three of us would squeeze on to a bench together, sharing the contents of my greasy bag. A certain *hombre* would always sit behind us. I guessed he was sweet on Ophelia, as she always got so giggly when he appeared. It was awful seeing her reduced to that. I vowed I would never get silly over a man. Maria told me he was our whistle-blower. Admittedly, I was intrigued. Our first night in Quito I could not sleep for the clicking and whistling and tweeting. Tony explained that the clicking and whistling were tree frogs. The tweeting was a man hired to roam the streets at night to deter thieves. All our neighbours paid him a monthly fee. Tony called it protection money.

As my mother realized I was going to be a complete failure in school, she enrolled me in the Conservatorio de Musica downtown, around the corner from the old house on Roca-fuerte. It was a once-elegant nobleman's residence, dating from the eighteenth century. Two hundred years later its balconies sagged and weeds grew in the patio, but I loved it. From every grilled window came the scraping of cellos, tinkling of piano scales and ah-ahhing of sopranos.

My violin teacher was a Frenchman who spoke some English. Upon meeting me he cried, 'Angermeyer? Angermeyer? But Mademoiselle, I read about your family in Paris magazine. The Robinsons of Galapagos. Your uncle is the pirate – what is his name – Gustav, no? And his woman is Lucrecia, the Inca princess. How they live in a cave and eat raw meat; how they dance naked and keep wild dogs who bite anyone who invades! I read also of how many people disappear on the island of Floreana! *Mais, oui*, I know them all!' I spent most of our first lesson trying to convince him that it was all nonsense – and hoping, oh, praying – that I was right.

At nine I would have eaten raw meat and danced in the nude with them, but now I was nearly fourteen. Life was serious. Worse, I was acquiring curves, though I always hid these under a heavy coat when I went downtown. I marched through the streets to the Conservatorio with my violin case pointed like a cannon. But the men on the street corners knew. They smiled knowingly and whispered, '*Gringa preciosa* – I love yooooo.'

Mother said to laugh, and perhaps I could have had I been a beauty. But I was not and I drew a mental overcoat around my sense of humour. I died a thousand deaths on the ancient streets of Quito and poured my moods and uncertainties into my music.

It did not take the animal-sellers long to find me. They peddled baby animals picked off the backs of speared or blow-gunned parents. When I learnt of this I tried to steel myself not to look into their gunny-sacks. I told Ophelia to send them away. I threatened to tell the police, which made them laugh. I went through torture every time one came, knowing there was some frightened, cold animal huddled out there at our gate. My hand would grip the doorknob and I would force myself to turn away. But many times I weakened and bought the poor creature, haggling the price down and giving the Indian a tongue lashing in miserable Spanish which he didn't understand anyway.

Other *gringos*, less aware that they were supporting the beginning stages of a lucrative rape of the rain forest, bought exotic animals, as one collects pre-Inca pottery to decorate the home. They soon discovered, however, that kinkajous were nocturnal and liked to roam the house at night, knocking over expensive porcelain or swinging from the chandeliers. That is when they brought them to me.

Emaciated parrots, armadillos with scraped noses, songbirds with pneumonia, an opossum with a broken tail. The vet could not help me much he said, he was only trained to treat dogs and cats.

My brother bought a car. A week before Mary was due to arrive, Mother prevailed upon me to lessen my sister's culture shock and return my fully recovered animals to the jungle. This meant everything but my ocelot kitten, who was not yet weaned. We drove to the darkest, deepest corner accessible by car and then walked for an hour. As we watched the beautiful birds fly away and the crawling creatures leave their baskets and steal their ways through dripping ferns and vines, I prayed they would run faster the next time man's footsteps were heard entering their forest.

It was a shame about Mary's room. It had looked so nice when we left for the airport, with the starched curtains, polished floor, sweet-peas in a vase and a welcome-home-Loli card from Johnny on her pillow. But it was a cold day so I set our old-fashioned kerosene burner on low and asked Ophelia to keep an eye on it. It is possible she did not understand me. Not wishing to hurt my feelings, when Ophelia did not understand my Spanish, she always nodded anyway.

We brought my sister's suitcases into the room and turned on the light but merely a dim glow shone in the gloom, like an eclipsed sun. Mary shrieked as black smoke billowed out. Tony crawled in on his knees to open a window. The next day, I was told, I would begin scrubbing the walls and ceiling. Ophelia was not to help.

Mary slept in my bed that night with Johnny, who wouldn't let her out of his sight. A little before midnight she tiptoed into the sitting room where I was trying to settle on the sofa, and asked why she kept hearing tea kettles and castanets. I ushered her back to bed in a sisterly fashion and explained that the castanets were male tree frogs. The females belched when it rained, that's how you could tell them apart. The blower, I said, relishing knowing something she did not, was sweet on Ophelia. That was why he always blew so long outside our gate. The bats in the garden were old rats who had sprouted wings. I looked closely to see her reaction to this but my big sister was fast asleep on my pillow. She looked as vulnerable as her little son curled up beside her.

The next day, as I scrubbed, I was told we were all going down to Rocafuerte street that afternoon. Well, I knew what a fuss they would make; every man in the bus, every Romeo on the street corners. Don Benito would take my sister's hands and say how much she looked like Father and I would be miserable. So I stayed at home and was miserable.

By the time they returned Ophelia (who had insisted on helping) and I had finished Mary's room and rehung the curtains. We laid a nice tea for their return. Ophelia bought fresh sweet rolls and I picked snapdragons for the table.

But they came home late. They'd already had tea: in the Hotel Metropolitano! Rudolpho the pianist still worked there occasionally, but Boris, the Russian accordion player, had gone.

My mouth dried up.

'You should have come,' Mother said unnecessarily.

I said nothing.

'One of the waiters recognized Mother,' Mary added, 'and told her the most bizarre story . . .'

She waited, as one does, for me to invite her to go on. My tongue was locked. I hadn't even been inside the Hotel Metropolitano yet. We'd been saving it, I thought, for Mary to come. We were all supposed to go together!

I threw a log on the fire and begged Mother with my eyes to tell me every detail. She understood at once.

'Well, remember I told you, when we used to sit out on the porch, that some members of Boris's band went searching for Atahualpa's treasure? When they did not return, Boris went after them, convinced something terrible had happened.'

'And . . . had it?' I croaked.

'That's just it. No one knows what happened to any of them. Boris hasn't been seen for ten years. But today the waiter reminded me of something. He said, "Señora, do you recall how red the Russian's hair was?" Yes, I said, it was quite unique. "Most unique," the waiter agrees and then he bends over our table and whispers, "If you go down to the Jewish curio shop on the corner, you will see a *tsansa* for sale. Oh, not one of those fake shrunken monkey heads," he says. "Oh no, everyone stops and gapes at this one for it has – long red hair. It is quite unique, as you say."'

Ophelia was getting fat. I stopped feeding her doughnuts at the movies, but it made no difference. Then one afternoon she and Mother had a long chat in the sitting room. I was told to serve them tea. Me! It wasn't that I minded, the disturbing thing was that Ophelia was so distracted she let me.

As I set the tray down, I could see the girl had been weeping. Mother's face was kind but firm. Later she told me Ophelia was expecting. I was embarrassed, remembering too clearly the candy-striped dress in the closet, Mother peeling onions, Mary placing the tomatoes on the blue plate. 'We must all be kind to her. She is so ashamed. The father is already married...'

It was the whistle-blower. The nerve! Flirting with her like that at the movies; her hero in white. He was forbidden to set foot inside our gates.

It rained that night. Snuggling down under my alpaca blanket I counted eight male tree frogs courting at least fifteen females out in the flower beds. Our family was, at last, complete under one roof again. Complete as it would ever be; there was little hope of finding Father living with savages down in the jungle. Galapagos was just around the corner. In two months, when school ended, we would board the first boat. I curled up with delight at the thought. The frogs outside my window stopped belching; a sign someone was approaching. The gate rattled, but Ophelia's light stayed off. The whistle-blower gave two blasts, swore and moved on.

The next morning was Sunday. As was customary, we took turns reading the Bible. We had reached Leviticus which I had been dreading, due to the men lying with wives and begettings and leprosy. To recover my composure, I sat in the sunny patio. Suddenly the doorbell rang. I glanced up as Ophelia went to answer it. There in the doorway stood Aunt Lucrecia, Uncle Gus's wife, the Inca princess.

If my aunt had looked faded on the black and white *True Adventure* programme, she made up for it now standing on our doorstep in an array of colour. Striding past me like a flamenco dancer, her wide skirts swirled like a carousel. Luxurious auburn hair was piled artfully on her head and secured with a green-and-gold scarf knotted on top. I helped her remove her bright poncho. As I hung it on the coat rack her peasant-style blouse slipped off one slender brown shoulder.

'I am Lucrecia,' she announced unnecessarily. 'You must be Yohanna.' I felt queer. I hoped I wouldn't be sick. Galapagos wasn't supposed to come to us! We were supposed to arrive at sunset...

'Where are the rest of you guys?'

I showed her into the sitting room. As she warmed her hands

by the fire, I was astonished to see she was wearing, not the black pumps that all genteel ladies wore, but spanking brand new, startlingly white basketball shoes with 'CHAMP' written on the sides in bold green.

At a loss, I picked up my ocelot kitten. My aunt reached over and stroked him, which impressed me as most people were afraid of Ati.

'Just like your dad, animals, animals. Always animals – better than people he always said. He said funny things sometimes.'

When the family entered the room there was much exclaiming in Spanish and loud American. It was all very dramatic. I guessed my aunt did everything fairly dramatically. Ophelia, fascinated, tore herself away to make coffee. I followed to heat a bottle for my kitten and saw Ophelia disappear into her room and emerge wearing her best blue uniform. The buttons wouldn't do up over her tum, but she looked pleased with herself, as though she were off to a party, as it indeed turned out she was.

Lucrecia wanted to know all about California and why we left such a wonderful place to come here and how much Mother earned as a teacher and what shampoo Mary used on her hair and how much rent we paid. She was on the mainland to see a dentist and buy, among other things, cement for Gus to finish her new house. This house, she said significantly, would be much larger than Marga and Carl's. It had a big veranda where they could have many parties. 'Yohanna! Your mamma is telling me you play the fiddle. Come, play music. We dance!'

Fiddle indeed I murmured, tightening up my violin bow. I turned to Mother. 'What . . . ?'

'*The Beer-Barrel Polka*,' she answered without hesitation.

'Hey you remembered! Yeah, my favourite!' Lucrecia leaped to her feet, pulling my startled brother after her so that he spilled his coffee down his waistcoat.

'"Roll out th' barrel . . ." Yeah, Gus and I dance it all the time!' she panted as they whirled past. Lucrecia was sounding less and less like an Inca princess. Over my bow I saw Mary beating a spoon against the coffee pot with abandonment, tapping her toes. Ophelia danced with Johnny clasped tightly against her big bulge. He surfaced for air periodically.

'We have a barrel of fun...' Tony's tongue crept out in concentration. He always had trouble keeping in step. 'One-two-three-Hop!' I heard him whisper as they bounded by. He needn't have worried, for Lucrecia deftly led him around the floor.

'And the gang's all here!' Lucrecia, Mary and Johnny sang out with crescendo fortissimo. They sounded like a bunch of hicks, I thought.

'Hey,' my aunt demanded breathlessly, 'when you guys coming to Galapagos?' Her hair had come unpinned and cascaded down over her forehead. 'Why you don't all come back on the boat with me? You bring your instruments – we have a big party – all the time parties!'

Mother pushed her bellows closed. 'Mary can go with you. She has no commitments. Tony has business on his hacienda and the rest of us have to wait until school finishes.'

'But Motherrrrr!' I whispered desperately.

She ignored me. Lucrecia jumped for joy in her basketball shoes. 'OK, man, I hate going on the boat with all those *hombres*. Mary can live in my new house on the cliff. It's gonna have a bathroom some day just like Marga's. Hey, you guys gotta bathroom? You gotta toilet, American-style? Let's look at your toilet!'

It was crowded in the bathroom with six of us staring at the toilet. 'Hey, that's beayoootifool! You got enough water to flush all the time? Fresh water, no? Can I flush it now? Gus says he is going to make me a box over a crack in the cliff but I say no, I wanna toilet. Oh, and you got a bathtub...'

I cornered Mother by the dirty-clothes basket. 'Mary can't go!' I hissed. 'We're supposed to go together, remember?'

'Would you keep your sister back?' She rescued the bath-mat from being trampled.

I reminded her how we were all supposed to sail into the bay together – it was the way it was going to be, that was all.

I shouldn't try to arrange everything, she said. Life was more fun with surprises. I stared at the toilet-paper roll. Surprises terrified me.

A week later I watched Mary pack. Mosquito repellent. Khaki shorts and safari shirts especially sewn by *my* seamstress. Seasick pills. Basketball shoes and, worst of all, a shiny Jim Bowie knife with a bone handle in a soft leather sheath on a belt. Who did she think she was. Jungle Jim? Sarcastically, I said all she needed was a pith helmet. She thought I was being nice and said it was all right, she'd buy a Panama hat in Guayaquil. I hated it when she was nice.

I hated watching. I couldn't tear myself away.

They left at five o'clock in the morning. The old locomotive had been made in Philadelphia. On its black side was painted G & Q, for Guayaquil–Quito. Optimists called it the Good 'n' Quick, but it would take twelve hours for it to travel the 462 kilometres down to the coast. The cars, made of wooden slats painted red and green, had wooden seats inside and windows which did not rise when it rained and did not lower when the smell of humanity overpowered the occupants. The engineer strutted on to the platform and spat orders to the filthy man who stoked a hellish hole leaping with flames. Fascinated, I moved closer to the engine's shining body. The fireman wiped his brow, bent over, grinned and hissed, '*gringa linda!*' Quickly I retreated to Mother's side.

Lucrecia and Mary found seats among dusty Indians with bobbed hair and red ponchos. They were headed for Riobamba high on the desert plateau where the people were called Pupa Arenas, or Sandy Bellybuttons, because the wind blew there incessantly. The Pupa Arenas couldn't take their eyes off my tall, blonde, well-fed sister. But Mary grinned and grinned, oblivious even to the chickens roosting on her Samsonite. The train belched, whistled hysterically and began to shake. Mary waved until they disappeared from view down the tracks, into the cold mountain fog.

A month later it took us twelve hours to drive down the

mountains through Machachi, where Mama and Hans had been married, over the high plains of Riobamba down into the jungles and over endless miles of banana plantations.

Guayaquil had been built over a swamp and still smelled like one. Every afternoon the inhabitants took a siesta to escape the heat. But by the time we drove into the city, the red tropical sun had dropped behind the hills and the streets vibrated with dance bands, pickpockets and precocious insects. Carpets of red coffee beans and cocoa pods were raked out in side streets to dry, their strange, not quite agreeable smell wafting through the humid air. Flimsy horse-drawn carts bent under pineapples, papayas and green coconuts the size of soccer balls.

Men lifted their T-shirts, exposing their beer bellies to any passing breeze. Women slunk across busy streets, daring cars to run them down. Malarial children with bloated abdomens darted through traffic selling lottery tickets or a handful of limes, blowing their noses into the street or squatting in filthy gutters.

Wealthy owners of chocolate factories, sugar mills or plantations lived out of town, where their airy houses caught the evening breezes. They drove American cars and made frequent trips to Miami for medical attention, clothes or tennis rackets.

It was said that Guayaquil made the money for Quito to spend and, although the port city had a contagious party atmosphere, the 'pearl of the Pacific' as she chose to call herself, was in truth as dirty as Quito was beautiful, as uncouth as the capital was elegant.

The captain of the *Cristobal Carrier* leaned out of the wheelhouse waving a beer bottle, beckoning us aboard. The gangplank sagged dangerously under a constant stream of black men carrying gargantuan sacks of potatoes, rice and cement bound for the islands, sacks which frequently burst open, dusting the men in ghostly grey until rivulets of sweat ran down their bodies, turning them to cracked statues.

The *Carrier* was a World War II landing craft. About 160-feet long, she was blotched with sickly shades of blue and white painted over varying thicknesses of rust. The old vessel leaned tiredly against the Malecon, the notorious strip which hugs the river Guayas, and allowed herself to be loaded throughout the night, sinking lower and lower into the murky water.

We were escorted across the foredeck, through the second-class section, up an iron ladder, into the wheelhouse and along an open passageway to our small cabin. Churning with excitement and intense relief that we had actually made it this far, we dumped our food boxes and suitcases and allowed the cook, doubling as steward, to conduct us back to the first class, where he served us tepid Coca-Cola in dirty glasses.

'I guess we should start calling this the stern,' said Tony, sitting gingerly in a threadbare deck-chair. A stalk of green bananas hung from an iron rung overhead. A ripped red-striped tarpaulin flapped lazily in the evening breeze.

Our captain, dressed in wrinkled whites, came to welcome us formally. We were the only first-class passengers, he said, except for a Jesuit monk.

'Must have done something bad for them to send him out to Galapagos, eh?' chortled the captain and winking conspiratorially at my brother. His big gut shook when he laughed. He looked like he could tell a dirty joke or two.

'*Bien,*' he said, flicking bits of tobacco from his tongue as he rolled a cigarette. 'Don Gus is your uncle, eh?' he said to me, taking in my age, vital statistics and unease with one white-slaver's glance. 'Your uncle and I are *gran amigos*! What a *macho* he is. *Que hombre!*' He paused, looked at me closely and asked, 'You don't get seasick, no?'

I shook my head emphatically. I had never been on a boat before in my life.

'I thought not, you being an Angermeyer.' He turned to Tony. 'Better lock your cabin door tonight. Word is out we got *gringos* on board and there are bad people out there, *gente mala.*' He tousled Johnny's hair and laughed until his belly shook. Hitching up his trousers, he grinned, flashing three gold teeth. 'We sail at 2 a.m. If I'm not too drunk that is. If we go in the right direction we should be in Las Encantadas in three or four days. Ha! Ha! Ha!'

When he'd gone I went down below to the bathroom, squeezing past a dozen seedy men playing cards with toothpicks in their teeth and cheap Cristal in their glasses. They fell silent as I appeared. The bathroom doorknob fell off in my hand. Inside I looked for a clean place to hang my towel. Brown water washed back and forth under the slatted floor with the ship's swaying. Feeling queasy, I flung my towel over my shoulder and turned on the tap. Yellow rust-water sputtered out, then hissed dry. The toilet reeked of creosote. I decided the chamber pots in our cabin were an indispensable luxury. Passing the gents' door I heard coughing and a low retching sound. The card players fell silent as I climbed the ladder. Their bloodshot eyes followed me. Someone made a remark. There was a burst of laughter.

Brushing my teeth with bottled Guitig water, I spat overboard, washed my face with 4711 and climbed into my bunk. Tony turned off the light. I fell asleep to faint scurrying sounds.

The next morning, as we were the only first-class passengers to show for breakfast, the cook was generous. Tony eyed his fried eggs, steak and greasy plantains and quickly departed.

The second day we spent rocking in our bunks. Johnny and I invented jingles in time with the increasingly violent heavings.

'Alley ooooop – and down again – alley –'

A feeble voice complained from the lower bunk. Tony missed breakfast again but later managed to rouse himself to get some fresh air. After fifteen minutes he returned, his face a khaki green.

'Six hundred miles of open sea and not one single lifeboat,' he said miserably, and crawled back into his bunk. 'There are men downstairs with haunted faces.' He took a deep breath. 'They sleep in greasy hammocks over the engine room. The fumes down there – I cannot tell you.' He turned his face to the wall, moaning quietly.

Lunch was fried pork, limp salad and watery gelatine pie. I returned to our cabin to reread Tony's ancient *Time* magazine, with President Kennedy on the cover.

'Are we there yet?' Tony asked weakly. 'Are we unloading?'

'You should eat something,' I said mercilessly. 'You're

becoming feeble-minded.' I handed him a box of crackers from our large box of food supplies.

'Yikes!' shouted my brother, opening the Saltines. 'We've got cockroaches! The place is crawling with 'em. Get a shoe! Don't just stand there, do something!'

He really was ill. Of all people to be afraid of cockroaches. 'You always said they were charming creatures and cleaner than us.'

'I only said they were as clean as the people they live with!'

I thought of the bathroom downstairs and got a shoe. But there were hundreds of them: black ones the size of mice, golden ones like almonds, fat hairy brown things with waving antennae.

Tony swung his legs out of bed, grabbed the cracker box like a football and dashed to the stern, zig-zagging and slipping over the wet deck in his stockinged feet.

'Don't throw our food overboard!' I yelled after him.

'Only the roaches!' he yelled back. But the *Carrier* rose, reeled and lurched. She groaned with each roll. Tony lost his grip on the crackers and they fell in. My brother stared at the place where they'd fallen for a considerable time. Then he returned, clutching the rail.

'Sharks.'

'Where? You're not going to tell me they ate your crackers?'

'Garbage. Cook threw a garbage pail out. I didn't notice at first – fins. Fins everywhere. They're following – our ship.' He sank into the bunk. I tucked him in.

The sea was deep blue. The waves all wore party hats and blew salty spray into the sunny sky. I gripped the railing and inched my way to the saloon for afternoon tea.

Johnny saw the horse first; a glorious silver beast with an iridescent mane tethered behind a row of diesel drums and onion sacks. Banging my shins on crates and sliding over spilled oil, I made my way to his side. The horse looked smaller close up and not so much silvery as shining with diesel. He sighed as I stroked his oily neck and stuck out his lower lip dejectedly. I wondered if horses got seasick. They certainly got thirsty, so I made a precarious journey back to the galley. The captain told the cook to give me a bucket of water and some wilted carrots, but they cost me a smile.

The poor beast gulped down the water and devoured the carrots. Until we reached Galapagos I would have to compromise and keep smiling. A wiry little man with white hair approached me. His clothes had obviously been slept in, probably in one of the greasy hammocks Tony had seen in the third-class section. I prepared to leave as he climbed over the onion sacks, but in spite of his clothes, the man looked dignified and he wasn't leering; he was studying the horse.

'The church sent him out to the priest on San Cristobal Island. You know San Cristobal?'

I shook my head. 'We go to Santa Cruz.'

'Ah yes, I know your uncles. Santa Cruz is a pretty island, your uncles chose well. The other Germans went to Floreana. It has a spring in the hills but the coast is dry and lonely. *El come gentes* lives there.'

'The people-eater?'

'*Sí*. People-eater. Many people have disappeared. There is something evil on that island. But San Cristobal Island also has evil in its past. Perhaps that is why the first church was built there . . . to dispel badness. I believe there is now a small church in the hills as well as on the beach. But the road to the hills is too muddy for a holy man in sandals. That is why the priest needs this little horse.'

'Why doesn't the priest simply catch a wild horse? There are wild horses, aren't there?' I asked fearing the answer.

'Oh, *sí, sí*. Plenty. But you need a real cowboy to catch one and a real *vaquero* to ride it. There was a Norwegian lady named Karin. She could ride anything, just like a man.'

'Really? Just like a man.'

'Oh *sí*, and every man who ever met her fell in love with her. She married the son of Cobos.'

'Who was this man – Cobos?'

The old man carefully rolled the frayed cuffs of his trousers as though they were custom-made, and climbed up on the sack of onions.

'Old man Cobos had this big plantation on San Cristobal

Island. It was a long time ago – maybe 1875 or earlier – a very long time, but Cobos is still hated. He owned much land on the island. With that land he was given men – prisoners from the penal colonies which then existed on some of the other islands. Many of these men were as young as you, señorita, if you pardon my impertinence. Strong men were broken, working as they did in the coffee or sugar-cane all day with little food or water. Cobos had a small railway to take produce down to the ship. The ship he also owned. He owned everything – he was *loco* with power. They say he rode his big horse all over his kingdom, armed with whips and pistols and surrounded by a pack of killer dogs. Any little thing that a man did wrong, Cobos punished with floggings, beatings, banishment to desert islands. Once a man named Cassanova was sent to Santa Cruz with a jug of water, a dull knife and some matches slipped to him by fellow slaves. There is a brackish well in Pelican Bay beneath a large poison-apple tree. For three years Cassanova survived there alone, eating raw iguana and fish. Ships came. He begged the crews when they put ashore, "Take me with you! Take me in the name of mercy!" But no one would take him.'

'Why not?' I asked. The horse's stomach made comforted sounds and he closed his eyes. The *Carrier* thudded violently in a trough of sea. I wiped the spray from my face, hating the way my hair blew wild. The old man's face glistened with salt, but he seemed not to mind.

'Cobos had a sign put on a tall pole. The sign said, in English and Spanish, "Do Not Take This Man Away. He is Twenty times a Criminal!" The tall pole from which this sign hung is still there today, but the sign, of course, is gone. Wretched Cassanova is gone. Cobos is gone.'

'What happened to Cobos?' I whispered.

'He was hacked to death.'

'Oh.'

'You see, one day Cobos went too far. He condemned a man to five hundred lashes on his bare back. Can you believe it? Five hundred! The slaves had seen too much. They made a plan. Now Cobos, he had a fine villa in the highlands. Outside he had a lovely garden where white roses grew. Every evening he wined and dined by candlelight at an elegant table. Now this particular night it was full moon, so they say. A band of slaves hid behind ferns near the house and waited in the moonlight for Cobos to drink enough to make him doze. But the pack of dogs smelled the men and barked, alarming Cobos, who went out to see. Then the desperadoes attacked with their only weapons – machetes used that morning for hacking sugar-cane. Legend has it, I have been told so, that Cobos was wounded eleven times. But you know, he rose each time with pistols and sword drawn, slashing this way and that, blood pouring from his wounds – until dawn he fought them off. His servants found him the next morning among his rose bushes, lying in a pool of blood. He was surrounded by three dead slaves and thirteen dead dogs.'

I said nothing. But I wished I hadn't such a vivid imagination.

'They say the white roses turned red with the blood and still bloom red today. You can see them if you go up there. Cobos was buried in the very spot where he had flogged six men to death. Vengeance belongs to the Lord.' The old man leaned closer. The smell of squashed onions was overpowering. 'But,' he whispered, 'Cobos never came from our Lord. Cobos came straight from the Devil.'

'You believe in the Devil?' I asked.

'I know there is a Devil,' he answered intensely. 'All bad comes from him, not from God.'

'What happened to the slaves?'

'They commandeered Cobos's ship and sailed to the mainland. Do you know, no one there would believe how bad it had been for them! In the mainland they do not want to know about Galapagos. It has always been so. We could all die and no one would care.'

'Where do you live?'

'In hell,' he answered smiling for the first time.

'I don't believe in hell. If God is love how could there be a place like hell?'

'I believe.' He paused. 'I believe there are places on earth where the Devil taunts God and where a man's spirit is tested and sometimes broken...' He tailed off, weary of story-telling. Easing himself off the sacks, he limped over to sit with a bony man with crooked teeth who was strumming a badly tuned guitar.

The next day the sea turned from nearly black to a lighter blue. A bird flew overhead at midday and we constantly mistook clouds on the horizon for islands. My clothes smelled of creosote and my scalp itched. We wearied of card games. Johnny drew pictures of fantastic ships, sea monsters and portraits of his Loli wearing high heels with rouge on her cheeks like apples.

I slept fitfully that last night, dreaming that my uncles chewed tobacco and had brown creases where it seeped down their chins. My aunts appeared to me in sleeveless, gaudy dresses, hairs growing out of moles on fat upper arms. I rose about midnight. Seeing the state of the sea from our porthole, I thought of the horse, cold and hungry, and took a patchwork quilt we'd packed and a precious handful of Sun Maid raisins down to him. As I descended the ladder I was dismayed to see our captain and the card players were still up. I strolled past them with all the dignity I could muster. Passing around a half-empty bottle of Rum San Miguel, they eyed my quilt with red-eyed curiosity. El Capitán called after me, 'I could keep you warmer than that horse ... ha ... ha ... ha!'

The sea washed past us like ink. If he followed me and we struggled – if I fell in – no one would ever know. Quickly I tied the blanket around the horse's neck and belly with bits of twine. He refused my raisins, so I ate them myself, spying on the men from behind the horse. Strange how a big animal made you feel protected, yet protective. 'Tomorrow,' I whispered into his fuzzy ears, 'we will be there. Then the next day you will be home too.' The horse tossed his head, knocking me in the teeth. Then he spread his rear legs and urinated all over the blanket.

7

The Island

I rose at dawn as the sun emerged red and huge from the sea. Sleepily, I hurried to where I'd tied the horse-blanket to a stem of bananas, hoping it would have dried. It had not. I folded it anyway and turned to sneak it back to the cabin.

It was then I saw the island.

I stood mesmerized as it appeared on the horizon, first in a low mist, then turning golden as the sun illuminated it like a painting in the Bible. Craters sat on its spine like squashed hats, tilted pots melted to one side while pouring out the earth's boiling content. I could see that the hills were just high enough to catch passing clouds, giving the island a green, rain-forest hat. Tied about the island's waist like a belt lay a fearful wilderness of spines, cacti and bare white trees sprouting from tangled lava churned out of the earth lifetimes ago, to hiss at the edge of the sea. Our ship seemed dangerously close to the shore, where the breakers pounded against steep cliffs, and I remembered how drunk and bleary-eyed the captain had looked the night before.

Our bow cut through ribbons of smooth, glassy water between the chop now and then and I remembered that out there the powerful Humboldt Current brought cold water to these shores, making them habitable for penguins, fur seals and cooling what otherwise would be a sweltering equatorial heap of ashes.

Quickly I stashed the smelly blanket in our cabin and woke the others. Then I hurried to the bow, climbing over the freight and gripping the rail. A huge chunk of the island had at one time collapsed into the sea, creating a sheltered bay of turquoise water, calm and inviting after the black depths we had just crossed. Sea-birds circled overhead. Our engines slowed to a thump-thump as we slid past a small islet; Jensen, I remembered from a map, where a colony of sea-lions posed on the beach.

Academy Bay was shaped like a horseshoe pried open. In the middle squatted, at most, twenty wooden houses set on a sandy area. To the left lay a small lagoon that Mama always called the bay of the Nimfas, from which rose a sheer inland cliff of maybe seventy feet. This cliff, or barranco, met the sea and formed the one side of the horseshoe on which my uncles lived: Angermeyer Point. To the right of the village was another inlet flanked by thick mangrove. Mighty coconut trees swayed in patches; there might have been twenty or so – not what I'd expected. I told myself to stop it; 'surprises were more fun.' I gripped the rail that much tighter.

Mother joined me and pointed to a trail leading up to the hills from behind some of the coconut palms. She said it took about two hours to reach the small village up there, 'but it is beautiful, with wild orange trees and ferns and exotic plants no one has ever named'. Once the early mist lifted, the remote farmers up there would spot the ship and begin loading donkeys and horses with bananas to trade in town for store goods.

We moved to let the crew drop the anchor. It plunged through the turquoise and settled on the sea's crystal floor. Tropical fish stared warily as it squatted huge and rusty among the sea stars.

'You're disappointed, aren't you?' asked Mother quietly. 'I know you always imagined a palm tree and waterfall island. It – it isn't Tahi –' Dear Mama, she looked suddenly so young and vulnerable. I was frightened by the devastation my next words could cause.

'It's . . . it's the most beautiful place I've ever seen,' I said. The strangest thing was, it was true.

The *Cristobal Carrier* belched dirty smoke into the bright clean morning as the four of us gathered our suitcases, bedding and crates of food, and assembled on the main deck of the rusty hulk, unwashed, weary and self-consciously marring the beauty of Eden.

No one stirred in the village on Angermeyer Point. 'You'd

think long-lost relatives arrived on every boat,' I grumbled, collapsing on to my suitcase. I felt sick. My back ached. My throat felt like it had when the boy in *Old Yeller* fetches the gun and goes out to the woodshed. Mama stood very close.

'You should have eaten breakfast. You look pale.'

I rested my head against her hip. Her breathing was confident.

'Isn't anyone going to come for us?' I asked.

'No one hurries in Galapagos, not even on boat day. I could never understand why, but there's always enough time...' She laughed. 'There's always *mañana*. It never made sense; every little task here takes so long to do but ... out here you get the feeling you could live forever...'

My eyes stuck to the barranco. The first rock house built on the very edge above the sea had a pink roof, with careless drips of tar all over it. The windows were Russian–German clean. I could see lace curtains and a bowl of flowers in the window-sill. A tabby cat sat on the veranda beneath a spectacular cherry-pink bougainvillaea. It was an artist's house, built by Carl for Marga; the half-finished one we had seen on the television, now completed.

Suddenly one of the blobs of tar sprouted legs and chased another down the roof, over the stone walls and into the sea. The rest settled down again on the roof. A bronze-coloured man in shorts emerged from the door carrying a white enamel pan. His voice travelled over the water as he called, 'Aneee-aneee-aneeee-aneee'. Immediately the mass of grey bodies broke into individual marine iguanas, some three feet long, shoving and kicking as they raced down the house, surrounded my uncle and attacked the enamel basin in the sand. Uncle Carl went inside and came out, pointing binoculars our way, waving with one hand. Timidly, I waved back. He was definitely the handsomest man in the world.

The second house up the barranco, the one Gus was building for Lucrecia, was also made from lava, and stood at the very edge of the sea. Larger than Carl and Marga's, only the ground floor was finished. On the veranda a recently planted bougainvillaea bent dejectedly as though not yet convinced it wanted to compete with Marga's magnificent specimen. Goat skulls lined a trail leading to a wooden shack on a slight rise behind Lu's house. Goat skins were nailed all over the outside walls. It was the sort of shack Ernest Hemingway would have written elephant-shooting stories in.

I almost missed the third house on the cliff, it was so small and camouflaged amongst the rocks like a forgotten bird's nest. Perched on a section of the barranco forty feet high, a sentry of opuntia cacti, feet embedded in tons of lava, surrounded it, warding off intrusion with shields of spines. The house's one visible window was boarded up and the Dutch door needed paint. A brown pelican preened its wings on the dilapidated roof. Spines grew from the chimney.

Out of Lucrecia's house strode a tall girl. She ran her hands through her boyishly cropped hair. Buttoning her safari shirt, she shielded her eyes against the sun, saw us and ran barefoot over the lava to the barranco. Her legs were longer than I remembered, her hair lighter. She was tanned gold. What had Don Benito said that day on Calle Rocafuerte? 'People would look at him coming up the hill, he was so golden.' My sister ran to a natural platform in the rocks, untied a rope attached to a large branch stuck into the cliff and pulled a rowboat towards her. Every house had such a landing place, with a dinghy tied to a branch. Three sailboats were anchored out in the bay, their rigging festooned with frigate birds all vying for the best view of the proceedings. Pelicans paddled beneath the ship's galley, competing with striped blowfish for breakfast scraps.

Back on shore, Uncle Gus trotted down the goat-skull path and joined Mary on the landing. She jumped in the boat, pulled up the anchor as though she'd been doing it all her life and Gus rowed out to get us, standing, pushing the oars forward with great speed. Within minutes they were alongside.

'Come! Pass down your gear!' My uncle growled beneath his moustache in a pirate voice. Was he displeased with us, I wondered? Did he know about the things I had said about him back on Arlington Street when we'd read his letter? We passed Johnny down to Mary first, then I descended the rickety rope-ladder, my knees wobbling as I reached the smaller boat. A strong grip steadied me as the longboat rose and dipped in the gentle swell. Zorba the Greek looked me straight in the eye.

'I,' my uncle announced grandly, 'am the King.'

'Oh,' I answered faintly, finding a seat in the bow.

'King of these enchanted isles,' he winked. 'And you, my girl, will be enchanted too once you step ashore. It may be paradise waiting for you over there – or it could be hell.' He paused, catching suitcases Tony passed down. 'Are you afraid? This is your last chance to get back on that rotten tin tub and go back to civilization – if you are afraid, Hanna.'

'I am not afraid,' I insisted, watching him closely. I clutched my violin case close to my chest with one arm and gripped the side of the bobbing boat with the other, muttering under my breath, 'And it's Jo-hanna with a J and an O.'

Tony landed precariously behind me, knocking one oar into the sea. Gus stretched out his leg and grasped the drifting oar with his toes. He had feet like mine. I didn't have funny feet!

'Hanna,' he growled again as Mary pushed off, 'don't hold on to the side of the boat. Your fingers might get crushed against the rocks and I haven't heard you play that violin yet. Tonight we have a party. You will play.'

I was going to throw up. It wasn't the rocking of the boat or because the water we were rowing over showed large fish circling us; it wasn't the huge red crabs on the rocks. I had a terrible certainty that the moment my foot touched my father's island, I would jolt awake to hear commuter traffic on Arlington Street or Miss Bean rapping her yardstick on the desk and demanding, 'How many jelly-beans if I take five?'

'Give me your hand!' shouted a brown boy, crouching to hold off the boat.

'Jump, Hanna,' shouted Gus. 'Hold your cousin's hand and jump.'

'Don't be afraid, I'll catch you,' said the boy.

'I am not afraid!' I repeated, leaping to shore and nearly pulling my cousin over.

'I am Johnny. It's easier to do that without shoes. You want to take your shoes off?'

'What, and walk barefoot?'

'Yeah.' He had unusual green-flecked eyes, with freckles on his nose. The rocks looked fiery hot, the sand rough. The path to the shack where our belongings were being taken was littered with sharp coral, shell, crab claws and pieces of dried cactus pad.

'I'll take my shoes off – tomorrow,' I said primly.

Gus and Johnny left us to help my other uncles unload the family's supplies off the *Carrier*.

Lucrecia had breakfast waiting for us. She met us at the door of the shack, her other house not being ready yet.

'Take off your shoes,' Mary said.

I gave her a disgusted look.

'What's wrong with you? Used to be we couldn't get you *into* shoes! It's the custom when you enter a house.'

I took them off. The floor was deep in goat skins. The house smelled of kerosene, fresh-ground coffee and a strong musky odour. I looked suspiciously at breakfast. The rough table was laid with an assortment of plates, jars and mugs with printed yachts' names. The bookcases sagged with paperbacks, dictionaries, writing paper, dusty shells, candles stuck into holes of naturally formed lava dishes. Two rifles hung over the door, a box of bullets on a shelf nearby. Cousin Teppi, a graceful boy my age, sliced a loaf of dense dark bread very thinly, eyeing me closely.

Conversation centred around how long the ship had taken, had we seen any cement sacks and concern that the family's mainland agent had got their orders loaded on board in time.

Tony spotted a large spider in the corner of a window, but Mother's eyebrows dissuaded him from catching it. His colour was poor. He looked like a man who had just reached the top of a mountain he hadn't wished to climb. Little Johnny sat bubbling on Mary's lap until a strange yell which seemed to come from the dense bush outside stopped him short.

'Tukka-tukka-tukka teeeeveleyssssss!' There followed a short silence, then a dark girl crawled out from under the table where we sat, ran out of the door and down the steps screeching, 'Teeeveleysss – teeeeveyless!'

'That was Ana Eva under the table; she's adopted. Cousin

Franklin was the one calling from the bush; he's shy. No one knows what "teeveyless" means.'

'Don't pay any attention to my little brother,' said Teppi, pouring coffee from a chipped enamel pot. 'He's crazy.'

Mary nudged me. 'Don't believe it. Anyone out here who is a little different is said to be crazy.'

In that case, it seemed to me, everyone I'd met so far was as crazy as a loon.

'Bread?' asked Teppi. He had a teasing smile. 'Smoked goat meat?' Sliced thinly, it was tough but delicious.

'White butter?' offered Mary innocently.

I spread some on my bread but nearly spat it out. It was pork lard.

'We will have yellow butter today if Alf comes down,' Teppi emphasized the name, watching to see Mary's reaction. She ignored him, and studiously mixed powdered milk in a plastic cup for Johnny.

'Jam?' asked Teppi. It was green and slimy, with little black seeds.

With my best Quito manners I asked what it was made of.

'Cactus fruit,' he answered.

It was the best thing I had ever spread on bread. I ate seconds of everything. Lucrecia was pleased. She cut me a fifth slice of bread and passed me a jar of honey which I spooned on liberally, hoping I would not appear too greedy. The honey smelled odd. As I bit into it, Teppi said, Fresh turtle oil, killed only yesterday.'

I gagged in silent dismay, gulping down scalding coffee and curling my toes to stop from retching from the cod-liver-oil taste. I looked under the table for a cat, or whatever it was Galapagueños kept as pets. At that moment a granite-coloured lizard ran across my foot, though I wouldn't have known if I hadn't been looking, so light was his touch. I slipped a small piece of bread down to him and, to my astonishment, he picked it up and ran off.

Lucrecia took us over a low coastal path lined with rough seagrass to the beach where we intended to camp. To my surprise she showed us a rock house built more from necessity than inspiration, and said we could stay in the Stewarts' house.

The Stewart family had joined a doomed group of Americans from Seattle who came to neighbouring San Cristobal Island determined to make a fortune from Utopia's coffee and fish. When the enterprise failed, two of the families came over to Santa Cruz to try again. But it wasn't long before they acknowledged defeat, leaving this and the lonely house I'd seen up on the barranco as proof that they'd ever tried.

'They were nice people. Their girls liked the life at first, then they got homesick. Lotta people come to live in Galapagos,' said Lucrecia, opening the door which fell off its hinges, 'but mostly they go. See, on this side we got no spring. If our rain barrels go dry we have to row to Pelican Bay on the other side for brackish water. Also we have to row over for supplies from the store. When the hunter comes down with beef from the hills, or farmers bring fruit, we usually miss out because the villagers get there first. Life is easier other places. Only crazy people stay here.'

There were three rooms, the largest being a kind of living room, with a long window facing the beach, Jensen Islet and Barrington Island beyond. There was a lopsided stone fireplace useful for cooking or feeling cosy on windy evenings, a decrepit bookshelf with mouse-nibbled Erle Stanley Gardner mysteries and three wobbly camp-beds with rusty hinges. The kerosene burner in the kitchen was rusty also, as was a crudely painted table with its legs standing in tin cans which had once been filled with diesel to keep fire ants away.

Arranging our belongings, we disturbed lizards, long leggy spiders and things which scurried in the rafters. Mother assured me that everything was harmless, reminding me that when Uncle Carl had built his house on rocks belonging to iguanas, he'd allowed them to move up to his roof.

Having a house when we had expected to camp was a blessing, even though it had no window screens, electricity, flush toilet or running water. Water was the problem. I kept belching cod-liver-oil taste and went in search of a drink. We had a rain barrel one-fifth full of green slime and teeming with aquatic creatures which appeared to be swimming round and round in tiny sleeping-bags.

'Mosquito larvae,' said Tony, enraptured. 'We'll have to boil this before we can drink it.'

'Drink it! It looks like avocado soup!'

'First we'll have to go to the village and buy kerosene for the old stove in there, if it works. Also, I must mend this bent-up guttering before the rain comes or we won't catch any water. At least we have the sea for washing.'

I ransacked my suitcase for half a chocolate bar reserved for emergencies, but a cockroach had found it first. His jaws moved, antennae waving excitedly. Disgusted, I threw chocolate and occupant through the window, but Mary made me fetch it back.

'Save paper for starting fires. That chocolate will make a roach trap. We need a bottle. Sometimes they wash up on the beach. You put something sweet inside and by morning it's full of cockroaches; breakfast for lizards. Don't throw anything away, first because we'll probably need it for something eventually and second, nobody wants garbage messing up the place.'

I sneaked down to the beach with the damp quilt and washed it in the sea, but it still smelled of horse. When I owned up, Mother said I could sleep under it, which did not surprise me.

When I could put it off no longer, I summoned courage and went to the privy at the back of the house. The hole in the crude seat was densely black. I shouted down it, trying to dispel any giant centipedes that, Mother had warned me, might be housed there. A little night gecko with bulbous eyes and padded feet ran out of the hole and up the rock wall. His translucent sides panted; you could almost see his heart pump. I felt sorry for shouting. The plank placed over the pit was rough. I prayed nothing would sink its pincers into my bottom. A stack of yellowed American movie magazines had been left in the corner. Each magazine had the name Stewart childishly printed on the cover with an address in Anaheim, California. When I opened the first one, silverfish darted out. Inside, someone had meticulously drawn hundreds of tiny red-ink hearts around every faded photograph of Elvis Presley, Tab Hunter and Ricky Nelson.

8

Dancing with the Duke

At mid-morning cousin Johnny rowed across the bay to the 'other side' in a graceful clinker-built longboat he and Uncle Gus had made. We decided to call him Big John although I, fascinated by his green-flecked eyes, said he would always be Goat-Eye to me. I meant it as a compliment, but in turn he threatened to call me Pig-Eye, which was unfair as anyone could see there was no resemblance.

Slowing his strokes as we skirted the base of the barranco, my cousin pointed to dramatic formations in the lava. One was called the King's Throne, in which you could sit at low tide; another buttress was shaped like a dragon, another like an angry woman shouting. 'My dad calls it nature's sculpture,' said Big John. 'Sometimes my dad goes out hunting for goats but comes back with a sack full of rocks instead. My dad loves rocks.'

Blue-footed boobies stared cross-eyed at us as we slipped below them. Big John said the males were the smaller birds and had smaller eye pupils. In the mating season the females honked and the males whistled, waving blue feet in the air and sky-pointing their beaks. Booby came from the Spanish *bobo*, or clown, and indeed their rubbery blue feet looked like they'd been stuck on by a toy manufacturer for a laugh. It suddenly occurred to me that God had a sense of humour.

Entering the shallow Nymph Lagoon we saw a great blue heron fishing among the rocks, a yellow-crowned night heron in the shadows and a little green heron hunting beneath the mangroves. Red Sally Lightfoot crabs hung like gaudy jewellery from the rocks. A grey gull with an idiotic laugh perched upon a tall pole; the one used to hang the warning signs about marooned Cassanova.

The village, so deserted earlier, now bustled with farmers down from the hills, shuffling about in mud-caked boots. Bare-chested fishermen unloaded the small boats which taxied supplies back and forth from the *Cristobal Carrier*. Women gossiped outside the store dressed in faded floral dresses and nut-brown children got in the way. Cowboys tethered rambunctious ponies beneath the tamarind trees and sauntered bow-legged up to Jerias General Store. When the sacks and boxes were opened, the crowd pressed forward good-naturedly, all shouting orders at once.

It was a one-room store piled high with galvanized buckets, brooms, sacks of onions (I recognized the one I'd trampled to get to the priest's horse) and bolts of gaudy dress fabrics. Coils of new rope and barbed wire cluttered the entrance. Shelves sighed under tinned peaches that were smothered in dust as they were too expensive for anyone to buy except for anniversaries or saints' days. Purple horse-medicine seeped over white baby shoes, sewing notions got tangled in fishing hooks. Jars of sticky sweets buzzed with flies, their lids rusted askew. A plump Indian woman named Piedad, the owner's wife number two, dipped her scoop into peanuts, flour and chicken feed with amazing dexterity. Expertly she measured pounds of this or that on squares of brown paper, twirling the edges to make leaky pack-ages. The filthy bills exchanged were worn, Scotch-taped and familiar to everyone, as they rarely left the island.

Tony, waiting patiently with his list, was shoved this way and that in a tide of women until Piedad, taking pity on him, sold him a broom, a bucket, ten pounds of flour, rice and sugar, lard, three lamps, kerosene, twenty tins of tunafish, four grass sleeping-mats, a stalk of bananas and a bag of salt.

'Salt? You bought salt?' exclaimed my cousin when he rejoined us. 'Man, you got tons of salt behind your house in the lagoon. Just take a bag and shovel it in. Bananas? Next time buy from the donkeys.' He pointed to a woman unloading heavily laden donkeys beneath the tamarind trees. The woman wore a shapeless sweater over a cotton dress, over a man's trousers

tucked into rubber boots and a frayed straw hat. By the time
we rushed over, other women had bought most of the papaya.
Mother crowded in and managed to get some cabbage and
yucca root. She asked for some oranges but the woman said the
garua season was late. The few avocados and oranges the farmers
had they kept for themselves.

We followed Big John to the post office. About a quarter of
the island's estimated population of 400 were congregated
around the tumbledown shack. My cousin said people you
might not see for months turned out of the island's darkest
corners on boat day. The hill people, on the whole, did not look
as healthy as the beach inhabitants; their faces were drained
of sun, their hands swollen, with yellow fingernails curving
downwards like warped piano keys.

Mother chatted with a tall, distinguished man wearing spotless
white shorts; Kuebler, I discovered, had once been married to
our Aunt Marga. A German diplomat sent to Spain before the
war, he and Marga and their young daughter Carmen had
moved to Galapagos, whereupon the marriage broke up and
Marga married Uncle Carl. Kuebler had a magnificent garden
with figs, vegetables, papaya and more coconuts than anyone
else, for he had a spring. He rarely spoke to anyone. A sign
hung from his gate saying, 'Keep Out. I Have No Time For
Visitors!'

Uncle Carl married Marga and Marga's daughter Carmen
married Carl's brother Fritz, so Carl was his own brother's
brother-in-law and stepfather, and mother and daughter were
sisters-in-law and it was all very confusing. I gave up trying to
make sense of it.

'Goat-Eye,' I said, leaning against his strong back. 'Why does
the postmistress have blood smeared all over her apron? It's quite
disgusting.'

He picked up his foot and studied his toe, bringing it closer
and closer to his nose until, using his fingertips as tweezers, he
yanked out a long spine. I sat upright; it was quite disgusting.

'I've been trying to get that one since last full moon. Blood?
Oh yeah, that's Señora Marina, she hunts wild bulls in the hills.
Her husband Victor Hugo waits with the donkeys in a safe place

until she shoots a bull. Then they cut it up and he brings it down here to sell. That's him over where Mary is.'

A little man one-third the size of his wife wielded a huge machete as he hacked off bloody chunks of meat tied to the back of a sleeping donkey. There was no method to his butchering. My sister indicated the general area she was interested in and stepped out of the way. Victor Hugo raised his machete, arms extended, legs poised like a matador. Incredibly, not a speck of blood reached him as he whacked. The donkey carrying the gory load seemed unperturbed, but I noticed it kept ears and tail well tucked in.

The postmistress dug into a huge post bag and called out, 'Kastdalen *y familia*!' A gigantic young man rose to collect a thick stack of letters and a Sears-Roebuck catalogue. He was over six feet tall. A carefully combed blond thatch sat vigilantly on his Nordic features. His bare feet stretched out in front of him like loaves of French bread.

'That's Alf,' Big John announced loudly. 'He can't find shoes in all of Ecuador to fit. He can't even find a horse big enough to ride. Donkeys can't carry him because his feet drag on the ground, so he walks barefoot – even down the rough old trail from the hills.'

The Kastdalens had come from Norway when Alf was about eleven. Alf spoke four languages fluently and knew more about the island's botany than the scientists. His family had the best farm in the hills.

My cousin moved closer and bellowed in my ear, 'Don't tell Mary, but Alf is sweet on her!'

I had a feeling my sister already knew, for the Norwegian was carrying Mary's big bag of meat and a large bulging sack of what I later discovered were precious avocados, especially picked for her.

Big John identified people as they rushed to claim their long-awaited post. One was an American named Nelson who was building a hotel. He was married to a slender Norwegian girl.

'Alf was going to marry Friedl, but this American guy sailed in on his yacht and she called it off. Everybody talked. I'm not saying what's right or wrong, but you don't have to marry somebody just because you grew up next door, do you? Maybe a person wants something different. Maybe a person wants to go somewhere and see things.'

I nodded, an ominous feeling rising within me.

'Friedl's brother is my friend,' he continued. 'I visit him on their chacra, their farm, sometimes. We sit up in the king-fruit trees and tell dirty jokes. You know any dirty jokes? You know the facts of life yet? Yeah, me too. You been kissed yet? I kissed the McGough girl once. Well, anyway, Sig and I get jokes from Nelson's American magazines. But one night we were laughing and laughing up in a tree and old man Horneman comes out and nearly shoots us! Sig said he was only after wild chickens in the avocado trees, but you would a thought he could hear us laughing and guess we weren't chickens.'

'More likely roosters if you ask me . . .' I mumbled.

He shot me a startled look, then saw my face and broke into a grin; a grin which would take him far, I thought to myself.

'I'm going to Miami Beach, Florida, United States. I get to go first because I'm the oldest kid.'

An elderly couple who had come through on their yacht had invited him to go to high school, get a driving licence, live in their house, swim in their pool, drive their car and have a television in his room. He would leave as soon as he and Gus finished the boat they were building.

As I had feared, now that I had finally arrived, all my cousins would begin to leave, seeking out the very things I had left behind.

Tony made a good effort at helping Big John row home, though he splashed us with every stroke. Mother shot me a look to keep quiet and told us about her chat with Kuebler.

'He has offered us coconut and figs whenever we want some. He was always kind to Johnny and me.'

'Who do you mean, Johnny?' I asked.

'My name for your Father was Johnny.'

'Even I knew that!' shouted Big John sarcastically over his shoulder.

I turned on him, flushed with resentment. 'I did too! I just forgot, that's all.' Of course, I had not known. Mother had started her story with Uncle Jacob the horse trader and ended it with her and Hans marrying. I still knew nothing of the time they had spent on the islands or – afterwards.

'Oh yes,' she continued, 'and Alf Kastdalen kindly invited us up to visit his family and see their farm this weekend.'

Big John shot me a knowing look, typically forgiving my former outburst instantly. My cousins Anne Liese and Maggie were also invited to help us find our way. There were no road signs on the island, no maps. You memorized the trails and did not stray or you ended up like a few others had – lost forever.

As we reached the landing and scrambled out on the barranco, Mary warned us about clumps of long black arrows just below the water's surface.

Mother said, 'Hans used to say if a spiny sea urchin stuck you, you must urinate on it.'

'On the place where it sticks you!' explained Mary, seeing Tony's puzzled expression.

'It must be the uric acid . . .' He stopped to ponder, one foot on shore, the other pushing away the dinghy. Mary yanked him out of his splits and on to shore just in time.

I was about to ask what happened if you didn't – couldn't – at that precise moment, but Big John said, 'Lotta sharks in this bay, every night about five o'clock they hunt. So it's a rule you don't go swimming off the barranco after sunset.'

Little Johnny hadn't said much on the way home; he felt very delicate as I lifted him to the shore.

'Do sharks bite?' he asked me.

Tony paused, no doubt about to expound upon some gory shark story he'd read. I hurried Johnny along saying, 'Everything is tame in Galapagos – it's just that sharks swim with their mouths open and things get sucked in.'

Mary looked at me, astonished.

'Mama says he mustn't be made afraid of swimming,' I explained in an aside.

'Fine,' she whispered back, 'now he's only scared to death of the giant vacuum cleaner of the sea. Besides,' she said, tying up the boat, 'no one's ever been attacked by a shark here. They're too well fed.'

Mama wore a mint-green blouse. Her hair blew off her face, showing how pink her cheeks were. Rolling up her trousers, she hoisted the broom and lanterns and set off for home. Her legs were white against the wet black rock; nice legs. My mother had nice legs. Funny I had never noticed before.

Mary would say I too would have nice legs if I wore my oxfords. She walked barefoot all the way home. Showing off, I called it. I saw her wince when we reached the white coral. Then she looked at the sun to see if it was time for lunch. I could have told her that, the way my stomach felt. It might be nice to marry her off to Alf, I thought. She could churn butter all day and I could keep horses in their pastures.

Mary's avocados were too green. The stove would not light. The sack of wild beef oozed blood so badly Mother doused it with salt and left it hanging outside in the eaves. We were going to die of thirst. And since we didn't know how to fish, hunt goats or wild bull, cook cactus jam or render turtle oil, we might starve as well. I wished Father were there to tell us what they'd done in the days before tinned tunafish.

By the afternoon we had made up some beds on grass mats, unpacked, located an emergency salami and mended the worst of the tears in the screens with a sacrificed pair of Tony's underpants.

Hearing a distant 'Halloooo – halloooo!' I looked out and saw a small group coming up the path. Aunt Carmen pushed a wheelbarrow with a jerrycan of water. Her daughters Anne Liese and Maggie brought bread and smoked fish. Marga, I knew her by her flaming red hair, gave us some beautifully roasted coffee, a jar of cactus jam and a teapot. Looking me over carefully she said, 'You are dark like your Uncle Carl, isn't it? Not like your father at all. I tell you, when the *Cristobal Carrier* came in last month I looked out and said, "It is Hans come back!" And you, Yohanna, are playing the violin, isn't it? You will bring it to the party. Normally we all write letters on boat

night, but tonight we will all get to knowing each other, no?'
She spoke with grace and polish. Tante Marga had brought *je
ne sais quoi* to the wilderness.

I didn't know I had a cousin Traudi. She and her husband
Bernhard had joined the family from Germany after much
hardship in the war. She and my mother seemed to have much
to catch up on, so I left them talking in German and strolled to
the beach with her young daughter Gundi, who chattered away.
I asked her how she'd learned such good English.

'My mother is teaching me and my brother Martin every
morning at home. I get so hot but now is better with garua
season coming. When it is cool it is more, how you say –
gemütlich to stay in the house, *neh*? Also we are having many
books in English. Some Americans and yacht people leave them
for our library. Come I show you.'

We took a sweeping path past the beach until we reached a
sturdy clapboard house in Divine's Bay.

'Hallooooo!' we called.

'Halloooo!' answered a woman through a screen door. 'Oh,
you must be Mary's sister. I heard you were coming on the
boat. And your mother? Did she bring her accordion? Oh
wonderful. We ladies can get together and play. You won't be
here for very long, five weeks or so?'

Gundi asked if we could see the library.

'The library? Well, I don't know. You two won't mess
anything up, will you? You won't disturb Margarita?' Doris
was not sure she'd made the right decision. An exceptionally
good-looking woman with long, ash-brown hair, glittering blue
eyes and a model's cheekbones to go with her figure, there was
a high-powered nervousness about her which hinted at a stifled
intelligence.

Margarita must be the maid, I thought, as we approached a
cement-block building. Gundi and I pushed open the warped
door between us. A stem of rotting bananas fell over like a dead
body; gnats rose in a cloud. A sack of chicken feed hung from
a cobwebbed rafter. There were four sagging shelves of books
along two walls and dusty boxes heaped with more books. The
room smelled of rat pee. Black bananas fallen from their stems

Grandmother Mari and my mother a few years after leaving Russia and emigrating to Nebraska in 1913. Grandmother's own education was cut short when she married, and she vowed her daughter would go to university and travel, little realizing what lay in store for young Emmasha.

Marie and Heinrich Angermeyer, who sold their home to purchase the boat on which their five sons escaped from Germany in 1935 and set sail for a life on the Galapagos Islands.

My mother Emmasha in about 1936, when she met her first husband Marco, an Ecuadorian aviator who was studying at the Charles Lindbergh Academy in Nebraska. He said that Emmasha was 'the only girl on the prairie who could dance the tango'.

My father Hans as a young man. As boys he and his four brothers had played Swiss Family Robinson and sailed on the Hamburg estuary. But this fantasy could hardly prepare them for the challenges faced on the Galapagos.

(*Above, left*) The dashing Capitán Marco Antonio Aguirre; (*above right*) Marco with his sister in Quito, Ecuador.
(*Right*) Marco at the controls of his plane; (*below*) My mother and grandmother about to be taken for a flight over Lincoln, Nebraska.

Hamburg, 1935 (*above*). The Angermeyer boys on board the *Marie*, checking the chart before setting sail for South America. (*Left*) All musical, the family have one last sing-song. The brothers planned to send for their parents once they reached the islands.

(*Above*) Grandmother gave each son a farewell photograph of herself, with a proverb on the back. My father's said: 'Unless a man builds with God, he labours in vain.'

The Angermeyers: Gus (second from left); Hans (fifth from left, partly
obscured); Fritz (seventh from left); Carl (right); Greta
and Heinrich (front).

Arrival in Galapagos. The brothers were in good spirits although they
had lost their boat and the eldest brother had had to return to Germany,
never seeing the islands. From left: Gus, Hans, Lizzie (Hans's first wife),
Carl and Fritz.

Hans

Gus

Carl

Fritz

(*Left*) My parents on the mainland, shortly after Mary was born. Their plans to sail to Galapagos were suddenly crushed with the news of the attack on Pearl Harbor.

(*Below, left*) Hans, my brother Tony and hunting dog Elmo on the *Marie III*, 1940.

(*Below*) Hans (left) with friend, on the *Marie III*, 1940.

(*Left*) Fritz, Gus and Carl not long after their arrival.

(*Below*) Uncles Gus and Carl as they appeared in the *Argosy* magazine article.

seeped in their own fermented juice on the concrete floor. I gasped as I stepped into something soft and mouldy.

'Shhhhhhhh!' warned Gundi. 'That is Margarita in that box. She is broody.' A red hen stared hypnotized into nothingness as we tiptoed by. Gundi pointed to the shelves. 'See? I told you – books.'

I was speechless. Before me was a treasure: thick novels by Steinbeck, Michener, Du Maurier, Dickens; slender ones by Willa Cather and Conan Doyle. Volumes of Robert Frost, fat how-to books, children's digests, Beatrix Potter, dictionaries, medical books and mysteries. I had not seen so many books since Mother gave up her job in the public library.

'Careful how you put your hands into boxes. Maybe "cien pies" inside.'

'Centipedes?'

'Very long, black. Bites hard.'

I thought I felt a tingle along my arm. *Oliver Twist* fell to the floor with an alarming bang. Margarita let out a screech. From the shed where 'Uncle' Bud, Doris's husband, was working a deep voice roared, 'You kids! Don't go bothering that hen!'

'Run!' hissed Gundi. Quickly I signed for *The Swiss Family Robinson*, *Jane Eyre* and *Beginner's Carpentry* on a rusty clipboard.

I caught up with Gundi in the mangroves near the beach. The sun was sinking and throwing a rosy glow over the sea. I tried to catch my breath. 'Why – why is there a chicken in the library?'

'Uncle Bud isn't coming, is he?' she gasped.

I peeked through the branches. No sign of him.

'The Library used to be the chicken house. When the books arrived on the yacht we had nowhere safe to put them. Bud moved Doris's chickens to a new house but Margarita remembers the old days, so she won't nest anywhere else. You have to be careful where you step in there.'

We lifted our feet in unison, exclaiming in English and German. Laughing, Gundi hobbled down to the wet sand to scrub her foot, returning seconds later to find me still struggling with the laces of my basketball shoes. Tomorrow I would take off my shoes and enjoy being a kid again.

'Be careful not to step in that sea-grass with bare feet. Scorpions. Little brown ones. They would rather run than bite. They don't bite hard.'

There was much to learn. I would ask Gundi to teach me how to row and fish and swim. We'd play around.

'This party tonight, at Uncle Carl's,' I ventured as we walked towards the Stewarts' house, 'what kind of shoes do the ladies wear?'

'No shoes. Much better to dance in bare feet.'

'Well, what kind of dresses do they wear? What will you wear?'

'Me? I don't go to parties! They're for grown ups.'

'Oh.' I was dreadfully disappointed.

'Oh, but you can go!' she shouted merrily scampering off for home in the twilight.

'Yes. Yes, of course,' I answered softly and went indoors.

Night falls quickly in the tropics. One moment you gaze spellbound at a sunset, the next you fumble around in the dark for matches. I stood before a cracked mirror. My hair hung limply, reeking of creosote. Bathing in the sea had left my face streaked with salt. My only dress was wrinkled beyond redemption. Could one iron with hot lava rocks? Tonight of all nights to look a wreck. It would have been easier to meet the Duke of Galapagos as a little kid; they looked good in dirt. When you became a woman everyone expected you to be gorgeous.

'Ouch. *Caramba!*'

'Pick up your feet then!'

'Watch it!'

'Slow down for pity's sake, I can't see a thing the way you're waving that flashlight around.'

We stumbled in the dark along the beach path towards Marga and Carl's house, each holding firmly to the one in front, like a chain of paper dolls. Mary led Johnny, who was afraid of the dark. Tony brought up the rear, carrying the accordion.

'What was that?'

'What?'

'Something scurried over the path.'

'Probably a centipede. Gundi says...'

'Do they bite?'

'Let's see if we can catch it.'

'Is that my accordion case you just bumped?'

'No, it was my toe.'

'*My violin*! I forgot it.'

'Well, you can't go back now.'

'I must. I have to!'

Mama understood. She handed me the small pocket torch with the low batteries.

'Keep the sound of the sea on your left as you go and on your right as you come back,' Mary cautioned.

'I know, I know!'

Tidal pools gurgled. Something went smack-smack-hishhh on the beach. Our house was ahead, with spindly trees waving back and forth in the dim glow of my flashlight; like hungry witches grabbing at the stars. There weren't many stars, the witches had gobbled them for tea. I skipped along the path. 'The witches had 'em for tea! The witches had 'em –' The torch dimmed and died. I slapped it on my thigh. It blinked back to life. A gust of wet wind hit my face. Garua! Thank you, God! We would have water for breakfast!

As I reached the house I checked Tony's guttering, mended that afternoon with bandages from the first-aid kit. I listened until I heard the sound I yearned for; water trickling down into our clean barrel.

I had left my violin on the bed roll. The flashlight flickered to show a spider sitting there the size of an English muffin. He clamped a moth in his front legs. The moth struggled. His antennae waved slower, slower, then he was still.

'Let him go!' I shouted. Tony had said we mustn't interfere with the natural food chain. I backed away. Using his mouth like a camper's all-in-one fork-set, the spider began to eat his dinner. Only he wasn't eating. He was sucking. Tony would have loved it.

'Git. Git away, shoo!' I clapped my hands. The spider did not move, but something on our tin roof screeched and flapped off. If I grabbed my violin case, would the spider run over to my arm, up my sleeve and into my bra? He would have pipe-cleaner legs like Tony's tarantula. I found a rusty coat-hanger, hooked the handle of the case and slowly pulled. The spider trotted away on his toes, clutching the moth's torso like a lunchbox and leaving a trail of silver-wing dust behind.

It was then that I noticed my sister's makeup case. Propping the light between my knees, I opened the lid. She hadn't been using it much; the mascara in the little red Maybelline box was new. I spat on the cake, rubbed it into a gooey paste and brushed it on my lashes as I'd seen Mary do. I smeared Parisian Glow on my cheeks. Freckles vanished beneath Tawny Peach Powder and I managed to add some lipstick before the light died. I slapped it on my thigh again. I needed to check my face one more time! Where were the matches? I ran my fingers over the rusty stove. Something slithered away.

'Keep the sea to my right.' Garua blew my hair over my face. I lost the outline of the path, tripped and nearly fell. The flashlight hit a rock and came back on. Thick red mud oozed over my shoes. I had wandered off into the lagoon. I got up and took off my shoes. Garua ran down my nose. My eyes burned. Breakers pounded ahead. I hobbled towards them, just making out the path. A few minutes later I saw the light in Marga's house.

No one answered the door, so I let myself into a small room lit with a lantern. White curtains blew at the window. There were His and Hers basins, clean towels hanging from a pair of goathorns and a bar of soap smelling of roses in a shell dish. The toilet was a throne set over the sea. A crab scurried sideways down the hole. A full-length mirror hung on the back of a second door which presumably led to their bedroom. A terrible sight stood in the mirror. Black eyes streamed down the hideous face. Blobs of powder congealed on the nose. I couldn't possibly wash in Marga's spotless bathroom, or use her clean towels.

I crept outside, leaving my violin propped against the house and found the steep steps down the landing where my uncle tied his dinghy. The bottom step was slimy. Cautiously I scooped up water and scrubbed my face and hands. Climbing the steps I gasped as something cut into my heel, but could see nothing. Straightening my dress, I knocked on the veranda doors. Through the window I saw Traudi's husband Bernhard pick up his concertina. Marga tightened her bow and Mama opened her accordion case. Kerosene lamps threw a rosy glow over the people sitting at a polished table. They all applauded when the music began.

A tall shadow broke from the clump of men and answered the door. I wiped my nose with my sleeve just as the door opened.

'By Jove, it is Yohanna!' exclaimed the Duke of Galapagos. 'We have been waiting for you – let's see – about fourteen years, isn't it?' His shirt was open down his chest, to where the hair was thick. He wore a red scarf about his neck and black trousers slit to the knee. He was as beautiful a thing as I had ever seen. My nose dripped again.

'Allow me to loan you my handkerchief. It is pretty clean, I think.' It smelled of sweet pipes.

'*Caramba*,' Gus joined us, glass in hand. 'What happened to your foot, woman?'

Numb with embarrassment, I looked down. My heel left prints of blood where I stepped.

'Here, I'll fetch a bucket of sea-water to wash it. No, don't you come, it's too dark and dangerous down on the landing. You should see the moray eel on those steps at night!'

He hurried back. I stepped into the bucket of cool water and blew my nose again. My heel exploded in salty pain.

'If ever you get bitten by an eel,' warned the King, 'don't yank away, Hanna. If he doesn't let go friendly like, chop off his head. You got a knife? Good. Where is it?'

'In my suitcase.'

'You going to live in your suitcase, girl? Wear it. Or are you too much of a lady?'

'I'm no lady!' I countered robustly, hoping all the makeup had washed off.

'Anyone can see she is a Galapagueña,' said the Duke, handing me a beaker of punch. 'That will warm you up!' He escorted me into the crowded room where people were singing in German. 'You could dry by the fire but there isn't one. Ani-ani sleeps in the fireplace on these cool nights.'

'Ani-ani?'

'My grandfather iguana. At least I think it's a grandfather. I haven't looked too good to see, ha, ha!' He showed me the sleeping form of a large grey lizard creature sleeping in the fireplace. 'Carmen's little boy, Fiddi, couldn't say iguana when he was a baby – he called them anee-anees. So I named them all that. They come when I call. Did you see me feed them this morning? Usually I feed them in the afternoon, but I had some rice left over. The scientists say they only feed on marine algae, but they forgot to tell this to my iguanas! Mine love rice. I thought maybe you were watching from the boat this morning. I saw you out there with my binoculars. You finished your punch already? Good. Maestros,' he sang out, 'Yohanna is ready to dance. Music please! We start with a waltz. You like waltzes?' he asked taking me firmly by the hand.

'I don't –'

'Good.' He swept me on to the floor. My first dance. I never felt my feet – not even the bleeding one.

A room full of paintings, books, some sculpture, heavy Germanic furniture and a full-rigged model of a ship in the rafters reeled around us as we waltzed.

In the musicians' corner, Bernhard bounced his concertina and Mother played as though she had never left. Tante Marga pursed her lips when she hit the high notes on her violin. I hoped she didn't mind that I was in love with her husband.

9

Ice-Cream by Parachute

The following weekend we set off for the interior of the island. Anne and Maggie gracefully picked their way over the tumble of rocks while we followed slowly, deliberating over every step. It was a mean choice between balancing on an ill-fitting jigsaw of lava or sliding in a dirt trail churned to red mud a few days previously by donkeys and mules weighted down with boat cargo.

Fragrant palo santo trees sprouted the merest hint of green leaf in immediate response to the arrival of garua season. The mist now wafted over the island every morning, giving us two or three inches of drinking water in our tank each time. After an hour's walking, we left behind the arid zone. Red-barked opuntia and jasminocereus cacti gradually gave way to Chinese lanterns, tall trees draped in black orchilla moss, morning glories and wild cucumbers, their orange fruit split open to reveal scarlet seeds.

A second hour of steady climbing brought us into a cool, canopied rain forest of enormous balsa trees and dripping ferns. Giant elephant-ear leaves dwarfed us as we left the four-house village of Bella Vista and walked a few hundred yards on a narrow road until we stood before a crooked gate with a weathered sign that read: 'Vilnis'.

Mary said it meant Wilderness in Norwegian. We paused for breath and she told us the Hornemans' story. When Mrs Horneman arrived as a bride from London, where she had worked, her new husband brought her through this gate, which then said 'Paradise'. It was a word Mr Horneman had presumably used often in describing his island of clear waterfalls and springtime orchards. However, after seeing the primitive state of the house and overgrown farm, his young wife had marched down with hammer and nails and changed the sign, or so the tale went.

The Hornemans were conversant in five languages and enticed many international scientists to their dining table.

The house was two-storeyed, the ground floor built of rock and concrete with an upstairs made from wooden planks. A slender man with a long Darwinian white beard greeted us and invited us in for refreshment in courtly English. We removed our muddy shoes and entered a dark kitchen. When Mrs Horneman smiled, her generosity extended to her eyes, which crinkled behind thick spectacles. She wore her long greying hair simply tied back, like a young girl's. After inquiring of everyone down on the beach, she returned to stoke the fire in her stove and put a kettle on to boil. The smell of wood-smoke and ground coffee, the cat curled on the chair, the dark panelling of the room, and the half-read books everywhere made me sink into the built-in seating behind the table and think of Gundi's word, 'gemütlich'. As the conversation hummed, I lifted up a volume on man's enlightenment in the nineteenth century. The print was tediously small but, curiously, nearly every sentence was underlined; the margins overflowed with notes and exclamation marks. The second book at my side was the same, and the third.

Our hostess produced a substantial brunch of her famous 'miches', deep-fried pancake nuggets rolled in sugar; all the more remarkable for the lady moved as if in constant discomfort, holding on to the table and moving with difficulty. I learned later that she suffered quietly from a hip disorder which kept her nearly housebound. She said I could lay the table from a drawer at the end of the long table full of miscellaneous cutlery. I laid things out meticulously, one thing I had learned in Doña Magdalena's cooking class. Considering that none of the knives and forks matched, I thought I'd done quite well, but Mrs Horneman became quite perturbed. Oh no, the silver fork went to Mr Horneman, the knife with the flowered handle was only used when their daughter Friedl visited, the small spoons were for visitors' coffee, that fork was for so-and-so. I was amused at this arrangement. Each fork and knife had its own personality, each waiting in the dark drawer until someone special came to visit. But for Mrs Horneman, a prisoner in her own kitchen, in a house full of twice-read books, on a farm set on a drenched hillside on an island in the middle of the sea, visitors meant everything.

A large dog strolled in, waving his long tail apologetically and grinning until Mr Horneman gave him a banana. The dog trotted off outside. From the window I saw him grasp the fruit between his paws and fastidiously peel it with the tiny teeth at the front of his mouth. A donkey in a nearby pasture pricked its ears and stuck its head through the wire fence.

'I am glad to see that burro showing an interest in food,' said Mrs Horneman.

'Why, is it ill?'

'I certainly would be if I were her. A few days ago she slipped and fell badly on the rocks while bringing cargo up from the *Carrier*. Fortunately it was just out here on the road, for her insides came out the back end. I didn't know what to do, so I took them in my hand and pushed them all back inside. Donkeys are tough little creatures.'

So intent was I in trying to imagine what I would have done in the same situation that I failed to notice Tony disappear with Mr Horneman. Mother dispatched me after them, for we were due at the Kastdalens'.

The view from upstairs was magnificent; Academy Bay glistened in the sun. Across the shining sea I could just make out the *Cristobal Carrier* making her lopsided way past Barrington on her mail route back to the mainland. Last night everyone had been busy. I remembered Uncle Gus's letter written so long ago: 'Tomorrow they say there shall be a boat so this is my writing night...'

I found Mr Horneman and Tony amongst piles of books, kneeling over a large Bible.

'Ah, but energy equals mass times the speed of light squared! Thus, matter can be produced from energy just as energy can be produced from matter – look at Hiroshima,' said Mr Horneman.

'Indeed. But the big-bang theory claims that chaos produces

organization. But do bombs build houses? "Every house has its builder but He that constructed all things is God." So it says right here in the Book of Hebrews.'

'It is too simple, my friend,' the odd man said slowly.

'Tell me then, if the vegetation around your house is not cut back, if the house is left to its own devices, given time, does it decide to add new rooms and mend its own roof? Or does it become overgrown and decay?'

Below in the awesome green world that surrounded us, a huge old avocado dropped its torpedo-shaped fruit to the leafy floor with a thud. The little donkey trotted swiftly to where it had fallen and devoured it. Whichever way you looked at it, life itself seemed too incredible to be true. Yet undeniably there it was at my feet; unadulterated life waiting for me on an island demanding courage and wisdom. Mrs Horneman had known it the day she'd changed the sign on the gate.

The Kastdalens' dogs always gave a dramatic welcome to visitors. Usually the pack of ten or so came snarling and barking, ran past and ended up calmly watering the rose bushes. But Johnny kept asking if they would bite, so Tony perched him on his shoulders. At our first 'Halloooo', a furry mass of legs and teeth rounded the corner of the pink house and stampeded towards us. Alf's mountainous shape appeared on the high porch and hurried down to greet us. He and Mother strolled ahead, heads bent as she asked him the Latin names of various plants she had collected on the hike up. Before I could warn her, a big, rangy, male dog, his neck mane bristling, sneaked up and sank his teeth into Mama's calf. His teeth just slipped in and out cleanly. Immediately, blood began to spout. Mama swore she never felt a thing.

'It doesn't hurt a bit!' she insisted, as the distressed family gathered on the porch armed with disinfectant and a bottle of brandy.

'Ach, but that is a terrible dog!' Mrs Kastdalen's light-blue eyes were kind and concerned. Her able hands had bound many wounded legs before.

'Oh, but such a thing to happen to a friend!' clucked Tante

Lala, Mrs Kastdalen's companion. She wrung her small sparrow hands, worry paling her bone-china face. She had been, and still was, a very beautiful woman. The tale told on the beach was that when the family had left Norway, Maya Kastdalen had been frail. Worried that she might not survive the rigours of life on the island, she had asked Lala to come so as not to leave her family motherless. But now, over twenty years later, it was Lala who looked fragile and Maya who blossomed with vitality.

Tante Lala poured Mama a glass of banana brandy, but she gave most of it to me, restoring my colour. Then we joined the others in the parlour.

'They dropped ice-cream by parachute,' Alf was telling the others. 'I was only a boy of seventeen, you understand, and had never tasted such a thing before, so it was something of a *beeeeeg* treat, I can tell you. You know Baltra Island, just north of here? There were nearly three thousand American men over there during the war, defending the Panama Canal. It was good for us, we traded our fruit for Spam. You know Spam? And they dropped our mail right out there in the rose bushes. Mail service has never been so good since! When they left, of course, we Galapagueños lost no time in bringing every scrap of wood and iron back here!'

'*Todas esas casas en la playa son hechas de madera americana,*' said Tante Maya.

'Oh yah, many of the beach houses were made from American pine. But Mother, we are speaking English right now,' Alf reminded Maya.

'I know, I know!' she said defensively. 'Was I not speaking English?'

'No, you were speaking Spanish.'

'Oh, *caramba.*' She shook her head and left to get more brandy.

To us Alf said quietly, 'If English-speaking people come here, Mother always speaks Spanish brilliantly. But if one of the Ecuadorian farm workers comes she speaks to them in Norwegian!'

'When first we come to Ecuador,' said Mr Kastdalen, chuckling, 'Lala looked around her and said, "Everybody here speaks Spanish? I cannot see why, Norwegian is so much easier!"' He laughed again. Then he said something briefly with Alf in Norwegian. They both nodded and the older man left the room.

There was a pounding on the floor. Alf said his mother was announcing dinner with a broom handle. We got up. I heard a shot crack. Then I observed Mr Kastdalen coming back with his rifle. I could not see his face but his shoulders slouched. 'We cannot have a dog what is biting people,' he said as we sat down to table. 'Yesterday he bites a scientist who was standing at the gate, doing no harm. No reason to bite. I have thought for some time that this dog was sick, going crazy in his head. On pig hunts he acted strange. Maybe brain parasites. Now he feels nothing.

'The other dogs in the pack will go bad also if we have one *perro malo*. Oh yah,' he said, taking in my startled face, 'so easy the animals here return to their wild state. Then they are dangerous.'

One shot. No lingering behind caged door, beseeching tail wagging while strangers paraded by the cells trying to choose a new pet. No unwanted puppies abandoned here. Your bitch had too many in the litter, the extras were killed at birth, quickly. It was a sad fact but an island, like the world, could support only so many.

Tante Lala ladled chicken soup from a pink porcelain tureen. Then flowered dishes appeared with bright green vegetables, hot crusty rolls, home-churned butter, platters of crisp pork, avocado, otoi-root pancakes, yucca dumplings, roast chicken and fried bananas with pitchers of sweet lemon juice to wash it down.

I was amazed and asked where they got it all from. It was the right thing to say, for Mr Kastdalen's face beamed.

'Wild boar, our chicken, our milk, our otoi root, our yucca, our avocados and our lemons – all from our farm, oh yah!'

'And the beautiful porcelain?'

'Norway,' Alf said, pointing to old photographs set in oval frames on the wall. Severe bearded men, stiff in their Sunday suits, sat beside corseted, unsmiling women. Another was a picture of wooden houses by a grim, cold sea. The harsh wintery scene was now browning at the edges from twenty-five years of Galapagos sun.

I tried to imagine the door of one of those houses opening and Alf's family, bundled against the wind, loading their possessions, these very dishes, into a horse-drawn wagon, clusters of shivering neighbours waving goodbye as the Kastdalens and Lala set off for the end of the earth.

'We brought what we could,' said Alf. 'When first we came in 1935 we made a little camp down on the beach. But we are not fishermen. Father was a farmer all his life.'

'Oh yah,' added Mr Kastdalen. 'And a carpenter. So we soon caught some donkeys and moved our things to the highlands. I searched all over, but when I stood on this spot I saw wild avocados, oranges, bananas and there was such a beautiful view of the sea. I said to Mother, "This is good."'

Maya gave me a second helping of everything without being asked. She paused, suspending a drumstick over my plate. 'We put up a big tarpaulin for sleeping, and a table. I remember our first Christmas; we had seven big Swedes with us who intended to settle. How it rained!'

'Oh yah, I remember,' joined in Alf. 'It was pouring down and all those Swedes were trying to fit under the tarpaulin and we were so happy singing carols while beneath our table was running a creek this wide!' Alf stretched his arms, dwarfing his fork to doll size. Then he sobered. 'When the Americans dropped ice-cream in the roses we had already been here ten years. In 1935 it was a different story; no treats. I would say it was not an easy life then. Our diet was poor. Practically we lived off the island, wild boar, fruit, roots. Later we tamed a cow for milking and got some chickens.'

'Were you able to order some things from the mainland?' asked Mother.

'We would put in a special order for Christmas as a treat.' Alf and his father exchanged amused glances. 'We got it for Christmas all right!' He broke into a wide grin. 'But one year late! Ha! Ha! Ha!'

'Well, I guess you learn patience in a place like this,' Tony said.

'I would say you learn many things. Here we even learned how to eat elephant eggs.' He laughed again and explained. 'First you grate otoi root. Then you mash it with, how you say *chicharrones* in English? Cracklins? Yes, then you mix this with lots of pig grease, put it into a *beeeg* cloth and cook it like a ball. That is really tasty, I can tell you.' He liked eeee sounds. Every time he pronounced big, pig and grease, he showed all his strong teeth. Such a sound seemed appropriate coming from big Alf.

Lala spoke. 'Mrs Horneman, she taught us how to make elephant eggs.'

'You must know the Hornemans quite well, being next-door neighbours,' chirped Tony unaware of Alf's ill-fated romance. I kicked him under the table and blurted, 'This otoi – could we get some to try and make elephant eggs?'

'Oh yah, but you must soak the root before you cook it. Otherwise the crystals of uhmn – a scientist told me once and I looked it up – I think it is calcium oxolate; yes; it will burn your tongue. The wild pigs dug up most of ours, but I tell you who has some is Old Moo just across the stand of avocado trees.'

'Also Gordon Wold has some,' said Mr Kastdalen. 'Old Moo doesn't see many people these days, but Gordon knew the Angermeyers well, he being a bachelor like they were, well, like most of them were. Gus, Carl and Fritz were something; always playing around, laughing and singing, never serious about anything. When first they came I said to Maya that, like the Swedes, they would never last.'

Lala passed plates down to Maya, refusing help. A short time later the broom handle pounded the floor and Alf rose, edgy as a boy about to open presents. 'Well, we can go down now for cakes and dancing!'

Tony disguised a startled belch and struggled to stand. Ignoring her protests, Alf carried Mother downstairs, embarrassing her into rattling off a detailed description of Russian–German basements in Nebraska.

It was a semi-basement with small windows looking out at the root systems of creeping plants eager to get inside and take over. Hundredweights of flour, sugar and chicken corn sagged drunkenly against the wall, as yet unstored in the rat-proof drums. A pail of milk stood in a pan of water, a butterchurn was shoved under the table out of the way. Mother settled in a chair, her leg propped on a milking stool.

Alf wound up the Victrola. Looking determined, he turned, slicked down his hair and approached my sister. Circumspectly, he took her hand and they began to foxtrot.

> '... if you no wanna love me ...'
> Mad I gonna be,
> 'Cause I wanna what I wanna ...'

'The Americans give it to us ...' shouted Mr Kastdalen to me over the crackling din.

> 'Why do you cooooo ...
> Pretty little things like you dooooooo ...'

Alf's feet, for all that they were shaped like shoeboxes, posed no threat to my sister, for not only was he barefoot, he danced expertly. Had his parents been coaching him down here all these years since the Americans left?

> 'When you wanna, I no wanna,
> So how we ever gonna make looooove!'

Soft light shone from lanterns hanging in the rafters. Tony took turns dancing with my cousins. Alf danced with no one but Mary. I was glad no one was in love with me. I remembered how ridiculous Ophelia had been over the whistle-blower.

Wandering about the room, I peered into a large wooden barrel. My hip bumped it and several dark chunks bobbed to the surface. Cautiously, I dipped my finger in. Rancid pork fat. Drawn to the Victrola, as I had never seen one before, I bent down to watch the old 78 whizz around in panic. The label on the box said:

The wonder of the 20th Century.
By appointment to the late Queen Victoria.
Gramophone by Imhof and Mukle.
New Oxford St. London W.

Alf wound it up again.

'You must have been a beautiful baby...'

They served thick black coffee, frothy milk and stacks of butter cakes on a tray. Alf would not stop dancing. He whirled my exhausted sister over the concrete floor.

'You must have been a beautiful child...'

I ate a fourth cake. I could not imagine my sister rising at dawn to milk mud-splashed cows. She loathed farms. I could not see her mashing otoi root with pig grease and boiling elephant eggs in a bag. Alf had never seen my sister in her beige high heels. He did not know that she wore pink foam curlers to bed; six on top and three down the sides. He didn't know that she liked to dance Persian belly-dances in the kitchen with finger cymbals on, or that she had a son. Yes, what were we going to do about that?

Hours later I snuggled under a feather bed, aware of a throbbing in my heel. Niguas throbbed; nasty little flea things which lived in mud. If the female got into a wound or under a toenail, she laid eggs there. The wound festered. If you cleaned the wound and broke the egg sacs, the niguas set up housing and eventually caused gangrene. Taking care not to rouse Mary, I lit the lamp by my bed and examined my heel. The bandage I had put there days ago was twisted and useless.

I got back into bed. What was the quilt stuffed with, leaves? I'd given up reading *The Swiss Family Robinson*. Mr Weiss had clearly never stepped on a real desert island; he made it all too easy: animals, tools and guns conveniently shipwrecked with them. Plenty of time for ostrich races. On a real island eating was a full-time occupation. And to think I'd hoped we would settle in Galapagos. We didn't know the first thing about building a house. Father and his brothers arrived without a roof over their heads or a general store to run to. Uncle Fritz had lanced his own leg. Mrs Horneman stuffed donkeys' insides back. Uncle Gus pulled his own tooth out with pliers. Could I shoot a wild pig if I were hungry?

Pigs. Pigs spread niguas in their excrement; Tony said so. How much pig excrement had I unknowingly trudged through today? I knew I had a hole in the sole of my shoe.

I closed my eyes. They amputated gangrenous legs. Decks of warships used to be painted red so you wouldn't notice the blood, Tony said. They filled you with rum and tied you down and then you died of septicaemia anyway. My foot throbbed me to sleep along with the wind in the avocado trees and the distant pounding of the sea.

The next morning we set off for the coast bearing gifts of butter and cheese to those on Angermeyer Point, all carefully wrapped in banana leaves. Tante Maya presented me with a special bundle of pig grease and cracklins for my elephant eggs. We would stop at Gordon Wold's for otoi.

The morning air smelled of rotting compost and the ground underfoot gave like a sponge beneath our shoes. Avocados lay everywhere, smashed or sprouting shoots. A pink, perfumy carpet lay before us that turned out to be rotting guayava. There is something about wild fruit going to waste, and greedily we began to stuff our sacks, but my cousins insisted the tender yellow fruit would never survive the trek home, so reluctantly we left it to the flies.

When it began to rain, we cut elephant-ear leaves for umbrellas. I used my knife for the first time, wiping it carefully on my leaf before I sheathed it. A vermilion flycatcher landed on my shoulder. He twisted his tiny ruby head and peered under my hat. I was speechless with delight, wishing the others would stop and look back at him. But as quick as he had come he flitted off into the moss-draped trees. I ran to catch up. My foot began to throb.

Before reaching the village we passed a house built in a dark corner of a wet wood. Graffer, my cousins said, was one of the first Norwegians to colonize. Rain pounded on the tin roof like a locomotive. There were words scrawled on the shack: 'Abode and Residium of Graffer', and, 'Headquarters of the Simian Hedgehogs'.

'What does it mean?' I whispered to Tony.

'Can we go?' wailed Johnny. Anne Liese agreed and quickly set the pace. Laughter rose from within the shack and two voices spoke simultaneously.

'Probably Old Moo,' said Maggie. 'Alf says he comes here to play chess a lot.'

I let the others go, not wanting them to notice my limp. The door of the shack opened and a grizzled toothless Ben Gunn, who I assumed was Graffer, waved to another man untying a donkey. This man had what looked like a radio wrapped in plastic under his arm. The other arm rose to wave, but then he saw me and froze. I raised my hand in greeting, but he pulled his donkey into the shadows; he'd looked scared to death of me. I caught a glimpse of his threadbare sweater, raggedy shorts and black rubber boots several sizes too large on his thin white legs as he disappeared.

Wold lived in a two-storey shack exactly like island houses in every adventure book I'd ever read. A crude ladder led to a sleeping room. To call it a bedroom would imply curtains, a chest of drawers and some degree of comfort. But Gordon Wold had developed simple tastes since his arrival in 1923. For curtains, the only ones there were thick cobwebs draping a lopsided window cut into the bamboo slats. What I suspected was his one change of clothes hung from a peg next to a bridle and a muddy length of rope.

I once had a doll with a faded face. It was my fault; for the only thing I could think of doing with the doll was bathing her, which I did so often she acquired an astonished expression every time I stripped her down and lathered her up. Wold looked faded like that doll; and just as astonished when we arrived.

Perhaps it was having six human beings on his hillside all at once.

He tended an open fire in a lean-to kitchen made of thin poles and slabs of tree bark. While attempting polite conversation in Spanish, he recovered enough to pull up four tree-trunk stools for some of us to sit on. When I asked to buy otoi roots for my elephant eggs, he looked startled and pulled what looked like hairy ivory tusks from a wooden box and stuffed them into my bag, refusing payment. The rain let up and we made moves to leave.

'You want frutas?' he asked pointing to a small tree laden with cherry-like fruit. 'You take what you like. Take. Take!' The others went to the tree but I stayed back, watching him remove a small black battered pot from its tree-limb hook and fill it from the rain barrel.

'I am Hans's daughter,' I announced. If Mother wasn't going to talk about him, maybe Wold would.

'*Sí, sí.*' He chopped some potatoes, not bothering to remove all the soil, and added them to the pot, with a spoonful of pig lard and a clump of sea-salt. He stirred the mess with a wooden spoon.

'You knew him in the old days – you knew my – Hans.'

Wold crouched deep in thought like an old man, though he wasn't much over fifty and looked fit, if a bit too thin.

'Tell me about him, won't you?'

He shuffled over to a hanging stem of bananas, picked three green ones and laid them in the ashes below the pot, to roast.

'It was a long time ago.'

'Yes. Well, not so long – surely you –'

'He was tall and blond.' He smiled as though this would appease me.

'Yes, yes, I know that already. I mean, what was he like?' I glanced nervously towards the others. They would soon be back. I smiled sweetly. He blushed. I was astounded at my womanly power.

He began haltingly. 'Well, Johannes was, I would say, a

thoughtful young man – maybe he thought too much. If you live with a woman – she talks too much. Galapagos is hard on a man, but for a woman – impossible. That is why I never married. Like Moo says, what is there out here for a woman? No pretty things, no clothes, nowhere to go at night.'

'Mr Kastdalen says you knew Hans in the old days,' I interrupted, trying to steer him back on course.

'Oh yah, he was the married one; a ballerina.' His eyes sparkled. Was it from the fumes of the mess he was cooking, I wondered. 'Like I say, nowhere to go at night. She used to come here; talking – crazy talk. She stayed too late. At first Hans came to get her. I wanted to marry once. Moo said, "No, look at Lizzie and all the trouble."'

I pulled my tree stump nearer. 'But what about Hans?'

'He got more and more quiet all the time; only talking to animals. He always had donkeys and dogs and cats and things. He had a horse, a wild thing – frightened me. I took care of it once when Hans took Lizzie to the mainland for a divorce. You see, Lizzie always said Hans didn't want children – crazy talk! Later Hans came back; much later, after the war – married to another woman. I never met her. He said he was happy, a changed man. They had children. He told me he was going to build a house for his family; the most wonderful house in the archipelago. I told Moo about it. Moo still said this was no place for a woman. "Forget women!" Then Hans and his wife left, don't remember why. He came up here to see me; in good spirits he was. "Look Gordon –" he was one of the few to use my name – "look, you keep my stallion for me till I get back." He was going to America, I think – somewhere like that – to sail a boat back or something. He was going to bring his children back to Galapagos. "You take the horse and in exchange for looking after him you can ride him down to the beach – it will be good for you to get some sunshine." But he never came back. That horse of his was useless. I couldn't ride him, nobody could – tore down my fences and went wild up in hills of Media Luna. Hans owed me for the fence.' Suddenly he swore in Spanish. 'Cursed bananas! They burn the minute you turn your back!'

'What do you call this fruit?' asked Tony, his mouth and pockets bulging. I tried one, but the milky sweetness didn't appeal to me.

'Norwegian cherries. You make jams. I brought the seeds from Panama forty years ago.'

'A long time ago,' said my brother.

'A long time,' agreed Wold, searching my face, taking in my youth, trying to recall what he had said, the things implied.

We thanked him and said goodbye. He watched us march down the slope to the road before returning to his cook-shed. I heard his axe chopping into the damp morning.

Suddenly he yelled after us: 'You! You watch out! Those fruits – they turn your teeth black – I forgot to say!'

10

Marooned

The next morning I felt unwell.

'It's rancid pig lard and Kastdalen butter,' Uncle Gus assured me. 'They're used to it, but I remember we had a party down here, oh, twenty years ago. Everyone brought food. The Kastdalens came down with fried pork from out of their grease barrels. It was a change from goat, so we ate and ate. But the next day? *Mensch*, we were sick. We were crawling with stomach cramps.'

I had gone to his shack after lunch to deliver the last bundle of melting butter. The interior was much changed, for Lucrecia had moved down into her new, though still unfinished, house. But Gus had decided to keep a room for himself where he could put 'pure thoughts down on patient paper'. At the moment he was typing a letter addressed to Washington DC on a very old typewriter.

'How do you spell in English un-ob-tain-able? A Dr Somebody from the Smithsonian Institute wants me to find him a rare cowrie.' He showed me a small photograph. It looked like every other shell on the beach to me. 'This American will pay a lot of money for it.'

'Never seen one.'

'Well, if you ever do, throw it back into the sea.'

'Why?' I protested. I couldn't help noticing that he needed new shorts and that the mosquito screens on his shack were full of holes.

'Why? You ask me why, Hanna? Look, things like shells will always be rare if fools keep yanking them from the sea. You ever seen stuffed animals mating in the museum?'

I'd never seen anything mating. I said nothing. He seemed

annoyed, biting the top of his moustache. I glanced at the dollar sign on the letter. Fishing for bacalao a few months of the year and selling it dried to the mainland for Easter soup did not bring in a great deal of money. We both knew what a cheque from America could buy. 'It's all part of life. My book will be about dreams and enchanted places; life. You understand, Hanna? You know what life is?'

In my fourteen years not many had asked me for my philosophy on life. I made a mental note to prepare something for the next time.

'Here on these ash heaps we try to make a life and be happy at the same time. It is up to each to find the roses between the thorns.'

'There are many thorns out there,' I said profoundly. 'Rocks, too.'

'Yeah, plenty. I love rocks, you know,' he went on dreamily. 'I like to touch them, move them.' He ducked under his desk and brought out a twisted rope of lava. 'Here, see this one? Look how nature is art. See, this woman is kneeling, her head to one side, no? Maybe praying. It is sad. But,' he turned the sad kneeling woman upside down, 'see now it is a man shouting, exulting as he walks alone through time and space!'

It didn't look like a woman praying to me, or a man shouting. The rock had a frying-pan look about it one way up and the other – carefully I took it, holding it sideways – it looked like the Oscar Mayer weiner car. On the television a midget chef used to hop out of a car shaped like a giant hot dog and start throwing free sausage whistles to all the kids in the neighbourhood. He never showed up on Arlington Street, so I never got one.

'Would you like to take it home? It is enchanted, this rock, I warn you.'

'For ever?'

'Yah, it's yours.'

'Thanks! If I take it home will it keep its enchantment?'

'That is up to you. It depends on how much enchantment you have yourself.' He held my eyes for a moment. 'Now,' he finished gruffly, 'how do you spell un-ob-tain-able?' I spelled it out, but asked him why he was still writing letters. The *Carrier* had sailed at daybreak.

'I'm going to catch up with her at Plaza Island. They've picked up some tourists or they wouldn't bother stopping there. A scientist asked me to take him over because he was bitten by a dog last week. I told him there is no rabies on Galapagos, but he is tired of counting wild tortoises. He cannot wait to return to hot baths and cold beer, poor guy. You want to come?'

'Me?'

'Sure, a little adventure. You haven't seen any of the other islands. Are you afraid?'

I didn't even bother to answer that, but said I would ask Mother.

'Why are you limping?' he called after me.

I showed the King, sitting on a hairy black goat skin on the floor and propping my foot on his knee. He peered at my heel through a magnifying glass, actually the lens of some broken binoculars.

'It isn't niguas,' he said at last. 'That hurt?' He poked, I winced. 'Yah, just as I thought. You cut it sometime on coral, no? Well, it's healed up over sand. Just open it and wash out the sand with puro, you know, cane alcohol. Soak it in the sea now and then, and wear a sock.'

'With my knife?' I asked, shrinking at the image of Uncle Fritz heating his big knife over the campfire after the wild-boar incident.

'Knife? What you think you are doing, taking off the whole foot, girl? Use a new razor blade. Soak it in puro. Pour a little down your own throat to start with.'

'Right!' I said, perhaps a little too heartily, for he let go of my foot, leaned forward and looked me straight in the eye.

'You going to do it or get someone else?'

'I'll do it, I'll do it!' I said testily, and got up.

'Good girl. Come back when you've done. We sail in an hour. We'll make a Galapagueña of you...'

I smiled wanly.

Mother said I should go, but she made me drink a large mug of tea and a bowl of porridge to calm my stomach. Hurriedly,

I belted on my knife and put a sketchbook and pencil into a knapsack.

I was relieved when the family all went down to the beach for a fishing lesson with Big John. I disliked writhing in public. Unwrapping one of Tony's new razor blades, I found the tomato-catsup bottle of sugar-cane alcohol and miles of sterilized gauze and tape. At the first swig of puro I knew that it had not been recommended as an anaesthetic but as a distraction, for nothing could be so painful as the raw dragon-fire scorching my throat, nasal passages and eye sockets. After I cut a shallow slit in my heel, I could see specks of fine sand in there. Gritting my teeth, I sloshed puro all over it. Our spiders, which had become quite tame, went into panic, running at top speed to hide in every available crack, while I hopped one-legged around the room, waving my exploding foot and yelling into a pillow.

The bitten French tortoise man was already on board the *Liv* when Gus rowed me out. His muddy hiking boots reeked and his filthy socks were festooned with clinging weeds and seeds. Cousin Franklin giggled as I got in the way of the coiling of ropes, stowing of anchors, raising of sails and cranking of engines.

Tante Marga appeared on her veranda as the *Liv* made her first eager lunges forward, like a dog who has been kennelled too long. 'Will you be back for our music practice tomorrow afternoon?' she shouted.

I called back that I would and waved goodbye as we sailed out of Academy Bay. I wondered where the Duke was; his boat was gone from its anchorage.

By the time the village faded in the distance and before we rounded Punta Nuñez, I was looking for somewhere to be discreetly ill, but Gus gave me the wheel, pointed the way to go and left me, thereby distracting me, and I began to enjoy the pitching and plunging.

The Frenchman sat beside me, propping up his bitten leg and telling me how the Kastdalen dog had tried to kill him; how wet and impossible the hills were once the garua started, how his food had run out, how the wild tortoise kept crashing through his tent and how the fire ants nearly drove him crazy.

'What is that island there beyond Barrington?'

He thought I was an island girl! I steered with what I hoped looked like casual expertise, trying to recall the map of the archipelago.

'Oh, you mean that one over there?'

'*Oui.*'

'That one you can barely see there to our right?'

'*Oui.*'

Gus joined us just in time. To me he said in an undertone, 'Right is starboard, *por favor.*' To the scientist he shouted over the engine, 'That is Floreana, *Isla de Misterios.* There is a spring up in those hills. The pirates spotted it from the sea over two hundred years ago – a patch of green in what is otherwise a pretty barren island.'

'Yes, I have read about it. There are caves. Have you been there?'

'I am the King, man, this is my, how you say – kingdom? Sure, I go everywhere. You can still see where the pirates carved niches out of the soft rock up there – shelves – benches to sit on – a fireplace. They used to go up there for water and giant tortoise.'

'What did they want with tortoise?' I whispered.

'Ate them. Those poor *criaturas* can live a year or so without food or water, so they used to store them in the holds of their ships, one on top of the other. Fresh meat when they wanted, see?'

'And you have some theory about what happened to the Baroness?'

'Ahh, the Baroness. I wondered when you would ask. Some people think she was the only human ever to live in *Las Encantadas.*'

'I have read that she had an entourage of men and proclaimed herself Empress of the Pacific, and that she shot a man so that she could nurse him back to health!'

'Going to be a good sunset. Look at those colours, man. But you should see them later in the year! You know, when my brother Carl went back to Germany not long ago to exhibit his paintings, they wouldn't believe his colours were true. Carl says that the northern sun is so faded, he could not convince anyone how *magnifico* our sunsets are. The oranges and pinks smear with the red across the sky. I never get tired of it. Never. Hard to starboard, Hanna. More. The currents through here are dangerous – steady as she goes. Good, keep her there.' Gus left us and went below.

The Frenchman continued. 'They say this Baroness came from Austria but that she met her lovers in Paris. Phillipson was the strong one, I believe and Lorenz the weak one. This woman took over the island, no? Everyone hated her, the Wittmers, Ritter, the dentist. He was a strange one. He had all his teeth pulled out before he left Germany and wore stainless-steel ones. His mistress Dora had her teeth pulled also. I hear they shared these, how you say, dentures?'

'What happened to all of them?' I spoke without taking my eyes off the point Gus had set as my target.

'The Wittmer family are still there,' said the Frenchman. 'Ritter died of food poisoning. Dora went back to Germany and wrote the book I read. The Baroness and Phillipson disappeared. Just like that!' He snapped his fingers. 'Maybe the jealous Lorenz killed them, maybe not. No bodies were found. Maybe sharks got them. They had no boat to escape. Lorenz was found on the beach of some northern island; Marchena, I think. The sun had mummified him. I saw a photograph once; it showed his hands – like this they were.' Graphically, my companion formed his hands in a grotesque grasp and twisted his rough-bearded face into a terrible death grimace. With that he limped over to his gear and stretched out for a nap.

Gus surfaced, looked to see if we were headed straight, but suddenly rushed back, took the wheel and told me to run forward. I held on to every fastened-down object and fell to my knees when I reached the bow. Below on either side were long silver porpoise, about six of them riding our bow wave, whistling softly to the smaller ones in the group and smiling up at me. Instinctively, I whistled back and they swam on their sides, whistling back, I thought, louder than before. I lay on my stomach, reaching as far as I could, willing them to come near enough to stroke their bodies, touch the scars on their backs. My stretching fingers came within inches of them and tears welled in my eyes from their beauty. The only sound in the world was the beating of my heart and the little gasps they gave as their blow-holes surfaced. Then, as suddenly as they had come, they dived and disappeared in the depths.

My uncle searched my face when I reached his side. He moved over, letting me take the wheel again. 'Steer with your feet,' he suggested, handing me an orange. We sat in silence as the sea churned past. The oranges were ugly dull green with scaly patches on the skins. I began to peel mine with my knife.

'We had oranges in California which you could peel and not get your hands messy,' I said. Gus nodded, having already ripped his orange open and sunk his teeth into it.

'The Original Navel Orange Tree lived down the street from us, in a cage with a plaque.' The peel fell off my orange in a thin green coil. 'They were navel oranges, you know – had navels on the bottoms. If you bought one with a navel you knew it wouldn't have any seeds and you could pry it apart neatly and eat the sections. That way you got all the juice in your mouth – just like M & M candies.' I laughed.

Gus made no response; he just watched me peel.

'– y'know, melt in your mouth, not in your hand?'

My uncle said he had never heard of them.

'No, of course not, silly me.'

'You want me to take the wheel while you eat that orange or are you going to peel it to death?'

I gave him the wheel.

'Your first Galapagos orange?'

I nodded. My first porpoise, my first orange. Disconcerted at being stared at, I took a tentative bite. Incredible sweet juice exploded in my mouth, choking me. I leaned over as juice ran down my shirt front, breaking into rivulets as it reached my waistband. I squirmed.

'Good, eh?' Gus grinned and wiped his mouth with the back of his hand. There were bits of orange caught in his teeth.

★

The ugly shape of the *Cristobal Carrier* lay anchored between North and South Plazas, two small, tilted lava faults lifted from the sea bed, separated from Santa Cruz by a mere hundred yards of water.

Gus took the tiller, explaining that South Plaza supported the most wildlife: swallow-tailed gulls, petrels, shearwaters and red-billed tropic birds, which nested on the cliffs. Sea-lions bred on the rocky coast; the tidal pools made play areas for their young. Land iguanas burrowed in the soft soil and marine iguanas draped themselves over the black shore, interspersed with Sally Lightfoot crabs.

The sky turned a delicate shade of violet with sparkling stars as we cut the engine. The passengers and crew of the larger boat leaned out of the saloon to watch us tie up alongside. The captain yelled, '*Don Gus, mi gran amigo!*'

'*Mi Capitán!*' thundered Gus.

To my horror, my uncle accepted an invitation to dine on board. I had no change of clothes I wailed but Gus insisted that *El Capitán* would be mortally offended if we did not all accept. We had to keep on good terms with the family's only link with the mainland.

There were but two other women on board, nuns in grey who eyed my shorts and bare legs. We were served macaroni and potato soup followed by tough meat, fried bananas and lentils with rice. The nuns wisely departed to their cabins before the appearance of the watery gelatine pie. None of the remaining men minded the way the green pie jiggled on the dirty plates like frog spawn, for they began to pass around the Rum San Miguel. Only my cousin Franklin, who sat in-communicado in the corner, did not drink from '*la botella de amistad*'.

The songs began by the time the second bottle was opened and immediately a cry rose up for Don Gus to sing. He got up confidently, drained his glass, told them a little story of a pirate on the Volga who has to choose between his loyal men and the love of a princess, and then sang *Stenka Razin*. His fine deep baritone was as full of vibrato as an old Caruso record. In a concert hall with ruby-red curtains and bejewelled ladies swooning from the boxes, he would have been magnificent. There among the scruff and green pie he was unbelievable.

When the third bottle had been opened, I asked Gus timidly if we shouldn't be going.

'Why Hanna, aren't you having a good time? Forgive me. Gentlemen? Caballeros, my niece, who studies real music in the capital, shall sing for you. Go on – one little song.' All the red eyes centred on me. Suddenly I hated it. I hated all the times I'd crept through the streets of Quito wearing my overcoat, suffering humiliation at every corner, constantly watching to make sure I wasn't followed home, suspicious of every smile, every whisper; in a sense, apologizing to myself for being female.

'You've had enough. You're supposed to get us home.'

'*Home*? I am home. Home is wherever I happen to be. You think my home is Lu's pile of rocks? That palace? Why do you worry so much? I shall sing one last song.' The cook twanged dismal chords on his guitar while his compadres sang a Spanish lament in drunken harmony to Gus's German ballad.

I shook Franklin's shoulder. 'Help me get him off.' Franklin opened his beautiful violet eyes. I pointed to the *Liv*, whose rubbing strake was cracking slightly against the *Carrier*'s baby-blue side.

'Gus, we must go.'

'*Nein.*'

'C'mon, you get up!'

'Relax, Hanna.'

I told him his boat was cracking up; feeling it was a justified exaggeration. Shaking hands around the saloon, Gus followed Franklin and me down the ladder. Franklin giggled as he untied the lines and pushed us away from the big hull. Now at the mercy of the currents, we began to drift towards the blackened shore. Sea-lions brayed noisily from the rocks. Rocks! I waited for the other two to do whatever you did to stop a drifting boat, but Gus had disappeared. After a few minutes I went below to find him curled up in his bunk, sound asleep. I shook him, shouting, but he was gone. The *Liv* gave a sickening lurch sideways. I ran back up calling Franklin.

'What do we do?' No answer. I could still hear singing aboard the *Carrier*. No use shouting to those drunken fools for help.

Finally Franklin suggested we throw out the anchor.

'Yes, but where do we throw it?' No answer. I picked up the heavy stern anchor, closed my eyes and threw it as far as I could, losing my footing and nearly falling overboard. I expected a splash, but got a thud and chink of chain as it landed in the wooden dinghy tied astern. I hauled it back, skinning my knuckles, and tried again. It was too dark to see what my cousin was doing but I heard a mighty splash from the bow. What were those dark shapes circling the boat?

'Have you fallen in?' I yelled shrilly. A giggle came from the bow, a snore from below. The *Liv* stopped lurching and settled down to bob and sway at her anchor. Sea-lions coughed and belched. The tide changed. The moon came out with a myriad of stars.

It was well past midnight. I needed a bathroom. Gus had said there was a tin somewhere on board, but I had no torch to look for it. I peeked down the hatch. Franklin was trying to read by a dim light over his bunk.

I experimented with projecting myself over the side, bracing my feet against the capping rail. Three dark shapes cruised below. Sharks? If I fell in – maybe that is what happened to the Baroness. People would tell my story for years to come: 'Never knew what became of the girl; she was on board one minute, gone the next!' I had begun to wish I was a boy when the *Carrier*'s engines started up. As they winched her anchor, she pulled nearer and nearer to us until I could clearly see the crew running here and there. Before I could jerk myself upright, her powerful searchlight caught me in its beam. I let go of my foothold and half fell into the water. My shoulders screamed as I held on, pulling myself up, squirming with pain as I banged my bandaged heel. At last upright and in a mean and ugly mood, I buttoned my shorts and stormed down below. Gus lay in the lower bunk, uncovered, his face like that of a small boy dreaming of island adventures. How many times had my grandmother looked down at him smiling in his sleep like that?

The night air cooled as the garua blew in. I reached down and pulled a blanket up over the King of Galapagos.

I awoke to a gentle rocking, a sunny blue sky and sparkling sea lapping at *Liv*'s sides. As I went on deck, prepared to demand to be rowed ashore to the nearest bush, Gus's voice bellowed from the boat's innards: '*Caramba*! Somebody left a light on last night!' Then followed a string of guttural oaths in low German. The little sermon I had prepared vanished as his face appeared through the hatch.

'You?' he roared in his best pirate voice.

I shook my head.

'Franklin!' But my cousin had miraculously vanished. 'Well, that's that. No spark, no engine. We go nowhere.'

'Do you mean we are stuck out here?' I squealed incredulously. 'For how long?'

'How long? You ask me how long? What do you think, I have a glass ball? Or maybe you think the *Queen Mary* will cruise around the point any moment and tow us home.' His tone softened. 'Some day it will be like that. This little island will be covered in tourists. You won't be able to step without bumping into cameras. Cruise ships in and out all day. But for now, we wait for some filthy fishing boat to come by.'

'Couldn't we make a fire to light on top of the island?'

'Like in the movies, eh? Sure, you go and make one. Only I hope you find enough driftwood on an island without any beaches. What is there below for breakfast?'

If I hadn't been so interested in the answer myself, I would have demanded to know whose fault it was we were landed in this mess. How was I supposed to know that Franklin's forgotten reading light would burn out whatever it was? Down in the galley I found four oranges, one of which was going mouldy, a bottle of iodine with a rusty cap and two packages of what appeared to be lentil soup imported from Turkey. I reported this.

'Franklin! Didn't you put that box of food on board like I told you?'

No answer.

(Photo: Daniel Angermeyer Fitter)

Academy Bay: view from the barranco

Santa Cruz

Carl's house: Angermeyer Point

Academy Bay from the highlands

Penguin on the Equator

A flightless cormorant

Masked boobies

Frigate birds and a red-footed booby (*right*)

View from Barrington Island

Marine iguanas

Devil's Crown

Tagus Cove

Opuntia cactus

I thought back to California on Saturday mornings when Mama used to take us to the supermarket. All the food she never allowed us to eat: sliced Wonder Bread, chocolate milk, Oscar Mayer bologna and Coco Puffs floated in a mirage before my eyes.

'You know how to fish?' asked Gus, handing me an orange. He knew I did not. 'I will show you today.'

'Have you any bait?' I wanted him to know that I knew the rudiments at least.

'We used to put a rag on a hook and haul in the biggest bacalao you ever saw. Fish are more particular these days. We'll catch some crabs and use the legs.'

I ate my orange as slowly as possible. In a week's time all of this would be a wonderful adventure. Some day I would bore people with the telling of it. Raking every vestige left on the bitter skins with my front teeth, I studied our surroundings. A narrow channel separated us from Santa Cruz. One could row over to the red beach there, scale the cliff and hike across the back of the island to the hills, down past the Kastdalens' farm and into Academy Bay for help. Or you could retrace the way we'd sailed yesterday, following the coastline.

'You try it either way and you will be a dead man. It's miles of hell in there. You would never make it.'

'I'm the only one with shoes,' I offered nobly.

'Yah, and a heel with a hole in it. You clean it out like I said?'

'Of course.'

'Bleed much?'

'No.'

Surprise, if not approval, crossed his face. 'Anyway, even tough leather boots would last only a couple of days in that bush. Here, take a look.' He handed me the binoculars. 'First you would have to climb Cerro Colorado.'

'What are those bits on the beach?'

'Some driftwood, maybe broken crockery left behind by pirates.'

'Go on! Pirates!' I scoffed.

'*Seguro*! They used to camp there. Plenty rum. When they got drunk they broke bottles around the fire.'

'Which reminds me . . .' I began.

Gus interrupted quickly, 'Then, once up on the cliff, you would have to balance over rocks as sharp as machetes, through thorns three inches long, in a blazing sun without water. And if you slip down into a crevice no one would find you in a thousand years.'

'Better than starving to death,' I mumbled.

'Relax, no one is going to starve. Below I have my .22, and have I not fishing hooks and line? For now, lie back and listen to the music of nature. This is paradise. Enjoy it!'

'I have to go to the bathroom. I don't suppose there's any water on Plazas?'

'You still worried? We have some water. Anyway, we can always drink the blood of sea-lions if nobody comes soon.'

'You crazy?' Mother would have been aghast at my speaking to him so, but he seemed to enjoy it and besides we were starving on equal terms now.

'It's not crazy. Back in 1906 some shipwrecked Norwegians walked halfway round Santa Cruz eating raw turtle and drinking sea-lion blood.'

'Raw meat – maybe. Blood – never. You're supposed to pour blood on the ground when you kill an animal – give it back to God or something.'

'You got a lot of opinions for a girl! Anyway, wait until you're thirsty.'

'I would sooner die,' I countered.

'Those Norwegians wrapped sea-lion skin around their feet; walked until their clothes fell away in shreds. They lost two men and left hundreds of English pounds worth of gold some-where when it got too heavy to carry.'

'Treasure? You're kidding.'

'I am what?'

'I said you are fooling.'

'No fool. I know where it is buried.'

'You do? Where?'

'Aha, now you want to be friends again, eh? Now that I know about treasure. Anyway, Hanna, what do we want with

146

treasure? Life is a treasure. Life! That is the name of my boat: *Liv*. Means life in Norwegian. Thor Heyerdal told me.'

Franklin rowed me to shore. I hurried behind a large opuntia with immense relief. I had not been there long before a golden dragon emerged from the thorny undergrowth, grinning and tipping his head endearingly. When I got out my pencil and pad to sketch him, the creature darted up my leg. Another land iguana joined us, and another. They all began to nod their heads like synchronized clockwork toys. One scaled my shoulder and stood upright on his back legs like a circus performer. Glancing up I suddenly realized they were after cactus fruit. With my knife I cut several blossoms off. There was a mad scramble accompanied by much head nodding. I cut blossoms for all of them, now there were about seven. Each dragon positioned the fruit beneath its foot and rolled it about in the sand, meticulously scraping the spines off. Then they ate, smacking lips. I gave them second helpings and tried eating one myself. The opuntia fruit had little taste; the texture being slimy and the juice was not really thirst quenching, but then, I was not really thirsty – yet.

Climbing the two hundred yards to Plaza's highest point, I stood above pale gulls with charcoal heads that hung motionless on the air currents, swooping to dizzy depths where breakers pounded the rocks. The horizon was empty. To my right, Santa Cruz baked.

As I turned to go, a tremendous roar broke from a brown rock at my feet. A huge sea-lion bellowed, his mouth armed with ivory knives. He waved his head back and forth trying either to smell me or attempting to rouse his heavy body from slumber in an attempt to flee or chase me, I knew not which. I smiled at his ungainly attempts, but amusement vanished when I saw the terrible gaping wound in his side near the back flipper. Flies tried to land on the exposed wound but the bull waved them off with his still-functional flipper. All of my instincts screamed at me to do something to help him. All those pat phrases, 'nature is cruel', and 'survival of the fittest', had not prepared me for this flesh-and-blood reality. The wound was white, about the size of a shark's bite, with bits of blood dried black. I did not smell death from where I stood; no rotting.

I bent as close as I dared, trying not to upset him further. Part of the wound had closed at least and the animal did not look thin, I comforted myself. I would have to leave. I could do nothing. Slowly, I walked away. The sea-lion, as though to put me at ease, yawned, let his head fall on the rock and went back to sleep.

Judging by the sun, it was midday. I wandered down to the coast where the sea glittered with diamonds. In a small cove, out of sight of the *Liv*, I removed my clothes, except for my shoes, and slipped into a deep tidal pool. The water was cold. With some trepidation, I explored the bottom with the toe of my shoes. A body bolted past me, and another. Floundering, I lost my footing and fell backwards. I shot back up, rubbing my eyes and gasping, trying to see what was attacking me. A small whiskered head popped up only three feet away; then another and another. I was surrounded by water puppies; baby sea-lions left to play in this pool while their mothers went fishing.

I was speechless with delight as they circled me, coming nearer and nearer until we peered into each other's faces. A second before our noses touched, they flipped backwards and disappeared in a Milky Way of bubbles. I floated on my back while they tickled my legs, deliciously, with their whiskers. Then I became bolder, meeting them underwater where they examined my flipperless body from top to bottom, thinking, no doubt, what an inadequate creature I was, while I was thinking that this was the finest moment in my life.

Then they taught me a game, one sea-lions must have known for thousands of years. My playmates swam tight circles around me, nudging my thigh or shoulder with their noses while I pretended not to notice. Then suddenly I turned and dived after them while they somersaulted backwards in mock hysteria, their eyes wide. Surfacing to sneeze, they then dived again to start all over, making me laugh until I thought I would drown.

When I reluctantly crawled out, they followed me like little black spaniels, sniffing my clothes as I dressed. When the smallest one wasn't looking, I gently stroked her body. Her soft coat felt warm in the sun. Then she dashed back to the water, joining her friends who floated in circles on their backs, using three flippers to propel themselves while the fourth fin was raised like a sail. When I turned for one last look, they were still there, drifting aimlessly in the sparkling pool.

Swimming had made me hungry. There was no sign of life aboard the *Liv*. Presumably Gus had not been fishing. Of course, I remembered, he needed crab legs for bait. There were Sally Lightfoots all around me. I eased my knife from its sheath. It would be easy.

'Don't think – just do it!' urged my stomach. 'A rock – use a rock – go on. One slam will do it, then pick off the legs.' I looked for a rock of a suitable size. Crabs scurried as I chose my weapon. I took aim. The crabs froze. Their legs had golden hairs at the tips. Each claw was perfectly designed for securing toe-holds against the pull of the sea. Their front claws never stopped nibbling at the wet rocks. When you squatted at their level, they looked like tiny Chinese cooks busily feeding themselves with bright red chopsticks.

I could not remember killing anything before. My heart pounded like an engine. It was all right, I consoled myself, I was simply entering the food chain. I clamped my wet hand against my breast to quiet my heart but the tuk-tuk-tuk grew louder. Then I spotted the yacht, brilliant white against the sea glare. Gracefully she rounded North Plaza and slipped alongside the *Liv*. The Duke of Galapagos was at the wheel, wearing his Robin Hood hat and waving. 'What are you doing here?' he called out. His three passengers leaned over the rail with drinks. They looked cool and clean from where I waited with my rock in the green slime of low tide.

Once I heard *Liv*'s engine turn over, I collected my knapsack and announced that I was sailing home with Carl. Instead of chagrin, the King met this announcement with amusement.

'Relax, girl. You see? *No pasa nada.* You take life too serious. We could have survived for weeks out here!'

Survived? I felt like shouting. Survive? Sure, I had a lot to learn. I couldn't even kill a crab, but my family and I weren't completely gutless. We'd already survived the paint-peeling poverty of Arlington Street; the liquor-store bottles wrapped in brown paper, the candy-striped dress in the closet, the Mrs Pearces and Miss Beans of the world – things that would have scared the pants off Robinson Crusoe.

11

Shanghaied to Hollywood

'Of course, you could have sailed the *Liv* home without an engine,' said Carl that evening back in his house, seated at his dining table spread with a lace cloth.

Sails! How could I have been so stupid? Gus had wanted to be marooned. Either he had wanted a break from finishing Lucrecia's bathroom or he had merely been testing my grit.

By the time Carl's boat had pulled into Academy Bay, his iguanas were climbing up to the roof for the night and the ladies of our orchestra were folding their rusty music stands and loading their instruments on to home-made wheelbarrows for the push home.

Carl had insisted Mother and I stay for his speciality. His crew man had dived for lobster that morning. I was relieved to see a sharp knife had been stuck through its head before it was plunged into boiling water. I was also relieved that my uncle's passengers had stayed on board for dinner; the blonde German woman in the bikini had made a fool of herself all the way home, giggling at Carl's stories. Naturally he had to be nice to her.

Carl entered the dining room bearing a platter of steaming rice under an exquisite creamy sauce. 'I turn ordinary *langosta* into "Lobster Velouté". Superb, is it not? Yes, I will admit I am a wonderful cook,' he said immodestly. 'My mother said to me, when we boys left Germany. "Carl, take good care of your brothers. Hein is oldest, so he is captain. Gus is for the engines. Hans and Fritz are for the deck. But you, you must cook, for you know best." One day I will tell you the story of the Christmas cake I baked for my brothers when we were ship-wrecked in St Mawes, England.'

'I remember when Hans and I lived out here in the forties,' said Mother wistfully. 'We never went hungry, but we sure missed certain foods. At night we used to tease our tastebuds, leafing through my *Betty Crocker Cookbook*. There was one mouth-watering photograph of fried chicken in a basket lined with a red-checked napkin. Now, someone had told me that iguana tasted like chicken, so one day while I was washing clothes in Pelican Bay I caught one by its tail and took it home under my laundry – this was before they were protected, of course! "Oh look, Hans," I yelled, "tomorrow's fried chicken!" I thought he would be so pleased, but he didn't seem at all enthusiastic. I was saving him from going out goat hunting. Oh well, I figured he was just tired from building our house all day. I turned my basket upside down and wedged a rock on top. But the next morning it was turned over and that heavy rock miraculously thrown to one side. I wasn't fooled when Hans said he must have got loose. Johanna is just like her father, cannot bear to kill a thing.'

I thought back to the Sally Lightfoot crabs I'd nearly smashed, but kept quiet.

'With me it was like this,' began Marga. 'It was back in the thirties. I was still Frau Kuebler then, but my husband must have been up in the hills – he did not enjoy social outings, you understand. Anyway, that day a big American warship came in to Academy Bay. The captain was a fatherly type and invited the twelve of us living on the beach on board. Oh, we had dancing and music with a phonograph and things to eat. Then an officer says to me in front of everyone, "Ma'am, what food are you most missing out here?" Well, I was feeling good with wine and music so in a very loud voice I says, "*OH, BUT I WOULD LIKE SO MUCH A PIECE OF BREAD!*" My English was not so good in those days, no? Well anyway, they must have thought we Galapagueños were really having a hard time, isn't it? But you see, I was really thinking of some nice dark German bread with lots of real butter and a bit of good cheese and maybe even sliced salami on top, with a pickle. Much later, when we was taken to shore, they handed us a big box, looked kindly at us and waved goodbye. When we all looked into this box, we found twelve loaves of bread! Gus could not wait. He taked his loaf, sat on a big rock for his feast and bit in. Oh, but his face. It was pinched like a prune. "*Papier!*" he groans. The bread, it was white, how you say, like *cartulina*? Cardboard? The Americans were eating white cardboard! We nearly wept. As that big warship sailed over the horizon, Gus just stayed there, squeezing his piece of bread into little balls and dropping them into the sea.'

'What I missed most in those early days,' said Carl, 'was sweets. Sugar-cane we had, but it wasn't the same – more like biting into bits of sweet wood. I dreamed, oh, I had visions of chocolate cake and sugary buns and *Apfelkuchen*. But bananas were the next thing and we never got tired of them. But back in the thirties again, when we first came and tried to farm in the hills, we had no banana plants of our own, so we had to hike many miles to where the pirates had planted them. We would camp there overnight and the next morning load our donkeys with wild lemons, avocados, papaya, oranges and many stems of green bananas – you know, you cannot carry ripe bananas or they get mashed. While those bananas were still green we boiled some like potatoes. When they all ripened we had too many, so we cooked them over a slow wood fire in a big pot until we had something looking like plum jam. When we had both ripe and green bananas, we made rye bread!'

'From bananas?' I scoffed.

'*Natürlich*. You grind twelve green plantains in a hand mincer, then mix in six ripe eating bananas. The really ripe ones act like a sort of yeast, you see. You shape this and bake it and it has a flavour of rye bread.'

'If you have not tasted rye bread in a very long time...' added Marga drily.

'Man, I tell you it was *delicioso*. Put in between a slice of roasted wild pig meat and sprinkle over some drippings and you have a sandwich almost like what we had back in Harburg. Even better with a drop of rum.'

'Hmph!' said Marga.

'Yes, we probably wouldn't have been in that fix over in Plazas if it hadn't been for rum,' said I, still unwilling to forgive.

'Rum was it, by Jove!' said Carl in mock disgust. 'I have seen rum ruin a good man.'

'Hmph!' Marga knew what was coming.

'Mind you,' continued the Duke, 'I have seen rum save a good man too.' He leaned closer. 'Did I ever tell you how I was shanghaied to Hollywood?'

'Hollywood!'

Marga groaned.

'It was 1947 – still a young man then, no? In those days Gus was working at the American base on Baltra. That's how he speaks better English than the rest of us. One day a huge gaff-rig schooner named the *Morning Star* – on her way to the Marshall Islands with two thousand Bibles – comes in to Baltra. Now a gaff-rig is plenty of boat to handle and the captain was a military man who knew almost nothing of sail. So he asks Gus to come along to the Marshalls. But Lucrecia had just given birth to your cousin Teppi, so Gus could not go.

'Well, I sailed into Baltra the next morning on my little boat *Rainbow*. I was invited aboard this big schooner. We had a little rum, as one does and got talking – *natürlich*. Then they invited me to stay for dinner. We had more rum. Then we had coffee, but with each cup they always put in some rum there too!'

'And you did not see this!' scoffed Marga.

'How could I? It was very dark rum – the same colour as the coffee! Anyhow, we got to singing that night and got very friendly. I think I must have been very drunk. I really think I was very, very drunk, because the next morning the captain comes to me and says we are ready to sail. I say, "Sail? Where to?" He says, "Why, to Hawaii, of course. You signed on as first mate last night and you sold your *Rainbow* to an officer for $250. You said you wouldn't be needing it anymore, since you were going with us."

'Well, I said, "I cannot go! I have a wife, man!" Then Gus comes along and says, "Last night you promised to take this ship all right. I heard you." Also, they showed me the log book. There was my name written down. I looked in my pocket; there was $250! "But I must say goodbye to my wife. She thinks I left to go fishing. I cannot just go off thousands of miles to Hawaii!"'

Marga broke in. 'I was standing where is now my veranda before this house was built, watching for any boat what is maybe coming in. Then I see it the fastest boat I have ever seen in my life. When I see my husband waving at me I say, "Oh, oh! Do not tell me he has crashed the little *Rainbow* on some cliff and the navy has picked him up!"

'I shout to Carl as he steps on the landing: "You all right?" He says he is all right but that he has to go right now to Hawaii. I say, "You are *nuts!*" but Carl says he is sorry and I could see he was. So I go to pack him a little seabag and told him to go.'

'And not come back?' joked Mother.

'No, no, I said why should he not go and see something of the world, a different island. Not much was happening here. Carmen and Fritz were living in a small house, two by one and a half metres wide, where your cousin Maggie was born – life was very primitive then.'

'Yes, yes, that is another story,' interrupted Carl. 'So anyhow, we sailed away on the *Morning Star*. Now forty days out to sea and four thousand miles to deliver our Bibles and tempers were getting short. On board we had a cook, a radio operator, some deckhands, but the only experienced seaman besides myself was a *huge* Swedish–American guy with hands twice the size of mine and shoulders like the yoke of an ox.

'One Sunday morning the captain comes on deck to give orders. I sent the Swede to slack off the sheet on the main tops'l. He went to do it. But the captain is watching us and says, "Hey you! When you receive an order I want to hear you say 'Yessir!'"

'Well, that night when I am on watch, the Swede comes to the bridge and says in a low voice, "I have had all I can stand of him. Tonight – he goes over the side!"

'I say, "Now wait a minute here, he is the captain, you can't just push people over the side. You know what that means? Mutiny, man, mutiny!"

'"Well," this huge guy growls, "I don't like the way he smokes his cigarettes." Man, he was in a dangerous mood. I told him to take the wheel and I went below to the captain's cabin.

'"You are going to be pushed over the side tonight," I say. "I don't know what you've done to make him so mad, but the guy is twice my size, I can't save you if he decides to get rid of you!"

'The captain turns pale. "What shall we do?" he shouts.

'"Shhhhhhh!" I tell him. "Look I'm sorry because I know you are captain and it's not customary but – well – you got to say you're sorry, man. Now wait – you got to because we are forty days off Galapagos and only God knows where you would swim to from here and I tell you, by Jove, you are going to the sharks!"

'So I rush out and tell the cook to make a big pot of coffee. I invite the Swede down to the saloon and I get a bottle of rum. I play the harmonica and teach him some German sea-songs and give him plenty cups of coffee, each time with a little rum – and the next morning the captain was still on board. You see? A little rum saved him, by Jove.'

Marga moaned.

'But how did you get to Hollywood?' I insisted.

'First we got to Hawaii. Everyone there complained at how primitive it was, but for me it was a big city by comparison. There was a yacht club. We used to go for midnight sails with many well-known wealthy people. One night there was a man known in Hollywood called Howard something or other. He didn't even know where Galapagos was and he couldn't figure out where I came from, so he began introducing me around as the Duke of Galapagos. Since then everyone called me that. He said I should go to the "studios". I did not know what he meant and thanked him but gave it no more thought.

'My plan was to get to California and catch a tuna clipper back home. While I was there trying to find a ship, another wealthy man invited me to stay at his home – you know they all have swimming pools full of fresh water – more drinking water than I had ever seen all at once. But anyway, while I was staying there a letter comes for me. It said I should go to Metro-Goldwyn-Mayer Film Studios for a "screen test". I said I would not go. My hostess said, "Hey, Carl, are you crazy? What a chance they are giving you. You know how many people live their whole lives in Hollywod waiting for a screen test? You got to go!"

'So I borrow a sports coat with stripes in the latest style and arrive at the big gates. I thought the guard would tell me to go away but he sent me to the big shot, Mr Selznick. When I got to his office, this Mr Selznick had big problems with a blonde lady screaming and shouting that she didn't want to get on a real horse. I didn't know who she was but the secretary said she was a big famous movie star. I wandered around while they got the problem sorted out.

'It was quite a place, I tell you; there were wild west towns and buildings with no insides, just fronts stuck on poles. They even had a square-rigger ship and they made it catch on fire in a heavy sea using fire hoses and a wind machine.

'Well, finally they took their test. They made me walk here and walk there and say this and say that. A little while later they called me to the office and I sat in a big leather chair and they said I should become a movie star.'

'What did you say?' I breathed.

'I thanked them very much but said I wanted to go home now. I found a tuna clipper whose captain I knew from before. I was glad to get back here I can tell you! I heard later that the *Morning Star* sunk soon after leaving Hawaii for the Marshall Islands. Like I said, the captain didn't know much about sail.'

Ani–ani rustled in the fireplace. Marga lit a hurricane lamp for us to take home. Carl hoisted Mother's accordion on to his wheelbarrow. I insisted I could manage it.

'We missed you at music practice today,' said Marga as we said goodnight. 'My violin needs help against all those accordions.' I promised I would not miss next week's practice. I was so tired and did not feel well; my foot bothered me slightly, but my skin itched and I found welts when I scratched.

Mother held up the lantern as I pushed through the deep sand, hitting half-submerged rocks and stumps, jolting my shoulders and nearly dumping my load. The worst rock was just outside Carmen's house – I invariably stubbed my toes on it. As Mother picked it out with the light, I paused to catch my breath.

'You think I take life too serious?' I asked her.

'Gus tell you that?'

'Yes.'

'Funny, he used to tell Hans that all the time.'

'Did he? Take life too serious I mean.'

'Serious*ly*; you are speaking English very strange*ly* these days. Ah well, what can I say? Life handed Hans responsibilities very early on; his first wife for example. Now that you are here, can you imagine how it was living with a person who hated Galapagos and constantly complained? It's hard enough when you love the islands. And then he was – shall we say – he was frustrated by incompetence. He liked to get the basics out of the way so that he could enjoy the pleasures of life. Mary has some of that. That's why she gets "bossy". As you both grow older she will learn tolerance and you will – well – you are so alike, you will probably go through the bossy stage too.' She smiled and gazed out to sea. 'Marga is right. The solo part of *The Blue Danube* really is too much for one violin against all those accordions.'

'And me?'

'What?'

'Am I like him too?' I whispered over the gentle surf. 'Am I like Hans? You said Mary was like him. I know already she looks like him, I've heard that enough times.'

'You may not have his blond hair and blue eyes, but in some ways I have often thought you were more like him. Mary is trusting; you are cautious. You look at a thing from five different angles. And when you were little and started taking in injured animals with such a vengeance, I was a bit surprised, for I could not remember telling you about him and his creatures. I used to think to myself, "Well, well, just like Hans."'

Why had she never told me? Would being here in Galapagos now unlock thoughts like this that she had never before shared?

We wheeled past Carmen's bright window. The lamp over the table had a poppy-red shade made from cloth left over from my aunt's new skirt. Uncle Fritz sat at the table with his family, their heads bent, each one involved in a different project. How strange it would be to sit like that with your father; see him so often you took him for granted, watch his hands carving a pipe or cleaning a rifle, hanging goat in the rafters; how delightful to weary of him repeating boyhood stories.

The new-moon tides had risen up and heaped sand over the path. The wheelbarrow's wheels were worn. Mother helped me push. I strained so hard my head throbbed. I crunched my sore heel into a piece of washed-up driftwood. The pain was exquisite. Mother made me stop and rest.

'Do you know what perception means?' she asked.

'I think so – I don't know for sure.'

'It means seeing behind people's faces – behind situations. Sometimes it means you see more than you ought. It can be – painful like that foot of yours. Hans was too sensitive.' She paused and looked out to sea. The moon was rising like a golden peach. 'I often thought – sometimes I thought he was like an artist caught in a battlefield. His mind worked overtime, he made plans, was so sure his dreams would come true if he could simply be in control of his life. Maybe that's why he and Gus –' The light in our house came into view. She walked faster.

'Yes? What were you going to say?'

Mother weighed her words out and placed them in small parcels labelled Handle With Care. 'You and your sister are so alike,' she repeated. 'You – you really must try to understand each other better than you do. Otherwise . . .'

'Otherwise?'

'You will lose out on so much that you could give each other. One day you'll look back and wonder why you wasted so much time . . .'

I waited.

'Your Grandmother Marie told her five boys to stick together. Hein was the eldest and very capable. Only Hein went home. The eldest always took command. Hans had difficulty in accepting that.'

'I bet Hans wouldn't have ended up marooned with three oranges and a package of stale Turkish soup-mix.'

Mother said nothing.

'I bet he wouldn't have drunk too much rum.'

No answer.

'But I guess men do that sort of thing.'

'Yes. Some do.'

'If Hans was sensitive it doesn't mean that – well – that doesn't mean he was a – a – sissy, does it?'

'Sissy? Good heavens, no!' she laughed. 'Why, your uncles used to tell of a boat race in Germany. Hans rowed so hard his calluses burst open. The rest of the crew wanted to give up, but he wouldn't. When the race was over, Hans could barely let go his grip on the oars, his hands were so shredded and bloody.'

I stopped as we reached the narrow path to the house, and centred the accordion so I wouldn't dump it in the mud. I fussed, hoping she would talk on. It was easier to talk in the dark.

'And there was a time, I remember, we were anchored in Plazas. Hans kept an eye on some sailors off a navy ship walking on shore among the sleeping sea-lions. A few little ones wandered up to them like puppies. I lost interest in watching them and began to talk about something else, but Hans told me to be quiet. "Something's wrong," he said. "I don't like the looks of them." The next moment he was proved right. The brutes began beating those poor gentle creatures over the heads with heavy oars. Hans jumped into the dinghy and once ashore tackled all six of them. Some he flung into the sea, others he knocked down on the rocks, cursing them in German and Spanish. The rest ran away, but your father had to put three animals out of their pain. When he came back to me I could see that he was also in pain – and outraged at the stupidity of man.'

I could find no words to tell my mother how much I loved her for telling me these stories. My hands met hers as together we pushed the wheelbarrow up to the house.

The door fell off when I opened it. It was truly strange how a tumbledown house on a beach with a dim candle burning, five garua-damp beds, a wobbly table and a smoking fire in the chimney could look so inviting.

The next morning, Cousin Teppi arrived with a foreleg of a goat shot that morning; we ate with relish. Then Fiddi brought us mullet which Mother fried. We ate that too, not knowing what else to do. In the tropics, without refrigeration, the safest place for meat or fish was in your belly.

It was unusual for the system on Angermeyer Point to go awry this way. Each household normally knew through the 'bajucco' (a tenacious vine) just when another hunter or fisherman was going out. In between times the children net-fished on the beach, then distributed mullet from house to house. When no one went out, we ate rice and avocado, when available, or tinned tuna, or bread if one had an oven. When someone got hungry, they took half the day off and took a gun into the bush. Sighting of goats were reported. Sometimes big bucks followed the house-goats home and were shot before breakfast from a bedroom window. Feeling guilty that our household never contributed to the system, Mother decided that until we learned the skill of staying alive on Galapagos, the least we could do was make an open invitation to whomever needed a place to stay in Quito, whether it be for schooling or simply a visit between ships. This was greeted with enthusiasm by the family. Big John would be our first guest *en route* to America.

That afternoon Mary said my hair smelled like a stagnant goldfish bowl and it was decided we should take our laundry and dirty bodies over to Pelican Bay for washing. Borrowing the most uncapsizeable and therefore heaviest of Gus's skiffs, we took turns rowing tight circles and zigzags across the bay, my sister, as usual, telling us what to do.

But it was Mother who remembered how to wash clothes, scooping up brackish water with a bent rusty can from the same crack in the lava she had used all those years ago, lathering the clothes with blue lye soap, rinsing them in a bucket and hanging them over bushes to dry. It was back-aching work. The lye burned our eyes if we brushed the perspiration from our face with our hands. The soap did not rinse out thoroughly and our perverse drying-bushes brushed the clean clothes into the red dust every time a breeze told them to.

Shampoo was so expensive that we washed our hair the islanders' way; squashing ripe avocados on each other's heads, sprinkling soap flakes over this and creating a pale guacamole lather. The oil was so rich that, once rinsed, our hair shone and our skin felt as soft as if we'd used the costliest soap.

Haeni, the Swiss carpenter, lived alone in a quaint wooden shack. A blond man going grey, he was compactly built and walked with a slight stoop which may have come from long hours at his workbench, for Haeni was industrious when he wasn't drinking. He had made his own windmill and built a well-equipped workshop, many of the tools hand-turned on his lathe. Also he grew grapes, melons and tomatoes, which he offered to sell to us. Haeni seemed lonely, the way he followed us down to our skiff speaking of his early years in Galapagos; how he missed his homeland sometimes, how fortunate he was to have such a benevolent piece of property.

'Plenty water – underground,' he said. 'Good earth.' He pointed to the three other houses in Pelican Bay. 'All have good earth – grow things.' It was true, coconut trees grew by each of the houses. One small white house was nearly hidden behind vines and green bushes. Haeni said a shipment of sprouted coconuts had been sent to Galapagos for planting. He had planted his, Kuebler his, quite a few in Pelican Bay had planted theirs for the future, but most of the islanders ate theirs. 'Imbeciles!' cried Haeni. 'Today our village would be shaded by coconut trees if they had not been such *idiotas!*'

'Is there any land for sale over here?' asked my brother. My mouth fell open in astonishment. Haeni said he did not know of any but he would keep his ears open. I dared not ask what Tony had in mind – I dared not think that, like me, he harboured a secret wish to live in the islands permanently.

Rowing home, Johnny announced that I had spots all over me. They all gathered close, tipping the boat to have a look down my arms, legs and face. One said it was acne, another an allergy. Johnny was sure something had bitten me. Tony said they looked like ulcers.

He took over the oars. 'I was just reading in the Bible the other night that when Job had ulcers he powdered himself with ashes and scraped himself with bits of clay pot – don't know why exactly – must have itched. Unfortunately I dumped all of our ashes down the privy yesterday.' He was not joking. Our first-aid kit did not cover skin complaints.

Margarita the hen had hatched her chicks. So, apart from a rather splendid endemic bush-rat who had nibbled bits out of almost every banana on the Divines' stem propped in the corner, I had the library to myself that afternoon. The rat watched me from Webster's Concise Dictionary while I looked up skin diseases in an outdated medical encyclopaedia. After comparing my lumps with the black-and-white photographs, I decided I either had skin cancer, smallpox, elephantiasis, impetigo or leprosy. The best thing would doubtlessly be to soak myself in the sea every day.

The medical book was grimly fascinating. I leafed through, A to Z, stopping at the ghastlier pictures: an appendix in the lid of a jar, an old engraving of a bubonic-plague victim, Siamese twins after surgery to separate them. There were excruciatingly explicit descriptions of cystitis, diverticulitis, emphysema, fractures – hernia, lumbago, meningitis, pleurisy, tetanus. Tuberculosis caught my eye: the disease which had turned Uncle Hein back to Germany and caused the brothers to lose the *Marie* and put Gus in charge as the eldest.

'. . . infectious disease caused by tubercule bacillus. Spread in saliva, possibly hereditary. Early symptoms: loss of strength, emaciation, coughing of blood. Middle stage: fever, nightly sweats, morning sickness, racking cough.' The last stages were shattering. I made myself continue: severe diarrhoea, subsequent dehydration; acute nausea, falling in of chest cavity. High fever, worsened sweats, coughing up of thick yellow sputum streaked with blood. Death usually occurred by pulmonary haemorrhage.'

I let the rat out of the door and walked home feeling weary. Mother was upset that I'd taken my ulcers to the dusty library. She marched me off to Tante Carmen's tiny kitchen-cum-sitting room, where all the more serious ailments ended up. Carmen could give injections, bind the ghastliest wounds, offer sound advice, and she had a fairly recent Merck manual. Leafing through the thick, well-thumbed book she decided I had impetigo.

It was four o'clock. Uncle Fritz came in from his workshop. My cousins put on the kettle. Carmen took fresh oatmeal cookies from the oven and read about my disease aloud: '– highly infectious, acute inflammation caused by streptococcal organisms characterized by running sores, thick scabs and yellow-brown discharge.' Undaunted, my cousins munched their cookies.

I needed mercurial zinc paste or steroxin ointment. Carmen pulled out the insect-and-mouse-proof box of medicines from under her bed. Inside, laid out with meticulous care, were sterile pads, syringes, tourniquets, assorted tablets and various tubes left behind by kind yachtsmen. To my immense relief and gratitude, there was a half-used tube of zinc ointment.

I was not to go near the sea. I must disinfect the privy seat with puro after every use, for that was most likely where I picked it up in the first place. I looked awful, my face, neck, arms, torso were covered in erupting miniature craters. Doris Divine, once she heard, came over with Adelle Davis's book *Let's Get Well*, but her diet recommended plenty of leafy green vegetables, fresh fruit and spring water. The highlands were blanketed daily in garua; the road a quagmire. Whatever milk, avocados, oranges, bananas and otoi leaves the farmers did not eat themselves, they would feed to the pigs and chickens until the road dried out.

For the next week I observed Galapagos from the window by my bed. I read, wrote dreadful poetry, watched baby spiders hatch on the ceiling and observed the feeding habits of wimbrells, stilts, wandering tattlers and ruddy turnstones in the lagoon which surrounded our house at high tide.

During the long days while my skin went through its metamorphosis, I watched Johnny become an island boy: learning to swim, playing pirates or sailing crude balsa boats with Martin and Fiddi in the lagoon at high tide. His feet became tough and his hair straw-coloured.

Tony learned to fish with a lead-weighted net. Once he and Big John caught a baby shark along with the mullets. When

Tony stooped down for a closer look, his glasses fell off and the shark, a mere foot long, clamped its jaws on to the earpiece, nearly breaking it in two before they wrenched the glasses away and threw the irritable infant back.

Mary went hunting in the bush with the King and returned dust-streaked, ankle sore and thorn-bitten, but she hung fresh meat from our rafter that night. Gus sent a message to me in case I wanted the skin, a particularly pretty black hide with tan markings down the legs. He would show me how to nail it on the side of his shack and I could salt it and scrape it to take home. But I wasn't allowed near salt, and when I went outside hordes of flies chased me. It was a good thing a breeze always blew through the house or they would have come indoors after me.

Unlike the Swiss Family Robinson who were marooned on a benevolent island, most of our daylight hours were spent gutting fish, collecting salt from the lagoon, cooking goat meat so it would not spoil, hauling sea-water up to the house, keeping the rainwater tank clean, mending screens and eradicating fire ants, which invaded our beds and formed endless queues along Mother's work counter in search of minuscule crumbs, blobs of grease or even drops of water. But we tried to leave our afternoons free. Mother took up sketching again, sitting indoors with me, correcting my compositions and teaching me to make a frame with my fingers and find pictures in the landscape. One blowing, wet afternoon I daubed what was nearly the last of the zinc ointment on my skin and tried valiantly to finish *The Swiss Family Robinson*. Worrying about what would happen when the ointment ran out, I found the book irritating with its donkey-swallowing snakes, irrigated fruit orchards, flowing streams of sweet water and gardens sowed in 'ground light and easy to dig'. I was desperate for another book but the others were busy sorting oranges brought down by Alf and making marmalade from the squashed ones. Johnny offered to go to the library for me, but he couldn't read, so I picked up the family Bible. Tony's marker fell out.

So Satan struck Job with a malignant boil from the sole of his foot to the crown of his head. And he proceeded to take for himself a fragment of earthenware with which to scrape himself and he was sitting in among the ashes . . .

Job's wife told him to 'curse God and die'.

In the seventh chapter of Job, his flesh became clothed with maggots and lumps of dust and his skin proceeded to form crusts and dissolve. Later his skin turned black and 'dropped off'.

I decided to switch to the mouse-nibbled Erle Stanley Gardner mystery we'd found in the corner. But when I got to page fifty-two, termites had chewed filigree patterns through the bit about the strangled bank-manager's secretary.

While the family continued to squeeze and chop orange peel, I filled a sheet of paper with little trees bearing tiny oranges. My drawings got smaller and smaller. In between their branches, with my sharpened pencil, I fitted miniature white horses performing airs above ground; then, as my pencil began to dull, I added spotted ponies with bushy tails, dappled greys and fearsome black stallions. The pencil snapped. Where were my wild horses? Could I so easily forget a dream? How were we going to get back to this island to stay? Mary wanted to. And the others? As Mother had said, once you got here, you felt you could live forever. Back in civilization, I would die.

I looked outside at the sunset over the Pacific and thanked Job's God for the thousands of miles we had come. But where were we going? I thought of tired people waiting in dirty depots for Greyhound buses, of black women trudging home in nurses' shoes with mended shopping bags, of picnics on Beer Can Beach, yellowed newspapers and old ladies with too many cats.

The marmalade cooked to a dark amber and tasted delicious. But we had no bread to eat with it.

12

The Grandparents

A few days later my scabs fell off, leaving telltale scars all over my body. The following day I was allowed out. Fortunately, it was a perfect day: garua had replenished our tanks and then moved on to the hills, leaving us in glorious sunshine. Diamonds sparkled on the sea, birds chittered at the window. I washed my hands and face with rainwater, combed my hair for the first time in weeks without my scalp wincing and ran outside to freedom.

Johnny chased me down to the beach to wash the breakfast dishes. We caught little fish, who came to nibble the crumbs, in a jam jar, let them go, waded out to where he had seen an octopus, made a sand-castle and drew giant bird tracks in the sand. After lunch we ran to the library and checked out five books.

I couldn't bear to take a siesta so I wandered down the coast, stopping at each tidal pool as the sea receded.

And God asked Job, 'Where did you happen to be when I founded the earth' and went on to say 'This far you may come and no farther and here your proud waves are limited.'?

My feet burned from walking barefoot over the hot rocks. I sat beside a particularly inviting pool and slid my feet into the cool water. The water magnified pinnacles of coral into spectacular Russian steeples. Little hermit crabs scuttled through the Russian streets wearing magnificent turbans. A brown crab chased a black crab, then climbed up my instep and sat on my big toe, contemplating the hair growing there.

Show your concern for the earth and the animals will instruct you. The winged creatures of the heavens will tell you. The fishes of the sea will declare it to you. Who among these does not know that the hand of God made all these things?

A voice called. I looked around. A figure beckoned from the window of Traudi's small house. Meanwhile, the brown crab gathered the hair of my toe in his claw and yanked it towards his mouth like a teething baby. I leaped up with a yell. The crab, claws poised angrily, slowly sank to the bottom of the pool.

'Come up for a nice cup of tea?' called Traudi.

It being my first social engagement since being smitten, I quickly inspected my arms and legs, feeling over my face to make sure there was nothing hideous left and then walked up the sandy path to my cousin's house. As I opened the door the glorious aroma of bread baking greeted me.

Traudi and Bernhard's little house was built of aged pine from the American base on Baltra Island. Certain floorboards sagged with obstinate woodworm, although Bernhard frequently doused it with burned diesel. The three rooms had a Black Forest look about them, as though a cuckoo would spring out of the tiny bedroom door every hour. The table was in a corner with benches on two sides. Once you slid in there and rested your back against the dark pine walls, you felt you'd been adopted. Gundi and Martin slept in an attic room with Hansel-and-Gretal furniture and toys produced in their father's immaculate workshop below. From their rooms they had one of the finest views of Academy Bay and distant Barrington Island.

Traudi wiped her hands as I sat down. 'We will have some fresh bread for tea. Just you and me. That will be nice.' She poked her fingertip into the dough rising in its tins, nodded with approval and slipped two tins into the oven.

'I wish we had an oven,' I said, trying to remember when I had last eaten bread.

'Yah? Well, next time you come you could build one. An old diesel drum on rocks will do.'

'Also we need a smoke house.'

'Yah, that too you can make from a diesel drum.'

'You had to learn to make a lot of things when you came, I guess.'

'Oh yes, but it was such an adventure – every little thing we made was such an accomplishment. First when we came I was impressed, sure, with the iguanas and giant tortoises and birds so tame they ate from your hand; then I have to say I also was disappointed – everything was so dry. We came during one of their driest spells. Many times I wished we could live up in the hills – have a garden with roses like the Kastdalens. Later, when we had this house, I tried to plant a little garden in front. I dug and pruned and fussed over some sad little sticks in the ground. Everybody said, "You must be crazy, this stuff is all dead!" And when it finally rained, it rained so much we ran out of barrels and pots and pans to collect it in. We took as many showers as we could under the guttering, washed our hair, our clothing, everything we could think of so as not to waste it. Then I woke up one morning and it was like a miracle; the bush was turning green. All the sleeping seeds out there came alive – except in my stick garden. It was truly dead. I would still like to have just one little rose bush . . .'

'Why couldn't you get a little soil from the hills and a cutting from Tante Maya?'

'Oh, I could, I could, but you see, it is the water. Now it is garua season, we have moisture every morning and things are turning green. But when that stops, and it will after you have gone back to school on the mainland, every drop of water has to be for us and the chickens, and of course for the goats when they give milk. We let them go every night into the bush and they come back in the morning because they expect water and food. But it is hard work to row across the bay and fill drums with brackish water. You count every single cupful.'

She took an old teapot from the shelf, filled it from the boiling kettle, set it on the table and sat gazing at the swirling steam rising between us.

'We had plenty of roses back in Germany. Pink, yellow, white, some the colour of wine. I can still see the seasons in my mind, you know?' There was nothing plaintive in her voice.

She was stating a fact, that was all. 'Our great-grandfather Angermeyer had a most wonderful rose garden, you know. He used to win prizes, although I imagine his gardener did most of the hard work.'

'What, you mean my great-grandfather?' No one had ever spoken of the man to me.

'Oh yes, being such a wealthy man, he had a fine garden and time for his hobby.' She chuckled, giving me a cup and saucer. 'Of course, you have heard already the story of Hans when he was a little boy – Hans and the manure?'

'Oh no,' I told her, greatly excited, for I could see in my cousin's face another natural story-teller.

'Well, it is a family joke now. Hans's papa, your grandfather, being the son of such an important landed gentleman, was supposed to enter a respectable profession like his brother, who was an architect and who later became mayor of the town. Also, Grandfather was expected to marry a socially acceptable girl, chosen for him by his parents. But being a real Angermeyer, he was stubborn. He liked working with his hands, making things. Then, to make matters worse, he fell in love with a little nobody called Marie. She was such a dark beauty, with sparkling eyes and long, dark-brown hair she could twist any way she liked. Grandfather's parents tried to bribe him; they argued, they begged, they threatened, but he insisted he would marry his little Marie. So he was disowned by Great-Grandfather.

'Time passed. Marie had their first child, a girl, my mother. Then came Hein, Gus, Hans, Carl and Fritz. Last of all came a lovely baby girl named Anne Liese. It was a large family to take care of, but Grandfather never asked his rich father for anything. He worked hard building boats, working in the shipyard on one of those big cranes. Imagine what his father thought when he heard! I think he felt sorry for disowning his son, but he was stubborn too. Already an old man, he would sit on the park bench and watch his grandchildren play from a distance. Of course in the beginning the children did not know who he was! Finally one day he softened and called Hans, who had blond curls and big blue eyes, and said, "You, boy! I need manure for my roses. If you bring me a bucket of good horse manure every day, I will give you a gold coin."

'My mother, being the eldest and almost a young lady by then, used to blush when she told the story of what happened next. Little Hans got a big shovel, bigger than himself, and a bucket. Then he hauled these things all over the town behind the huge cart horses what pulled the beer wagons through the streets. Every time the horses stopped, Hans stopped and waited. The shovel soon felt very, very heavy and he became so tired carrying the big bucket. After some long time, the horses stopped on a busy street full of shoppers. Hans got fed up. He went to the front of the wagon. He shouted at the top of his voice to the driver: "Man! Why don't you make your horse – !"'

Traudi laughed so hard her hand shook as she poured our tea. 'Of course – of course Hans's father found out about it – everyone in the town of Harburg was laughing and laughing about it. And our grandfather put a stop to the manure business pretty quick!'

'Did our grandfather and his father ever make up?'

'Well, as so many times it happens, they made up too late. So many years were wasted. Many words unsaid and not time to change his will before he died. Great-Uncle Anton, the mayor, inherited the factories, the estate, the stables and the land. Our grandfather got a small piece only, which was a large house and some land that they later sold to buy the ship *Marie* for the boys to sail away in.'

Traudi opened the door to the oven, tapped the top of the bread, turned it round and sat down again. 'A few minutes and she is ready.'

I stirred sugar into my tea. A fire ant rose to the surface. I scooped it out with my spoon.

'The funny thing is,' Traudi went on, 'the funny thing is – our grandparents were disinherited because Marie was of the wrong class. But you know, much later, when the Nazis investigated Marie, as they did so many if they thought they were Jewish or gypsy – or somehow different – they discovered she really had more of an aristocratic background than the

Angermeyers. Her great-great-great-grandfather was a French nobleman who escaped from France with his family disguised as gypsies.'

'No!' Gypsy wagons tumbled down the roads of my mind, with nobility in the back trying to change their clothes, tossing pince-nez, powdered wigs and satin breeches out the back as revolutionaries scoured the countryside searching for guillotine-fodder, in turn chased by the Scarlet Pimpernel.

'– and they sold their title to the gypsies and paid them a great deal of money to take them safely into Germany! On the documents dated back to the eighteenth century, it says they entered Germany as "sellers of rags"!'

Possibly Uncle Carl really was a duke! We were noble! If only Miss Bean could hear it!

'Of course Marie never put great store by such things, but she was more noble than her father-in-law on his grand hill.'

'You remember Marie?'

'So clearly. You could not forget such a woman as that easily! I remember when her sons left she would not let herself be heartbroken. She collected all their letters and photos and news-paper clippings and kept them in a soft leather handbag which she never let out of her sight. I remember the handbag, it had beautiful cut-out leaves, very artistic it was, in browns and forest greens – I shall always remember her small hands clutching that bag. Often I would beg her to open it and show me all the pictures. She would undo the clasp and say, "Now then, here are my boys on the *Marie* in England. Here they are giving a concert to buy their new mast – my boys, they sing so beautifully – Here they are in Denmark – There is Hans, here is Carl, how young they look, no? Here is Fritz, serious as always. There is Gus making jokes, Hein is there and there is Greta.'

'What was Greta like?'

Traudi took the bread from the oven, tapped it and set it on a rack while she put in another loaf. Over her shoulder she said, 'Greta? Well, she had been a model, that is how she and Hein met. He was a very gifted artist: sculpture, portraits, illustrations for magazines. Greta was how you say – eye-catching. Like a movie star. I remember how people's heads turned when she walked down the street.'

'You remember so much.'

'Yah, yah. I was the eldest of five sisters when the worst of the war came. You are fourteen. It is a good age for noticing things, no? Things you will remember all of your life.'

I nodded.

'This bread will be cool enough to eat soon. I will make more tea. Bernhard is out fishing, he won't be joining us until suppertime.'

'Did you – did you never wish you had sailed away on the *Marie* also? I mean, you were stuck in Germany when the war started.'

'I suppose we wished it. Nobody realized how quickly things would happen, such terrible things – For the brothers so far away, it was bad because they could get no word from home and such dreadful things was reported – horrible things that was happening: bombings, no food and no hope that it would ever end. Then your father's youngest sister, Anne Liese, got very sick. She faded before our eyes. Only nineteen.'

'What happened?' I whispered hoarsely.

'I was sitting one day on the staircase of our home. The war was bad; good food, medicines, impossible to get. At least my father still had a job working at the bank. My mother was upstairs. Grandfather came in and rushed past me. I rose to speak but he just touched me with his strong hand on my shoulder and went up two stairs at a time to Mother's room. They were in there for such a long time. At last Grandfather came out. He was looking like a broken man. My mother behind him looked suddenly shrunken and old. He left. Mother's door closed. I waited outside of her door for two whole hours. Finally, she came out, remembered me and said, "Anne is no more."

'Later, Grandfather told me everything. Anne Liese knew she was dying. She barely had any voice to speak. She raised her head just a little and told her Mama and Papa, "I am not afraid to die." She said she trusted God that it was time to go. She said she had read in the Bible that one day there will be a new earth where there is no more death. One day, she said, when God

173

says it is time, she will come back to that clean earth – and then she closed her eyes and – It was terrible the way Grandfather told me – the way he remembered every word she spoke. He said he would never forget those words just like I can never –' Her voice broke on the edge of memory.

I looked down at my empty cup. 'What –' I cleared my throat. 'What did she die of?'

'Consumption. Hein had it also, but he did not die from that. My father became worried; he was convinced there was a weakness in the family. He searched all over to buy liver so my sisters and I could be strong, but it was almost impossible to buy such luxuries, food was so scarce. Finally he decided to move us to the country where we hoped it would be safer, not so many bombs. Even if there was not much food in the countryside there was clean air.'

'The grandparents stayed in Harburg?'

'Yah yah; with Hein and Greta. By this time they had a little child. You, I hope Yohanna, will never know what it is like to be so hungry – starving. No food. No clothes. No transportation even to look for food. We lived like refugees in our own country.' She put the warm loaf on a board before me.

'Right at the end of the war, of course we did not know it was the end then, only we hoped and prayed it would come soon. One day Grandmother Marie came to visit us in the country. I went to Harburg to fetch her and bring her back. It took all day catching one train and waiting for others who came full of soldiers and never stopped or never came at all. There were no schedules. Everything was crazy. You sat and hoped one might come going in the right direction for you. When we finally got out of Harburg the train left us far from our house. We had a long way to walk.'

Traudi's bread was exquisite, the tea was made from sweet rainwater.

'Ah yes, we walked and walked. I could see even Grand-mother was getting tired. She was not young then of course, but still beautiful, her hair still long, her skin clear and fine. Finally a cart piled high with furniture came, pulled by a weary horse. Even the driver looked weary. He saw Grandmother and stopped and let her get on. She climbed up over the furniture and sat on a big armchair facing the back. I did not get on because the old horse had enough to pull. I remember it was a beautiful spring afternoon, warm and kind. There were flowers growing by the roadside. It seemed impossible that flowers should grow among all that violence and misery. Something must have touched Grandmother's heart because she began to sing. She had a lovely voice, too. She sang to the tired old driver and the poor thin horse and to me, trailing behind – all the way to our house. I have thought since that it was like – like she was trying to tell the birds "You must keep singing no matter what happens."

'For a week she stayed with us. We had such fun. But she missed Grandfather because never were they parted since the first Great War. We all knew how they felt about each other still, after so many years, although they never – you know – kissed, or suchlike in those days in front of the children. But I tell you, one afternoon we children were sitting on the front steps and looking down the road. We saw a tall, fine gentleman with a moustache riding a wobbly bicycle towards our house.

'"Grandfather, Grandfather!" my sisters and I shouted. Grandmother heard us and came outside. I tell you then we had a shock. She ran down the front steps of the house like a young girl, skipped down the path and threw her arms around him so his bicycle fell over into the flowers. And you know they kissed! Right in front of us.' Traudi gazed fondly at her piece of bread. Then, absently, she drank her tea and put the cup down, still smiling.

'What did they say? Can you remember?'

'Oh, like yesterday. Grandfather put his face in her hair and said, "You were gone a week – but for me it was ten years." He had ridden that terribly rickety bicycle all the way – oh, I cannot remember how many miles, but many, many.'

We chewed contentedly. I had to stop myself from wolfing the bread down.

'And they lived with you then in the country?' I asked, my mouth bulging.

'No, we were one week more laughing, singing and joking

together in spite of the hardship. Grandfather made friends everywhere. He was comfortable with people from any social class – poor farmers or wealthy bankers – and he became friendly with a rich man nearby who drove an elegant coach with horses. How he kept the horses from the army I do not know but anyway, when it was time for the grandparents to leave, this gentleman offered to take them the many miles to the railroad station where they had the best chance of getting a train back to Harburg.

'It was now early June. It was so sunny and peaceful; no sounds of war anywhere. Flowers were coming out between the cracks of the pavement, in the garden, on the fruit trees. We all stood with the grandparents out by the gate. We looked down the road. Over the rise of the hill came the most wonderful sight: beautiful shining horses pulling a magnificent carriage for a queen, like something from a fairy-tale. The gentleman stopped the carriage by our gate. Grandfather gave his hand to Grandmother like she was a grand duchess, and helped her in. She sat down and took off her hat. The pins came loose and all her hair came undone and spilled down her back like a young bride. We stood waving for a long time as they went down the road. Through an oval window in the back of the carriage we could see their heads bent close together like they was just married.' Traudi paused, looked a long time at the tablecloth. 'It was the last time we ever saw them.'

Twigs in the oven crackled irreverently. I could see their fiery glow through cracks in the black iron grate.

'What happened?' I was unable to swallow. The bread turned to dough in my mouth.

'A week before the war ended. Bombs over Hamburg and Harburg.' She picked up her teacup, then put it down, turning it round and round on its saucer. Her voice became galvanized. 'The only body they got out whole was Hein. Dead. Just as well, really. But I think the others – maybe not – well, maybe the grandparents did not suffer because they – they were in a bad state when they were found. But Greta. Greta was found with her small child – her arms cradling him, trying to protect him at the last –'

A clock ticked in the background. Outside Gundi rattled a tin of corn for the chickens. Little hens came running.

She went on. 'Bernhard at least came safely home from the Front. We had nothing, but we got engaged. He was a master carpenter but of course there was no work. We fixed a date anyway for the wedding. Secretly – I wished so passionately for a dress to wear for my marriage. But there were no dresses for sale and in any case, we had no money. My only skirt was two sizes too big. I had an old blouse. It did not close very well in front, but it would have to do. Now, what I will say seems, even to me this day, quite unbelievable, again like a fairy-tale, but I tell you it is true. One day just before my marriage, we received a package through the Red Cross. On it said the words: "From Lincoln, Nebraska, United States". We were scared to open it. We knew no one in America and where was this place, Nebraska? Opening it, we found to our joy and astonishment, some dress material and heaps of clothing! One dress was my size. It was so lovely! I wept, I wept for joy! I wore it for my wedding and I was so proud. At the bottom of the box was a letter, a very kind letter in German from a lady we did not know. She signed her name Mari Vogel.'

I swallowed the bread in my mouth but the lump remained. So that was why Traudi and Mother had spoken so animatedly in German the day we'd arrived! From some obscure corner of my mind I remembered Grandma Mari showing me a photograph from the shoebox. Five young, pretty but sober-faced girls wore identical checked dresses, their hair plaited German-style. Grandma Mari had said, 'Once when there was a war, your Mama was in Ecuador. She sent me the address of your Papa's people in Germany. I sent some things what I could find. I was always sorry I could not send more. It was so bad there. Isn't it nice they sent us this picture.'

Young Martin came through the door carrying a balsa boat he had just finished making in Bernhard's workshop. It had an anchor made of twisted wire, a tiny winch and a perfect minia-ture bowsprit. Traudi told him in German to call his father for coffee. She put the boiling water in the coffee pot. I cut some bread and laid out cups and plates, 'white butter', some smoked mullet and a pot of turtle oil.

'Three years later, you know, things in Germany were still very difficult. So when Martin was a baby we packed the few things we had, Bernhard's tools and his accordion, and came to Galapagos. It was so isolated, we had no shops and no money. But we didn't care. Sometimes I would hear Bernhard singing in his workshop and I would stop doing my chores and say, "My God, I have so much!"'

It was getting late. Traudi lit a kerosene lamp. The light cast a Dutch master light over her face. Bernhard came in carrying two large fish he had just caught, followed by the children. I went to the door. I would have to hurry home. Mary would be saying I had twisted my ankle and fallen in a hole or something.

Bernhard called '*Ein moment!*' from the small, dark kitchen. He rushed out, holding one of the skipjacks by a gill, his other hand catching the drips. 'For your supper tonight, eh, Yohanna?'

The dead fish had iridescent peacock colours. I held it under its belly as though I were about to slip it gently back into the sea instead of into Mother's frying pan. They would be pleased at home: I felt like a breadwinner. Someday I too would hang a leg of goat from the rafter, catch a fish for supper.

I paused, hand on the home-made doorknob, my fingers tracing the slightly square, uneven grooves left by Bernhard's lathe. I wished I wasn't so bad at saying things.

I thanked Traudi. 'I hope I haven't stayed, y'know, too late.'

'Yohanna! Stayed too late? Here, you will learn, in Galapagos, if you go for coffee at four o'clock you stay at least until the lamp is lit. Any sooner means you don't like us!'

Outside the moon was riding galloping clouds, waving a silver wand over thorn trees, Gus's beloved rocks and the small patch of ground by the door, still waiting for my cousin Traudi's rose bush.

The next day a small fishing boat came in from Wreck Bay in San Cristobal Island. Her captain reported that he had overheard a radio message from the mainland. The *Cristobal Carrier* had nearly sunk on her return passage to Ecuador. The owners were sending her back to Galapagos two weeks early, for she urgently needed a major refit. She would be out of operation for many weeks. It would be our last chance to get back to Quito.

Big John was ecstatic. On the next sunny day at high tide, he launched his beautiful clinker-built longboat, complete with centreboard and sail. Everyone from the Point came to see. Gus, who had passed down his own father's skill, looked on proudly as the boat bobbed merrily in the turquoise sea. Later on, when the excitement had died down and my cousin and I sat on a rock watching nothing in particular, I told him that the States was not like the pictures in the *National Geographic*. But Big John packed his cardboard suitcase a week early anyway.

We all felt low the day the *Carrier* limped in past Barrington. It was a cool, drizzly day, our water tank was nearly flowing over. We would, at least for our last few days, have plenty of water for drinking and washing our faces. Tony must have been thinking of the long voyage home, for he had no appetite for breakfast and wandered off towards the barranco before we had finished.

To make up for time lost with impetigo, I went swimming as I washed the dishes, throwing cups and saucers into the sea and then diving to retrieve them. When I got back to the house, Tony had returned. He had been to the barranco to see Harold. I had seen the German only once, at Marga's party. A short young man with fair skin and an expression as though he had just been slapped, Harold never said much, but as he and Tony had sat on a rock and watched the *Carrier*'s arrival, they began discussing life and the future of mankind and Harold confessed he was unhappy. Galapagos was no place to live alone. He would return to Germany as soon as he could sell his house.

'It's not much of a place,' said Tony, 'pretty run-down, but sturdy. The tin roof leaks and it's quite far up the barranco, but the view from there is superb. I don't know what you think — it would take quite a bit of work . . .'

And so we set off, hiking up what could only be described as a goat trail winding behind Lucrecia's new house and up a wobbling rock section of barranco to Harold's front door. Once our eyes adjusted to the gloom inside, we could see that goatskins were tacked over the windows, which had no frames or glass. The fireplace overflowed with rusty tins, a bent kettle and a doll's head. Harold said the Americans who had built the house had thrown rubbish out of every window; he had been collecting it for months. His cooking area was primitive and charmless, with a greasy oilcloth on a small table branded by scorching pans. The bedroom area had a sway-backed sleeping-cot in one corner. The back door opened to a formidable lava flow seven feet tall which had, a thousand years before, stopped dead in its tracks and now gave the disconcerting impression of a pet brontosaurus begging to be let in. Finches, lizards, mockingbirds and yellow warblers flitted in and out through the doors, eating crumbs left on the table next to a half-melted candle embedded with roasted moths.

Harold kept a wreck of dinghy tied at the bottom of a steep landing. The privy mid-way up the path was a loosely constructed rock turret at the edge of the barranco. One squatted over a gash in the rocks, with a view of the sea pounding twenty feet below. On a goat horn embedded in the rocks was a wad of blue-grey tree moss for toilet paper.

We gathered up at the house to talk it over. Harold sat on a rock ledge and watched the *Carrier* being unloaded to give us time alone. From the Dutch door, you could lean out and observe yachts appear over the horizon, sail past Barrington and into the bay. To our left you could watch lazy happenings in the village on the other side. The zones of the island were clearly marked in a gradual palette of colour: the pastels of the bush giving way to the dense green of the rain forest, and at the very top, Half-Moon Crater with its feet in red bracken.

It would take a considerable investment to transform Harold's house into a home, even one for vacations. Not one of us knew how to plaster, lay rock, repair roofs, mend window frames or build furniture. It wasn't realistic to buy this house. Tony could not promise to come out every summer. How would we women cope alone with a fallen-down shack on a cliff edge? What if we ran out of water? We must be honest with ourselves and wait to buy something over in Pelican Bay, where there was at least water and soil.

We looked back at the house. It was an awful mess. We decided to buy it.

13

Return to Galapagos

Our return voyage to Guayaquil took five long days. The *Carrier*'s old engines broke down repeatedly and once we drifted in open sea for six hours. Big John was the only thing that made the suspense and boredom bearable; joking with everyone on board, making even the dour cook see the funny side of burned rice.

I watched my cousin's face as we reached the port city, wondering what his reaction would be to cars, telephones, running water and a city full of strangers, but he took everything in his stride; a sailor's stride so long I had to hang on to keep up.

The drive up through the jungle zone to the Andes was hot with six of us in the car. Heavy rains during our absence had washed out the road in several places, making it necessary for us to get out and leave Tony to manoeuvre as close to the precipice as he dared. Perhaps to distract me, Mother said that when Tony was a few months old and Doña Aguirre was being particularly troublesome, a friend, Anita Restrepo, invited her to escape from Quito to her family's vast estate at the foot of the volcano Tungurahua. The hacienda could only be reached by horseback along a mountain pass. The road, a bare two feet wide in places, had been gouged out from frequent mud-slides. Señorita Restrepo insisted it was safest to strap Tony to one of the barefoot servants' backs. As Mother's little horse lowered its head and measured every footfall, she gripped the saddlehorn, unable to take her eyes off the Indian's cracked, flat feet plodding inches from the edge. Each step seemed closer to death than the last. But, her hostess insisted, 'Indians never fall.'

When Tony drove the car to safety Mother sighed, 'Don't tell your brother's illustrious relatives, but he must have Indian blood in his veins.' I searched his face for telltale signs, but his hair was wavy brown instead of jet black and his nose, rather than being flat, had an aristocratic beakiness – or was that from where he'd been hit by a baseball? Contemplating my brother's profile, I realized his jaw looked firmer, stronger. Startled suspicion made my mouth drop like a drawbridge. Was my brother handsome? Had Galapagos done this in four weeks? Mind you, just like an Indian, he couldn't seem to grow a moustache. A moustache would have helped.

Quito was swaddled in fog. When Ophelia came out to open the gate she looked ill. No, her baby boy was fine, she insisted, taking our bags, no, the whistle-blower had not been shouting at her for not letting him in. It was the '*animalito*', my ocelot, she said.

I found Ati lying in the bathtub. The newspaper beneath him was streaked with excrement. Ophelia had tried to keep him warm with a fan-heater and hot-water bottles but he would not eat. He had terrible diarrhoea. I crawled into the bathtub with him. His body went rigid with cramp. He passed blood. I stroked his head and heaving rib-cage. He groaned.

The vet, Ophelia said tearfully, had told her to stop feeding him meat and chicken as I had instructed. He was getting so big; he growled too much. *El doctor* had insisted that milk, bread and tunafish would tame him. She had stopped giving him vitamin drops in his milk. Then he had sickened. Ophelia, watching my face, began to wail. How could she, a mere *muchacha* from the country who couldn't even read and whose parents still wore rope sandals tell *el doctor* what to do?

I laid Ati on a bed of soft, clean rags. Tony ran to the *farmacia* in the plaza for medicine against infantile dysentery. I mixed the powder with boiled water and dribbled liquid frequently down Ati's throat. He needed an intravenous drip – I knew not what to give or how. I cursed my ignorance. If only I had knowledge! There must be a vet somewhere who could treat wild animals. What would I do if I were in Galapagos? I racked my brain in desperation. Tante Carmen would know, or Mrs Horneman.

But then, in Galapagos a wild animal would never have been captured in the first place.

For the next few days my family tiptoed around the house, using the spare bathroom, warding off draughts, bringing me cups of tea. On the third morning Ati's eyes opened. I cleaned his matted coat very gently, tracing the swirling patterns of his once-magnificent fur with a baby brush. He recognized me then. By afternoon he lapped chicken broth from a spoon. Then he crawled on to my legs and settled there, weakly kneading my thighs and purring. His once-booming voice now sounded like a tractor mired in some distant field. We stared at each other. My head throbbed with guilt at having left him. I saw grey porpoise in the depths of his eyes, gentle sea-lions in his whiskered face. I do not know what he saw in my eyes or found in my face.

That night I kept myself awake speaking of islands where wild animals would never be captured. I promised that when he got well I would set him free in an emerald forest. Ati just sighed, put his head on my arm and slept. Around midnight the cramp and diarrhoea finally ceased. His breathing steadied contentedly. Overjoyed, I gathered a second blanket about us both and we slept, propped up in the bathtub.

Mary quietly opened the door at dawn the next morning. I smiled up at her.

'Look,' I whispered, 'he's much better.' Gently, I pulled back the blanket. Mary tiptoed over to see. Ati was dead.

Big John and Johnny dug a grave in the snapdragons. Mother gave me a soft blue flannel she had intended for a bedjacket. Tony constructed a rather crooked box from bits of the crate the refrigerator had come in. When we buried Ati, Mary had the same look on her face as on that morning when she had saved my duck.

Cousin Johnny, thinking he was out of earshot, asked my mother if she thought I would like Ati's beautiful skin to remember him. Dear Mama said she doubted I would need help remembering. My cousin meant it kindly. He was used to skinning things.

★

Big John and I were sent everywhere together over the next weeks, arranging his passport and visa. I found it odd that entrance to America was so difficult for one so keen to get there, while we had had such a struggle to get out. The Romeos ceased to bother me while I had my tall brown cousin bounding at my side as though the whole earth were a rolling deck. Johnny never looked before he crossed streets and I fancied I saved his life more than once.

One day while walking in the park, Big John referred to his father as 'my old man'. I became very self-righteous and said he was lucky to have a father. If I had one I certainly wouldn't call him an old man, and so on and so on. As usual, he took my outburst well. We sat quietly for a long time. Then he said he remembered my father. When he was little and they lived on the American base over on Baltra Island, there used to be many parties in the Officers' Club – dinner dances and so on. His mother used to love to go and she and Gus would stay out late once he was asleep. But sometimes he would wake up and hear the music from a distance. One night, he said, he woke up, looked out of the window and there was my father – just standing there.

'I don't remember what we talked about. But he held my hand through the window and told me not to be frightened of being alone – you know, I was just a little kid, really little, they get scared easy. He promised to stay until I fell asleep. I never forgot that. When I heard he was dead I felt real sorry.'

'Did he look nice?' was all I could think of to say.

'Yeah. He was kinda thin, I remember. Guys don't remember how people look like girls do.'

'No,' I said.

It was a warm afternoon, sun and gentle rain had made the 'city of eternal spring' blossom forth unashamedly. As we strolled home past fine houses, flowers cascaded over every wall, obscuring the broken glass. Tea roses and fuchsias hung down and caught in our hair. Big John picked a bouquet for me. When we reached our own gate he suddenly suggested we get married. When he returned from the States, he added hurriedly.

'I'll be twenty-one then and you'll be eighteen. Carmen and Fritz were younger than that when they married.'

I said I didn't think we could marry.

'Why not?' I was relieved to see that his hazel eyes did not mock me. I explained it had to do with children; I'd read somewhere that, well, they came out all wrong or something.

We both blushed. It was my first marriage proposal.

A few days later, minutes before he boarded the plane for America, when no one was looking, Big John kissed me. He said he bet it was my first kiss. I assured him hotly that it was not! When I was eleven, I had been kissed by a stocky boy named Keith who had a snake – we weren't sure if it was a king snake or a deadly coral snake, so we went to the public library to look it up in the Encyclopaedia Americana, but the librarian got so hysterical when Keith took his snake from his pocket and laid it on the snake page that we couldn't make a positive identification. Anyway, Keith used to walk me home from school every day and he would give me baby birds and orphaned house-mice to rear, but he began beating up boys if they talked to me so I stopped kissing him.

When John's plane took off I felt terribly lonely. The summer was over. My brother sold off some property and took a trip around the world. Before he left he grew a moustache. About the time he sent a postcard from Rangoon, school started up again.

My family had changed. I had changed. School had not. The calluses I had striven so hard to develop soon smoothed to a delicate shell-pink. While we señoritas filed our nails during cooking class, Doña Magdalena continued to feed us meringues and stuffed eggs. For exams we still squeezed more baby booties from our icing nozzles. Every Monday morning we older students assembled in our ill-fitting maroon jackets while the national hymn was played, and visiting dignitaries made mouth-gargling speeches. On one occasion, a well-known senator arrived with America's handshake to the Ecuadorian people.

Washington had made a special request that a convertible be put at the senator's disposal. There was but one such car in the entire country; a magnificent white Cadillac with flash red upholstery and tail fins. A friend of the ambassador from some obscure country managed to borrow it for the day. The senator had a heart-warming response, riding with the top down through the cobbled streets, smiling and waving to the crowded balconies. The Quiteños cheered, bands oompahed, old ladies twittered and even surly young men smiled. Washington had not expected such a favourable response.

When it was over, the white convertible was quietly returned to the well-known madam of the most exclusive brothel in town.

Encouraged, the American embassy increased its staff. '*Gringo*' kids came to school wearing blue jeans, smoking, dancing the twist to Chubby Checker and swearing like veterans. Our school now provided some classes in English, but the Americans were bored by 'Ecuadorian Culture in the Sixteenth Century', even if it did mean release from the classroom to tour the ancient streets of Quito behind our professor, a philosopher of great reknown whose English, I must admit, was unintelligible. Strolling past my beloved Conservatorio de Musica and Calle Rocafuerte with a dozen or more *gringos* cracking jokes about the blind accordion-beggar only isolated me from them. However, somehow I picked up their swearing, like a dog catches fleas. Four-letter words had an uncanny habit of falling out of my mouth when I least expected.

Mother was offered a good position at a new school, teaching music, art, drama and dance. She was torn between going that summer to the islands and staying to set up her new programme. The *Cristobal Carrier* had new engines but her service was erratic; she kept going up to Columbia where, it was rumoured, she could make better money bringing black-market Nescafé back. Mother could not afford to get stuck out in the islands.

Mary and I insisted the two of us could go without her. I guess we never really expected Mother would say yes. After all, we were only fifteen and twenty-one respectively.

'About Uncle Carl's age when his mother let him sail from Germany to Galapagos,' said Mary in a stroke of genius. We agonized while Mother thought it over. Finally she sat us down, rather formally, I noticed with foreboding. She had a list written out before her.

'All right, you can go. However, HOWEVER,' she called for silence, 'there are certain "points" to go over.'

'Point number one: Mary must try to be more tolerant.'

I glanced smugly at my sister.

'Point number two.' Mother's eyebrows looked at me, one raised, the other crouching. 'You are to be less mule-headed.' She pronounced it like the Ten Commandments.

Mary snickered.

Point Three. Mother was weary of our bickering. If two months of trying to survive on a heap of hot rocks didn't teach us to understand each other, she doubted anything would.

Point Four. If we could spare any time for self-improvement, Mary should get up earlier in the mornings.

I snorted.

– And I should stop swearing.

Mary smirked.

'– there are better words in the dictionary,' Mother continued. 'And speaking of books –' she glanced down at her notes and then looked at me with what I hoped was a tinge of compassion – 'this brings us to the subject of your algebra grade. I was never good at math myself, but your father was. What's put in the dough comes out in the baking, so maybe you'll take after him.' I would have to re-sit my exams in October. It was up to me whether I packed my textbooks or not.

'Mary is not to nag you about studying or complain when you practise your violin.'

I smirked at my sister.

'Naturally, you will practise it when it is least likely to get on your sister's nerves.'

Mary snorted.

Then we got to the nitty-gritty. I should have known by Mother's eyebrows that she was leading up to something earth-shattering.

Johnny was going with us. He was now six years old and very bright. Did Mary not think it was time things were explained to him? Did she want her to do it or would she? Mary said she would – once we were out in the island, when the time was right. Mother said she knew she could trust us to take good care of him and ourselves.

I convinced Mother that we needed a dog to protect us on our travels. She agreed on condition that it should be a hunting breed and we must train it and leave it in Galapagos: the city was no place for an active dog.

We made meticulous lists of things we had neglected to take the first time.

      cement
      nails, all sizes
      hammer, saw, etc.
      kerosene lamps and extra chimneys
      toilet paper
      two pairs of canvas shoes each
      khaki for extra shorts
      straw hats
      fishing line and hooks
      purple dog-medicine

Then my sister suggested we take plenty of cotton wool, knee bandages, aspirins, ointments, ankle supports, iodine and Sloan's liniment for me. My hackles rose.

'Then who cut her foot open during the first week in the islands? Who got it so inflamed with sand she could barely walk? Who was the only one to catch impetigo from a privy-seat everyone used?'

Mother just watched. When we had finished we sat back down and completed the list.

      large and small cooking pots
      boric-acid powder (against roaches)
      bay leaf (against weevils)
      rat traps
      insect repellent
      plastic window screening
      buckets, dishes, cutlery
      new primus stove and spare parts

    violin strings
    needles, scissors, thread
    mirror

Lastly, we knew we would need advice on lining water tanks, mending roofs and mixing cement, so we bought gifts of goodwill: fabric, colouring pencils, medicines for Tante Carmen's metal box, pipe tobacco, oil paints, violin resin and a typewriter ribbon for Gus. Mother threw in her old *Betty Crocker Cookbook*, two salamis, three large cheeses and the Bible with Colossians, chapter 3, verses 12 to 14 underlined.

Then she gave us Father's old brass binoculars, given to him by his father when he left Germany. She looked excited for us when we said goodbye. For a minute I even thought she was glad to get rid of us. She promised to write.

We flew down to Guayaquil, obtaining unprecedented permission to take Gypsy – our newly acquired pointer puppy – on the army plane at the last moment, because as often happened, some colonel remembered Capitán Marco's widow.

The *Cristobal Carrier* was now painted pirate black. I preferred baby-blue. Not surprisingly, the captain leered at us when we boarded and offered to show us to our cabins personally. It was so hot and humid, I guess you had to excuse him for sweating profusely. We put Gypsy in the lower bunk nearest the cabin door. He growled five times during the first night, but it might have been cockroaches or mice, which he'd never seen before.

Our voyage was uneventful. Gypsy got seasick with my sister. This I hoped would bring them closer, for Mary wasn't entirely sold on the dog yet. Three days out of Guayaquil we rounded the southern point of San Cristobal Island and entered Wreck Bay. The tips of a pair of masts stuck out of the water, the only visible remains of an English steamer that had ripped her bottom on a submerged reef and sunk, some time during the First World War. Three raucous blasts announced to the population, some thousand people, that we had arrived. A few ran out of little wooden houses, across a fine sweep of golden sand and assembled on a rickety wooden pier. It was a sleepy little village of some

charm, but without the vibrant contrast of black cliff and deep blue which made Santa Cruz so dramatic.

Mary and I hurriedly strapped on our knives, grabbed three hats, water bottles, home-sewn knapsacks and prepared to go ashore and explore the highlands while the ship was being unloaded. But, it being the capital of the islands, here the port captain was '*un hombre muy importante*' and when he came alongside, standing precariously in the bow of a sinking motor-boat, he ordered that no one was to go ashore until his cement was unloaded. We wondered what the cement was for. The only sign of concrete was a bust of Charles Darwin standing forlornly in a heap of sand.

Finally our captain, in a foul mood, bellowed that we could go ashore. Between us, Mary and I quickly carried a trembling Gypsy down the ladder and scrambled into the tender. Halfway to shore the captain said he didn't like dogs in boats and threw Gypsy overboard. Johnny screamed. I grabbed for his collar but Gypsy went under only inches from the boat's propeller and disappeared. While I tore off my shoes and prepared to jump in and save him, Mary berated the captain in fractured Spanish, which restored his good humour. Gypsy paddled to the old rickety jetty, climbed out, and, when we landed, shook himself all over the captain's whites. After this Gypsy's hackles rose and he gnashed his teeth whenever the crew came within feet of one of us.

The islanders were friendly enough when they thought we were tourists, asking in broken English where we came from. But when we, as modestly as possible, answered in Spanish that we were Angermeyers, like magic caps were doffed, hospitality offered and glasses of coconut water brought out on trays.

I praised one deaf old lady for planting the many coconut palms in front of her house.

'No,' she shouted shrilly. 'It was Señor Cobos who planted them! Many years ago. The only good thing he ever did.'

I asked how we could reach the village of Progreso. She pointed to a dusty red road leading through a dry wilderness. I asked if Señor Cobos's house was still up in the hills.

'No!' she shouted again. 'He is dead and gone to the Devil!'

'*Sí*, but his house, his hacienda? Does it still exist?'

'Gone to the Devil!' she repeated.

'Can you tell us where the wild horses are?' I asked her once Mary had walked on.

The lady, baked brown as a fruit cake, shouted, 'Too far. Much too far. Why you want to ruin your nice white skins by going up there on such a hot morning? Stay down here – swim – take a siesta – I give you my hammock.'

I thanked her but insisted I must know about the horses.

'Well, if you must, once you reach Progreso village, there is a trail leading into a valley of grassy hills. Cattle and donkeys graze there. You will see first the volcano of San Joaquin. You walk up the side and will see the lake of El Junco down in the crater. Wild horses sometimes drink there. Come back when you get tired!' she cackled after us.

We followed a relatively good road deep in volcanic gravel, through scrub with an occasional poisonous manzanilla tree. Finches pecked at seeds on either side of the road and, as we soon entered a cool transitional zone between beach and highland, vermilion flycatchers landed in branches mere feet from us, their colour startling against the bleak vegetation.

At about 900 feet we entered a refreshingly cool cloud where gnarled ciruela plum trees grew covered in black moss. Small yellow flowers appeared timidly between clumps of not very green grass. Then straight out of the *True Adventure* film we saw the wild orange trees, growing so nonchalantly beside the road we couldn't believe they were real. Their trunks and branches were armoured with vicious two-inch spines, as the Original Navel Orange Tree had been protected by an iron fence. Grinning foolishly, we cut off as many oranges as we could eat, sat on rocks and stuffed ourselves. The dog lapped the juice as it ran down our dust-streaked arms and drooled until I gave him one which he ate, anchored between his paws. I thought back to the first island orange Gus had given me; its skin so scaly and rough I thought it was inedible until I found the surprise of sweet juice inside. I must have been a laughable creature, nibbling daintily, straight from my fancy school with my refined manners.

would – once we were out in the island, when the time was right. Mother said she knew she could trust us to take good care of him and ourselves.

I convinced Mother that we needed a dog to protect us on our travels. She agreed on condition that it should be a hunting breed and we must train it and leave it in Galapagos: the city was no place for an active dog.

We made meticulous lists of things we had neglected to take the first time.

cement
nails, all sizes
hammer, saw, etc.
kerosene lamps and extra chimneys
toilet paper
two pairs of canvas shoes each
khaki for extra shorts
straw hats
fishing line and hooks
purple dog-medicine

Then my sister suggested we take plenty of cotton wool, knee bandages, aspirins, ointments, ankle supports, iodine and Sloan's liniment for me. My hackles rose.

'Then who cut her foot open during the first week in the islands? Who got it so inflamed with sand she could barely walk? Who was the only one to catch impetigo from a privy-seat ~~everyone used?'~~

~~...~~re had finished we sat back

~~...~~ches)

~~...~~s

192

At about 900 feet we entered a refreshingly cool cloud where gnarled ciruela plum trees grew covered in black moss. Small yellow flowers appeared timidly between clumps of not very green grass. Then straight out of the *True Adventure* film we saw the wild orange trees, growing so nonchalantly beside the road we couldn't believe they were real. Their trunks and branches were armoured with vicious two-inch spines, as the Original Navel Orange Tree had been protected by an iron fence. Grinning foolishly, we cut off as many oranges as we could eat, sat on rocks and stuffed ourselves. The dog lapped the juice as it ran down our dust-streaked arms and drooled until I gave him one which he ate, anchored between his paws. I thought back to the first island orange Gus had given me; its skin so scaly and rough I thought it was inedible until I found the surprise of sweet juice inside. I must have been a laughable creature, nibbling daintily, straight from my fancy school with my refined manners.

...against the bleak vegetation.

...between beach and highland,

...road and, as we soon

...anzanilla tree.

> violin strings
> needles, scissors, thread
> mirror

Lastly, we knew we would need advice on lining water tanks, mending roofs and mixing cement, so we bought gifts of goodwill: fabric, colouring pencils, medicines for Tante Carmen's metal box, pipe tobacco, oil paints, violin resin and a typewriter ribbon for Gus. Mother threw in her old *Betty Crocker Cookbook*, two salamis, three large cheeses and the Bible with Colossians, chapter 3, verses 12 to 14 underlined.

Then she gave us Father's old brass binoculars, given to him by his father when he left Germany. She looked excited for us when we said goodbye. For a minute I even thought she was glad to get rid of us. She promised to write.

We flew down to Guayaquil, obtaining unprecedented permission to take Gypsy – our newly acquired pointer puppy – on the army plane at the last moment, because as often happene some colonel remembered Capitán Marco's widow.

The *Cristobal Carrier* was now painted pirate black. I pr baby-blue. Not surprisingly, the captain leered at us v boarded and offered to show us to our cabins person so hot and humid, I guess you had to excuse him profusely. We put Gypsy in the lower bunk ne door. He growled five times during the first ni have been cockroaches or mice, which before.

Our voyage was uneventful. Gypsy go This I hoped would bring them closer sold on the dog yet. Three days ou the southern point of San Cristol Bay. The tips of a pair of masts visible remains of an English st on a submerged reef and sun' War. Three raucous blast thousand people, that v wooden houses, acros on a rickety woode

'Sí, but his house, his hacienda? Does it still exist?'
'Gone to the Devil!' she repeated.
'Can you tell us where the wild horses are?' I asked her once
Mary had walked on.
The lady, baked brown as a fruit cake, shouted, 'Too far.
Much too far. Why you want to ruin your nice white skins by
going up there on such a hot morning? Stay down here – swim –
take a siesta – I give you my hammock.'
I thanked her but insisted I must know about the horses.
'Well, if you must, once you reach Progreso village, there is
a trail leading into a valley of grassy hills. Cattle and donkeys
graze there. You will see first the volcano of San Joaquin. You
walk up the side and will see the lake of El Junco down in the
crater. Wild horses sometimes drink there. Come back when
you get tired!' she cackled after us.
We followed a relatively good road deep in volcanic
through scrub with an occasional poisonous
Finches pecked at seeds on either side of
entered a cool transitional zo
vermilion flycatcher
colour st

Suddenly we were startled by a shrill yelling and thudding of hooves. Three cowboys rode towards us in a cloud of dust on wild-eyed ponies. When they spied us they spurred their mounts into an insane downhill gallop, stumbling over rock and uneven earth. The cowboys' saddles were harsh wooden seats, meagrely cushioned on the horse's back with thin sacking. A rough rope passed beneath the tail to secure the saddle. An old rag had been stuffed there to keep the rope from cutting into the flesh, but even as they flashed by the scars on the animals were visible. The stirrups were haphazardly tied on with bits of twine and wire, the reins one-sided affairs with a knotted loop squeezing the horse's lower lip.

A short while later the road ended at a grassy clearing with four or five deserted cane houses leaning wearily on stilts, their occupants down at the ship. A few chickens scratched among hibiscus bushes; a brown speckled pig rolled in the dirt. We sat down for a quick rest. As I shook the gravel from my shoes I noticed thin, bent rusted bars amongst the sugar-cane.

'Cobos's railroad!' I exclaimed. 'Look, they lead on into that plantation!' With great excitement, we followed the trail into cultivated banana trees, but soon lost it beneath rotting timber and leaves. Wandering on, we found the cow in the clearing the old lady had mentioned. The air smelled of wine where yellow fruit fell unloved to the ground, spilling out its shocking-pink insides. It was an orchard gone mad. There is something irresistible about wild, forgotten fruit. Whipping off our straw hats we filled them greedily, slipping and sliding, churning the ground to rosy slush.

On close inspection, the guayavas all proved to be fly-bitten, so we tried picking the best from the tree and soon filled our knapsacks, but the fruit seeped through the canvas and stained our shirt-backs. Reluctantly, we dumped them all out again, all around some rose bushes which grew along the ground and over stumps. Realizing we were propagating more guayava, we quickly scraped up what we could of the slush away from the roses, and dumped it on sand, where hopefully it would not seed. The legend swore that Cobos had planted white roses. These were blood red.

I don't know what I expected to find beneath the roses; the thigh bone of some forgotten convict perhaps, a rusted machete, some sign at least of the struggle between *les misérables* and master. Johnny was tired. Mary said if I wanted to wander on a bit further, they would wait back in Progreso for me. She said she didn't like the feel of the valley. Gypsy was tired but he insisted upon plodding after me. I was pleased. Mary had a son. The dog was obviously going to be mine.

I quickly gave up hope of finding remnants of Cobos's grand hacienda. Not even a tarnished candelabra was to be found in the weeds. As we continued uphill, the earth became moist and oozed over my basketball shoes, staining them red. I walked for another fifteen minutes, thinking I would just reach the top of the rise and then go back. But at the summit I was stunned to find I was looking at the sea – the other side of the island. Unable to move for the mud on my shoes, I took a stick and began to scrape them. Gypsy growled. I immediately feared we had been followed by some unshaven member of the crew. But then I froze.

Below in a small valley stood three horses. They were small bays with tangled manes and long tails. Wild horses! I grasped Gypsy's collar firmly and crept forward. They did not move, so I assumed I was downwind of them. Suddenly Gypsy lunged forward, broke my hold and gave chase. I bellowed at him, but it was no use. The horses raised their heads in alarm but did not bolt. Instead, the largest backed up and prepared to kick Gypsy in the chest. Then I saw why the animals had not fled; they were hobbled. I nearly wept. Slipping down the hill after Gypsy, I caught his collar, tied him to a tree with my belt and sat down disheartened. What was the point of a world without wild horses? The trio eyed me warily, but their hobbled forelegs did not take them far. Perhaps they had been wild until recently and someone was trying to break their spirit by leaving them to half starve on scrub. In a few weeks the mare would feel a cruel wooden saddle on her back; in a month her flank would be scarred by spurs.

Speaking softly, I managed to catch hold of the first mare's long mane to prevent her turning on me, and bending slowly I

eased my knife free of its sheath and slashed the knots close to
her fetlocks so the dirty rope fell to the mud. Inching my way
towards the colt, I cut him loose. The third animal proved more
wary, hopping a few feet each time I neared. But she was large
with foal and soon tired.

It wasn't until I waved my hat and gave chase that they
realized their freedom, leaping over the tufts of grass towards a
worn volcano long since tamed by the centuries. I galloped up
the side, secretly mounted on the grey I used to ride to Miss
Bean's class. I had forgotten him for all these years! My foot
struck a hidden rock; my ankle twisted, my arm lashed out to
stop my fall and I grabbed a handful of nettles. I hadn't sworn
for ten days. I immediately vowed to wash out my mouth with
sea-water when I reached the beach.

I limped up the last few yards to the rim of the crater and
gasped. It wasn't merely the lonely beauty of the little lake
sitting there like a perfect saucer on top of a plum pudding, but
the mystery, the miracle of so much fresh water on Galapagos.
There were no apparent streams running in or out. The horses
paused for a drink, keeping a watchful eye on me, their sides
heaving with grateful slurping. Then they were off, up and over
the rim. My heart swelled at the sound of their thudding hooves,
at the sight of the heavy mare kicking the sky. The last I saw
they were galloping down towards the other side of the island.
From where I stood panting, you could just distinguish the sea
glittering silver and turquoise beyond.

14

The Cliff Dwellers

'T-shirt. T-shirt. Teeeee-shirt.' Finches congregated on the roof, their twiggy feet scratching like fingernails on a blackboard. The sea lapped the base of the barranco. Otherwise there was silence; blissful peace after so many days of the *Carrier*'s interminably thumping engines. We were now cliff-dwellers.

I threw back the covers on my cot and ran to open the top of the Dutch door. Our view. From our house. Just in time I remembered the three-masted brigantine anchored not fifty yards off and ducked behind the door to slip a shirt over my head. Father's binoculars hung on a nail beneath my clothes, handy for sightings of yachts. Propping my elbows on the lower door, I fiddled the knobs and focused on the most splendid sailing ship I had ever seen; fifty-two feet long, with romantic olde-worlde lines, a sturdy mast and complex rigging. The *Beagle II* had sailed all the way from England to become the new Darwin Station's scientific ship. Uncle Carl, her captain, said she was a jackass-rigged ketch. My three uncles were unashamedly infatuated with her; so much did she remind them of their beloved *Marie*.

Into the lens appeared a leg, then a broom and a hairy chest. The '*Beagle* Boys' were up early and already scrubbing the decks with buckets of sea-water. The rhythm of their brush strokes was accompanied by strange frenzied screaming: yeah-yeah-yeahs wafted over the water and smacked our little house in the face.

'I wanna hold your hand – I wanna hold your hand –'

I'd never seen an Englishman before, except in old movies where they shuffled around in fog with black umbrellas. But these were in colour; Julian had a blond, bushy chest and a curly beard. He wore white cream on his sunburned nose. His lips formed words as he sang along with the noise: 'and when you touch me I feel happy – inside'. Then I focused on a foot, a most Godly foot, and long limbs jerking to the music: Richard. Such splendid English names.

'I've been up for hours!' Johnny boasted marching up the path in search of breakfast. Mary yawned behind me.

'It's rude to watch people through binoculars,' she said sleepily, and snatched them from me.

'That one with the beard is cute,' she said.

'Yeah, but have you seen the other one?'

'Too pretty,' she said with the voice of expertise. 'Oh look, they've got a monkey or something – it's climbing around in the rigging – ugly little thing . . .'

I grabbed the glasses back. A tiny creature jumped down from the rigging into the gorgeous one's blond hair and held on.

'It's a marmoset, I think.'

I pumped the primus but couldn't get it going so we ate a cold breakfast of stale rye bread and jam we'd brought with us, out in front of the house with our hats on against the sun. It was about eleven o'clock and there wasn't a cloud in the sky. The *Beagle* Boys disappeared below deck and reappeared with mugs in their hands. They waved. I ignored them. Mary waved back.

Although dirty with dead insects and smelling of rat pee, the house was much more attractive than I'd remembered. Once we tore away the goat skins, which were infested with maggots, termites and cockroach capsules, we realized our windows framed three views: one of the sea, one of the hills and another of thorny bush. Grey Darwin finches, yellow warblers and lava lizards darted in and out of the thick scrub, making straight for our house whenever we opened any food tins. The back door opened on to a glob of lava so large that in the moonlight it looked like a wild beast with gleaming obsidian fangs. Our fourth window was really a porthole to one side of the door, a perfect peephole for detecting visitors coming our way – though over the next weeks not many ventured up our path except nimble children distributing fish or meat. All the rocks wobbled like loose teeth in a skull. One foot put wrong, especially in dim light, would send you tumbling into the breakers below. After getting caught out the first night and having to grope our way home, we learned never to leave the house in the afternoon without a hurricane lamp in case a tea party tarried into the night.

Harold had left us a small table painted sickly green, an ugly pale-pink wardrobe with three rusty hangers, a wooden settee with a lift-up seat for storage, a chair and a stool. The fireplace was still full of tins and the doll's head still stared vacantly at the rafters.

That first night we slept badly. Rats poured through the windows, up into the rafters and over the roof, chattering bitterly at our presence. Endemic rats were not dangerous, nor were they filthy, but they were messy: chewing books, candles, any food left out, and sometimes leaving drops of blood where they debated whose territory our house really was.

The following day we three tied kerchiefs about our heads and made a smelly bonfire of the goat skins, setting them alight on a natural rock platform above the house so as not to catch the dry bush on fire.

Then we made exhausting trips down to the landing to fetch buckets of sea-water to scrub floors, walls, ceiling and furniture. Our nearest neighbour, Lucrecia, had generously sent up two large jerry-cans of water to start us off until the garua arrived. But the sky showed no sign of mist and the island's dry face simmered in heat.

By mid-afternoon we had unpacked, filled the kerosene lamps, and stored our food, candles and soap in large biscuit tins, protected against rats and roaches. Able to postpone it no longer I went to our privy on the cliff-edge armed with a bottle of sugar-cane alcohol. Glancing at the impetigo scars on my wrists, I so drenched the privy with puro I could have set it alight. Fire ants staggered from the seat in drunken stupor. When I sat, the whole barranco seemed to shake, but I hoped this was merely an optical illusion caused by the rising tide washing below. Peering through a gap in the rock wall, I spied the *Beagle* Boys and Uncle Carl taking tea under a tarpaulin with what looked like a sea chart spread out before them. I had heard that they were going off on a scientific voyage with new biologists who were staying in the Darwin Station. I could see the new UNESCO buildings on the far side of the bay. At its inauguration, speeches were made saying that scientists would be the saving of Galapagos. But Gus said they would be our downfall, one day bringing tourists and trouble. I felt this could never happen. Surely there wasn't enough water for tourists.

When the tide was up, we went to our landing on the barranco to wash, but didn't undress in case the *Beagle* Boys had binoculars. It was so hot and the water so clear, we could not resist a swim. But before we jumped in, Mary gave a little lecture on sharks. We were, she reminded us, no longer swimming at the shallow beach. Large white-tips and even hammerheads entered the deep bay and hunted along the base of the barranco. They were well fed and harmless so we must never panic if a shark appeared curious. If one came too near, we were to stick him in the nose. With that she gave each of us a flimsy looking short stick with a nail fastened to the end. Johnny was still unconvinced, so to prove there was nothing to fear, we all slid into the water and cupped jam jars to our eyes, surveying the sea floor twelve feet below. Dark shapes cruised past and I knew from the way my skin crawled that if a shark had arrived, I would have dropped my stick, panicked and surely drowned; but the shadows were merely gentle leopard rays drifting by like golden leaves in the shafts of light. Then a kaleidoscope of tropical fish appeared, swimming through our legs like shining jewels. Some were peacock-blue with mustard-yellow stripes, others were iridescent green, like butterfly wings, still others had pink clown-lips and bulging eyes. As this new world opened before us, we began to feel at home in the sea and learned to jack-knife to the sandy bottom, picking up sea stars and stroking fish as they gathered round. But when the sun began to leave shadows behind on the cliff face, we remembered the rule about swimming after five and crawled out, laying back on the rough steps. What was left of the day's sun dried us like three happy fried eggs on a sidewalk.

The next morning we rowed to Pelican Bay. After we'd washed our clothes and filled our water cans, Adolfo Haeni tottered after us, saying he was selling some window frames cheap. He'd made them for Mrs Horneman, but he must have drunk too much rum the night before he went up to take measurements, or else her windows had shrunk. The frames weren't very much too big, he'd told her; she could have nailed them to the house and no one would have noticed, but Mrs Horneman wouldn't have it. We said we'd see if we could afford them and slowly rowed home.

I had never realized how heavy water was until we had hauled it out of a hole in the ground, over wet rocks, through the slime of low tide, into a tipsy boat, across the bay, up the barranco and over the burning-hot sand to our front door. By the time we got home I was thirsty enough to drink the lot. We fell into our cots that night exhausted and reeking of liniment.

I do not know what we would have done without rocks. Fish were gutted on the big one outside the door. We heaved another flat one on to two square ones and made a table for our 'veranda'. Small ones with interesting shapes became candle holders, book-ends and paperweights. I began to see why Gus loved them.

Our list of repairs and improvements grew longer every day. The most urgent was cement-washing the inside of the rain barrel so that when the outside finally rusted away, we would be left with a concrete tank. We measured out one bowl of sand to two bowls of cement, dribbled on precious brackish water and stirred it with a stick. Two hours later, our hands stiff, hair grey, nostrils clogged with cement dust, we stepped back and admired our work, only to see it let go of the barrel's interior and slide *en masse* to form a grey, wet, unyielding mess on the bottom. It lay there drying before our eyes so, with tears of frustration, we quickly scooped it up and stuck it on again. And again. Finally, about sunset, when we were on the point of hysteria, it stayed put. Utterly exhausted, we took buckets down to the landing in the dark and stripped and washed before we fell into bed again.

Last thing at night we would discuss our priorities for the following day, trying not to let tempers flare. Everything took so long to do, and we only had two months to do them in. Water, food, rats, windows and tin cans in the fireplace were our main concerns. In spite of the blisters on our hands, twice a week we would have to borrow a dinghy and row over to Pelican Bay for water. Brackish water tasted foul and did not keep; tiny organisms died and after some days stank, making the water fit only for washing, but it was all we had until garua came.

Our diet would not be very healthy until fresh produce came down from the hills and, again, this depended on garua. But Mother had told us to look after Johnny, and oats three times a day was not what she'd had in mind.

The bush rats would still not accept our presence in the house. Gypsy showed no inclination to chase them so, reluctantly, we borrowed a trap. Every morning Mary rose to throw limp bodies over the cliff into the sea and every night more rats came back.

We knew that if garua ever did come, mosquitoes would begin to hatch and without windows we would go crazy. So we rowed back to Haeni's and bought his bargain frames, aware that they were too small for the spaces in our walls. It took us two days to collect thousands of tiny rocks and another four days to fill in the gaps with what looked like an intricate mosaic, held in place with cement. Halfway through this job our hands became so sore, we had to stop and sew clumsy gloves from denim cut off from our blue jeans.

Unable to bear the sight of tin cans and the doll's head staring at us any longer, we borrowed a dinghy from the *Beagle*, rowed out to the middle of the bay, stuck the tins full of holes and sank them where they would eventually rust away. We weighted the doll's head with a rock and ghoulishly watched her sink.

The *Beagle* Boys became more and more neighbourly over the weeks; especially Julian, who often bounded up to loan us Penguin paperbacks from the ship's library or invite himself to tea, bringing his own fresh water, teabags and crackers, which he spread with a disgusting black goo called Marmite.

We were a bit wary about accepting gifts. Before coming we had vowed that we would not be a burden to our neighbours this time. But we needed meat. Our two salamis and one smoked cheese were strictly for emergencies. The time had come when one of us would have to hunt and the other cook.

'You choose,' said Mary.

Doña Magdalena had not prepared me for goat stew and turtle steak. On the other hand, I hated death. I couldn't imagine fixing my eye to the sights of a rifle and shooting a goat in the heart. I said nothing.

'You afraid of the bush?'

'Of course not.'

'It's pretty rough in Devil's Kitchen. Your ankles might slow Gus down.'

'There is nothing wrong with my ankles!'

'Good, then we'll take turns. I'll hunt this month and you cook, heaven help us,' she muttered, crawling into her cot.

The three of us lay in the dark; a little thirsty, a little hungry, very sore and, though we wouldn't admit it, homesick for Mother.

'Remember how the two of us used to share a bed in the days on Arlington Street?' Mary said at last.

'Yeah.'

'We called it snuggling like spoons.'

'Yeah.'

'You always used to wait until I was nearly asleep to ask questions.'

'Yeah.'

'You're probably old enough now to read the letters in the shoebox.'

But I no longer wanted to read them. They were about death. And I felt very much alive.

I usually awoke at seven, unable to stand my hard camp cot any longer. After dashing to the door to see if any garua had fallen, I made oatmeal with powdered milk for Johnny, myself and

Gypsy. A lava lizard usually shared breakfast with us and finches flew down on our heads to eat rice from our hands.

Johnny had always been up hours before I awoke. Curious, I watched him one morning. Very quietly, he slipped a large piece of paper and crayons from the lift-top settee. Unrolling the paper, he anchored it on the floor with shells, then sat on his knees, with his tongue stuck out in rapt concentration. I dozed off then. When I awoke, he was rolling up the paper and securing it with a rubber band. Then he moved a stool over to the pink wardrobe, stepped up and commenced rifling through our carefully washed and folded clothes. He slipped my white blouse over his head, draped four or five colourful headscarves about his throat, tied Mary's best belt around his middle, pushed his feet into my black rubber mud boots, drew an eyebrow-pencil moustache above his lip and, after flexing his muscles in our small mirror, slipped a wooden spoon into his belt. Then he gathered his papers and clumped down the path and out of sight, whistling the theme from *The Comancheros*, his favourite movie. An hour later he returned, quietly undressed, folded everything neatly and stowed it away.

The *Beagle* sailed off for a two-week cruise around the archipelago. I watched Mary's face and knew she would miss Julian's visits. The bay looked empty without the *Beagle*. No yacht had sailed in since our arrival and I began to wonder what was happening in the rest of the world. Gus stopped by to discuss a hunting day with Mary and said he'd heard on the BBC World Service that the Americans were sending a man to the moon.

'Maybe you could make me a picture of that, no?' said Gus, tousling Johnny's hair. Then Gus said he'd been very pleased to find the picture of a Chinese junk crewed by pirate birds with machetes in their beaks under his door that morning. Everyone, he said, was talking about Johnny's wonderful pictures. Mary and I looked blank.

'You mean you don't know? Johnny is knocking at everyone's doors early in the morning and delivering pictures. Carmen heard a tapping at six o'clock last week. She thought it was chickens and got her broom to shoo them away but found

Johnny on her doorstep dressed like a pirate with a picture of a magnificent sailing ship with rigging such as I never saw.' Doris Divine received a train full of bears shooting cannons, Marga, a two-headed dragon flying over what looked like a fruit bowl. Mary and I found this very embarrassing, but people said they now looked forward to finding a pirate on their doorsteps first thing in the morning.

'I am not a pirate!' Johnny would insist. 'I am Monsewer Paul Regret!' But unlike Johnny and me, who had seen the movie *The Commancheros* five times, no one on Angermeyer Point knew who Paul Regret was.

The next day Mary and Gus bagged a large billy. The meat was a bit stronger than usual. I was just wondering how to cook meat that smelled like sweat when Gus pulled from his bag a pair of magnificent curved horns over two feet long and a musky black goat skin for me.

We salted the hide and nailed it to the outside of the King's shack. Every day, once my chores were finished, I visited the shack to peel off the dry bits. From within the thin walls I could hear my uncle slowly tapping on his old typewriter.

'You type?' He called to me through the slats.

'Yeah, I learned some in school.' I continued scraping the hide.

'You type German?'

'No.'

'Ach, sure you can, I will teach you.'

He was writing most of his book in longhand on endless stacks of paper covered in spots. They were the same spots I had noticed on the letter he'd sent us on Arlington Street.

'Spider drops. You cannot housetrain spiders. My book will be covered in them; they will become my trademark.'

And so I began to type, but German, like Spanish, refused to enter my head through osmosis. In desperation, Gus acted out the stories, playing the roles of his four brothers sneaking out of Germany, being shipwrecked off Cornwall, arriving in Galapagos, hunting boar. I would sit there, fingers poised in amazement over my keys, listening to the most incredible tales. But when it came to writing them all down, Gus always looked tired – more than he ever did after a day's hunt in Devil's Kitchen. Writing was a lonely, exhausting endeavour he said. There was so much to tell. 'If only I could put pure thoughts down on patient paper.'

He was amazingly patient with my inability to learn his mother tongue, though inwardly I think he despaired.

'But Hanna, your father was German! He spoke it as a baby, that's how easy it is! Now think, girl, what does *traum* sound like to you?'

'Uhhhhmmmmm – traumatic?'

'What does traumatic mean?'

I fetched his dictionary. 'Traumatic: an unpleasant experience from which neurosis develops.'

'*Nein! Nein! Traum! Traum!* It sounds like dream, *nicht*? That's what it means – *dream*, girl! You see how easy it is?'

I tried my best not to look stupid. I borrowed his old English–German dictionary and tried to memorize some words so he wouldn't be disgusted with me. I forgot to study algebra. As + Ys had so little to do with rain barrels, goat skins, rats and rocks.

Julian returned from his cruise with wonderful tales of fur seals, penguins, whales, lakes of flamingos, and flightless cormorants. Tower Island had boobies with red feet instead of blue and frigate birds that puffed their throats into huge red sacs to attract their mates. There were waved albatrosses on Hood Island and thousands of marine iguanas on Fernandina.

'And you should meet Bryan Nelson and his wife,' he told Mary. 'We left them alone on Hood Island, where they will be studying synchronization in breeding sea-birds compared to nesting sites of nidifugous birds versus the nidicolous.' On the *Beagle*'s voyage, Julian said, they had seen evidence of many specialized ecological niches of endemic species, plus one or two examples of carboniferous activity.

When Mary walked Julian down to the landing that night and Johnny and I lay in bed, he told me that Julian talked like that because his parents were 'imminent naturalists'.

'Mary said so. She said they write books.' I went to sleep wondering if we would ever see the fantastic places Julian had spoken of. Fernandina Island sounded a thousand miles away. Uncle Carl might take us some day – if the *Beagle* had space. The only reason my other uncles ever ventured far afield was to fish bacalao. Fishing season was a long way off. We would all be back in school by then. Unless some catastrophe happened, some minor one to prevent us going back.

15

Rock-flying

'Easy breezy! Easy breezy. Eeeezy breezy!' Finches squabbled at the window screens, waiting for their morning handout. It was still dark outside, surely it was too early. My face felt damp, my bed clammy. I leaped up and looked out of our seaward window. Garua! Sheets of wet clouds were crawling into our bay, wetting the iguanas on Carl's roof, soaking every house, dripping steadily into echoing rain barrels.

Johnny had gone on his morning rounds and was then to spend the day with Martin. Mary's cot was empty, her knife gone from the peg. She and Gus must have slipped away before dawn, a mighty feat for her. Goat stew would make a welcome change from fried mullet and rice. If only we had some potatoes, carrots, celery, peas and a sprig of parsley, all of which the *Betty Crocker Cookbook* said I needed for lamb stew. We hadn't seen a fresh vegetable since our arrival, for the garua in the hills had not been dense enough for crops; but all that would change now. On the sloping sides of Half-Moon Crater moisture hung like strips of gauze. Soon avocados would begin to swell, bananas and papaya grow plump, wild-tortoise ponds fill with sweet rain and pastures turn bright green. If you listened closely you could hear a cow chorus of thanksgiving. Alf and his father would no longer have to chop down banana plants for their livestock.

Every day the hills had beckoned me. But the earth up there would be too dry to detect hoofprints. I knew it was foolish, this horse thing. For that reason I kept it in a pocket of my heart and took it out only when I needed to reassure the child within me.

'When the grass at the base of Half-Moon Crater turns green, I promise I'll take you,' I told the nagging kid. 'We will hike to the very top and I will show you that there aren't any wild horses on this island any more.'

Slipping on my shorts and shirt, I went outside and let my face be washed. The earth smelled rich and good. The sea lay calm beneath thousands of droplets.

Gypsy eased his black-and-white spots from some blissful dog dream and padded over to the big tin, tail waving expectantly. I pried open the rat-proof lid and measured out raw oats, rancid milk powder for us both and a handful of Sun Maid raisins as a treat. I scattered a handful of rice to the finches outside. 'Easy breezy – easy breezy!' Did finches change their call from 'T-shirt, T-shirt' to 'easy breezy' when the weather changed, I wondered?

In the five weeks we'd been in the house, cooking had been a problem. Leftover soup turned sour, fried fish grew whiskers overnight and rice sprouted weevils in spite of the bay leaves I kept in the tin.

But this afternoon I would lean over the Dutch door and try not to look too smug when Mary came up the trail, dusty and sweaty, with a dead goat on her back.

I opened *Betty Crocker* to 'Wonder White Bread'. A fat cockroach ran out of page 82. Horrid thing. I hated their hairy legs, the way they got into everything, their smell. I dusted some boric-acid powder on the 'Quick Bread' section. They always went for the drips on my banana fritter recipe.

Betty Crocker smiled at me from her photograph near the 'easy step-by-step instructions'. 'See Your Husband's Eyes Light Up When He Comes Home From a Hard Day at the Office and Gets a Whiff of This!' I heated brackish water on the primus stove, then let the yeast bubble for five minutes. 'Use Crisco Angel-Light Homogenized Shortening in all your baking.' I dumped in a dollop of Kastdalen pig lard. The recipe wanted fine granulated sugar. I poured in dark molasses. Three petrified mouse-droppings floated to the surface. I then added a chunk of flamingo-lagoon salt the colour of Pepto-Bismol. Would it, I wondered, turn my bread pink? I measured out flour. Fourteen

(*Above*) The barranco as seen from our path, looking towards Angermeyer Point. Note the marine iguanas on Carl and Marga's roof.

(*Left*) Carl, Gypsy's daughter and Gus. The barranco and village as seen from Angermeyer Point.

(*Below*) Our second house, where my mother, brother and I settled in 1971.

'We still have our parties, music – music. Everybody plays something,' Gus wrote to us in California.

This impromptu dance (*below, left*), took place in Tante Carmen's kitchen.

(*Above, left*) Alf Kastdalen with future hunting dogs.

(*Above, right*) Maya Kastdalen and her lifelong companion, Lala.

(*Left*) Fritz with two of the original Norwegian settlers: Gordon Wold and Graffer.

A dinghy-ride below the barranco, habitat of unique wildlife, unafraid of man

When Carl Angermeyer built his house on the barranco, the
iguanas moved up to the roof. Today they dumbfound scientists
by coming when called and eating the dog's leftovers.

(*Above left*) Gus's wife Lucrecia
and their sons Johnny, Teppi and
Franklin in front of the old
house. Elmo's great-grandson is
on the right.

(*Above*) Fritz with Carmen and
their daughter Anne Liese.

(*Left*) Carmen's first kitchen.

Carl with friend.

(*Above*) Tante Marga with Anton, the sea-lion who slept indoors.

(*Right*) Carl with Ani-Ani, the grandfather marine iguana who slept in the fireplace. The reptiles are harmless and feed on sea algae.

(*Left*) Mary, Tony and me in Nebraska shortly before moving west to California.

(*Below*) The year after Miss Bean. I'm fourth from the left in the top row.

Johnny.

Mary (*right*) and me collecting plants in the highlands.

Tony with his son.

Mary, Julian and their son Daniel.

(*Top, left*) Carmen and Fritz with their daughter on the edge of the bush. Shoes were reserved for goat hunting or treks to the highlands.

(*Top, right*) The 'muelle' – the dock where dinghies were tied up while we shopped in the village. The pole is the one from which hung the sign warning everyone to leave the marooned Casanova alone.

(*Below, left*) Carl on his boat, the *Indefatigable*.

(*Below, right*) Fritz and Carmen sawing timber dragged from the bush.

freckles moved up and down the mound like tiny slaves at a salt mine. Weevils. Miniature elephants in white booties. The flour sieve left behind by Harold was cloaked in cobwebs. I wiped it out with the tea towel but the bottom fell out, leaving a dry molehill of rust on the flour. The weevils continued to trek up and down, in and out of the white mountain. I hadn't put enough bay leaves in the flour bin. I'd never get rid of them now. Carmen always said weevils would flee if left out in the sun, but there was no sun today, so I dumped the flour into the yeasty mixture. The elephants dog-paddled to the sides of the bowl and climbed out. I kneaded it, then laid it in a greased bowl, covered it with a tea towel, put it on a table in a corner where the garua wouldn't reach and set the table legs into four tunafish tins full of paraffin against ants. I looked about me in dismay. Garua was indeed a blessing, but it was drifting through the windows all over our bedding, books, violin case and furniture.

Now all I needed was firewood. Belting on my knife, I grabbed the canteen and half filled it from the rain barrel. There was barely two inches in the bottom. Gus never took water, but then, he never got lost in the bush, and I might.

Carl had told me about 'the Donkey Lady' who went after firewood one day. Deeper and deeper she went, filling her *costal*, or sack, hoping to find some nice hard matazarna wood. But she did not mark her trail and she took no water. She picked up a piece of wood here and there, wandering further into the scrub. The cacti got taller, the trees thicker. Her donkey wearied of stumbling behind her; he got hungry. When finally she turned round to load the animal, she found he had wandered on home. 'We formed search parties. All over the bush we were looking. Nothing. Years later some hunters found her.' Carl had paused to sip his coffee.

'And?' I whispered.

He lowered his voice. 'A white skeleton sitting, how you say? Crosslegged? Crosslegged in a palo santo tree. Her bones blended in with the white branches, you see. She was sitting there just like she was waiting to catch a bus, I tell you. The hunters only spotted her because of the mass of hair blowing — only it wasn't her hair – it was pale green moss growing out of her skull!'

You never knew when to believe Carl.

Putting on my oldest canvas shoes and grabbing the woodsack, I hooked Gypsy's lead to his collar. He shrank back as I opened the back door and faced the lava monster waiting there. I found footholds and pulled Gypsy up behind me. Fifty yards of petrified coiled rope, swirls, bubbles and daggers extended along the barranco. Gypsy yanked away and tried to slip back home.

We entered the foggy bush through a spiderweb door. A shimmering net of raindrops lay over bare trees, cacti and blue lichen. A thousand years before, molten liquid had poured out right where I stood. Now the rocks lay cool and still, harmless until you tried walking on them. Then each took on its own perversity, wobbling left, slipping right, snapping at your ankles like a terrier or sending you headlong into thorny thickets. As we walked, bizarre shapes emerged from the black floor. There was no trail leading to where I needed to go. You chose the direction of the least spines, turned your face against whipping branches and bulldozed through.

I knew I must keep the sound of the sea pounding into the barranco to my right. Devil's Kitchen was far to my left – where Gus and Mary were now. She was safe. The King never got lost, though he was known to run off if he wounded a goat, chasing it for miles through the bush until he finished the job. Although she'd never admit it, Mary was probably gasping at this moment, trying to keep up with him, some bloody carcass strung over her shoulders, slipping on the wet rocks but unwilling to beg for a rest.

When Gypsy and I reached a river of arrow-sharp lava, he flatly refused to proceed. I gave in and carried him across. 'Just this once!' I warned. The book I had at home on dogs, in the chapter 'How to Choose Your Dog', said, 'Pointers are all-weather companions; stout-hearted, eager to please, a real friend of the active sportsman.' Gypsy whined when I set him down. I inspected his paws. How long did it take a dog's feet to adapt to such stuff? The lava had gouged the rubber soles of my shoes like a huge cheese-grater. Blood oozed from criss-crosses on my ankles. I dare not go too far I told myself, because my dough would be rising out of its bowl.

Suddenly my armpit was ablaze with a hundred cigarettes, then my breasts! Fire ants! Rain-washed from leaves, they were known to sneak down your shirt-front and spray their acid in the most sensitive places. I jerked my shirt up, flicking them from my skin, but they rolled up into tiny defensive balls the size of pinheads.

They began stinging around my waistband, on my back. I nearly broke my buttons getting undressed. I shook out all my clothes, but on close inspection they were still infested. I hadn't time to fool around. Was it so bad to walk naked in the bush where there was no one to see me but God. Was I so much worse than his other creatures? Garua washed over me and my skin sighed with relief. I tied my clothes high in a palo santo tree as a marker. I must not get lost. It would be indecent to greet a search party in the nude. I held the rough sack in front of my body against the spines, but soon the cat's claw thinned and was replaced by stands of palo santo trees. Here there was a bit of wood, most of it rotting. Gypsy began to relax as dead leaves and mulch cushioned his feet. The mist grew thicker, blotting out where we'd been and the way forward. I could hear no trace of the sea. I began to mark my trail, a pile of rocks here, crossed sticks in a tree. Ground finches stopped squabbling. Lizards waited in hiding to see where I was going to place my foot so they could jump to get there first, upsetting my balance and making me stumble. The scent of palo santo, holy stick, wafted stronger in the wet air. I broke off a twig and crushed it between my fingers. It made me think of Quito. Outside the cathedral the incense-seller balanced on his crutches, one hand raised, cheap paper alight, its pungent smoke spiralling into the thin air. Even on rainy nights he stood there as umbrellas rushed past, his medieval wares burning, cheering the crowds with scent as they splashed home in the cold.

I crushed the stick behind my ears and on my wrists, and stuffed more in my sack for that evening when we three would celebrate the arrival of the garua and my fresh bread, sitting before the fireplace, watching roast meat sizzle in the embers.

Darwin's finches of all beak sizes and shapes watched from the trees and hopped from branch to branch as we penetrated deeper and deeper into the unknown. Dark humus smelling of pipe tobacco collected in small pockets between the rocks. The lava gentled and turned to red earth as we entered the transitional zone between coast and rain forest. Here there was an abundance of firewood though it would be a long way to carry it home. Bushes sprouted leaves and Chinese lanterns dripped moisture. All the weeks we had been waiting for garua, seeing it appear on the horizon only to blow over our heads to the hills, it had been dragging its feet through this transitional zone just enough to get life started. Morning glory vines and wild cucumber draped over rocks and climbed tree trunks which, though temporarily stunted by the dry spell, now held up branches of tight-fisted leaves about to unfurl. Tiny blue blossoms like designs on English teacups sprouted hand in hand with wild cotton smelling of prairie flowers.

I listened for the sea but heard a mockingbird. A few more steps, I promised myself, then we would turn back.

Parting silvery curtains of lichen, I stepped into a small clearing. The sun shone weakly for a moment and illuminated there before me, like a picture in an old Bible, the most beautiful wild garden I had ever imagined.

Gus had once looked up from his writing and said, 'You, Hanna, will discover places, wonderful secret places in the bush, where no man or woman has ever walked since the birth of this island. You will find them only once – never again. Such is the wildness of the *Encantadas*. And, if you are a true Galapagueña, you will know when you find one. You will know.'

A part of my heart which had never before been touched began to ache for the innocence of Galapagos, where my kind had yet so little to be blamed for and still so much to learn.

What was I supposed to do now? Were mine the first footsteps ever to enter this garden? Finches eyed me from the trees. Lizards stuck like Bandaids to rocks and stumps, cocking their heads, waiting for an answer. Above my face a lemon-and-black spider peered down from her spinning. What did one say to creatures who had never seen a human before? One shout, one pugnacious stomp in the name of mankind, and this naked little god could shatter the spell forever. What wise words had the great Creator whispered to Adam when he rose from the dust to wander through Eden?

Gypsy sighed, sank in a patch of sunlight and gratefully licked his paws. I sat beside him, an eavesdropper in a silent world. A few moments passed. Then, suddenly, the yellow spider resumed her weaving and the finches returned to squabble over white glue-balls in the Mu Yu Yu tree. I had been accepted.

Had Father ever found such places while wandering in those early days? When he married Mother, had he taken her by the hand to some secret haunt and smiled at her surprise? Some moments in life needed to be shared.

My uncles rarely spoke of Hans. When the family story was told late at night to visiting yachtsmen, I noticed it was always 'we three brothers', not four, not five. I guessed it was easier that way. I was the daughter of a memory.

I drank from my canteen and poured some water in the cap for the dog. It was time to go. My bread would have risen. Midday sun was steaming through the garua clouds now, lacing the tops of trees with diamonds and drying the puddles. A yellow warbler landed on a twig so near I could see the breeze ruffle the rust-brown flecks on his bright breast. His black eye blinked and he threw back his head in song, while his paler mate splashed a bath in a cactus leaf. I nudged Gypsy and grabbed the woodsack. It felt rough on my shoulder, so I picked some long strands of lichen, inspected them well and draped them over my body like a soft gown.

I always seemed to be turning for one last look at places – it came from those days as a child when I'd stare out over the top of a U-Haul trailer, as another town, another rented house, another temporary school receded into our past. I took a long look at my secret wild garden. Perhaps I would never find it again. Perhaps no one would.

Finding the trail home was not difficult, for I had broken branches and upturned rocks as I went. I kicked rocks back into their holes as I passed. No one would ever retrace my footsteps.

I found plenty of wood once I really looked. My sack became almost too heavy to carry. Weaving drunkenly through the thickets, I stopped to catch my breath as we neared the coast and, with relief, spotted my clothes waving in the tree. But I rather liked my lichen garment and I was very dirty, so I tied my clean clothes round my waist, making sure all the ants were gone. It was when I hoisted the woodsack back on my shoulder that I felt the legs; millions of them. Caught in my hair! They weren't twigs because they moved! They thrashed in frenzy, going nowhere! I gave a yell and grabbed a stick. Gypsy stared in amazement. Thinking I was mad at him, he ran to hide behind a break-the-pot tree. Panicking, I stirred the stick in my scalp, twitching like a medicine man. I would have gladly unscrewed my head and thrown it over the cliff. I heard myself shouting, 'Get off! Get off! Get off!' To my horror the berserk creature slid down my neck, over my body and thudded to the ground. I backed away, flicking my hands over my skin, trying to erase the memory of the giant centipede legs. It was at least ten inches long and thick as a hosepipe. The monster had probably been stuck to the underside of a log I'd picked up, and then crawled out of the woodsack and up on to my head. Hurriedly I grabbed the sack, wanting only to get as far away as possible.

Gypsy's head, wreathed in leaves, emerged from his hiding place. I barely recognized him. He bristled, he growled, he quivered. His tail stretched out, his forepaw rose to meet his chest and he pointed! The centipede, taking no notice of this phenomenon, hastily searched for a hole.

Gypsy rose like a grizzly bear, slobbering and snarling. 'NO!' I shouted, lunging for his collar. The centipede rose valiantly, hairpin legs gleaming in the sun, pincers opening and snapping shut like maniacal elevator doors. 'NO!' I hollered. But Gypsy, so foolish, so brave, attacked. A soft-mouthed bird-dog hadn't a chance. The pincers lashed out, grabbed Gypsy's upper lip and hung on. The dog thrashed his head, yelping, his eyes bulging with pain. I grabbed my knife and tried to knock the beast loose. Again and again I slashed, fearful of stabbing Gypsy, who was now going wild. I slashed again and hit the centipede. It fell, running crazily into the undergrowth. I caught Gypsy, held him close and forced open his jaws. I let out a yell! The head still held on! I pried it off with the point of my knife, but one of the pincers remained embedded in the tender pink flesh. Gypsy's eyes closed wearily. His legs folded; the pith of his soul disintegrated with shock and self-pity.

'Urinate on sea-urchin stings.' Mother's words echoed. But how could I, at a time like this, get Gypsy to raise his leg on his own head?

Grabbing my sack I started off, urging, cajoling, begging him to follow. He moaned and staggered aimlessly behind me. Heartlessly, I trudged on. It wasn't so much further. 'You can make it. Come on, don't be such a sissy!' I glanced back. He sat on a rock, his face sagging like a puppy. When I reached his side, I saw his eyes were swelling shut, and his nose growing to an alarming proportion. I pulled him along, he stumbled and fell. I could stand no more. Slinging the sack over my shoulder, I hoisted Gypsy under my other arm, settled his rib-cage into the curve of my hip, revved up my legs and took off. I flew sweating, itching, bleeding, scratched and half-naked, down the barranco; over lava, through cat's claws, down and up, up and around. I stumbled, but the more I stumbled, the faster I went until with startled delight I realized I wasn't slipping so often or pausing for balance every time a lizard darted across my path. I had mastered the art of rock-flying!

Fifteen minutes later we were home. I lay Gypsy down on his mat and spooned rainwater past his puffy lips. My dough had risen up over the bowl and covered the small table. A mockingbird stood up to his ankles eating the last of the weevils and pooping on my Wonder White Bread.

I needed ice for swelling. That was ridiculous. No one in the entire archipelago had ice! A raw steak? We had no meat. Digging through our supplies I found an onion. Having nothing better, I sliced it in two and heated half over a candle. I placed this on his lip while heating the other half and kept this up for twenty minutes while the bird continued to poop on my dough. At last Gypsy's head sank on the mat, the worst of the swelling reduced. I dissolved one of Johnny's baby aspirins and forced it down his throat.

The mockingbird shrieked abuse as I sent him out the back door. Tante Carmen would have started her own baking by now, she'd be wondering where I was. Quickly I rinsed my filthy hands and punched the dough. It gave a mighty sigh and sank to one-third its size. I pulled and pushed, pulled and pushed like I'd seen Grandma Mari do. Then, cutting it into quarters, I squeezed out the bubbles and slammed it willy-nilly into four borrowed tins, black with someone else's expertise. Betty Crocker smiled benevolently from her glossy page. 'Dear Homemaker, here is an easy way to shape a pretty loaf!' Behind her would be a cake-mixer, hot and cold taps, a big refrigerator – inside it would be a large pitcher of cold strawberry Kool-Aid and ice – and she'd have newspaper on the floor because she couldn't housetrain her Pekinese.

I put my dough babies into a basket. They had a slightly grey tinge. I covered them with a cloth and, clutching the woodsack and the basket, I rushed out the door. I had gone halfway down the trail before I remembered to run back indoors and put some clothes on.

16

Bread

Chickens poked and pecked beneath Carmen's Mu Yu Yu tree and occasionally, lifting their feathered petticoats, made graceless leaps at what was left of well-picked turtle shell hanging there. A fawn-coloured nanny goat suckled her new kid with one foot in a pan of drinking water and raised her head to watch my ungainly approach.

With the bread basket in front of me and the woodsack on my back, I could not see where I was going at all, and sympathized with all the world's pregnant women. Usually I stubbed the ball of my foot on the 'bruising rock'; this time it was my toe, the big one I'd stubbed four times in the past quarter of an hour during my perilous journey down the barranco.

The bruising rock, with its tip only inches above ground, was rumoured to be the very foundation of the island. Carl said once that he, Gus and Fritz had tried to pry it out of the sand after stubbing their toes 132 times apiece. As the crowbar began to shift the rock, it was reported that the island was felt to shudder as far away as the Kastdalens'. It was said that if you moved that rock, our island would be cast adrift into the Humboldt Current and swept westward to Tahiti. Of course Gus swore the rock was enchanted and that it changed position every new moon. That was why every time you thought you had memorized where it was, you smashed your toes into it again on a moonless night.

I handed Carmen my bread and then turned to scrape my feet clean on a root. I should have washed my bumped toe in the sea, but the tide was way out and I was becoming so very, very tired.

'I'll just check and see if my bread is done yet.' She opened the oven door, slid out a dark German loaf and thumped it. The smell nearly made me faint. I'd had no lunch.

'The oven is nice and hot. I see you managed to find some good firewood,' said my aunt, looking into my woodsack and at the same time taking in my sweat-stained, rumpled clothing, scratched legs and bleeding toe.

Fiddi slumped over his arithmetic at the kitchen table. He folded his long music-stand legs and poked at a thorn long gone from his calloused heel. 'Yah, the oven is so hot it is burning a hole in my brain.' It was true his freckles were redder than usual. His lower lip protruded at the injustice of schoolwork on baking day, especially now that the garua had gone and the sun was blazing. He watched his mother move about the kitchen, hoping his sorry state would soon be noticed.

'Ah well, go on then,' Carmen sighed at last, wiping her hands on her apron. 'The garua has lifted. Go finish your little boat in the workshop. You can try her at the beach when the tide comes in.'

I could hear Uncle Fritz hammering away in his workshop. He could make anything; his graceful sloop *Nixie*, this house, these cupboards, beds, dinghies, a smokehouse, even the oven we were baking in. I opened the fire door and added wood to the glowing embers. A flat tin of coffee beans lay on the oven floor, turning golden brown. By the time they were dark, the kitchen would be filled with enough smell to make your stomach leap for joy. With growing optimism, I slid in two of my loaves. When next I opened that door the pale grey goo would have turned to wonderful golden bread. I hoped.

I wandered to the window and picked up the binoculars always kept there for sail-spotting. The day had cleared so much you could just see San Cristobal's outline behind Barrington. I focused on Anne and Maggie way out at the sea's edge, washing up their mother's baking dishes, ankle-deep in a tidal pool.

On the way back to the house, the girls paused often, dishpans rested on their slender hips, to look for shells. Then Maggie pointed towards Barrington. I followed her hand with the binoculars. A yacht! A large, white motor-yacht, dipping in the swells — too far away to see her flag. How beautiful she was. Now there would be news from the outside – new faces – maybe even a party. I had one clean dress – my hair, despite the horrid thing that had been in it, was basically clean, I could wear it in one long braid down my back. Shoes were a problem – mine were wearing out and had to be reserved for walking in the bush. Anyway, I was more comfortable barefoot.

'I thought I would make a cake to help use all that good heat,' Carmen was saying, unaware of the yacht. 'We're a bit low on flour since the *Carrier* didn't bring out our full order last time, so I've thrown in some oats.' The mixture looked a questionable orange-brown colour; a real Galapagos cake – everything thrown in and hope for the best.

'Did anyone ever die of a centipede bite?'

'Only geckos and cockroaches, as far as I know.'

'I guess a dog would survive all right.'

'Oh yah. Gypsy get bitten then?' she asked chirpily.

I was cautious. My uncles did not have a very high opinion of my dog in the first place. 'Well, I think he thought he was defending me, see.'

'Well, he's young yet. Give him time. So much to learn in Galapagos.'

I smiled. Carmen was always one step ahead of everyone else.

My cousins came in and took up the binoculars. 'I can't see the flag, she's rolling too much.'

Maggie took a look. 'I bet she's American. Remember that American who built his yacht around a grand piano because it was too big to fit down the hatch?'

'Maybe she's British. They tell such good stories.'

'I bet they are Australians and they'll swear the house down when they find there are next to no supplies to buy over in town. They'll drown their sorrows in Carl's punch.'

'Will there be a party, then?' I asked.

Carmen took the binoculars. 'She's a good size. I think she is American. Party? I suppose we could if they stay long enough and if they're our kind of people. Gus and Carl usually go out and make friends first, then we'll see. We should soon be getting oranges down from the hills to put in the punch to make the men dance,' she laughed.

'Well, that's another thing,' said Maggie, putting the dishes away. 'The English are such hopeless dancers. Have you noticed how whenever British yachtsmen come to our parties they hide in corners and talk of nothing but Seagull outboard motors?'

I knew this was going to inspire the question that had the bajucco humming lately.

'Oh, I hear Mary is teaching Julian how to dance up at your place?'

'Oh yeah,' I said casually. 'He brings his record player sometimes.' There followed a disappointed silence. The whole Point was buzzing over rumours of Julian's frequent visits up at the barranco. I tormented them with a long pause before adding, 'Of course, they don't only dance – sometimes Julian grabs the broom and tries to kill our rats. He goes crazy, sets the dog barking, jumping all over the room, breaking things – I've already had to mend the broom twice. Of course when there aren't any rats, they just make a fire and drink cocoa.'

There was a meeting of eyes in the room.

'Mary went hunting with Gus this morning.'

'We know,' they joined together, disappointed at the change of subject.

'She wants the exercise,' I added. 'She wants to whittle two inches from her waist.' A long pause. 'Though I happen to know Julian likes her the way she is.'

'Yes?'

'Well, he calls her Honey-Bun and she calls him Curly . . .'

Maggie grinned, opening her sewing-basket and laying out a new dress pattern.

Anne met her mother's eyes as she went outside. She returned with the baby goat. Soft brown like its mother, at once it set out at a gallop to explore the house, hoofs clicking on the wooden floor. I resolved not to tell them that Julian was now kissing my sister goodnight after he helped her toss dead rats over the barranco.

'Well, hunting will improve the figure all right,' said Tante Carmen, extricating the kid from the lower cupboard where it was knocking over pans. It stamped its hoof impatiently and made a sideways leap with a mid-air twist. Yes, I thought, admiring my aunt's slender waist as she put the goat outside; hunting, fishing and keeping up with Fritz and his brothers all these years hadn't done her any harm at all.

Outside, along the shore, the tide began to creep in, casting a seaweed smell that mingled with roasting coffee, bread and cake. The fragrance wandered around the kitchen, then out again, catching Fiddi, Martin and Johnny just as they ran past towards the beach, balsa boats under their arms. The next moment they were through the door, remembering at the last moment to wipe off their sandy feet. Squeezing behind the table, they watched in awe as tins went into and came out of Carmen's oven.

My loaves baked to perfection; domed, high and crusty. I shook them from their tins and set them on their sides to cool in the window-sill. Carmen shook the coffee beans to see if they were evenly roasted. Then she tested her yellow cake and put it beside my bread. Maggie folded her sewing and began to grind coffee. Her slender brown arm cranked with a steady rhythm. Anne took the plastic bag of milk from the cupboard. She always mixed the milk. Always. I averted my gaze down to my big toe. The nail was split down the middle. It oozed blood and sand. Anne's fork whipped and whipped in the plastic cup. I knew it was the red cup – she always used the red cup. She added a drop of water from the pitcher. Then more milk powder. I couldn't watch... The fork slowed as it struggled through the thick paste. I hated it – I hated what came next; the silence as she licked the fork – all that horrid thick milk paste stuck in the prongs. Sometimes my cousin ate dry milk straight from the bag. I had learned to not watch her do that – it was so fascinatingly awful. I squeezed my toe. Blood dripped out. I said 'ouch!' Anne said 'Ummmmmm', raking off the prongs with her teeth and smacking her lips. She couldn't help it – she'd never drunk cold bottled milk straight from the doorstep, with two Oreo cookies on a blue willow-pattern saucer after school. You couldn't really expect her to know how awful milk powder tasted.

Uncle Fritz filled the doorway. It was nearly four o'clock. He grinned, taking in the fresh coffee, baking, his pretty daughters and hungry boys. He nodded my way. I blushed. It was a lot from my silent uncle.

Taking his carved pipe from the abalone shell on the window ledge, he aimed the binoculars on the approaching yacht, said something in German about how many knots she was doing, then joined the boys behind the table, propping one bare foot on the cushion so that the boar-hunting scar on his shin glowed in the afternoon light. He lit the pipe, puffing first with his lips, then clamping the stem between his back teeth. We had an old sketch at home, one that Mother had made of Hans, less than a year before I was born. It was dated in faint pencil in the bottom right-hand corner. This tall, confident man puffing on his pipe looked more like Father than his two brothers; the chiselled lips, eyes that dipped down at the ends, the long nose with a slightly bulged tip, the determined jaw.

'Yohanna? Yohanna,' Tante Carmen was peering into my face, 'will you have some coffee? Nice and fresh.'

I thanked her, but I had to go if I was to beat Mary home by sundown. Besides, I wanted to be there when that yacht came in; our first yacht since moving into the cliff house. I wrapped up my bread, leaving one loaf as a token for the use of the oven; the island way. Before I left I looked again through the binoculars. The ship was flying the Stars and Stripes. She was quite large, over a hundred feet long and just sailing past Jensen, using the chart no doubt, and keeping Carl's pink roof to port.

I managed to miss the bruising rock on the way back, stopping now and then to watch the yacht and peering down at my newborn bread, the perfume of which nearly made me giddy. As I strolled past Traudi's I could hear her singing in German. It was something by Verdi – the slaves' chorus, I thought.

I moved on, humming the tune. Rounding the sandy bit behind Carl's house, I stopped singing. He was bent over a dinghy, holding a bucket of paint. I blushed. What was I going to say? What would he say? My skin tingled at the way he shone bronze in the afternoon sun. I stepped forward, nearly tripping over one of his iguanas.

'Ahoy! Who goes there?'

I tried to look nonchalant.

'What's in the basket – no – let me guess.' He sniffed. 'Bread,' he sighed. 'Wonderful bread. When did I last smell such beautiful bread? Was it 1937? 1947 maybe – still before you were born, no?'

Pain. Why did he have to remind me of my youth? I pretended to ignore him but he blocked my path, brandishing his paint-brush like a pistol.

'Now, if you give me a piece of bread, I might let you pass without trouble.' His eyes teased.

'You are as crooked as that water-line you are painting,' I said shyly.

'Don't change the subject,' he growled, 'or I might keep your bread and fling you to the sharks which I keep right there in that lagoon beside my house.'

'Aha, but if you throw me to the sharks I won't be able to bake any more bread.' I lifted the cloth. 'Want to see it? It's still warm!'

'I could not bear it.'

'But I'm going to give you some.'

'Oh no, Yohanna, I was only joking. Don't you know when I am joking?' He looked embarrassed, actually vulnerable!

I insisted. Clucking like a hen, I sat down on a closed can of paint and cut off a nice thick wedge for both of us with my knife.

'Too bad we have no butter,' I said, handing him his piece.

'You mean that yellow stuff what is coming from cows?' he said wistfully.

We chewed in public-library silence. The bread was warm, tender and delicious. The Duke's eyes focused on a memory of some other place, some other time, perhaps some other girl my age, I thought jealously.

'Did I ever tell you the story of the Turnip-and-Vitamin Cake? No?' His eyes widened with astonishment. I told myself to relax. Gypsy would be all right for a little while longer. Carl leaned against a boulder and I sank down in the soft sand.

'It was 1935. Already Germany was unrecognizable from what we knew as boys. Work was hard to find. We boys were in trouble for not joining the Youth Movement . . . People were staring at us all the time. So, you know already the old story of how our parents sold the house and helped us buy the *Marie* and sneak out and so on and so on. But first, before we left, my mother says to me, "Well Carl, you are the only one knowing how to cook, so you must take care of your brothers."' He smiled. 'And you know that is still what I am doing today, eh? Well, the important thing about cooking is to make something with nothing and make it tasty. You learn a lot here in these *Encantadas* where you cannot just row to a store and find what you are wanting. If there is nothing around, you just use your imagination.'

'That's what I do all the time when I cook.'

'Quite right, by Jove. Back to 1935. After we rescued a man, Heinrich Kubele in the North Sea – that is another story for next time – we had seven people on board the *Marie*. Off the Cornish coast we hit a helluva storm, as you have heard. No warning. By Jove, the waves were taking us twenty feet high and then dropping us sideways into a deep trough. The wind was gale force ten at least and the main mast snapped like a little stick, so the sheets got tangled in the rigging and the weight was dragging us over to port and we knew we would sink and so on. Well, that's when Fritz, only oh, about sixteen then, takes an axe and chops the mast down. We heave it over just in time, for we were about to crash on the rocks where so many fine ships have been lost. As you must know, there used to be wreckers – wicked people with lanterns – but that is another story.

'Now then, we safely put into St Mawes, a little fishing village. The authorities said, stay as long as you like but you can't work. Sure, we had some money put by, but not enough for repairing the *Marie* and eating – seven people on board eat a lot. Well, after our picture came out in the newspaper, we were invited here and there for cocktail parties. You ever been to a cocktail party? You stand around and talk about the weather and painting and tell amusing stories and smile and try not to stare at the trays what they are passing around. And when the tray comes to you you must politely say, "Oh, just one if you insist!" The English, they like good manners and so do we, but not so much when your stomach is growling. Well, in this way we made many friends.

'One night our hostess puts on the gramophone, an old record. Gus starts to hum along. Soon all of us, with tears in our eyes, join him, thinking of home. Our hostess says, "Oh, you know this song?"

'Oh, many times we have sung it! It is our favourite from home! *Stenka Razin*, the Russian pirate and the princess. Well, right there we acted out the story for her. She says, "This is fantastic! You must give a show in the village hall ... invite everyone and earn the money for your new mast!"

'It was a good idea. So Hein drew some posters:

3 SEPTEMBER 1935
ANGERMEYER BROTHERS TONIGHT: *STENKA RAZIN*

'I never imagined there was so much talent in that little village! They made beautiful costumes. We had a chorus. The daughter of some wealthy yachting people, who was very pretty, dark, you know – offered to be our princess. We even built a ship on stage.

'Now Stenka Razin, the pirate, had a loyal crew. But he fell for this princess and there comes the problem, for he must decide between that lovely girl and the sea and his crew! Gus was Stenka, of course. He looked the part, as you can imagine. The day before the performance, in rehearsal, he takes the princess in his arms and kisses her – and what a kiss. By Jove, that was some kiss! Anyway, the crew wait for his decision – them or her. Stenka decides. He must throw her overboard – phhhhhhtttt – on a mattress hidden below. So everything goes perfectly and Gus cries, "Mother Volga, take her! You never had such a treasure!" To the crew he joyfully sings, "Boys! Sing – Vodka and Life!" Then twenty ladies, one of them an opera singer, join in the chorus. A second time they rehearse, and a third. Gus is so good! He is perfect, I tell you and gets into the part. But the fourth time he cries, "Mother Volga, take her!" he throws the princess too far! She – how you say? flips! Misses the mattress and nearly breaks her arm, poor girl!

'The whole village is hearing about this and the next night, everyone, but everyone, is crowding into the village hall, a little theatre up a very old cobbled street. The children must sit in the windows, for there is no room even for one more. All the townspeople hold their breath when the time comes because the princess now has a bandaged arm – she insisted she wanted to go on with the show, no? Maybe she wanted to be kissed by a pirate again, eh?

'So when we come to the part of "Mother Volga, take her!" Gus wraps his arms around the little princess and kisses her for the last time – but he feels so guilty about yesterday that he lifts her – and oh, so tenderly plops her down over the side. Then there is a roar of applause and everyone shouts out, "The pirate is a gentleman!" *Un caballero*! Ha, ha, ha!'

A plump marine iguana waddled up, stopped and smelled my basket.

'They know it's time for the dog to eat his rice. I should go. It must be past coffee time.'

I plucked off a piece of bread and gave it to the iguana, a sacrifice to keep the flow going.

'You haven't told me about the Vitamin-and-Turnip Cake!'

'I haven't told you – *Mensch*, you are right! Well, we put the *Marie* into a little boatyard and got enough money together to buy her a new stick. But still we did not have enough to eat. Soon Christmas was coming, you know, the time when everyone eats special treats. I thought, I really must serve these guys something good. But how? Well, around St Mawes there were many turnip fields. I thought, turnips are not so bad if you prepare them properly and the farmer had so many, so I took some home.

'In the ship's saloon of the *Marie* I set the table with all our best china. It looked very elegant. I thought, *Mensch*! I must make them a cake. But with what? Into Hein's cabin I went. He

226

and Greta were living on shore. I looked into a little box which had this and that. There was a big bottle of a kind of vitamin powder. You know, in those days you did not take a pill, you took powder and mixed it with water. I tasted some. "Not bad," I thought. I had no time to read the label how to mix it and so I just added some water and with my hands went pit-pat-pit-pat and soon I baked it and we had a little cake. I called the boys in and they admired the table and said how grand it all was. Then I served each a half of a turnip with my special-recipe mustard sauce which I will give to you some day. It was *delicioso*!

'But! Then I bring in the surprise, the grand finale no one was expecting. My cake. My brothers could not believe their eyes! "Where did you get that from?" they ask. I say, "Don't ask questions, just eat. Enjoy!" And we did.

'So later that night we were all invited down to the town for mince pies and sherry and cocktails. There were trays and trays of little lady sandwiches, how the English like them with the edges cut off and not much inside. We were saying all the time, "Yes, thank you, no, thank you." We went from party to party, at last getting full.

'It was moonlight when we finally started walking back to the *Marie*. The four of us had to walk through the turnip fields. It was very still. I began to feel a bit queer. I could hear my stomach growl. I thought it was just because it was full for a change. I looked around for my brothers, but they had all disappeared! I could just make out dark shapes amongst the turnip plants. Someone groaned out, "*Mensch*! Man! What did you put in that cake?" They said other things too, but as you are a lady we will not say more.

'Well, so it was all the way back, dashing in and out of the fields. When we reached the ship which was slipped up on land, we did not feel any better. They made me go and get the bottle.

'"But it's just vitamins!" I said. "Vitamins are good for you – you only ate vitamin cake. I tell you, turnip-and-vitamin cake!"' But they were looking at me with evil in their hearts. I showed them the bottle. Hans turned up the lamp and read aloud: "... one teaspoonful daily for adults ... *Do not exceed prescribed dose!*" he yelled. I tell you I would have been a dead man but the vitamins saved me; just as they were about to grab me, they all groaned and clutching their stomachs, ran off into the turnips again! Ha, ha, ha. Oh my, I can still see their bare bottoms out there in the moonlight!'

He rose, still chuckling, and daubed a bit more blue on to the dinghy's water-line with a stubby old paintbrush. The blue ran down over the freshly painted white. He would go over it again later with white and cover the blue drips.

'And if the white then runs down over the blue when you turn her right side up?' I asked smiling.

'Oh, that won't matter, she will be in the water, so no one will see.'

'I guess that yacht is anchored by now,' I said casually.

'Yacht? Yacht? What yacht?'

I laughed. 'She's American. I saw her flag.'

'By Jove, she's American, eh? I'd better get changed.'

Carl waded through his iguanas, who were still waiting for the dog's rice. He limped more than usual.

'This knee!' he called over his shoulder. 'It's getting old ahead of the rest of me.' He stopped and turned. 'That reminds me. Did I ever tell you the story of the white-slave traders? No? It all started when I was in hospital in Denmark with this knee. Come anytime, anytime. I will tell you. I will show you my paintings. You still sketching?'

I nodded.

'Good, good. My older brother Hein used to say to Hans and me – "Draw everything – everything you see."' He grinned and waved goodbye. I picked up my bread basket. As his wide, tanned shoulders disappeared around the bougainvillaea I could hear him already calling, 'Ani – ani – ani – ani –'

17

Cocktails and Carcasses

Gulls screamed their old-men-on-the-porch laugh when I neared our landing. A brown pelican hurried a few feet overhead to join the frigate birds dive-bombing for titbits thrown up at them. Lucrecia's five cats joined me on the trail, tails pointed straight up, their noses taking them to fresh meat. Mary was home from the hunt.

'Hanna!' Gus called up from the lower steps, waving a bloody knife. 'There you are! We were just thinking you must have got lost out in the bush.'

A goat carcass hung from a branch stuck in the barranco. My sister, considering her arms and legs were flecked with blood, looked quite composed as she helped Gus skin it, though her nose was corrugated.

'Did you have to go far?' I asked, avoiding the headless spectacle by looking intently at the yacht. Nothing much was happening out there, only the port captain inspecting their papers. I wondered if the yacht's captain knew he was expected to give the official a bottle of Johnny Walker.

Mary threw a scrap up to the gulls. 'Naw, we nearly tripped over this buck this morning. He must have followed some of the house-goats home.'

'Then where have you been all day?'

'Sitting in the shade of a cove this side of Turtle Bay, cooling our feet and discussing the origin of the universe. The place was teeming with turtles and sharks. We only took that there.' A burlap sack sat motionlessly on the bottom step.

'That's for you to clean,' said Gus, straightening up. 'Good practice and you won't get many more chances.'

'Gus says there aren't as many sea-turtles in the pools lately.'

'Used to be plenty. Some months ago I saw a wild pig dig up eggs on the beaches as soon as the old female laid them. The few that hatch have to get past mockingbirds, frigates, gulls. Last year I saw a nest of – probably fifty baby turtles eaten as soon as they ran for the sea. I caught about a dozen in my hat and put them in the water, but there were sharks waiting for those – no telling how many made it to the open sea.'

'What's in the basket?' asked Mary, her nose still crinkled.

'A surprise.' I lifted the cloth and peeked at my tame and domestic day's work. 'Can I have that goat skin or does somebody else want it?'

'You don't want another smelly buck skin, Hanna!'

'I do! I like it.' It smelled of musk and palo santo trees. In a month's time when I dragged myself out of bed to go to school, my toes would sink first thing into tangible proof of these past two months. I ran my hand down the buck's fawn hide, avoiding the ruby droplets that gathered along the slit belly, sorry that vegetarianism was impossible in Galapagos.

'Come, Hanna, here is a treat to put hair on your chest! Heh, heh, heh!' He held up a blueish-red goat liver. Cutting off a bit, he threatened to eat it raw before my eyes, which I shut in time. When I opened them the meat was gone. He grinned wickedly, pretending to wipe his chops. 'Better than chocolate! You should try some.' But I knew better. I had heard the smack of the pelican's beak as he caught the titbit mid-air.

'You'd better get started on that turtle.'

I ran up to the house to stow my bread and get my knife. Gypsy whined at the door. His face looked awful, eyes nearly shut, nostrils distended, lips puffy. I gave him another half a baby aspirin in some rainwater, and massaged his face. He sank back on his mat and slept.

I grabbed a knife, ran back to the landing and retrieved the goat skin just as Mary removed the last bit. She'd done a good job, nicking it only once. I folded the skin in a square. Later I would rub salt into it and tomorrow nail it to Gus's wooden house.

'Next time, Hanna, you and I go hunting, no?' He was talking to me!

'When?' I asked, covering my trepidation with a nonchalance even I did not consider convincing.

'Well, with all this meat we won't have to go hunting for some time. Why, you so bloodthirsty you want to go right away, eh?'

'No, no – I was just asking.' I stuck my hand in the bag and dragged the turtle out. It was heavy. I couldn't think how they had carried a turtle and a goat through the bush when a bag of wood had been enough for me. At the water's edge, Gus showed me how to start. Then he returned to the goat while Mary took a rest. Blowfish formed a half-circle in wait. The belly plate had been removed, and thankfully, the head. I didn't think I could bear to look at a turtle's dead eyes. I poked a flipper with the point of my knife. It waved back! Slowly, back and forth, back and forth like someone wishing me *bon voyage*!

'It's not dead! You haven't killed the poor thing properly!' I wailed.

'Nonsense girl, they always do that – it's their nervous system – like chickens when you chop off their heads they sometimes run around. *Mensch*, girl, you look pale. If you're going to be sick, be sick in the sea down there. Look, I shot it and chopped its head off – it can't be alive.'

I was just tired, that was all. I splashed my face with sea-water and got started.

Johnny appeared, carrying a balsa boat he said he'd made 'all by himself' with Fiddi's help. It was a good first effort, though the mast was crooked and it was top heavy. I feared it would sink the first time he tried it but he, like the other boys, would learn with practice and someday he would be building real dinghies.

'That's a splendid tuk-tuk boat!' said Mary.

'It's not a crummy old tuk-tuk boat, it's an American yacht like that one.'

'I see Carl is out there already.' The Duke had changed his paint-shorts and put on a shirt against the late-afternoon breeze. He climbed aboard, shaking hands with the Captain.

They disappeared below, presumably for a bit of coffee with rum.

I would never get used to cutting up twitching meat. Did anaesthetized human bodies quiver under a surgeon's scalpel? I held my breath, but after cutting out the liver, a delicacy, and feeding useless scraps to the waiting birds, crabs, fish and cats, I saw beauty in the open carapace. The organs fit together like a cubist painting: the flippers perfectly designed for life in the cool sea.

Those going down to the sea in ships,
They are the ones who have seen the works of God.

By the time I had filled two buckets with meat, the sun was balanced on the sea's edge like a monstrous orange balloon, turning the bay golden, pink and mauve. A powerful motor started up. Out at the yacht, Carl's dinghy was gone. People were climbing down into the yacht's tender. I thought of hiding too late.

'Hi! Howyadoin?' they chorused. They were not the usual windblown, khaki-clad, crinkle-eyed, barefoot yacht's people. These were dressed too well.

A bearded young man holding the bow-line called, 'We were told we would find the King of Galapagos and two princesses over here.'

'You thought so, eh?' rumbled the King, straightening up and sharpening his big bloody knife on the cliff face.

'Is this where we land? We're heading for the Duke's tame iguanas before it gets too dark,' said the young man.

'Yah, you better wait till morning. They will be going to sleep now.'

'Do they really sleep on the roof?' asked a woman in a yellow pantsuit.

'Yah, yah, you see, my brother has powers,' Gus growled. 'He has tamed the dragons but I warn you, those are the only tame creatures on these Enchanted Isles, heh, heh, heh.' The Americans looked nonplussed. I was tempted to tell them not to worry, that he spoke that way to everyone. I tried to rinse some of the blood off my hands and pushed the hair from my eyes, wishing my braids weren't so frizzy. 'Oh, look, they're killing something!' exclaimed a large lady. 'Here, Howard, take a picture – hurry the light's fading!'

'Don't rock the boat, Gladys!' shouted Howard. 'Just siddown willya? For Pete's sake, where's my light meter?'

One by one they got out of the boat, posing beside our bloody work, asking questions slowly, to make sure we understood. Gus refused good naturedly to pose. He once told me never to pose for a camera. 'Make the photographer step into your shoes and walk around in your life. They get better pictures and you won't feel like such a donkey.'

The *Wanderer* was an expensive, glossy motor-yacht; about 130 feet in length; one of those where the passengers pay for the privilege of working their way across the Pacific to Tahiti, island-hopping. Most of them had little yachting experience, so it was the adventure of a lifetime. They didn't have long and they wanted to see the best of Galapagos.

Gus pointed to the hills, quite eerie in the waning light. Up there were the giant tortoises if they wanted a six-hour hike. Or they could go to Plazas for sea-lions, land iguanas and tropic birds. There were blue-footed boobies on Daphne, red-footed boobies on Tower, flamingos on Floreana, hundreds of marine iguanas and maybe a few penguins on Isabela; flightless cormorants on Fernandina, fur seals on James. My head swam as he told them of the outer islands, the mysterious places I had yet to visit. They might as well have been on the other side of the world.

The young man took a small pad and pencil from his pocket and made notes. Then they clambered back into the tender and took off for Carl's house. I knew they would be too late for the iguanas, but Carl would paint a few seascapes in his studio by lamplight while they watched. He would give the painting away with a story. Almost out of earshot the Americans shouted an invitation to us for drinks on board at 8.30. Mary accepted, waving her knife.

Just before the sun plopped into the sea, Gus sent Franklin and Ana Eva off on rounds to deliver meat. He said he might go out to the yacht later on but he had some writing to get ready for me to type. I promised to come the next morning.

Mary and I sat down to try and wash off the blood, sweat and billy-goat smell. The sea was green and heavy with phosphorescence; it swirled like a deep Milky Way at our feet. I dipped my hand in, gathered diamonds on my wrists and let them sparkle against the *Wanderer*'s lights until Mary pointed out how many sharks were cruising past, attracted by turtle guts and goat scraps. She left me there, scooping up water and trying to flush the sand from my stubbed toe by the light of a torch.

I heard the tuk-tuk-tuk before I saw the little fishing boat. Then I recognized the *Corsario* leaving the bay. Her skipper often brought sacks of oranges over from San Cristobal. He was deeply tanned, with a big smile and white teeth. He shone a torch on me when I called '*Buenas noches.*'

'*Muy buenas!*' several voices called back.

I shone my light on them. There was a woman in a pink dress and headscarf. One or two figures behind her waved. A young man standing on the bow in a sailor's cap did not wave.

'*A donde?*' I called.

'*A San Cristobal, no mas.*' The young man's mother was dying, shouted the captain, rather crassly I thought, considering. I didn't know what to say so I just waved, adding, 'Bring us some nice oranges next time you come, no?' The captain said sure, he would, real nice ones. They tuk-tukked out into the night.

Back at the house, Mary and Johnny gasped in astonishment at the three loaves of bread I produced from my basket. My plan to make a cosy fire and roast succulent bits of meat was scrapped when Mary said we barely had time to get ready. I had to admit I wasn't as hungry for meat as I had been; the turtle flesh in the bucket still jiggled unappetizingly when poked. But I said Carl had told me all about cocktail parties. Why didn't she and Julian go out? I'd just as soon stay home with Johnny and the dog.

To start with, she said, Julian was on watch that night, as the *Beagle* was dragging her anchor, so he couldn't come. Secondly, she said, seeing straight through me, no one, least of all that splendidly handsome young man from the yacht, would mind my wrinkled shirt, bare feet, bloody toe or the merthiolated crisscrosses all over my legs. I mustn't lose all the social graces I'd acquired at school; they would stand me in good stead. One day I would thank her for insisting I come along. Gypsy would be all right. Johnny would come with us. We wouldn't stay late.

I cut a large slice of bread for each of us and took down the sack of emergency cheese from the rafters. Such simple fare looked delicious in Cinderella movies but in real life, despite the romantic lamplight, it lacked an apple, a pickle and a piece of salami, the last of which we had finished two weeks previously, after trying for days to catch a fish off the barranco.

We changed into our least rumpled clothes. I combed John- ny's hair, Mary braided mine so tight my eyes pulled. Gypsy could not have been suffering too much torment, for when I immersed my hand in the turtle meat and administered a chunk to his face to reduce the swelling, he gulped it down before it could work. Poor Gypsy. We could hear him howling as we rowed out into the coloured lights of the *Wanderer*.

Before we climbed on board, I gripped the ropes of the boarding ladder and said, 'We going to let them know we're American?'

'I'm not going to blow a horn, if that's what you mean!'

'But promise me you're not going to do your Russian peasant accent.'

'Don't be silly. Just get out, will you? This dinghy has a leak and it feels like it's going to tip over!'

'Yeah, but then are we going to let them know we aren't real island girls at all?'

'You think they're going to ask for our life story the minute we set foot on board? Will you get out? I can see a big shark fin out there and I tell you, this dinghy is taking water.'

I got out, wincing as I slipped on the slimy bottom step, banging my sore toe and skinning my knee.

'I don't believe it...' Mary muttered under her breath. As she tied up to the deck cleat I heard Frank Sinatra.

Moonlight in Vermont . . .

'If you do an accent I won't admit we're related. I swear I won't.'

. . . ski trails on a mountain side . . .

'All right, all right. Is your knee bleeding all over the deck? Wow, look at that, I think it's teak.'

. . . Telegraph cables they sing . . .

'We going to mention Arlington Street?' I whispering, daubing my knee with spit.

. . . People who meet in this romantic setting . . .

'Look, I don't care who knows about Arlington Street. All that doesn't matter any more. What matters from now on is where and what we are.'

. . . Evening summer breeze, the warbling of a meadowlark . . .

She sounded ready to tell Johnny. Now I was not.

Everything aboard the ship gleamed and smelled of Spic 'n' Span. To gain composure, I went into the loo. There was a Pine-Forest deodorizer stuck under the seat, soft pink paper and a sign by the shower: 'Save Water – Bathe with a Friend.' I washed my knee from the tap and then cupped my hand and drank some. It was fresh. I hadn't drunk tap-water for over three years. Even in Quito Ophelia had to boil the drinking water. I slurped a bit more. Then I made the mistake of looking in the mirror. Oh, why had I come? I was so tanned I looked dirty. My face was sprinkled with freckles. I didn't look sweet sixteen at all. I looked like Tom Sawyer in braids. I undid them, twisting my hair into one long braid, borrowing bobby pins from the sides, and made a French bun on the top of my head with two spit curls on my cheeks.

Everyone was gathered on the open-air lounge in the stern. A jovial black man who turned out to be the cook, pushed an aluminium trolley loaded with Ritz crackers, Philadelphia cream-cheese spreads, sweet gherkin pickles, smoked oysters and pretzel sticks. The captain manned a bar gleaming with bottles and glasses of every size and shape. I sat down in a deck chair so deep I feared I would never escape and observed thirty or more passengers.

Smoked oysters only served to whet my increasing appetite. I thought back to Carl's Cornish tale of, 'Oh no, thank you', and 'oh, just one more'. Fortunately the cook took a shine to Johnny and wheeled the trolley our way often, laughing when Johnny helped himself to handfuls of peanuts and cashews in spite of my scoldings.

I'd forgotten how open and friendly Americans were. They plied us with questions, but I soon realized I had a meagre supply of scintillating answers.

'Don't you young things get lonely way out here?' asked a big-boned man in a Dodger's baseball cap and Hawaiian shirt.

'What do you do for fun?'

I said we were doing up our house and had just put in windows and hoped soon to start on a new privy. The response was muted.

'I study algebra some days, and practise my violin. The three of us read the Bible at night.'

Ice clinked in glasses. '. . . And I baked bread this afternoon.' They waited for more. I said that we spent a lot of time hauling water across the bay.

'But that'll get better now that the garua has come,' I added quickly.

'The what?'

'Garua. It comes most mornings, starts on the beach, then works its way up to the hills.'

'Did she say gorilla?' muttered the baseball man to the lady I knew was Gladys.

'I dunno – do they have gorillas here?' she hissed back.

There followed a silence as we crunched pretzel sticks. Mary, her social graces being less tarnished, saved me.

'Oh, you wouldn't believe how much there is to do. We sketch a lot and watch birds, and we fish, swim and snorkel.' (I was relieved she didn't tell them we wore jam jars on our eyes.)

'We play volleyball on the beach almost every afternoon and sometimes make a bonfire on the beach with dancing. The ladies have a little musical group – everyone plays something.'

'And what about this little guy here?' said the captain, bouncing Johnny on his knee and making him turn green – too many peanuts. Why do kids close up just when you need them to be charming?

'My little – brother paints pictures every morning and dresses like a pirate –'

'Paul Regret!' shouted Johnny like a precocious little brat.

'– er, like Paul Regret every morning and delivers these fantastic pictures to our neighbours –' Our lives were sounding more dull and aimless by the minute.

'But where you gonna find husbands way out here?'

'We don't need husbands!' I blurted out.

'Oh, we'll worry about that when we're older,' finished Mary diplomatically.

Then they asked it; the question I'd been dreading.

'So, were you born out here?'

I told them.

'Oh, you're American then! Howard, they're American!' Gladys belted out, like we'd committed treason.

'Then why are you way out here?' I never knew how to even begin answering that one. Whereabouts in the States had we lived? What did we miss most from 'back home'? Funny how they always assumed the States was home.

I knew what I wanted to say, but I also knew toilet paper was a vulgar subject at a party so, thinking how long it had been since we'd eaten vegetables –

'I miss green beans,' I answered.

Someone handed me a tall glass with a paper parasol spearing a maraschino cherry as Mary, seeing a chance wasted, took over. I stared in open admiration as she listed 'egg-powder, best-sellers, Bandaids, tinned peaches, Ponds Dry-Skin Cream and number 3B art pencils.' Still hungry, I wished I'd added cold milk, Oreo cookies, butter, blackberry jam, crinkled potato chips, white salt, shoes and a new dog collar.

★

There was a big fuss as Carl and Marga came aboard, both awesomely elegant. My aunt's red hair dazzled under electric lights. They wore city shoes I'd never seen before.

The young man brought me another pink-parasol drink. He introduced himself as Franz Harper-Stubenrauch. He was half German, half English. His mother was a dress designer in London. Franz was an artist living in San Francisco.

A blonde in shimmering green pyjamas sat down next to me. Her name was Monica. Her face was expertly made up and I noticed her nails hadn't scrubbed any decks lately. I became acutely aware of my freckles, torn fingernails, iodined legs and bloody toe. I folded my feet one over the other as I'd seen Franklin and Teppi do on social occasions. But then I took a closer look at Monica's feet, difficult to do without being rude. They were rather pudgy, white and shapeless. I looked back at mine. My ankles weren't weak. My feet weren't 'funny', as the school nurse had claimed. All those tears over wearing clumpy oxfords. All that nagging about never going to wear high heels and twisting ankles – and being careful! I had hammer toes – rock-gripping strong brown toes and feet. My uncle's feet. I looked at my hands. Mother had a sketch of those hands. Father's hands.

Courageously, I unfolded my feet and stuck them out. My legs were brown, the hair blonde. There were three cat-claw spines embedded on the shin. An old scar glowed on one knee, the latest scrape oozed on the other. Mary was right. Arlington Street didn't matter any more.

Monica swirled her martini, poking the olive with a finger wearing a large diamond. She smelled of hairspray and clean sheets, and she was downright nosey: how old was I, and where had I gone to school, and how old was Uncle Carl and what did he do for a living and where did he meet Marga and when had he and his brothers left Germany and why? I thought at first that she was merely another female adrift under the Duke's charismatic spell, but Franz looked uncomfortable and tried to turn the conversation to giant tortoises. Annoyed, Monica dispatched him to fetch her cigarettes. When he had gone she asked if my uncles had left Germany before or after the war and had they been back since and were there any other Germans living on the islands? She reminded me of Mrs Pearce. When Franz returned with her gold case and lit her cheroot she even squinted through the smoke like her. Amused, I dodged Monica's questions as artfully as I had our neighbour's six years previously.

I was thankful when Carl expertly took over the evening's entertainment, telling the story of how they caught their first live pig up in the hills and how she weighed so much that when they swung her on a pole, their shoulders ached so they had to make cushions with their clothes and walked home naked through the bush.

Oddly, Franz remained by my side. He asked if I'd ever had Irish coffee San Francisco style. I pretended to have to think a moment. Coffee, I thought, sounded like a good idea. I had drunk two parasol things and was feeling lopsided.

When we reached the bar Franz said quietly, 'Watch out for Monica. Don't answer too many questions.' Mixing cream and liquid from an amber bottle, he whispered, 'Some of us on board think she's with the CIA.' I presumed this was some kind of department store but humoured him, promising to be cautious. He poured our coffee into two white ship's mugs. It was very sweet. My legs felt strange when we went to lean against the ship's railings with our mugs.

The moon came up an apricot colour, silhouetting the cacti on shore, and weaving gold into the calm sea. It's strange what tropical moonlight does. I began to talk; feelings well guarded and rarely divulged suddenly expressed to a man I barely knew. I even told him about the wild horses – and immediately felt a fool. But no, he insisted, he would love to see wild horses – could we not go up to the hills the next morning to look for them? He in turn said this cruise had helped him see things clearly for the first time in his twenty-six years. (Oh no, I sighed to myself, he was ten years older than I.) His dream was to work hard for the next year, buy a boat, probably a trimaran, and sail the world with his cat. When he found the best place in the world to settle (it would have to be an island) he'd build a house and spend the days painting in his studio with the stereo quietly

Frigate birds

Lone mangrove: Turtle Bay, Santa Cruz (*Photo: Michael and Barbara Reed*)

Blow-hole: Hood Island

Transport, Galapagos style

Fruit from Santa Cruz highlands

Wild oranges: Santa Cruz

Fern zone: Santa Cruz highlands

Palo santo tree and cactus: dry coastal zone

Sally–Lightfoot crab

Marine iguana in breeding colours: Hood Island

Galapagos tortoise: Santa Cruz

Sea-lions

Sea-lions

playing all day and night. He rested his mug on the ship's rail next to mine. His little finger touched my thumb.

From the *Beagle*, anchored not a hundred yards away, came a shout and flash of a powerful torch. The captain hurried to the bow. I could hear Julian's voice – something about swimming. The captain shone the ship's spotlight down into the bay. Everyone gathered at the ship's rail beside Franz and me to watch.

'Oh look, it's a baby sea-lion!' said someone.

What timing, I steamed. Fancy Julian shouting about a sea-lion! He had probably been spying on Mary with his binoculars, had seen Franz and me standing close and wanted to tease, miserable because he was left on watch.

The captain followed the creature with the light. 'The guy on the next boat says it's been swimming around the ship for the past hour.'

Strange behaviour for a sea-lion, I thought. Then I saw the spots. 'It's not a sea-lion, it's my dog!' I ran to the ladder, untied the dinghy and jumped in. She nearly capsized as I took an oar and frantically paddled out to Gypsy. His nose was barely visible, blowing a few bubbles. I tried to haul him up but couldn't get him in without tipping over, so I tied him up by his collar and rowed back to the yacht with mighty strokes. Five pairs of hands reached down to pluck him from the sea. His legs buckled. He didn't even have the strength to shake himself. Gladys appeared with a fluffy blue towel from her cabin, talking baby-talk as she dried him. I could almost feel the towel on my own face, soft and soothing, not like the stiff grey ones we used at home, washed in brackish water. Someone appeared with a mixing bowl of water but Gypsy wasn't thirsty, which I did not find surprising.

The cook appeared with a huge ice-cream carton. 'It's only leftovers, I'm afraid, but we don't have no dog food on board. Poor devil, he's going to have to build up his strength after all that swimming.' He looked at Johnny, then winked at me.

Franz squeezed my hand and kissed me in front of everyone when we said goodnight. His beard was soft.

We rowed home, very carefully. A big shark fin followed us.

If, like cats, dogs had nine lives, Gypsy had just used up one of them.

The party lasted until one o'clock. We knew because we stayed up till then. I opened Gypsy's carton, expecting scrapings from plates. Inside were carefully stacked corned-beef sandwiches, hunks of Velveeta cheese, Parker House rolls, golden fried-chicken breasts and three pieces of rich chocolate cake with gooey icing, all meticulously wrapped in waxed paper. On the bottom, wrapped in foil, was an enormous T-bone steak with a scribbled note: For the Dog.

By midnight garua fell heavily on the roof. Mary made a fire with palo santo twigs. We moved the grass mats near the warmth and ate our picnic.

It was ten before I woke the next morning, kicking myself because Franz and I should have made an early start. Garua swept over the bay and hills, completely obliterating Half-Moon Crater. Franz and I would not spend our day chasing wild horses after all. I opened the top half of the Dutch door. The *Wanderer* was gone.

With a heavy heart I fetched the morning bucket of water from the landing. There was a cardboard box on the top step. I lifted the flap cautiously. Inside were tins and boxes. I ran back up to the house. 'By Jove,' I called, 'look what they left behind!'

'You better not say that,' said Mary, fumbling into her clothes, her eyes half-mast, in need of her usual cup of coffee.

'Say what? Look, I'm telling you they left us a box!'

'By Jove,' she said yawning. 'It's swearing – the same as saying by God. If I have to get up early like this, you have to stop swearing, remember.'

'All right, all right, only look!'

'Vegetables?' Johnny screwed his nose and lifted the biggest tin of green beans I'd ever seen from the box. There was also dried egg-powder, two fat paperbacks, a Peter, Paul and Mary record, Pond's Moisturizer Cream, some freeze-dried apricots, soft sketching pencils, a book on the history of art and a white mug with a note rolled up inside, addressed to me.

Captain decided early this morning no point staying due to mist. Couldn't change his mind. Would have loved to spend day in hills with you. Going now to Plazas as your uncle suggested. Will write from Tahiti. Thought mug would remind you of Irish coffee ... and me with any luck.

Cheers, F.

18

Hunting with the King

Two days later a small fishing boat came in full of orange sacks. We bought them straight from the boat at our landing. But selling oranges was not the purpose of the visit. The *Corsario* had never reached San Cristobal. It should have taken no more than seven, eight hours, even with San Cristobal's strong off-shore currents. Boats went out to search. Nothing. Maybe they had fallen asleep and crashed into Barrington – but there was no wreckage. Or their motor had failed and they'd gone adrift in the current, or they'd been hit by a whale. A radio message would be sent from San Cristobal to the mainland as soon as they could get the generator running. Meanwhile we searched the horizon every morning hoping for some sign of the little *Corsario*.

Fruit and vegetables began coming down from the hills. All we women rowed to the other side on Saturdays and bought or shared sacks of avocados, papaya and cabbages. Our water tank was filled to overflowing with good, sweet water and dear Bernhard agreed to make us a new privy. It was nice to have a man working on the property, to see his strong back bent over rock and cement, to hear the sound of sawing and hammering and, now and then, humming. The finished privy was lovely, with a galvanized roof, goat-horn paper-hook and winding path leading to it in the bush.

'You see?' said Mary, surveying the privy the day after its completion. 'We couldn't have done that. You can't live decently out here without a man. I know you won't face facts, but it is true.'

'You going to marry Julian?'

'You crazy?'

'Well, anybody can see you're sweet on each other.'

'Don't worry, Julian plans to sail around the world. In fact when we go back to Quito, he's coming with us – to get his travelling papers sorted out.'

'I bet he won't go around the world without you.'

'What do I want to go around the world for? Besides if I want to get rid of him, all I have to do is tell him about Johnny.'

We stood in awkward silence. I had never thought about that. Would no one ever marry my sister? Would she be blamed for something which wasn't her fault for the rest of her life?

'There's Alf,' I ventured.

'Dear Alf.'

I could tell by her tone that she wasn't going to marry Alf.

The following Monday I was coming home from Doris Divine's house, where we 'ladies' had practised our music when I saw a speck on the horizon. I ran up the trail with great excitement, crying, 'The *Corsario*, the *Corsario* is coming in!' But when we got out the binoculars we got an even greater shock. It was the *Carrier*. At first elated by the thought of letters from Mother and supplies, it hit us that we were expected to go home on her; three weeks early!

She had sent us a wonderful package of salami, canvas shoes, homemade kolaches wrapped in foil, Tony's postcards from all over the world and a thick letter for each of us. School would start in October. If we went home now we'd waste a whole month sitting around and waiting. We rowed out to the *Carrier*. The captain managed to give us a straight answer without leering and assured us he would be coming back in a month. But as we left, thanking him, he called out, 'You are welcome, my sweet *gringas* – I would sail this ship to China for such beauties as yourselves!'

'We can't go home yet,' I said to Mary.

'I have to get ready for my teaching job.'

'It's a month early!'

'We'll radio Mother!'

'What if she says to come home?'

'Then we will.'

'I don't want to go back.'

'Neither do I.'

'Never?'

'No.'

'Well then!'

'It wouldn't be fair to Mother. We can't ask her to keep working and send us money for rice and bananas. All she and Hans ever wanted – These things have to be planned. God will show us how.'

Was she right? I remembered the words on the back of Grandmother's photograph: 'Unless a man builds with God he labours in vain.'

We nearly capsized in the turbulent entrance to Forrest Nelson's Hotel on the other side of the bay. On the way to the radio shack, he told of his plans for sunken tubs, bar and a penthouse suite. Girlie magazines lay casually on a coffee table in the large lobby. A picture window faced the bay. You could barely see our house on the cliff – camouflaged like a small, nesting wren.

Mother was a bit flustered at talking on the radio; she kept forgetting to say 'over' and, aware that hundreds of hams listened in whenever Galapagos came on the air, our conversation was somewhat stilted.

'Are you still having a good time? – Over.' She meant were we getting along, was Mary getting up in the mornings, had I stopped swearing and were we feeding Johnny properly.

'Yes. – Over,' we said.

'How is Johnny? – Over,' meaning had Mary been able to talk to him.

'Fine. – Over,'

Conditions began to break down. I grabbed the microphone. 'Can we bring the dog back? – Over.'

'What? – Bring what?'

Mary took the microphone back. 'She says can we bring the dog back, because he's like one of the family now.'

'Tell her he doesn't want to be a hunting dog,' I nudged.

'Shhhh ... What? Did you say O K? And can we bring an Englishman home too? – Over.'

'A who? – Over.'

'An Englishman – I wrote you about him.'

'Yes, yes – all right.'

I took the microphone. 'Anne and Maggie want to come too! Is it all right if they live with us and get jobs? Tante Carmen is going to write you.'

'Yes, yes – all right. – Over.'

'Only we don't want to come home on this boat because everybody's not ready. – Over.'

'What if you miss school?'

'I don't want to be a vet anymore. – Over.'

'You – change – so – be – Over.'

'Repeat, repeat. – Over,' burst in Forrest. 'She's fading. Better make it quick.'

'Can we stay one more month? – *Over*.'

'O K – O K – O K – miss – tk – care – *Over*.'

A deep voice crackled in: 'C–Q ... C–Q ... C–Q ...'

'Come in, breaker,' said Forrest.

The breaker was an American tuna boat, the *Caribbean*. They had found a small craft adrift with *Corsario* painted on the stern. Was this the local boat they'd heard was missing?

'Roger, go ahead.'

They had found her drifting, not a soul on board, no note, no sign of violence, her dinghy still attached. They had hauled the little boat aboard. They refused to give their position. This meant they were fishing within the 200-mile zone claimed by Ecuador. If caught, they would face heavy fines. If no questions were to be asked, they would bring her in.

Everyone turned out to watch the huge vessel come into the bay. By comparison the poor *Corsario* looked like a tragic toy, with her scuffed sides and crudely painted water-line, barnacles and weed, now exposed to the world. The port captain went on board. Deals were made, bottles exchanged, no doubt. The *Corsario* was cut loose and splashed into the very sea that had cost the life of her passengers; those smiling friendly people I had waved goodbye to on the landing. When the grim little show was over, we turned and went inside.

Big men with tattoos and flip-flops roamed the village, smiling at the girls and issuing a general invitation to the entire island to come on board that night for movies and ice-cream – at least, that's the invitation I heard.

With great excitement we went out that night. Two foreign ships in one month! Carl, Marga, Anne, Maggie, Mary and I formed a group for a tour of the *Caribbean*. The roaring engine room was huge, immaculate and painted yellow. The engineer explained how everything worked, but we couldn't hear a word he said. Up in the stainless-steel galley, the cook broiled steaks the size of Panama hats for the crew. In the cupboard were jars of peanut-butter the size of wastebaskets and squashy white bread.

We sat out on deck under the stars. There must have been a hundred of us, farmers, fishermen, old and young, perched on coiled ropes, net-hoisting machinery or lifeboats. While the screen was dark we made small talk:

Wasn't the bay choppy lately?

About normal for garua season.

The price of cement was going up.

Gus had better hurry and make that cave he kept talking about.

Big John wrote on the last boat. He was building boats and going to school. He had a car and a girlfriend.

So-and-so's goats were eating so-and-so's banana stems. So-and-so threatened to shoot them if it went on any longer.

Mrs Horneman's hips weren't any better. What she needed was sunshine; it was much too damp for her up in those hills.

So-and-so met so-and-so on the path the other day. So-and-so 'did not greet'!

No! Because of the goats?

Natürlich.

Have you met that new colonist, Max Christian? Is he Swiss or French? Did you know he was once an acrobat in a European circus? Well, that's what I thought he said – he was turning cartwheels at Marga's party last week.

He and the De Roys were talking about making jewellery from black coral.

Who would want jewellery out here?

Have you seen the Darwin Station's new director?

British?

Could you not tell with that pipe and cravat?

I hear he wears socks with his sandals.

No!

The subject of the *Corsario* was broached in whispers. Had they been washed overboard? Had the engine broken down? Had they tried swimming ashore to Barrington? Were they out there now, waiting for help? Had they been tipped over by a killer whale? Or fought over the inadequate lifeboat? Little did we know then that the mystery never would be solved. Several people had disappeared without a trace and I was probably the last person ever to see them alive.

Vanilla ice-cream cups with wooden spoons were handed round. Mary, Julian, Johnny and I kept ours closed until the moment the picture began. The screen filled with glorious Technicolor, trumpets blared – the same unfailing chill ran up my spine, the same thrill I'd felt every single time Mary and I sat down for the Saturday matinée at the 20th-Century-Fox theatre. Suddenly Johnny leapt up. He gabbled unintelligibly, throwing his arms about as if in a fit, nearly tossing his ice-cream cup overboard. Then he stood on his coiled rope and shouted with abandonment: 'It's Monsewer Paul Regret! It's Paul Regret!'

'Of all the pictures –'

'What's wrong with him?' asked Julian.

'It isn't . . .' began Mary.

'Yeah,' I sighed, 'it's *The Commancheros* all right, and I've seen it five times!'

Johnny was enraptured, speaking John Wayne and Stuart Whitman's tedious lines to the letter, bouncing when the blue-eyed Indians attacked, groaning when the baddies fell from their horses.

He wasn't the only one – I watched the faces of Carl, Gus and Fritz. They were six years old again; their ice-cream nearly

'Did you hear goat?' he whispered.

'No.'

'I smell goat. A buck has been through here.' He bent down, pointed to fresh droppings and ducked through a small gap in the scrub. I scratched my legs following him. A branch hit me in the eye, making it water. The sun came out without cloud, without breeze. The gun became heavy; the burlap sack rubbed my sunburn raw. Flies buzzed at my shirt, after the wound.

On and on we trudged. Heat rose in waves from the rocks. My stomach growled for want of breakfast. On and on, up and down, in and out, over and under. By noon my mouth was too dry to speak. I could feel the sun burning the top of my head.

He stopped.

'They seem to have stayed near the coast. We'll just check a place I know where they often look for shade.'

'OK,' I croaked.

They weren't there.

'If I spot one, freeze. We have to see that the horns aren't painted – those are all house-goats. I need a clear shot. If I wound one it means we have to track it down until we finish the job. I won't have an animal walking around wounded.'

'No.'

'You all right, girl?'

'Yes.'

A goat called. I froze. So did my heart.

Gus answered; a perfect imitation.

Phhhhhht! A large buck with horns appeared through ghostly trees – too far away, I knew. Phhht! He stamped his foot on a rock, warning the others and vanished. A nanny streaked out from the bushes, suddenly saw us and swerved. Her eyes were panicky, a tiny kid at her side, so close to us I could see its dried umbilical cord. A perfect, clear shot. Gus raised his gun and followed her. My heart banged in my throat.

I gripped my own rifle to keep it from shaking in my hands.

Gus lowered the gun.

'Do I remind you of Zorba the Greek?'

'Whha . . .' I cleared my throat.

'Someone I met on a yacht sent me a letter on the last boat with the book *Zorba the Greek*. Said I reminded him.'

'I – I – saw the movie.'

'You don't say!' He turned and led me from the bush. In a few moments we were back on the open coast. A small beach shimmered there. The water looked cool and clear.

'Now! Tell me. What is this dance of Zorba?'

'You want to know the dance?'

'Yes.'

We wrapped our rifles in the burlap bags and stuffed them under a bush away from sea-spray. I took off my shoes and waded into the water up to my knees. The scratches burned deliciously. I washed off my scorched face. The King watched, as fresh as when we'd left that morning.

'It's a man's dance – the Greeks – if I remember right, stand in a circle, arm in arm. Then you put your right foot forward – step with the left. No, no, you bend your knee, see like this.'

'Like this.'

'Yeah, that's right. Now left behind right – step. Left in front of right – step – remember to bend your knees.'

'That's it? So easy!'

He went off without me, left over right, left behind right, until he ran out of beach.

'Hanna!' he called. 'Bring the guns!'

'Oh gosh . . .' I ran and grabbed the bags, raced back to him, looking everywhere for the goats.

'Oh, there aren't any goats here. I just want to teach you how to shoot that thing. I should have showed you this morning but I forgot you didn't know. Now. Get it into your shoulder – so. See that little ridge on top? That's the sight – line it up – steady – release safety – and squeeze the trigger. So easy.'

'Easy.'

'Now, see that rock out there with the crabs?'

'No – yeah – now I see it.'

'Shoot the big crab in the middle.'

'Now?'

'When you're ready.'

When I'm ready, I repeated in my head. My hand started to

tremble. Then I made myself stop. I steeled my head – my hand – aimed – and fired. The rock became void of life.

'I've killed them all!' I said, horrified.

'Noooo. The bang scared them off.'

'You mean I didn't hit anything?' I said, even more horrified.

'Nooooo. You got one right between the eyes. From this distance – I'd say that was – surprising.'

'I don't believe you –'

'Take a look.'

I walked slowly to the rock, through the shallow tide pools. I hoped it wouldn't still be wriggling. I'd have to kill it by hand then. Somehow a steel barrel between you and life made it easier.

I found the crab. The biggest one. Shot clean through. Such a big hole it made in such a fragile shell. I picked it up and took it back to him.

'You going to stuff it?'

'Didn't you say the legs were good for bait? I'm going to catch a fish with it when we get home.'

'Well, I'm hungry for goat.'

I put my shoes back on. 'Why didn't you shoot that nanny then?' I asked quietly. Silence. I thought he hadn't heard, so I let it be.

He picked up my spent cartridge. 'I guess that kid was born last night. Seemed a short life.'

I wanted to hold his hand so badly – and close my eyes – and then, when I opened them, Father would be standing there –

We headed for home. A few hundred yards from the crack he stopped suddenly. I froze and planted my feet, my gun steady. I was ready this time. Now I could do it, now that I knew there could be decency to hunting.

'Hanna!'

'Yes!'

'Right over there –' he whispered. 'You see it? You hear it?'

I raised my gun slowly, leaving the safety-catch on.

'You hear it calling?'

'No.'

He put his gun down and ran over to a bunch of black lava. He picked up a piece the size of two fists. 'Look at this. I told you it was calling – rocks, I love them. They call out to me to be found. What do you see here? Come, come look at it the way I first saw it. There. Doesn't that remind you of a man's fist? *Mensch*! And here, here is the woman's hand. See? One way it is power and cruelty – the other gentleness and calm. War and peace. Torment and slumber.' He dropped the rock in his sack.

'We'll take it home for my cave.'

19

Old Moo

It was October when the doldrums set in. We had plenty of bananas, the tank was full, our house was comfortable; we had time to read and sketch and play but something, we knew not what, was missing. The sunsets grew oranger; the breeze wafted down from the hills and the sea turned warm; all signs of rain, but no promise.

My sister and I became compulsive horizon-watchers. At first it was for fear the *Carrier* would come back for us. By November, we wondered if she had forgotten. Not that we wanted to leave. Mary still insisted a woman could not live in the islands without a man. I asked her if this meant we had to return to civilization until we found husbands. She did not answer.

'Well, I'm never going to marry. And if I were, where would we find husbands to come way out here?'

She didn't know.

'I have to admit, a pair of strong arms would be useful now and then.'

'Oh,' she said wistfully, 'I didn't mean that. It's just – well, look at us. You don't see married people watching the horizon like we do.'

So I began watching Half-Moon Crater instead. Like Gus's rocks, the hills beckoned me and every evening when they turned purple in the twilight I vowed I would go up there the next morning. But in the morning, when I had filled my canteen and put on my shoes, the trail to Half-Moon looked too long and hot. So I'd empty my canteen, choose a banana from the stem and settle back against a rock to watch the horizon.

We decided that just because I had given up on algebra and was going to grow up ignorant, it didn't mean Johnny should too. Mary began teaching him at the table every morning. I took comfort, as I tidied the kitchen, from seeing their heads bent together. They filled a notebook with pictures; 'If six blue-footed boobies dive for nine fish and five frigate birds steal four of the fish, how many fish do the boobies have left?' But they did not discuss the things Mama had said they must.

One afternoon Johnny came running up the path, holding his overalls high. Mary had sewed them for him but forgot to put in a barn door, so he always had trouble and often left things too late. I rushed down to meet him. Mary was hanging washing in the trees and joined me. We each fumbled with a strap and at last pointed him towards a bush, but he yelled in protest, pointing towards the landing and babbling gibberish.

'A whale!' he finally got out. 'I saw a whale on the landing!'

'You are not supposed to be on the landing alone!' Mary scolded. He insisted we come. At first we saw nothing, but suddenly a huge black-and-white body emerged, blowing bubbles at our feet and smiling. He made a hussssh sound as he sank back into the sea.

'Killer whale!' we gasped. The creature was so beautiful we could only look on in dazed admiration as he moved further out in the bay. Over in front of the Darwin Station his mate surfaced, and between them they combed the bay thoroughly, and then vanished. It was then that I saw Gus rowing by in his little peapod dinghy, coming from town.

'Did you see that?' I exclaimed. '*Mensch*, were you lucky he didn't tip you over!'

'Tip me over? What for? He came in here to see me, don't you know? Puts his head out of the water and looks me over. I just stare him in the eye. Finally he says, "Hiya, King!" and I give him a wink.' Gus rowed on home. I knew then that I was going crazy, for I no longer found the King's stories farfetched.

That night I told Mary we shouldn't feel guilty about Johnny missing school. How many second-graders had a killer whale visit the classroom?

★

Life was peaceful. A new German family had arrived on the last boat. They moved into the Stewarts' house. Erna Sievers was amazingly elegant, considering she lived in a lagoon. Mr Sievers spoke no English, but he sang a song about 'Yohanna' every time we met on the trail. He had walked home from Siberia after the war, and I wished I could speak to him and ask him about such a feat; but maybe he didn't want to remember. Their son Rolf was single, which caused a stir and, along with the *Beagle* Boys, inspired many a 'young people's beach party'. We still played volleyball every afternoon and had tea parties and we ladies still got together once a week to play Strauss.

It was after one of these sessions at Marga's that Carl began showing me the scrapbooks from his successful visit to Germany. All the major newspapers and magazines appeared to have interviewed the Duke. Robinson *von* Galapagos made the headlines. There were glossy photos of him dancing beneath a chandelier, drinking champagne, sniffing a rose, having his face powdered for the television cameras. He was an interviewer's dream: witty, debonair and unbearably romantic and virile. For weeks the ample German bottoms had sat on the edges of overstuffed armchairs to hear his tales. Survivors of a fallen empire, victims of the Third Reich, their rapt faces looked so vulnerable, so eager to believe in Grimm's happily ever after. It was surprising that boatloads of *hausfraus* hadn't arrived already. I feared what I saw in their faces; it had been in mine that night on Arlington Street when we'd switched off the television. There were many people out there still searching for paradise. How long before the world caught up with us and trampled Eden to death?

'You know, Yohanna,' said Marga, pouring me coffee, 'when we was in Germany that time, everyone was taking us to this fine restaurant and that with music and candles. We was sitting one night and our host says we shall have a very, very special dessert. I am thinking, what can this be? Blueberries? Strawberries? They turn off the lights. In comes the waiter and lights a match and sets on fire our special dessert. When the lights come on I see what it is: pancakes! What we are eating in

Galapagos every other day when we cannot get nothing else better!'

'Like bananas, I cannot get tired of pancakes,' said Carl, closing his scrapbook reluctantly and returning it to the shelf. 'In the beginning we fried them in tortoise oil, you know. Old Moo taught me the recipe. You just render down the oil, then you take —'

'Who is this Old Moo?' I interrupted, remembering the odd, pale figure I had seen scurrying away from Graffer's house.

'Oh, his real name is Jensmoo. He was an officer —'

'He came from a good family,' said Marga.

'Old Moo came out with Gordon Wold and the other Norwegians back in 1926. But he left his sweetheart back in Norway. He always told Wold that a man should not live alone, so he went back to marry the girl. Only when he got home he found she had married his best friend. When he returned to Galapagos, he swore he would never marry, so he lives alone. It is not surprising, he is a bit — well, he lives like a hermit. Grows the best pineapple I ever ate, though.'

I asked where his house was. Carl said it wasn't far off the trail to Half-Moon Crater, past an avocado grove, down a gully with ferns and along a trail covered in wandering Jew.

'But if you ever go up there, whatever you do, don't eat his pancakes.' Carl paused to pour a capful of rum into his coffee. Marga frowned.

'Moo had a problem,' he continued. 'You see he — how you say it?'

'*Er sabbelt immer*,' said Marga.

'Yah, yah, in German I know — anyhow, take my word and don't stay for breakfast.'

'Or lunch,' said Marga.

'Or supper,' said Carl.

'But he is a very, very nice man. He gets up with the chickens and also goes to bed with them.'

'Old Moo,' said Carl, 'has a big chacra but never hires any helpers. *Mensch*, he grows everything on his farm. Back when the Americans were over on Baltra they used to buy fresh stuff from him. He must have made plenty of money. They say he's got it hidden between the walls of his house.'

'Oh Carlie, that is just a rumour!'

'Well, remember the radio?'

'What radio?' I asked.

'Remember I told you I was shanghaied to Hollywood? Before that I met the Duke of Sutherland out here on his yacht, and he said if ever I had the chance to buy a radio, I should get a Signet. So in 1948 I bought a little Signet in the States, just like he said. When I got back here I went up to the Hornemans' to say hallo. That radio was little, just like a suitcase, so when I got up there Mrs Horneman says, sit down for coffee. Gordon Wold and Graffer and Jensmoo were already there. I sat down and put my little suitcase under the table. When we were quiet, I turned it on with my toes. Music came out. You should have seen them jump! *Mensch!* But the most excited was Jensmoo. He said, "Oh look, oh look!" just like a little boy. I told him, "You should have one, man – keep you company. Music morning, afternoon and night. Only you must turn it off when you go out of the house to save the battery." Well, a Signet wasn't cheap but he found the money right away to give to Bud Divine and asked him to order one from Sears-Roebuck. And so he had his music, his chickens, and his pancakes. He seemed a happy man then.'

That night Mary forgot to tell me she'd sharpened the knife. As I began cutting cold goat meat for supper, I nearly took the top section of my finger off. I knew it was bad by the way it hurt. The dishcloth turned red in spite of my holding my hand over my head. Mary made me show her. Even in the candlelight you could see the bone. She said it needed stitches. I said no one was going to stitch me up – since seeing the movie *Old Yeller* the thought of stitches had always made me ill. The best we could do was clean it well and try pulling the flesh together with tape.

Afraid Mary might take me down for Tante Carmen to stitch me up the next day, I rose early, filled a canteen, put on my shoes, tied a sack to my back for any vegetables, wrapped a banana and a hunk of goat in a cloth and set off. I did not meet a soul on the old trail; I could have been the only human on earth. By 10.30 the sun beat down mercilessly, through my hat, on my head, into my brain. My head pounded; so did my finger though I tried to keep it up as I marched. An hour later I got to the village of Bella Vista feeling sore and thirsty. A cane house on the corner had a misspelt sign on the door offering cerveza.

I bought a bottle, feeling like a cheap hussy sitting on the steps, drinking as the villagers found excuses to come out and cast friendly but curious glances at me. The beer was warm and nauseous. I never liked it even when it was cold, thinking back to all the empties I'd cleaned up from behind the sofa when Mr E. lived with us.

I hiked on past the entrance to the Kastdalens' farm and paused at the old gate to 'Vilnes'. Mrs Horneman's kitchen would be cool. She would make me a pitcher of sour-orange juice – she would be glad of company. I forced myself to plod on.

When people had told me how to reach Half-Moon Crater, they hadn't mentioned a fork in the trail. I chose left, passed an avocado tree and walked for half an hour before I realized the trail was taking me west instead of north. I doubled back. It was dreadfully still and hot; I could feel my face peeling. I longed for the sea breeze. Sweat trickled down my back and into my eyes, stinging them. I tried to ignore the sound of water sloshing in the canteen. I returned to the fork in the road. But the avocado tree had turned into a mango tree. I saw whisps of smoke in the distance. I had made a circle. Climbing under a barbed-wire fence nailed to guayava trees, I cut through a field which I hoped would take me up to the island's backbone, up to Half-Moon. Thigh-high gorse tore at my legs. Then I felt a soft breeze on my cheek and turning to revel in it I saw a magnificent view spread out before me like a feast. I couldn't believe I'd climbed so high. It was as though you could see the whole world pass below. The sea sparkled blue and silver. I could see Carl's pink roof. Something rustled behind me. I turned, slipping on a cowpat. When I regained my balance I saw a large brown bull had emerged from the greenery. He stopped short when he saw me, lifted his two-foot horns and stared. Was he mean or just curious? He looked mean to me – and moody. I'd heard grim tales about the early settlers tangling with wild bulls; the infamous Baroness had made a sport of killing them, splitting their hearts in two with one bullet.

Could this one smell that I meant him no harm? I stepped back; the fence was only a hundred yards behind me. I ran. The bull followed with awkward, heavy steps, pausing to swipe at flies along his back with horns as sharp as swords. I had seen pictures in *Life* magazine of wounded matadors carried from the ring in agony, their purple *pantalones* stained black with blood. My shoe got stuck in another cowpat. I bent to put it back on, my eyes never leaving his. The beast began to trot, his heavy flesh bouncing at every step. I could hear his breathing as I fled again. Then I faced him. He stopped. I picked up a large stick and beat the air with it, but this only seemed to antagonize him for he roared. If only I had a machete! Stupid, what would a machete do against such a beast? I would never make it to the fence. The bull pawed the earth. He threw back his head and bawled again – an agonized, dismal wail. I walked backwards. A tree! I'd run for a tree, but there were only orange trees, covered in spines. It was spines or horns. I tried to climb the tree using the thorns as footholds, but they snapped off and I realized that even if I could get up I'd only be four feet off the ground. I had read about an African girl who was chased up a tree by wild bulls – but she did not get high enough. The bulls gathered round and licked the bottoms of her feet until she bled to death! Another roar came from the top of the field. The bull turned, arched its tail and galloped off through the tall weeds.

I ran as never before, rolled under the barbed-wire fence and just lay gasping in the wild-cucumber vines, now dried by the relentless sun. My canteen sloshed encouragingly. I unscrewed the cap and drank deeply, my hands trembling.

The sun stood at noon. I would not make it to the top of the island with enough time to get home before dark. Everyone knew there weren't any horses up there anyway. The bandage on my finger was grimy. I took it off and poured water over the wound. Looking at it made me queasy. I ate the banana but could not bear the thought of eating hunk of meat and threw it to the ground, wrapping my finger with the cloth.

On the way down I entered a dark, shaded avocado grove, found the deep gully Carl had mentioned, walked along a path nearly submerged in wandering Jew and came upon a wood-and-bamboo shack. I knew it was Old Moo's place when I heard the radio. I paused. One needed an excuse to visit a hermit.

'Do you have any pineapple to sell?' I asked in Spanish when he came to the door. He eyed me for a moment, then beckoned me closer with a wave of his hand. He was as pale as I remembered.

'Come inside. It's too hot. Too hot.'

I walked up three steps. A hen fled in panic when I stepped into a large room. Chickens preened themselves on a table. Still others dozed beneath a chair. Another perched on a sack of potatoes slumped in a corner. Hens balanced in the windowsills and on a cupboard.

'Forgive me one moment,' Moo called from a side room in Spanish. 'I was just making my lunch.'

I apologized and rose immediately to go.

'No bother, no bother.' He emerged from the kitchen and pulled aside a curtain leading to a small room with a bed and a table with an object covered in a blue velvet cloth. Lifting the cloth, he turned the radio down.

'Is that the radio you ordered from Sears?' I asked, to make conversation. He hadn't answered me about the pineapples yet.

'Lovely, no?'

I came nearer as he fiddled with the knobs. He tuned in to Holland, then switched it off. He moved the dial again and turned it back on. Spain. He turned it off. Turned it on. Moscow. Turned it off.

'Doesn't it work well?' I asked curiously.

'Works fine. Fine. Battery lasts forever because I turn it off each time like Carl said I should.'

'I – I think he meant you should turn it off when you go out – you know, to feed the chickens and so on – you don't have to turn it off when – when you turn the dial – not with these modern ones.'

'Is this a modern one?'

'Oh yes, I would say this was definitely a modern radio.'

'So I can leave it on, eh?'

I nodded. The radio pip-pipped.

'We are a little early for music – the news will be next. Can't stand the news. World's going crazy out there. Did you know they're having another war? Somewhere called Vietnam, I think they said.'

Lillibuelero tinkled out from the set. Deep booming bells followed.

'This is the World Service of the BBC. Here is the news at thirteen hundred hours read by – weeeeeeee,' said a cultured voice through a sea of interference and wailing.

'I normally eat earlier,' called Moo from his small kitchen, 'but I was out all morning looking for my cow.'

'– In Britain's recent general election, which produced one of the closest results in Britain's electoral history, the Labour government had a working majority of only four – wooooooo.'

'And did you find her?' I called out against the din.

'*Que?*'

'Your cow!'

'– investigative committee a year after late President John F. Kennedy's assassination in Dallas – woooeeeeee – no evidence that Lee Harvey – weeee – conspiracy either domestic or spisssss.'

'No, I looked everywhere, *baca mala!*' Whissssssssss.

'Senator Everett Dirksen – Civil Rights Bill – weeeeeoooooo.'

'*Caramba, ese radio!*' He asked me to turn it off. I was disappointed, for I hadn't heard the news in four months – or was it five? An old *Time* magazine had said boys little older than myself were being sent to Vietnam.

'I have no pineapple. Need rain. Should rain today, wind's from the hills. You came a long way for nothing,' said Moo, wiping his hands on a clean but ragged towel.

'No matter, I was going to the top anyway; to Half-Moon Crater.'

'You a scientist?'

'No! I was looking for –' I cleared my throat. 'I was just exploring. But I got chased by a wild bull.'

'*Caramba*! I told them there would be trouble if they brought in that new stock. What did it look like? Big white thing with a hump on its back?'

'No, no, it was much worse – sort of dark brown with two-foot-long horns and a wicked look in its eye.'

'Did it have a white square patch over one eye?'

'Yes, that's right!'

'My cow,' he called out as he rushed back to his kitchen.'Where was the brute?' Spppppp-whissssss-sppppp!

'Your – you mean, I ran from a – cow?'

'Good thing too. Cows more dangerous than bulls. She's mad; calf died. She went off searching for it. Won't let me milk her, so she's hurting. Ever you get chased by a cow, you run. Take bits of clothing off, leave them on the ground.' Spppppppp-whisssss! 'Take her a second or two to horn each piece while you get away.'

The radio was off. What was that sound? I got up and stood in the doorway to the kitchen.

'You remember where you saw her?'

Old Moo dipped a ladle into the smooth batter and lifted it over to a hot black frying pan. Pancakes! 'Whatever you do, don't eat his pancakes!' The batter swizzed in the hot grease. Moo must have been hungry, for he drooled a bit as he watched it burst its bubbles. A speck of silver formed in the corner of his mouth – 'Jensmoo has a little problem –'

'Yes, I remember, it was a second fork in the road to the left by a mango tree, a weedy pasture, orange trees to the west – I guess that sounds like every other field up here –'

'I know it.' The silver formed a thread. It ran down his pale lower lip and fell to the griddle. Spack-whisssssss!

'*Er sabbelt immer*' meant dribble? Moo drooled into his pancakes?

'*Sí*, that used to be the Angermeyer place. Was sold back in ohhhh' – whissss – 'can't remember – '48, I think.'

'Which Angermeyer owned it, do you know?'

'*Seguro*. Your father – Johannes.'

'How do you know he was my father?'

'Wold said. I was playing chess with him over at Graffer's

one night. He said you had come up asking questions some time ago.' Spppp-whissss. The pancakes burst their little bubbles and Moo turned them expertly. Chickens began congregating in the doorway like women at the first day of a sale. One flapped up to the shelf beside the stove.

'*Caramba! Carajo!* Get out of here! Out! I warn you I will fry you next!' He turned to me and said most graciously, 'You will stay for lunch?'

I was actually tempted. I liked him. But I said, 'No, no, I would like to but I must go. If I'm late down my sister will worry –'

'Suit yourself, suit yourself. Your uncle never liked my pancakes, but your father ate here once. Was very excited, showed me some plans he drew for a big house he was going to build up there where you say my cow is. Looked pretty ambitious to me. You can't be ambitious on these islands. Simple. Simple life is best. You see, chickens and my radio, that's all I need. Once I thought I needed much more – but that was when I was a young man. You think differently when you are twenty. I am an old man now.'

'No!'

'I feel old. Teeth going; hair. No one comes up here. They will when I die though, to search for my money. They say I'm *loco*.'

'They don't say you're crazy!' I lied.

'*Bueno*, a man who cares what people think will go crazy out here – crazy. It's a good thing I don't live alone. No person should live alone on an island. It's crazy, crazy.' He loaded an enamel plate with pancakes and carried it to the table. The hen on the bed jumped down and waddled over. Those under the table hopped up on the bench, clucking cajolingly. Old Moo whistled shrilly. Suddenly chickens and cockerels descended from the branches of the trees outside. Others emerged from bushes. Running flat out, flying in spurts, they flew in through the windows and landed on the table in a flurry of dust and feathers. To my further amazement, Moo began tossing pancakes right and left.

'I have no pineapples yet but you can take some otoi – lovely otoi growing by my gate out there. Cut off the tender, curled leaves. Take all you want.' Marga was right; he was a nice man, a gentle man.

I thanked him. He raised his voice over the din of cackling and shrieking. 'You know, of course, that you must rinse the leaves in boiling water and then pour it off. Otherwise it's poisonous.' He shielded his plate. 'Get away! Get off. *Caramba!* The rest is mine. *Caramba!*'

I waved goodbye. When I reached the gate I could still hear the hysterical luncheon party. I cut a big bunch of taro and wrapped it in two large banana leaves to keep it fresh. Was Jensmoo right? Would I go crazy if I lived out here all alone? I thought I had counted twenty-seven chickens on Moo's table; but I could have been mistaken.

Heavy rain came from behind the hills. It followed me down the trail, bending branches as it fell and forming rivulets at the side of the trail. At home our tanks overflowed and we rejoiced that night in the moonlight, taking showers at the roof's edge and shampooing our hair in glorious sweet water.

The next morning there was a speck on the clean horizon. It looked like a large yacht and we all became excited; Mary hung her best skirt on the damp bushes to get rid of wrinkles in case there was to be a party.

An hour later my sister brought her skirt back inside. The *Cristobal Carrier* was back. I took a long look through the binoculars to see if she appeared any more seaworthy than the last time, since we would soon be her foolhardy passengers. I saw a thin figure slumped over the railing of the first-class section.

'Mary, Mary, come quick!' I shouted.

When she rowed out to fetch poor Tony, I watched as he nearly capsized the dinghy when he got in. I ran down to the landing to help unload his suitcase, but ended up helping him out as well. He was sickly green. We took him home and fed him porridge and weak tea for breakfast.

Having been all the way around the world, my brother said that the last six hundred miles had been the hardest. Once he regained his colour, he wanted to know all about Mary's 'Englishman'. Actually, the way he said it didn't sound like he wanted to hear about Julian at all but, rather, that he'd suffered three days of nausea simply to check up on what we'd been doing for the past five months. I found this rather touching. My sister did not.

He was very impressed with what we'd done to the house. I was greatly relieved, since most of it had been done with his money.

Mary caught our last rat the next morning. As usual, I cringed when I heard the trap. When she stood on the chair to remove the corpse from the top of the wardrobe, she moaned.

'Ohh, poor thing.'

'You mean we've mangled one?' It was what I had been dreading since we started the wretched trapping business. I joined her on the chair, nearly tipping it over. The rat, a sleek endemic animal, looked truly pathetic, caught by his front paw. Carefully we pried open the trap's jaws, placed the rat in a moss-lined box and daubed antiseptic cream on his paw. He did well on Kastdalen pig lard and milky corn pudding.

Five days later when the four of us, plus Mary's Englishman, cousins Anne and Maggie, and Gypsy, boarded the *Carrier*, the rat was well enough for us to let him go in the bush, where he presumably slept rough one night and then wound his way back to house-sit until our return.

My cousins adapted to city life better than I did. Floundering in school and unable to catch up, I constantly found my eyes wandering six hundred miles past the standard school-typewriter keyboard to the toothy grin of Gus's ancient model, his shack smelling of goat skins and the King shouting, 'But Hanna, German is easy, your father spoke it as a baby!'

It was Mary and Julian who returned to Galapagos first. When Mary told her Englishman about Johnny, he did not flee as she had predicted. As I had said, he refused to sail around the world without her. His Gran back in England nearly disinherited him when he cabled home that he was going to settle in Galapagos and marry an 'island girl with a seven-year-old son'. Mary made him send his family a photograph showing she did not wear coconut shells or chew betel nuts. The day they sailed back to Galapagos, I felt I'd lost a sister I'd grown close to, a little brother and a small house on a cliff next to the sea.

Mary and Julian wrote with every boat. The day came when they were expecting their first child. Julian had leased a fishing boat, cleaned it up and was beginning to take a few adventurous tourists on cruises. Johnny was fine, still flexing his muscles in the mirror every morning, taking over chores while his father was away.

Franz Harper-Stubenrauch wrote from Tahiti. Then from San Francisco. He said he would go mad if he had to live in that rat-race. His thirst for adventure had only intensified since cruising on the *Wanderer*. He could no longer bear the fog and his former soul-destroying materialistic existence. We lived in a crazy world. Had I heard of the war in Vietnam? There was a movement towards awareness in the young in America. Everyday there were new protests. America now had 181,000 men – boys actually – being blown to bits in rice paddies over there. The system was rotten. He apologized for the intensity of his feelings, but wasn't it time to work for a better world? He lived for the day when he would have enough money saved to throw his kit-bag on to the deck of his boat and sail away, to have time to think.

I was eighteen. My letters back to Franz sounded terribly mature when I read them over. Secretly I felt this honest-hearted man was a godsend, my ticket to the enchanted isles. We would sail around the world and not find anywhere like Galapagos, so we would return to settle there and build a house, make a life together. Surely, if a woman had to have a man, Franz was the one for me.

I left school and got a good job teaching kindergarten during the day. In the evenings I walked the wealthier streets of Quito with my guitar case, giving lessons to everyone from eight to eighty. I began to save the money to go to San Francisco.

Months passed. Mary and Julian had a baby boy. He weighed ten pounds when he was born and looked like Winston Churchill. Johnny was sprouting new muscles every day. They all sounded so happy. Tony helped them finance a boat for chartering. Tourism was coming to Galapagos. I began to panic. It would all be changed before I got there.

Franz phoned long-distance. When was I coming? As if reading my thoughts he said the world was changing. He had bought a boat. There was no time to lose; he wanted to be able to recognize paradise when he saw it.

I had the money but I was scared to death. Writing letters was one thing. What was I getting myself into? Suddenly Mother and Tony said it was time they saw the States again. We would all drive across America together in a camper. I suggested we could end up in San Francisco. I would have told them exactly what I planned to do there if I'd known myself.

Then he did not write for a month. Finally he rang saying he'd been terribly busy. His commercial-art business had taken off. He was a success. He had bought a boat. It was time to go.

I needed my own passport, proof that I was not wanted by the Ecuadorian police, that I'd paid my taxes, and I needed a smallpox vaccination. It would take weeks to get it all sorted out and would require my birth certificate. The key to the strongbox was kept in Mother's jewellery box. The strongbox was kept under the bed.

I hadn't really forgotten about the shoebox. But my life was full of promise and the shoebox merely full of memories. It was larger than a normal shoebox. On top it said: Gold's Department Store – Galoshes – Size 5. The old string snapped when I tried to untie it.

20

The Shoebox

There were photographs: Grandma Mari wearing a muff, standing proudly beside her Oldsmobile, the one she bought after the first was hit by the train. Three dark men stood beside her. The tallest had his arm draped over Emmasha's shoulder. It was snowing. The date on the back was December 1935. There was another of Capitán Marco in his plane, goggles pulled up over his forehead. Another of Tony wearing a miniature air-force uniform. There were the clippings I'd already seen about the plane crash, some medals with the ribbons twisted and dry.

Then there was a studio picture of Emma and Hans wearing tropical whites. She sat, a Panama straw bag on her lap; Hans stood behind, his hand just touching her shoulder. They looked young and happy. The date said March 1941. My sister had been born a few weeks earlier.

The diary began two months before that. All the entries were in Mother's generous, schoolteacher's handwriting. Normally I would never have looked inside a personal diary, but this seemed not so much a pouring out of intimate thoughts. It was more like an account – expenditures, appointments – of the months soon after Hans and Emma got married in Machachi – where Mother had left off her story of coming home from their wedding in a taxi without headlights.

Guayaquil, December 1941
We are at last becoming used to the change of climate from lovely Quito to clothes-dripping Guayaquil. Johnny, after searching up and down the coast, has found a boat, a most beautiful yacht. He

has named her (of course) the *Marie*. Selling the house on Rocafuerte was worth seeing him this happy and soon we will sail off to Galapagos. Little Tony is as happy as a bee, imitating everything Johnny does. I can't believe our good fortune even as I sit here on deck. I am not allowed to help much and in my state I wouldn't be much help anyway, not being able to see my feet anymore. It is a good thing his brothers have come in to help get the *Marie* ready and sail her to the islands. They are great fun. Yesterday their hunting dog, Elmo, tried to attack the bronze statue of a wild boar in the park alongside our mooring.

7 December
News is bad. The Japanese bombing Pearl Harbor has affected us more than we ever imagined possible. Germans in South America are being interned. We think Johnny and his brothers will be safe. They have influential friends in the navy to speak for them, but we won't be allowed to sail home to Galapagos now. The American forces will be leasing a small island to the north of Johnny's island – making an airstrip to protect the Panama Canal. Everyone believes this continent will be invaded by the Nazis very soon.

Thursday
Americans are being told to go home. I have told the consulate that I will stay. This is my place. We will live on the boat until this blows over. Money is getting short as prices rise.

1 January 1942
Spent five sucres on baby clothes. I will embroider this bodice in red and blue – Russian style – which will suit a boy or a girl.
P S Just realized it's the new year.

3 January
If only we had not been waiting for the baby to be born we would have been out in Galapagos by now, instead of stuck in this miserable hot hole waiting for the officials to decide our fate. Johnny would not have let me have the baby out there. If he had experience with Ecuadorian hospitals he might think a desert island better! The officials wouldn't let me fly in this state anyway. I don't know what

the brothers will do. I feel so awful that they are trapped like this. They say that they will try for work up on the coast near Esmeraldas in the balsa-wood factories.

5 January
Americans are actually being forced home now. The man at the embassy says Johnny will not be allowed to enter the States with me because he is German! Have you ever heard of such stupidity? If only they knew his feelings about Hitler and this war –

10 January
The *Marie* will have to go. What a blow for the brothers after finding such a beautiful yacht, only to have her slip through their fingers. But we have invested so much money in her and a boat is a luxury unless she can earn her keep, Johnny says. He planned to use her initially for fishing, but says one day tourists will come to see the Enchanted Isles, as he calls them. We could have chartered her. She is so sleek and fast.

3 February
Mary Lisa was born. We named her after our mothers jointly and Johnny's younger sister. She has her daddy's big blue eyes and hair.

6 February
American Embassy adamant. I must leave as soon as baby strong enough. This is out of the question.

8 February
Tony pleased with his new sister. Needless to say, Johnny is over the moon! Actually, he doesn't look well, at least I don't think. I suppose it's worry catching up with us all. It's hard to imagine our peaceful little country being overrun with Nazis, but the Americans say it's only a matter of time. What will happen to men like my husband who fled Germany out of disgust of the Reich?

16 February
Spent: 2 sucres on rice
9 sucres cough-medicine

3 sucres toy car for Tony (is jealous of baby)
10 sucres for ad. in paper (sale of boat)

17 February
Johnny very worried about parents. He doesn't say but I know. No news but reports of bombings in Germany awful. Have moved into rooms in apartment building, pretty old and depressing but cheap.

19 February
Embassy is getting difficult. I will put off leaving Johnny until last minute. I don't want even to think of what a wrench like this will do to him – to Tony. To me. We have been so happy even though there is so little money.

27th
Tony four years old.

March
There has been a terrible earthquake in Guayaquil. People ran screaming out into the streets in panic as buildings caved in. Thank goodness we live in an old house. It swayed sickeningly, but newer ones collapsed. A woman next door was standing only feet from her daughter when it hit. The poor girl plummeted to her death while her mother was left untouched. I was terrified thinking of Johnny alone down on the quay. Didn't know what to do first. Ran out to plaza looking for Tony but *muchacha* already had him safely outside. I am ashamed that only then did I remember the baby. She is so new! I rushed back up the swaying staircase to grab her from the cot. Johnny ran all the way from the *Marie*. I'll never know how he found us among the crowd in the plaza.

Entries in the diary after that were erratic, the handwriting hurried, sometimes illegible. Then a month later:

Johnny is in hospital. I told him he's been working too hard. Suspected kidney stones. In much pain.

Days later:

Operation went well but Johnny pale. Embassy ordering me to leave. I must be the last American here. Must wait to see J. recover. Mary is too small for such a journey.

Following week:

Americans repeat impossible Johnny come with me as is German. How can this be since he is married to an American? If I were the man and he my wife would they leave a sick woman to fend for herself? The world is going crazy. Must I say goodbye to my beloved husband in his hospital bed? He is so pale still.

A day later:

They have threatened to take the children.

Lincoln, Nebraska

3 May 1942

Dearest Johnny,

I hope this finds you much better and sitting out in the shade fanning yourself in the heat while we shiver in the Nebraska spring showers. Lucky you!

We arrived safely but not without difficulty. Poor little Mary broke out in scabies on the plane. In Panama when the Americans found out from my documents that I was married to a German, they detained me. For one glorious moment I hoped they were going to send us back to you but after an hour I was escorted like a criminal on to the plane. Tony keeps asking why you didn't come too. It's so hard to explain –

The rest was in German and, I assumed, personal.

A newspaper article dated May 1942 said the Japanese now controlled the Pacific: Malaya, Hong Kong, Singapore, Burma and the Philippines. Experts were saying that Hitler had made his biggest error in declaring war on the United States. He was now faced with the vast resources of the USSR and the British Commonwealth together with the immense potential of the USA.

There followed a letter in a handwriting I had never seen before, very European, almost spidery, like the writing on old

Mozart manuscripts. I couldn't read most of it, for it was in German. It was signed 'Johnny'.

Dear Johnny,

    I am so relieved that you are out of hospital and that the operation was a success, but now you know that I wasn't exaggerating about post-operative care. How is your cough now that you are up and about?

Another letter in spidery handwriting. I could not understand a word. There were some cartoons – one showing a curly-headed sailor waltzing with a huge scorpion and the sailor shouting, '*Mensch*! What a love bite!'

Dearest Johnny,

    Black scorpions are more dangerous than brown ones – I told you. They are hideous creatures. Please don't wade about in the bilge anymore. It isn't funny! Are your glands still swollen? I know you don't like doctors, but you really should have gone to one rather than sweating it out in your bunk for three days. I am happy to see you are using that sketch paper I left behind to help while away the days. Yes, please play my accordion, otherwise both of you will get musty. I am looking for a teaching job. Mama will take care of the children.

Dear Johnny,

    I am both saddened and elated that you have sold the *Marie*, at least we know Señor Estrella will have the money to keep her in good shape. They say the war will soon be over. As soon as it is, I agree, you must come up here. Like you say, if we work hard together, we can find another boat and sail down to the islands as a family.

    We had such a laugh at the cartoons you sent. I stuck them on the wall to cheer us up. Spring is so slow in coming. The children are fine, except Tony has the most vivid nightmares and has taken to sleepwalking. Also, he draws terrible pictures of war planes on fire.

May 1943

Dearest Johnny,

I have a job as a stripper! (In a printing shop!) Mary is talking non-stop now. I took your suggestion and Tony has fewer night-mares since I stopped him listening to the news on the radio. For a five-year-old he is so aware of the war. I am sure all of this is going to affect him for the rest of his life. I just cannot imagine what it will do to children (and adults!) living in the middle of the horror. Yes, I too have seen haunting pictures of old and young poking through the rubble looking for food. Please send me your parents' address so we can send packages through the Red Cross as soon as it all ends. It may reach them — worth a try.

The letter ended in German.

The diary resumed in the summer of 1943:

Received letter from Johnny and sketches. I am amazed how good, how excellent they are. When he comes up I think we could exhibit his work — especially the seascapes of Galapagos. They are like nothing on earth. His letters are cheerful. Too much so? I wish he would tell me exactly what is going on.

They say the recent battle at Midway will be the turning point. You hear so many conflicting reports of how it really is over in Germany but the raids on Hamburg have been devastating. I only hope Johnny does not hear too much of this news. We have been parted for over a year. Seems like much longer.

Dear Johnny,

I am glad you moved back to Quito. You must tell me how it all looks, the Hotel Metropolitano, the fat ladies eating pastries. Is the Russian still there? I don't suppose you ever see Doña Aguirre or any of that clan. I wrote concerning Tony's inheritance but have received no reply. Don Benito wrote. He says you went to have a drink with him. I wish I could have seen his face when you showed up on Rocafuerte. But he says you look thin. I wish you would tell me the truth — are you really better? If it's still that cough, the thin mountain air won't do you much good, though I imagine living in a garret (by the sound of it) will inspire your painting.

277

The last work you sent was excellent. My not being there to distract you is obviously good for your work!

The rest was in German. I would not have read it even if I could have understood. You could tell it was personal.

Another letter in German. And another. Both were dated 1944.

I emptied the shoebox. There were curling newspaper clippings; one of determined soldiers up to their knees in water, the famous photograph you saw in countless history books.

D-DAY LAUNCHED

6th June, 1944 – 326,000 men with tanks and heavy trucks landed on a sixty mile stretch of Normandy beach. Over three million troops landed!

FRANCE LIBERATED

Reports of the assault on Germany followed. There were no letters from Hans.

THE BATTLE OF THE BULGE

made the headlines of the *Lincoln Sunday Journal and Star*.

No letters from Hans.

HITLER DEAD. GERMANY SURRENDERS!

Still no letter from Quito.

6 August 1945:

ATOMIC BOMB ON HIROSHIMA

Three days later:

NAGASAKI. JAPANESE SURRENDER

Estimated 84,000 killed in Hiroshima. 40,000 die in Nagasaki.

Editorials followed: blaming, justifying, explaining, accusing. The war was over.

Dearest Johnny,

I have been beside myself with worry. No, I did not receive any of your letters either. In my heart I knew your letters were simply

getting lost in all the confusion but not knowing, not hearing for
so long. I cannot believe it either, the war is behind us, the whole
nightmare. Soon we will be a family again. Let me know how you
plan to come up. I can meet you in Florida, New York – anywhere!
Mama is so excited that you will be joining us after four long years,
she doesn't know what to bake first! Just think! We have survived!

A letter came back from Hans, again the writing hurried.
The diary:

October 1945
Even dead, Doña Aguirre is up to her old tricks again. Johnny
cabled. He was having a cup of coffee in the Metropolitano when
he spotted an announcement in the *Comercio* calling all heirs of the
Aguirre estate to appear in court to state their claim. Something
about anyone not appearing will forfeit etc. Johnny cannot represent
Tony because he isn't his legal guardian!

Dear Johnny,
    I am leaving in one week but it will take me several days as the
plane stops in Florida, Jamaica and Cali. I have been saving as much
as possible from my odd jobs but as you say, this won't go far
towards the legal fees even if we find a lawyer who hasn't been
bought already. They will be shocked to see me in court.
    I am so excited at seeing you. Only I wish the children could
come, though of course it is too expensive, as you say. We have to
save every penny to come back! What a reunion it will be. Mama
is so excited for us. She has been wonderful about helping with the
children. As you know, with my parents' divorce, Mama has more
time on her hands, although she still works supervising the bakery.
My father remarried. He seems to be happy with his new family.
I have to remind myself that I don't have to envy other parents
with their children any longer, for soon we will be a normal family
again.
    We received the address you sent. We have collected things to
send to Germany for the past month, so now Mama will get a
parcel ready and mail it. Just think, you may get me before you
get this letter!

There were a few old recipes in the bottom of the box. Then a hideous sight as I unfolded crisp newspaper clippings. Ragged skeleton creatures with mummified expressions standing in lines stared out at me.

21

Letters

Galapagos
27 December 1946

Dear Mammushka,

Like you, I can't believe I am in such a wonderful place as this. It is so peaceful and clean here. Thank you for your letter with the good news that you and the children are fine. But you must stop paying Mary a nickel to eat her oatmeal every morning.

We arrived a week ago after a gruelling five-day voyage on the dirtiest, smelliest old tub you could imagine. You would have had your scrubbing brush out on the first day! Johnny promises that the next time we sail out here it will be all of us on our own boat!

It was the right decision, coming out here. Johnny's appetite has improved already, although I have to learn how to cook skipjack (a type of tuna) and shark steaks and lobsters. They tell me one can eat these strange sea iguanas which are all over the rocks, but Johnny isn't keen. He still coughs at night but in this nearly perfect climate it will be only a matter of time before he is completely well. I knew Ecuadorian hospitals were poor, but I never imagined he would catch pneumonia in that horrible Clinica where he had his operation.

We had a bad shock on our trip out here, even though we knew the news would come some day. A fellow passenger, a tactless, ignorant man, when he heard Johnny was one of the Angermeyers, shouted out during the midday meal that the boys' parents had been killed in the bombing raids over Hamburg, also the oldest brother Heinrich and his wife Greta and their child. I could have pushed the horrible little man overboard. Of course, the brothers out here had already heard the tragic news, but Johnny had been up in Quito all this time, waiting for me.

Well, that's the bad news. On a slightly happier note, at long last Tony's inheritance is safe for him. He can claim a great deal of valuable land when he is twenty-one but, ironically, we have spent nearly all our savings on legal fees and haven't enough money now to get back to the States. We have several ideas. There is a man farming up in the hills, named Jensmoo, who has made some money selling vegetables over on the base. But the Americans don't like to hike up there and this Norwegian doesn't like to come down, so Johnny plans to see him and other farmers and make some deal where we sell their produce for them. We will bring it down by donkey. Also we could sell fish and make jams and cakes to sell as soon as Johnny makes me an oven.

On the ship coming out, believe it or not, there were other Americans! One couple, the Conways, were here once before, on Floreana, but now hope to settle on James Island, where no one lives. They are nice and at least realistic. They know what they have let themselves in for. I cannot say that for the hillbilly from Arkansas and his frail auntie! It is true! A real hillbilly who says he has come to live on 'Paradise Island'! Those two came with one suitcase between them and a pair of shoes each. The Conways and Johnny told them that the most important possession out here is a sturdy pair of shoes, but they insist they will live on fruit from the trees. He says, 'I reckon we'll git along jist fine.' I can't believe how bizarre this all sounds as I write it to you. I am learning that islanders are all bizarre, romantic and a bit crazy. I miss you all very much but I am so happy. I enclose separate letters for the children.
Love,
Emmasha

There followed a drawing of a wonderful palm-thatched hut on a beach. Galapagos creatures formed a circle around a buxom lady who danced in the centre. Ballooned cartoon words came from a tortoise who shouted, '*Que alegría!*' A donkey brayed, 'I am in love with her!' and a grinning marine iguana said, '*Mi corazón.*' The border of the drawing was decorated with hearts and X X Xs and Johnny had pencilled in, below the shapely lady, 'My beloved one.'

At the bottom was written, 'Johnny says this is the effect of those pretty shorts you sent me!'

Galapagos
May 1947

Dear Mammushka, Tony and Mary,

We are so sorry you have not heard from us in so long. There has been no postman, since we haven't seen a supply ship for over five months until one came yesterday with all your lovely letters. Well, Tony you are nine years old now. At least I am happy you got the card Johnny made for you. We would love to see you ride your new bicycle. And Mary, do you like kindergarten? We liked the pictures you sent so much. They are good and remind us always of how much we both miss you.

The American sailors from Baltra come over frequently to buy our fresh fruit or trade it for spam, which is very useful when no one wants to go hunting or fishing. We built a grass hut for trading – something right out of one of those corny island movies we used to go to. Our neighbour Herr Kuebler sells his coconuts and figs. He is very kind and suggested we might have some little thing to put up in our hut to make the Americans feel at home. Of all things, in my trunk I found my University of Nebraska red and white banner! We had a good laugh when we saw the looks on the Americans' faces!

I enclose a map of Academy Bay and a sketch of our shack, which is very comfortable now. But it won't be a shack for long. Johnny designs beautiful house plans by kerosene lamp every night – a house for the beach and one for the hills (he says he knows a perfect spot up there). They are spacious, wonderful houses big enough for all of us, with wide windows to catch the sea breezes and to let the moonlight in . . .

We have made friends with the commander of the American base and his wife. I haven't been feeling too well so I went over there to see the doctor. It's probably only a bit of jaundice, quite typical in the tropics. Anyway, the houses there have electricity! And they use fresh water for flushing the toilets, if you can imagine!

I saw an iron and asked my hostess if I could iron her laundry for her. She had a good laugh and said I was the first person who had ever made such a request. I did enjoy myself – we've been ironing our clothes by spreading them out on hot rocks.

Johnny can barely stand to walk around the base because of the waste. He says he has seen mechanics in the plane hangars wipe their oily hands on good T-shirts and then throw them away!

Johnny is still thin, but then he is the tall, lean type. I tell him he looks more like Joseph Cotten every day. His hair goes lighter in this perpetual sunshine.

We are sketching a lot and playing music under the stars every night – like one long honeymoon. I cannot believe that you and he have never met, Mamma. It is the saddest of all that he and the children have not seen each other in five years. We are making reasonable money now, trading with the base. Our plan is to leave Galapagos once we have saved a bit more and come straight to America. There will be no problem now with Johnny being German, don't you think?

By the way, the hillbilly I wrote you about got serious fungus on his feet from the damp in the hills. He and his auntie nearly starved to death up there. The Americans stepped in, thank goodness, and sent them back to Arkansas. Poor people, they were only looking for a good life.
Love,
Emmasha (Mama and Daddy)

Quito, 1947

Dear Mamma,

As you will know from my cable, it wasn't jaundice. The baby is expected in February. I wanted desperately to have it here, which would allow me to stay with Johnny under the circumstances. But he spoke to our friends on the base and they say our chances of getting him into the States are better if I go up first and work on the officials from that end. Johnny insists America is a place of justice, that they will understand our plight if I simply explain. It isn't that he is naive – it's just that he cannot – will not – accept that he is so ill. He coughs a lot now.

Dr Ovalle was very kind. He says if we can just quickly get

him into one of those clinics in Arizona that have been curing tuberculosis, it doesn't have to be fatal anymore.

The Diary:
Lincoln, Nebraska, September 1947
How I put on that bright face when I said goodbye at the airport I will never know. I swore I wouldn't let him see how worried I was if it was the last thing I ever did. He gave me his mandolin to take to America, said the climate would be better for it. I think he knows he's dying. On the plane I cried and cried. I will never cry again.

December 1947

Dear beloved Johnny,

I am so relieved to know you got the package of goodies. Tony is at last out of the stage where he draws nothing but war planes. As you can imagine, he worked long hours on those pictures of ships, which he knew you would like. Mary is showing so much talent too. You can see from the photographs how much she looks like you. She is stubborn like you too, but at least we no longer pay her to eat breakfast.

The winter is bad here. I have a temporary job working in a department store wrapping Christmas presents. Jobs are scarce with so many veterans returning.

Now for the news I don't want to tell you. My hands shake with anger as I write. I have found a good lawyer. With his help I write to our congressman every week. But nothing seems to get me anywhere, I am sick to death of their vague answers to my direct questions. I have also contacted top people in the Red Cross and they say they are going to make a petition to the president if that's what it takes. But officialdom is so busy at the moment with their season of 'Peace and Goodwill' that they don't want to hear me out...

The rest of the letter was in German. Hans's letters back were entirely in German. I cursed myself for not having learned when Gus was trying to teach me. I couldn't understand a word, but I noticed the letters now came from El Hospital San Juan de

Dios in Quito, on Rocafuerte Street, and the writing was small and urgent.

Letters flew back and forth. The congressman said this, the Red Cross said that. The answer was maybe, the answer was no. The answer was definitely no.

I found Mother's old German–English dictionary. I went through the next letter word by word. Some sentences I couldn't get.

> Quito, 1948
> Hospital San Juan de Dios

Liebchen,

What is the matter with the top officials there? Can they not recognize that I am no threat to the American people? It is too comical, is it not? You have walked miles and written countless pleas to get permission for this wicked German to enter your country of freedom. Now that you have permission, the German is too sick for them. Is there nothing else we can try? I curse myself for lying here so helpless, surrounded by incompetent fools! Tell me, what is happening to us, to our dream? Tell me where is God? Even Christ, I was reading in the Bible my mother gave me, even He said on his dying stake, 'Where is God?' So this I must also ask. Because we have to face I am dying too. Funny about dreams, how intangible they are.

The Diary:
Lincoln, February 1948

We have named the baby Johanna after her father. Johnny says he likes the name. She has dark eyes and will have dark curls. From the photo I sent him he says she looks like his mother Marie. She is a quiet baby as though instinctively she knows she must not get in the way when there is this urgency. She smiles a lot. I don't think Mary likes her. Poor child, she asked for a baby doll that drinks and cries and wets for her birthday and got a baby sister instead. Imagine the baby being born on Mary's birthday. I have tried to explain to Mary that right now we just can't afford a doll. We can't afford a baby either. Every penny must be saved so I can go to Johnny, but not until he says that this battle is hopeless. How can

I be the one to say it is time to give up, that I must go down to him? Or would I make it easier by saying it first? He never could bear to admit defeat.

I got the dictionary back out.

Quito, October 1948

Hospital San Juan de Dios

Dear Liebchen,

The missionary who visits me is very kind. He has gone to the American Embassy to speak to the ambassador himself. They say the same here as from where you are. No one with tuberculosis can be admitted to America. If only I could get to Galapagos, but never mind.

Don Benito came to see me. We spoke of old times.

The American missionary, Mr Klingensmith, comes every day, did I tell you? We speak of the Bible. Strange, I had not read the Bible for years until he came. Too busy before, I guess. I was surprised to hear that he has my mother's belief of an earth cleansed by God's own hand one day – turned back into paradise for the righteous – as it was intended. Liebchen, you and I had paradise for a while, out on our island under the moonlight. *Kleine* Johanna is the proof, no?

I keep your letters and photographs of you and the children beside me, also the little one of my mother that she gave me. I often read the words on the back. I have a few sketches I'd like you to see –

I could not read anymore.

November 1948

Dear Mrs Angermeyer,

I cannot tell you how sorry my wife and I are . . .

The letter continued; there was no more she could have done. The missionary knew because he also had tried repeatedly to find some loophole in the law concerning immigrants with tuberculosis. He had seen to it that Hans was buried. The photos and Emma's letters were enclosed, also a photograph of Mr and

287

Mrs Klingensmith standing before a tomb in a wall. The plaque read simply:

JOHN ANGERMEYER
born 6 November 1912
died 5 November 1948

. . . a day short of reaching thirty-six.

The missionary's letter was still in the original envelope. As I studied the postmark, something slid back and forth inside. A small photograph of a dark-haired lady fell out. I knew what the words on the back said without looking.

22

Dreams

Siesta-time was just ending when I reached Calle Rocafuerte; shutters being thrown open, white-aproned children returning to school, wares being placed out on the pavement. I stood in front of the basket shop and took the slip of paper from my raincoat pocket. There was no mistake; to have my smallpox vaccination, I had to report to the Departamento de Inmunización, Hospital San Juan de Dios.

I must have passed the large ugly white building countless times before. I'd never taken much notice of it – healthy people don't stare at hospitals.

A corpulent woman in a greasy apron two doors down from where I stood threw a pailful of dirty water into the street, blew her nose into the gutter and went back inside. I glanced down at my high leather boots and recently dry-cleaned raincoat.

It was an old hospital which had been used to nurse soldiers wounded at the battle of Pichincha over a hundred years ago. Weeds grew out of cracked plaster. Years of damp and rot blackened the very foundations. There were bars on every narrow window, even at the very top, where no thief could ever have hoped to reach. But of course, the bars were not meant to keep thieves out.

I would have put off crossing the street for much longer, but the smell of urine against the wall behind me bade me move. I climbed the eight stone steps with a man I'd often seen begging down in the Plaza Grande. He was unmistakable by the holes in his face. It couldn't be leprosy; they didn't allow lepers to roam the streets, did they? Lepers lived in an asylum, down in the valley behind our house. I held the door open for him because his hands were covered in gauze.

There was no one in attendance at reception. The frosted window looked like a dead eye as I tiptoed past. The beggar knew where to go. I followed him down a hall towards the sound of voices. My boots sounded empty as I walked. I thought back to the Divines' library and the medical description I had found by chance.

Tuberculosis: Infectious disease caused by tubercule bacillus. Spread in saliva, possibly hereditary.

The medical book had described it so dispassionately.

Early symptoms: . . . emaciation, coughing of blood. Middle stage: fever, nightly sweats, morning sickness, racking cough. Last stages: sunken chest, severe dehydration, violent coughing, pulmonary haemorrhage.

Why had the words engraved themselves so clearly on my mind when I'd read them that afternoon in the library?

There was, thankfully, a short queue outside the door beneath the Inmunización sign. Poorly dressed women with wretched, runny-nosed children stood, eyeing me overtly as I joined them. A pious Virgin Mary stared down at us from otherwise bare walls. I smiled at the women, endeavouring to meet their eyes, but I was too well-dressed and their answering smiles were ingratiating and insincere. Grand señoritas like me didn't know what illness and suffering were all about. I didn't belong here.

A wail came from within. Strange, I thought, these women didn't look like the typical travellers getting smallpox jabs for flights out of the country. Not one of them had my same slip of yellow paper. I asked the woman ahead of me if she was waiting for a smallpox vaccination. I said it in what I thought was fluent Spanish, but she seemed to think I was a dumb *gringa*, for instead of a straightforward answer, she gestured with a dirty forefinger, poking a clockface pattern on her ample stomach. I had to admit I did not understand.

'*Rabia!*' she hissed through her missing teeth.

I stepped back; her meaning clear. Rabies injections were given in a circular pattern around the victim's navel, and I was standing in the wrong queue.

As I retreated down the cold hall, more doors with frosted-glass panels opened to my right and left. Granite-faced nuns wearing pigeon-winged headgear emerged carrying enamel basins and see-through plastic bags full of soiled gauze and bloodied cotton wool.

The nun did not answer me when I asked for directions. A pale white hand appeared from her grey habit and I thought she was going to bless me, but she pointed down the hallway. There was less light from fewer windows towards the rear of the hospital. Low, sagging cots and chamber-pots lined the passageway. Relatives of those too poor to pay for a bed squatted on the floor spooning broth into the gaping mouths of the infirm and feeble. One old woman rocked a child with a bandaged head, chanting 'Santa Maria' over and over. The child was silent. Disinfectant did nothing to mask the putrid smell of decay, mould and neglected mankind.

My face felt hot. My clothes disgusted me; my conspicuous leather boots squeaked as I turned and fled the abhorrent corridor. I found the right door further to the front; I should have known that rich people travelling to the outside world would not have been asked to wander down disgusting hallways filled with miserable scenes. I handed in my yellow paper, got my arm scratched and my paper stamped.

I walked briskly past the old house. I couldn't meet Don Benito today. He would only say something ridiculous, like 'the heart must weep before the guitar can sing'. I did not seek his pity or understanding.

At the top of the hill I paused to gulp at the thin air. 'I should have brought flowers,' I gasped. 'I should have come here the very day we arrived.'

I resumed climbing, turning left where normally I went right to violin class. I could see the waterfall cascading down the side of Pichincha in the brilliant afternoon sunshine. Too brilliant – I must hurry before the rain.

The cemetery lay stark and grotesquely white. Dots and

crosses sprawled like roadside litter on the mountain's green feet. Somewhere in there was my father. In a few moments I would stand before his tomb – closer to him than I had ever been before.

'I should have brought flowers,' I repeated, 'or at least one of those out-of-tune mourning bands to follow me down the hill.' Funny, turning up for your father's funeral twenty years late.

I remembered something Tony had said a long time ago, when I asked him if he remembered my father. Instead of telling me all the nice things I'd hoped to hear, he said, 'I remember when I was about ten years old. Mother got a telegram one night. She didn't say anything, just put on her old winter coat and went out. When she came back hours later, she said she'd been to the movies. I thought it was strange she couldn't remember what picture she'd seen. Grandma Mari told me to run along and not ask questions. The next day she told us he had died. Mama was changed after that. I'd never realized how much in love she and Johnny were.'

I approached the gate of the cemetery. Down the hill I could see a band of Indians carrying a small coffin on their shoulders. I would latch on to the end of their funeral.

> No more money in the bank.
> No sweet baby we can spank.
> What's to do about it?
> Let's turn out the light and go to sleep.

It was a silly little song Mama used to sing. Why had I remembered that song now of all times? A sudden vision gave me a chill. Filmy lace curtains blowing over a child's bed; streetlight coming through the window; a quilt kicked aside. How far back could memories journey and still be considered reality. A figure bending over me pulled off the quilt, lifted me gently, hand supporting my head. A nightly ritual once the rest of the house was asleep. A song sung over and over. Back and forth we paced, being lulled to sleep. Back and forth. I wanted to sleep but she kept pacing, holding me tight, singing to herself.

Later, much later, when I'd asked her with a child's bluntness, she had answered honestly. 'You don't have a daddy because he was very ill and so he went to sleep in a faraway land.' Later she had told me what the illness was. Oh yes, I'd known all right.

The band of Indians shuffled by carrying white lilies in their hands. I passed through the iron gates, my hands empty, unlike my heart. The Indians stopped to ask directions. The coffin wobbled as they all tried to start off together. They were drunk on chicha. I paused before a large, crudely painted sign; many of the words were misspelled.

> Esteemed relatives of the departed souls are respectfully reminded that unless the annual fee is paid, tombs will, regrettably, be reoccupied.

Mother hadn't known; she'd never sent any money. There was no JOHN ANGERMEYER in there! I began to laugh. The handful of Indians plodded on, their pathetic white coffin swaying as they went. I felt like shouting after them, 'Hey! Don't bother to bury your kid. They'll only dig her up in a year or two if you don't pay the annual fee!'

Where did they put a dead man when they 'reoccupied' his tomb? Down the muddy banks of the river Machangara? Sounded like a song. It didn't really matter I supposed. What had Traudi said? 'Our grandparents did not want their sons to end up dying in some muddy field far from home.' I guess we'd all been avoiding the truth. Hans had never escaped the war. Hitler had followed him all this way. The debris of my father's life lay scattered halfway across the world *en route* to paradise. But Father hadn't really been searching for paradise. All he wanted was a house on a beach big enough for us all, with windows wide enough to let in the moonlight. Was it so much to ask?

I walked slowly down Rocafuerte Street. At the bottom of the hill the rain began to fall. I looked at my watch: 3.05 in the afternoon. Like Don Benito said, every day the same. The blessed rain fell on my face. Big drops. So no one noticed the tears.

Franz Harper-Stubenrauch had a white wall-to-wall carpet in

his living room and a glass coffee table. There were glossy magazines beside a large brass lamp; magazines Big John and the Horneman boy would have sniggered over as they sat up in the avocado trees. He had a square black bathtub with golden taps in his black bathroom. He kept a brandy decanter on a ledge above the loofah sponge. On the ceiling over his king-sized bed Franz had installed a mirror. He was extremely proud of this and kept asking what I thought of it. But even after driving three thousand miles, eating oranges in Florida, peaches in Georgia and drinking Arkansas well-water, I was still suffering from such acute culture shock that I didn't know what I thought about anything anymore.

San Francisco lay under the spell of beads, braids and incense, while the television showed monks in Vietnam pouring gasoline over their heads and setting themselves alight. Outside the White House demonstrators shouted, 'Hey, hey, L.B.J., how many kids did you kill today?' Crowds of women my age burned their bras. Two men married each other; they put two grooms on their wedding cake and a priest blessed them. The comic strips weren't funny anymore. Men on windy San Francisco street corners didn't say a word when I passed. I was tired.

The night Franz and I went out to dinner, Tony watched me get dressed in my black-lace dress and stiletto heels. It wasn't easy getting ready for your first date in the back of a camper, especially when every time you looked in the mirror you jumped at the sight of a stranger. The woman at the beauty salon insisted I would look 'pixie-ish' in short hair.

Franz wore a baby-blue dinner jacket and a white bow-tie. We drove into downtown San Francisco in a blue convertible with the top down. The car matched his jacket.

A violinist dressed like a gypsy played *Otchi Chornya* in my ear so I couldn't hear what Franz was trying to say. In silence we drank Black Russians. When the violinist left us in peace I asked Franz how his boat was. He said he'd sold it. It was too small he said – dowdy was the term he used. His business was going so well, in four or five years he would have saved enough to buy a sixty-foot trimaran.

'Couldn't you sell your house?' I asked, assuming he'd want

to leave the rat-race as soon as possible. No, he was going to hang on to his house; property values were really skyrocketing in 'the City'. He had just made a downpayment on a gem of a little Victorian house. He would gut it and redecorate the whole thing. It would fetch a bomb when he finished.

We ordered.

How much did a sixty-foot trimaran cost? I asked. Franz said he could buy one right now but it would mean giving up his houses, which would be madness. A person had to have some income – one couldn't just up and sail away.

'Oh no,' I agreed heartily. One couldn't.

We ate.

Franz asked about Galapagos in the way you inquire after someone's aunt following a hip operation. My mouth was full of fried piroshki, so my comments about the islands could not have been construed as inspiring. He said he'd like to go back sometime for a visit.

I asked Franz what he thought about the Vietnam War. He didn't watch the news much any more, he said. For one thing he was too busy, and anyway there wasn't much he could do about it. 'Yes, in about five years I'd say, I'll be ready to retire for good. The golden sands and palm trees for me!' He smiled. I smiled.

We drove back to the Golden Gate Bridge, where Tony and Mother were going to wait to fetch me. It was late. Franz stopped the car. He whispered in my ear, in my hair. As the lights of our camper approached Franz said he wanted to take me home. We could work together towards our dream. But it wasn't our dream anymore. It wasn't even Father's. It was mine.

Epilogue
Half-Moon Crater

I hoped my nose wasn't broken. I knew of no one on the island who could mend noses. Gingerly, I touched it with my filthy fingers. Dark blood oozed out over my hand. My knuckles were scraped raw, my wrist rope-burned from where the horse had pulled me through the avocado trees.

Rising painfully from where I had been hiding in the ferns, I surveyed the island below me, tempted again to give up and go home. It looked so peaceful down there in Academy Bay, with the turquoise sea shining behind our house. Well, you couldn't actually see our house from where I was, near Half-Moon Crater, but I could see Pelican Bay, and our property was just there behind the coconut palm. Mind you, it wasn't much of a house, yet, just three badly shaped rooms with a roof stuck, or rather, unstuck, on top. But we'd only been there three months – there was time yet for Tony to break in his brand-new toolkit.

Seeing no sign of the horse, I brushed off my knees and pulled the weeds from my shoes. Which way to go? I squinted at the sun. It was nearly four o'clock. About now Uncle Carl would step back from his latest canvas, wipe his paint-smeared hands on his shorts and go inside to join Tante Marga for coffee. In an hour he'd limp back outside, rattling the dog's rice dish, and his iguanas would begin their daily scrape and slither down the walls.

I could see a stick on the horizon past Barrington. I bet it was the *Bronzewing*. Julian was expected in today. Mary would be looking for him every so often with binoculars. I smiled. Married people did watch the horizon. My sister would be taking fresh brownie cake out of the oven about now and stirring coffee beans in the pan ready to grind when she saw Julian put down his anchor. Johnny and little Daniel would row out to greet his passengers – Americans this time – Sierra Club, the more adventurous types. Thank goodness we didn't have huge liners cruising around in our lovely clean sea yet.

My nose stopped bleeding. Wrapping my handkerchief around my hand, I wished I'd brought my canteen. Tony had never imagined I was going to get into this much trouble when he'd sent me up here this morning. All those knowing looks between him and Mother when young Gonzalo showed up at the house with his rope, and my being whisked out of the door, and Mother insisting I needn't finish her mangrove chicken coop today as I'd promised.

By now Mother would be hanging up her machete, filling the kettle from the rain tank and making a pot of lemon-grass tea for them both. They'd sit down on the wobbly chairs under the coconut tree in the afternoon breeze and say, 'Well, I guess she's galloping all over the hills by now.' Then Tony would look concerned and say, 'Has she ever had any riding lessons?' And Mother would say, 'No, but when she was little she read every library book I could find on the subject and anyway, I'm sure Gonzalo will give her a few pointers.'

Gonzalo was poor; at twenty-five he was the eldest of twelve children and his family had no money. He spent a lot of time with my brother, discussing life. But he'd said less than a youth on his first date as we'd hiked up the old trail together, and I certainly hadn't known what to say, not even knowing why we were being sent to the hills together. It was only when we got to a farm near Old Moo's place and Gonzalo, lifting strands of barbed wire, told me to climb through, that I spoke.

'Isn't this private property?'

'Don't worry, your brother has arranged everything.'

We stopped by a grove of guayava trees. Gonzalo put his two little fingers to his lips and whistled. Nothing happened. He whistled again, louder. Elephant grass from the far end of the pasture rustled. A golden head emerged, ears pricked. Everyone knew Gonzalo's horse. Once a week he rode the stallion down from the hills, prancing and dancing and turning the girls' heads. Gonzalo always tried to look blasé, but he knew the girls eyed his one-horse parade. No man could fail to look *muy macho* mounted on such a beast, the sire of the first colt on Galapagos big enough for Alf Kastdalen to ride: Campeón, *el numero uno*, who had been challenged to many races but never beaten.

Gonzalo's prized possession tossed his shining mane and galloped over the field towards us, tail arched in a question mark like the one churning in my stomach.

The young man uncoiled the rope from his shoulder, looped it twice over the animal's quivering nose, deftly passed it over the ears, making a halter, and handed me the rope.

'I'm going to the mainland,' he said harshly. 'He is yours now.'

I was speechless. The rope felt coarse and rough in my hands. I gave it back.

'I couldn't–'

'Don Marco paid a good price. He says you have always wanted to own such a stallion as this.' His eyes softened. 'I also have a dream – your brother has taught me much. Now I want to leave this place, learn more – I want to become someone of whom God will be proud.' He took my hand and curled my taut fingers about the rope. 'You, señorita, and I are merely exchanging dreams.'

I looked away as he buried his face in the horse's thick mane. Without a word the young man strode down the hill. The soles of his boots were full of holes. There was mud on the trail.

The horse watched him go with flared nostrils. A deep rumble in his chest turned to a wet snort as he eyed me. I eyed him. Apologetically, I led him to a fallen avocado tree, and tried to remember which side to get on. I hadn't worried about such things with the dream-stallions of my childhood. Just as I swung my leg over his back, he sidled away. I landed in a heap on the ground. The horse set off at a trot. I held fast to the rope. He broke into a stilted canter, slowed considerably by my hanging on behind, bumping into stumps and rocks. A barbed-wire fence loomed up ahead; he'd have to stop now! But Campeón knew where the posts had rotted away and he merely stepped over the fallen wire. My sock caught on a strand and the barb bit into my ankle. As we ran towards a tree, I darted left where he went right. I fumbled with the rope, trying to tie a granny knot about the tree's waist, but Campeón lunged, caught my hand and crushed it to the tree. I yelled and let go. He disappeared through a wall of tangled hibiscus and wild coffee. That's when I got mad. I whipped out my knife and slashed my way after him.

That had been five hours earlier. I had followed him for miles. When we reached the trail to Half-Moon I should have quietly circled around to head him off, then gently herded him downhill. By confronting him, I merely spooked him uphill. Now, with all this open country, I would probably lose him. I'd feel pretty foolish if I had to get Gonzalo to come all the way back up here to whistle.

Shortly before sundown, Mother would check the time on the watch pinned to her shirt pocket. Tony would fret that she was about to ask him to climb up the old trail to look for me with the hurricane lantern. My brother was still suspicious of adventure. His glasses were broken and fell off if he bent down suddenly. He'd never think to look way up here. Anyway, the moon was coming up to full. I would need no lantern tonight and I didn't need anybody's help. Two hours before sundown. Two hours to decide what to do.

I marched up through the bracken towards the worn-down crater. I never imagined it would be so beautiful, open and wild up here, like the postcard Tony had sent from the Scottish Highlands. How odd of my brother to go all the way around the world and then settle out here. I mean, with me it was probably a family thing – Robinson Crusoe in the genes – but my brother? The gentleman farmer?

I had no idea the day Ophelia called us to lunch – it must have been a Saturday, for we were all at home – that things would turn out like this. On returning from San Francisco I went back to teaching and enjoyed it. But sometimes, when the children laughed and hung on me out in the playground, I thought back to Mari Katrina in the schoolyard of Wiessenmüller and how she'd always dreamed of faraway places.

And I remembered what her teacher Irina Avdyeevna had told her: 'You can make things happen...' And so, that Saturday I made my announcement.

I'd given it a great deal of thought. I would work for two more years and save enough money to build a little house on Galapagos. There were now fortnightly flights landing on the old airstrip of Baltra, bringing tourists. I would make exotic jams and cakes to sell to the cruise yachts. Once I knew enough about the islands, I would become a guide, working six months of the year. The other half I would paint.

'You see, it will all work out. I have no intention of ending up like that fungus-toed hillbilly from Arkansas.' I hoped I ended on a light-hearted note.

Ophelia served coffee.

'Well, I think it would be the most wonderful adventure,' said Mother. 'I'd do the same if I were twenty-two, with plenty of energy and no responsibilities.'

We sat looking at the fire. My brother had removed his glasses and rubbed the bridge of his nose where he had two perpetual pink spots. I knew he was disappointed in me. He put three teaspoonfuls of sugar in his coffee. Usually he took one. He crossed his legs. His suspended foot jiggled. 'If you could build a house anywhere in the world,' he finally asked Mother, 'where would it be?'

'Oh, I'd do just what she's doing if I were younger...'

He sipped his coffee. It must have tasted ghastly, but he didn't even make a face.

'OK. I'll build you a house in Galapagos. Wait, let me finish – I've been thinking it over for some time. If you and Hans hadn't spent your last cent to save my inheritance, I'd have nothing. But we can't rush into this. We'll have to plan, give ourselves a year – do everything right. We'll make – er – lists – lists of things to buy – things to sell. We'll meet every week and see how we're getting on.'

'What do you mean, we?'

'You can't possibly go out there alone!'

I had not read the Bible for a long time – because I'd been too busy, which is another reason to move to an island. But sitting there, looking into the fire and hearing my brother say these things, I could only think of the words of Solomon.

> As apples of gold in silver carvings
> so is a word spoken at the right time for it.

I could find no such word.

Mary wrote saying there was a house in Pelican Bay with coconut, fig and papaya trees. The house was 'airy'. The roof leaked. It had a lot of 'potential'. There were no frames in the windows and no door on the privy but there was plenty of land to build a new house and the land there had water, like old Haeni had said, 'it grew things'.

My children at school didn't understand when I said goodbye, though I drew pictures on the blackboard with coloured chalk to explain. Ophelia wept when we found her a new job. She couldn't bear to stay, but she couldn't bear to come either. She'd seen photographs. She knew the islands were covered in lizards. Everyone knew the Devil kept pet lizards in hell to eat the flesh of the eternally damned.

We hoisted huge crates on to a truck – even Mother's piano – and set off through the jungle for Guayaquil. There wasn't much room in the cab, so Gypsy and I sat in back wedged in between the sofa and Mother's well-travelled Russian chest. Like Grandmother Marie twenty-five years before in Germany, perched in the back of the furniture cart, I sang the whole way, at the top of my voice.

I tripped over a grassy stump. My nose began to bleed again. It felt puffy. I couldn't see any horses. I'd seen a few geldings earlier, turned out on common land by the hill people. I wouldn't make the same mistake as before and get all excited, thinking they were wild.

My hand was swelling. I might as well give up; after all my brother had promised me this horse over fifteen years ago, when I was a kid. I wasn't a kid any more.

'For crying out loud, you're not going to turn into some sniffling, whimpering adult, are you?' complained the kid at my side. Where did she think she was, back in Show 'n' Tell?

I challenged her: 'So what would you do?'

'I'd use my head. What does a stallion adore more than anything else in the world?'

'Grass?'

She rolled her eyes.

'Bananas?' I ventured.

'Bananas!' The kid snorted just like Miss Bean.

'You're so smart, you tell me.' I wasn't afraid of Miss Bean anymore.

'Mares! Mares! Stallions like mares.'

My shoes bounced on spongy moss covering the sides of the crater. I reached the rim and looked down. It was good of the kid really, to go to so much trouble; after all I hadn't treated her very well over the past couple of years. Like Father had once said: 'Funny, how we pretend to be grown up, denying the child within each of us, refusing to let it come out and play.'

'There's your horse,' the kid whispered.

What had Father said? 'When I saw that beast just standing on the hill – shining like a golden statue . . .'

'Well, don't just stand there. Now is your chance, you ninny.'

But my golden statue was nuzzling up to some skinny-legged, dusty mare with a long, scraggly tail.

'Shall I whistle?' I asked.

'You crazy? Sneak up on him – downwind. Then pounce on his rope.'

I crept down like she said. The rope halter was still on his head. A length of rope stretched out to one side, matted with weed and debris. Campeón, irritated at the mare's indifference, pawed the red earth. I loathed him for breaking away from me that morning; I admired him for it. He insisted the mare notice him. His beastly male conceit was charming, but it would be his downfall. I slid down the side of the crater and scrambled towards his rope.

'Grab it!' screamed the kid. I took hold of it. The horse took off.

'Hold on!' she hollered.

'Whoa.' I pulled back, using my body as a lever. The brute

stopped. He looked over his shoulder quite innocently as I cautiously pulled myself abreast, hand over hand.

'Now what?'

'Get on.'

I scrambled up and nearly fell off the other side. He had no bit in his mouth, but when I pulled on the rope, his head responded. I squeezed my legs ever so gently. He trotted off at a crab-walk, nearly snapping my neck. I gripped with my thighs, crouching over his neck, sliding back and forth. I fell off. He stopped. I got on. I fell off. We pranced sideways. The sun was beginning to set. The whole island was turning red and gold – the bay, the bush, the bracken – even my filthy arms and my shining horse. I urged Campeón into a faster walk. A little faster. He trotted. I squeezed again. He cantered. I stayed on. Faster. He galloped a few paces. I reined him in.

'Did you see that?' I yelled at the kid. 'Did you see that?'

But the kid was gone.

I was wrong that day in the cemetery when I said that standing before my father's tomb would take me the closest I'd ever be to him. I was closest now, with this golden beast taking me over the folds of the island Father had loved.

'I wound my hands into the horse's silvery mane. His ears twitched. I squeezed his flanks.

I finally managed to climb on his back.
Then we went like the wind, I tell you,
Like the wind!'